Jonathan Hall lives in Yorkshire, where, after more years than he'd care to remember, he has just retired from being Deputy Head of a Primary School.

His plays have been produced in theatres across the UK as well as for radio, the most recent being the BBC Radio 4 series *Trust* starring Julie Hesmondhalgh, the fourth series of which has just aired with a fifth currently in production.

His first novel, the international best seller *A Spoonful of Murder*, introduced us to the unlikely crime-solving trio of retired teachers, Pat, Liz and Thelma. Their sleuthing adventures continue in *A Pen Dipped in Poison* and *A Clock Stopped Dead*.

Also by J.M. Hall:

A Spoonful of Murder
A Pen Dipped in Poison

A
CLOCK
Stopped
DEAD

J.M. HALL

avon.

Published by AVON
A division of HarperCollins*Publishers*
1 London Bridge Street
London SE1 9GF

www.harpercollins.co.uk

HarperCollins*Publishers*
Macken House
39/40 Mayor Street Upper
Dublin 1
D01 C9W8

A Paperback Original 2024

1

First published in Great Britain by HarperCollins*Publishers* 2024

A catalogue copy of this book is available from the British Library.

ISBN: 978-0-00-860692-3 (PB)
ISBN: 978-0-00-860693-0 (TPB)

Typeset in Bembo by Palimpsest Book Production Ltd, Falkirk, Stirlingshire

Printed and bound in the UK using 100% Renewable
Electricity by CPI Group (UK) Ltd

MIX
Paper | Supporting
responsible forestry
FSC
www.fsc.org   FSC™ C007454

To Simon.

CHAPTER ONE

On the afternoon of a Blue Day something strange is experienced.

Fog – dense, freezing fog – lay all across the Vale of York and around the town of Thirsk during those early January days. On the second Monday of the month – so-called 'Blue Monday' – it seemed thicker than ever. Patchy in some places, impassable in others, it shrouded the sprawling flat fields around the town, reduced the trees and farms to sinister silhouettes and slowed the traffic on the A19 to a cautious, growling crawl. As the all-too-short afternoon began to fade, people peered out through steamed-up windows at the ominous grey twilight and felt glad to be indoors.

It was the perfect afternoon to encounter something strange . . .

'*TransPennine Express would like to apologize for any inconvenience caused.*'

It was the regret in the announcer's weedy voice that Marguerite found most aggravating – as if some highly paid company official was thinking 'we really *ought* to say sorry'.

What a load of numpties!

The display monitor on the chilly platform added to her

mounting annoyance. '*Cancelled, due to a shortage of train crew*.' She felt a desire to grab this mythical company official by the lapels and shout: 'Never mind apologies – get your blumin' work rotas sorted!' As far as she was concerned, unions and train operators were – to use a favourite phrase from her teaching days – *all as bad as each other*. The bigger picture of contracts, fair wages and the rising cost of living was rather lost on Marguerite, faced as she was with the prospect of being stranded in Thirsk station in the freezing fog, with no train back to Northallerton for the best part of an hour.

She sighed. If only she'd gotten the train at half past as she'd planned. It wasn't as though her mother even knew she'd been there (bless!). But it had been so cosy and peaceful sitting in the armchair amongst all the other dozing people, looking out at the muted trees by the racecourse . . . And the cake being served with tea had been really rather yum. She patted her handbag appreciatively, thinking of the two pieces she'd snuck in there before heading out the door.

And then of course Gary had posted some new pictures on Facebook that she'd wished to savour in peace.

Her thoughts turned – as they generally did – to her one-time lover. *If he'd been here now* . . . he'd have been over the concrete footbridge quicker than what-have-you, demanding refunds, taxis and the radar key to the disabled loo. But then if Gary was still on the scene . . . Marguerite sighed again. She wouldn't have been at the station at all, but sat in his 4x4 with the traffic-light air freshener, hand on his thigh, as she had been so often during those brief, glorious days twenty-one and a half years ago.

The Facebook pictures showed him to have put on even more weight – *quite* the spare tyre – and his hair was almost all gone . . . Both clear signs he wasn't happy; surely he *couldn't* be.

The slam and shock of a train thundering north shattered her thoughts. She spun around, alarmed, in time to catch fragmented images of lit carriages, people within reading, chatting, snoozing, safe from the fog and vagaries of TransPennine staff rotas.

Nearly an hour until the next train! Had it been the other platform (to York, Leeds and Manchester) it wouldn't have been so bad, as there was a proper building with light and warmth. But she was on the northbound platform (in the direction of Northallerton, Middlesborough and Newcastle), which was isolated away over the mainline, a bleak length of concrete with a decidedly spartan brick shelter, usually locked (as it was today). She could take a taxi, but on a part-time wage this wasn't really an option. And what's more, she was all alone in the fading light, with only the thundering phantoms of express trains for any sort of company.

Plus, she realized, she really did need the loo, and the ticket office over on the other platform would be closed by now.

A sudden thought slammed into her head with the force of a passing train. *The Junction!* She'd often thought how inviting the pub looked as she'd walked past it on her way to Hambleton Grange, and of course it was where she'd gone that time with Gary on one of their early dates. Sneaking away from the staff meeting, then sitting tucked discreetly away in that nook by the fireplace, the tang of real ale in her mouth, warmed by the log fire and possibilities. It'd be the ideal place to wait (and use the loo). She could even, if she dared, send a Facebook message to Gary saying *'guess where I am . . .'* The thought warmed her more effectively than any log fire as she clattered up the open concrete steps to the main road.

But the pub, like the ticket office, was closed – only on a more permanent basis.

There was something infinitely forlorn about the dark building with its fringing of portable builders' fencing, a board trying to tempt people into a 'Prime Retail Opportunity'.

3

Marguerite sighed to herself impatiently. What was the world coming to? It really was too bad!

Setting off back to the station another thought came to her. *Hang on a tick, wasn't there* another *pub just down the road into Carlton Miniott?* She had a vague memory of some staff do, more years ago than she cared to remember. She set off, urgency in her step. The main road was very quiet for teatime, only the occasional car gingerly braving the deepening murk.

At the crest of the slight rise by the station drop-off point she paused, disorientated. No pub, only dim houses. Except . . . there was a side road branching off to the right. Could it be down there, maybe?

She took a few steps down the path, and as she did the tarmac broke rapidly into a cinder track, a belt of trees and bushes fringing it as it ran parallel to the railway lines. Was the pub down here? It didn't look at all promising, but then, if push came to shove there were always the bushes . . .

Others might have thought twice about walking down an unlit foggy track as the light was fading, but Marguerite (as those who knew her would say) was never much of a one for thinking of more than a couple of things at a time, and right now her memories of Gary and her need for the loo were more than enough to drive out any sense of possible peril.

How far had she come?

It was the oddest thing. She couldn't tell if she'd walked twenty or two hundred yards; it felt like both. She was aware of a deep silence, tangible like the fog – no traffic on the main road, not even the distant sound of the trains. She frowned, peering forward.

Lit windows.

Hanging, glowing in the gloom . . . There was something inviting and comforting in their ethereal glow. But again, walking towards them, Marguerite was filled with an odd sense of

4

walking through a void, the lights hanging, not seeming to come any closer.

And then they were right there in front of her.

But the building was too small for any sort of pub. Some kind of shop? In the window was a disparate jumble of household objects. *A charity shop? But what was it doing here?* That was her first thought. Her second: *I bet they'll let me use the loo.*

She pushed open the door, immediately becoming aware of the sound of a clock; a steady, reassuring pulse.

She stepped inside.

When something is wrong, it is generally by degrees that our senses feed us the information. What seems at first merely odd, is joined by another sensation, and another, until some inner red light is triggered. The first thing Marguerite registered was the smell – an overpowering reek of tobacco: pipe tobacco, of the sort favoured by her late Uncle Kev – which was unpleasant but not in itself alarming. Someone had obviously been flouting the smoking ban. Then there was the merchandise on display. She could see no women's clothing – no blouses, no tops or shoes – just men's jackets and shirts and blazers all hanging with no sense of order. And it was so *dim*. The items on sale – books, pictures, plates – seemed to be almost *floating*; blurry Yorkshire landscapes . . . hazy shapes of brown and orange crockery.

Central amongst these was a pendulum clock, the sort you'd find on a mantelpiece. With a gaudy, golden face and ornate numerals it was the obvious source of the ticking. Only it was running a few hours slow. Maybe it was broken? A thought darted into her mind: *Gary would know where to take it to be fixed*. A sudden clear image drove everything else out. Gary opening a parcel, unwinding bubble wrap, a wistful smile playing round his lips . . . She peered at the clock, trying to discern a price. She frowned.

Wait a minute. That was odd!

But before she could pursue the thought, the lights dimmed further. It was now so dark she could barely make anything out, just a glow from a door at the back of the shop. Had there been some sort of power cut?

'Hello?' she called out uncertainly, but her voice was as it was in dreams – breathless, insubstantial.

There was a click that sounded both far away, and yet almost in her ear.

The noise of a door being locked.

And with that click all of these strange elements coalesced in her mind, giving her a flush of cold fear.

'Hello?' she called again, now with a shrill pulse of panic muting her voice to barely more than a croak.

It was then she became aware of a figure at the rear of the shop, a bulky, backlit silhouette. 'Who's there?' she whispered again, her tones suddenly those of a tearful, frightened girl.

'Why did you do it?' The voice was husky, resonating. *'Why?'*

Marguerite exploded into movement across the shop, rattling on the front door with ferocity. 'I don't know who you are,' she shouted, adrenalin injecting shrill volume and strength into her voice. 'But I demand to be let out!'

Just as suddenly as they'd gone out, the lights came back on. Marguerite turned, and as she did the door behind her released, and she propelled herself out into the fog on legs that couldn't move quickly enough as she retraced her steps back up the cinder track.

As she neared the main road it felt as though she was waking up, the elements of the real world reasserting themselves. The noise of cars, the amber fuzz of streetlights on the main road, the distant, tinny tones of the tannoy announcing the imminent arrival of the seventeen fifty-six to Middlesborough, calling at Northallerton, Yam and Thornaby.

As Marguerite stumbled towards light and sound and reality, twin beams from a car cut smoky, dazzling lines through the fog, forcing her to sidestep, foot plunging into the icy shock of a puddle . . .

'And it ruined my shoe!' Marguerite shook her head as she finished her tale. 'So at least *that* bit of it was real.'

Pat frowned. 'What d'you mean *real*?'

'Well, *corporeal*. It was the clock that made me realize.' Marguerite looked significantly at Pat, obviously expecting some kind of reaction, but for what exactly – the shoe, the clock, or the whole experience – Pat wasn't sure as she had rather lost track of Marguerite's point. She shivered. It was rather chilly in Mrs Hall's Larder, as it was in so many cafés this winter with everyone worried about the cost of heating. She looked at the woman she used to teach alongside. (The term 'friend' she always felt was putting it a bit strongly.)

'And this all happened yesterday?' she asked.

'If you can use such crude temporal terms as "yesterday".' Marguerite leaned forward intently. 'I've been reading up about it on t'interweb. Apparently, people like me can develop this gift in later life. I've always been instinctive; you know that—' Pat nodded, even though actually she'd have said the exact opposite '—but now, it's like what was latent has emerged.' Marguerite gestured significantly to the blue and pink crystals in a gauze bag that lay next to her coffee cup. 'Tantric crystals. They help nurture psychic energies. Twenty quid on Amazon Prime.'

Pat felt, not for the first time, a tug of sympathy for her one-time colleague. What had been charmingly kooky at twenty-seven was some twenty years later becoming decidedly threadbare. The curly blonde hair now liberally wired with grey, the fussy print dress, the unmatching glass beads . . . It all looked

7

more than slightly tired. It was, she thought, as if Marguerite had been frozen physically and sartorially at the point of her short-lived affair with Gary the photocopier man before he had gone firmly back to his wife. Now she was looking out at the foggy market place with the slightly superior air of one who flies above the mortals.

'People like me, we walk a lonely path,' she said serenely.

Pat sighed to herself and glanced down at the stale scone she didn't feel at all like finishing. These 'natter o'clock' sessions which had started when Marguerite dropped to part-time work were trying enough at the best of times – the complete opposite of her regular meetings with friends Liz and Thelma at the garden centre. The usual format was ninety minutes of Marguerite holding court about her favourite subject – Gary the photocopier man, and how she still, deep deep down, cared for him. Pat had hoped that dropping to part-time work would lead to Marguerite finding other things in her life – things to replace this obsession and although this seemed to have happened there was something in this strange tale Pat found deeply unsettling.

'It was the clock,' continued Marguerite, fingering the tantric crystals. 'You know how Gary loved collecting clocks, and this was just the sort of thing he'd have liked.' Pat nodded, not liking to point out that what Gary collected now, and what he'd collected twenty years ago, could well be two different things. 'I only remembered later that it was saying ten to three. I remember that because it made me think of being at school . . .'

Pat felt totally lost, and not a little impatient. 'And?' she said.

'I could hear it ticking, this big loud tick,' said Marguerite, her voice excited. 'It said it was two fifty, so I thought it was running slow, but when I looked closely at it *the pendulum wasn't moving! Nor were the hands!*' She sat back, a triumphant smile playing round her lips. '*That's* what made me realize the whole psychic episode had to be a sign.'

'I'm so sorry,' said Pat, 'I'm obviously being very thick here. But I don't get exactly *what* this psychic episode you had *was*.'

'I've just been telling you!' said Marguerite, sounding more than slightly aggrieved.

'Your train was cancelled yesterday, so you went for a walk and found this weird charity shop, saw a strange clock, got locked in and then got out again?'

Marguerite's podgy hand flew to her mouth, almost batting the tantric crystals clean across the scuffed floor tiles of Mrs Hall's Larder. 'Oh goodness gracious me,' she said and gave a neighing peal of laughter. 'You must think I'm a complete numpty!'

Pat smiled faintly, making a considerable effort not to look as if she agreed.

'*I went back*,' said Marguerite. 'I wasn't working this morning, so I went back to the charity shop. I wanted to go back and see how much this clock I saw cost. At that point I hadn't twigged that it wasn't real.' She paused dramatically.

'And?'

'It wasn't there!'

'The clock?'

'*No, the whole shop*. When I went back this morning, *the whole shop had just vanished!*'

CHAPTER TWO

Tension in the garden centre café leads to fact finding and a sad discovery.

'You mean the shop was shut?' said Liz, puzzled.

'No,' said Pat. 'The shop was *gone*.'

'It had closed down?' suggested Thelma.

'No, I mean *gone*-gone. Not there. Vanished.' There was a defensive note in Pat's voice. 'I *know* it sounds totally bonkers, but that's what Marguerite *said* – she went back the next day and there was no trace of any charity shop. Of any shop at all, come to that. Not even any *building*. Just waste ground.'

There was a pause and Pat allowed herself to relax into the mundane, oh so comforting soundtrack of the Thirsk Garden Centre Café: the murmurs of chat, the clink of crockery, the plaintive call of 'Tuna melt?' from a waitress. And the warmth! Such a contrast to Mrs Hall's Larder. She looked at her two friends, Liz in her faded maroon fleece her face a worried frown, Thelma regarding her steadily from behind those large glasses. Both so blessedly, reassuringly normal in a world that had lately been feeling as muted and uncertain as the foggy countryside. Something about Marguerite's tale had chimed with Pat's own uneasy feelings and the small hours had brought a jumble of dreams about charity shops, tantric crystals, and clocks . . . remorselessly ticking clocks. Dreams that had left her tired and scratchy with a dull feeling of disquiet. 'Blue' Monday might have been blue, but this Thursday wasn't feeling any more cheerful.

With an effort she pulled herself back to the conversation in hand. 'Completely gone,' she reiterated. 'That's what Marguerite said.'

There was another pause, during which she guessed what would be going through the minds of her friends. It was Liz who eventually spoke. 'I'm not being funny,' she said with her trademark worried frown, 'but this *is* Marguerite McAllister we're talking about here.'

'I know,' said Pat irritably. 'I do know.'

There was another pause, this one eloquent with unspoken understanding. There was no need to retell the story so well known by the three of them: how Marguerite had single-handedly conducted a campaign of sabotage against the school photocopier in order to secure repeated visits from Gary the repairman. They all remembered clearly how every time the warning light appeared Marguerite would be the first to say in airy tones that she had absolutely *no clue* why the chuffing thing was packing up every verse end.

'I know,' said Pat yet again. 'It's just . . .' She paused, unsure whether to actually voice the thought, the one mulled over during those restless small hours. 'What if it *was* some sort of supernatural vision? These things do happen.'

'Not generally in that much detail.' Thelma spoke immediately and decisively. She sounded damping and not a little dismissive. 'A usual component of any sort of vision is a rather blurry sense of not knowing where one is or where one had been. Marguerite seems to have been very precise.'

'So, you're saying it's all rubbish?' said Pat flatly.

'I'm not saying *that*,' said Thelma, though it was apparent to both her friends there was no sort of endorsement in her voice. A constant during all of the years Pat and Liz had known her had been her reactions to anything and everything connected with the supernatural, be it Halloween, *Most Haunted*, and even *Casper the Friendly Ghost*. Perhaps this was only to be expected from the wife of an ordained vicar, and for ninety-plus per cent of the time it hadn't proved any sort of issue. However, there had been times – such as that infamous occasion when Pat had erected a Witches' Kitchen in the Key Stage One library – that Thelma's views became crisp and uncompromising.

'This *is* Marguerite McAllister,' said Liz again, aware of the sudden frosty tension.

Pat looked down at her Melmerby slice. For whatever reason, it felt important to her that there was the possibility of *something* in Marguerite's story.

'People *do* see visions,' she said stubbornly. 'And there are things like seances.' She looked defiantly at Thelma whose face had closed the way it did when anything was mentioned that she had an aversion to – reality TV, social media, the infamous Melmerby wife-swapping circle . . .

'I guess we'll never know,' said Liz soothingly. But Pat did not want to be soothed.

'I just think—' she started, but suddenly realized she didn't know what she thought, other than that a bubble was being burst that she suddenly felt it was important to keep intact. To her horror she felt her eyes filling. 'Excuse me,' she said, rising smartly and heading off to the toilets.

Inside the ladies' Pat took a deep, steadying, potpourri-scented breath. Her knuckles whitened, splayed on the edge of the sink as she took another deep breath. *Get a grip, Pat!* The slightest thing seemed to set her off these days! What was wrong with her? Sixty was just a number! What was it they were calling it these days? The new forty. Only with both her and Rod hitting that milestone next month within a few days of each other, it felt significantly more than just a number and it had been preying on her mind. That morning had brought another reminder as she'd renewed her driving licence and saw with a cold shock that she was only ten years off having to reapply for it at seventy.

'Get a grip, Patricia,' she said, aloud this time. With a feeling of pulling herself together against all the odds she looked at herself in the mirror. Not too bad, all things considered. That new green top really did go with the conker highlights, and she made a slightly smug and guilty comparison with Liz's greying helmet of hair, and Thelma's bob, both of which – in her opinion – could use a touch of colour.

You can still carry it off, girl, she said to herself, but her words felt far from confident, and she found herself having to take another deep, steadying breath. Outside in the garden centre she could see the sad last remains of the Christmas stock jumbled together; where there had been a glittery, twinkly tunnel of Christmas lights were now unspectacular rows of seed potatoes. It was a sight that seemed to sum up her life.

'I'm sorry,' she said brightly, sitting back down at the round table in the corner. 'I just needed a moment.' She smiled, hoping her friends would confuse emotion with the sudden urge to wee.

'You've nothing to be sorry about,' said Liz.

Pat knew she'd fooled neither of them. She shook her head. 'I slept badly,' she said. 'And for whatever reason this tale of Marguerite McAllister has somehow really got under my skin.'

'About that,' said Thelma. There was something in her tone, something softer and more conciliatory.

'As you say,' said Pat, 'it's just Marguerite being Marguerite.'

'Even so,' said Thelma, 'it couldn't hurt to go over to the station and take a look for ourselves.'

* * *

13

Thelma drove, the other two piling into the mussel-blue Corsair for the short trip across town. As they drove down Station Road alongside the racecourse, the traffic began thickening and slowing.

'Roadworks, it must be,' said Pat. 'They're always doing something along here.'

'There was an accident down here the other night.' Liz rubbed the window and peered down the foggy road. 'Derek said the traffic was backed all the way up to the market place. He ended up going round by Sowerby.'

'What night was that?' said Thelma, changing down a gear.

'Tuesday, I think.' Liz bit her lip. 'Yes, it was Tuesday because our Jacob was over.' There was a distinct undertone to her voice that both of the other two noticed but didn't comment on.

'Tuesday,' mused Thelma. 'Wasn't that when Marguerite had her—' she chose her word with precise care '—her experience?'

By now they were crawling past the closed pub and the entrance to the station. 'Pull in on the other side of the bridge,' said Pat. 'At the drop-off point, if there's space.'

As the cars inched forward, Thelma nipped across the traffic into the triangle of tarmac by the entrance to the northbound platform steps. As they got out of the car, the reason for the delay became obvious – temporary traffic lights on the other side of the bridge. Figures in bright orange hi-vis jackets were unloading bollards from a lorry, the focus of their attentions a section of wall to the left of the road that had been smashed and fragmented like Lego bricks, the gap webbed with black and yellow police tape. Visible on the surface of the road were crumbs of shattered windscreen and the tell-tale black scrawl of tyres. Obviously, the site of Tuesday's crash.

Just down from the carnage was a young woman, a plump figure in an inadequate-looking jacket, standing there regarding the mess with a rather blank stare. As they walked down the other side of the road she stooped and placed a rather cheap-looking bunch of flowers by the surviving section of wall. Despite the workmen and the traffic, she struck all three women as being intensely alone and isolated.

'Derek did say he thought someone had been killed,' said Liz sombrely.

'It's down here,' said Pat. They looked doubtfully at the cinder track leading off into the trees and bushes.

'Are you sure?' said Liz.

Pat shrugged. 'That's what Marguerite said. The first right turn after the drop-off. A cinder track running parallel to the railway lines.'

The three set off down that track. After about twenty yards or so it broadened into a wide, puddled expanse that was neither track nor road nor even waste ground. To the left, backing onto some allotments, were three decrepit units; low, flat-roofed, plastered with posters and obviously unused. Opposite them, against the security fence running parallel to the station, was a hut half submerged in brambles and bushes, which looked as if it had at one time belonged to the railway. Ahead the space seemed to fade uncertainly into misty bushes. There was certainly nothing that could have been construed as any sort of charity shop.

'This is it,' said Pat.

'How peculiar,' said Thelma.

'If this *is* the right place,' said Liz doubtfully.

The fog had somewhat lifted, but nevertheless it was a desolate place to be as the winter's day wound down. 'I should have known it was all a load of hooey,' said Pat, resigned irritation evident in her voice.

'Except . . .' said Thelma. Her friends both looked at her. 'Marguerite said when she came back the next day, the shop had gone. And there's certainly no shop here.' She began walking purposefully over to the flat-roofed units.

15

Liz began walking after her, picking her way round the worst of the puddles. She could feel the cold starting to seep into her D&M pumps and wished she was wearing her gardening wellies. Supporting Pat was one thing, charging about in the freezing cold of a darkening afternoon quite another. It was the sort of afternoon when all you wanted was to be at home with lamps on and curtains pulled, maybe making vegan flapjacks for her grandson, Jacob.

Jacob. The thought gave her a jolt as unpleasant as the cold puddles. Despite the afternoon chill, Liz could feel her cheeks growing warm as she remembered that last awkward conversation with her son, Timothy. *I don't care what's gone wrong with you and Leoni, you just go back and put it right. Think of Jacob.*

That had been a few days ago. The fact that everything had gone quiet she was choosing to take as a good thing. That, plus the steady stream of emoji-outraged WhatsApp messages from her grandson – GRANDMA, YOU NEED TO SIGN THIS PETITION TO STOP FRACKING NOW – made her hope that not much could be amiss. But what had been the matter with Tim? All that talk about him needing to be on his own . . . It wasn't like him to be so . . . *mopey*. Her mouth tightened in a gesture both her friends would have recognized. When she got home she'd ring and check that everything was as it should be.

Mind made up, she quickened her pace to catch up Thelma, who was standing staring intently at the low units, which were plastered with posters in a bright kaleidoscope of auctions and concerts and circuses. It was obvious to Liz the place hadn't been used in years. They were wasting their time. She sighed, eyes roving round the site. Over in the scribble of brambles was the inevitable tangle of dumped rubbish, bin bags, the soggy sad remains of a sofa . . . and something else – a splodge of colour, bright against the grey vegetation.

She walked over, more to keep her feet from going numb than from any real sense of curiosity. A discarded packet? No, it was a paperback book. The one-time school librarian tutted as she bent to look at the damp and puckered object. A rather evil-looking Nazi officer leered at her from the front cover, beneath a prominent orange swastika; the words 'Gestapo Reckoning' written in blood red. She smiled as the brief fancy came to her of recommending it for her friend Jan's book group.

She looked over at Thelma who was also bending down. 'Have you found a book too?' she called.

'A piece of paper.' Thelma held up the pale scrap, also distorted by damp. In the fading light it was possible to make out squiggles of writing, blurring across the paper. 'I think it's from a notebook.' Gingerly she put the scrap in her handbag.

Liz looked at the low buildings in distaste. 'They can't have been used in years,' she said. 'No way are any of these any sort of charity shop.' With a mitten-encased hand, she tried one of the doors, but it refused to budge.

'Padlock,' said Thelma. She stepped back. 'And the windows are covered over,' she said, gesturing to the mosaic of posters.

'So?' said Liz. From the tone of her friend's voice, something significant had obviously been shared.

'It's what Marguerite said. *She saw the windows shining in the fog.* So, it can't have been any of these. But over *here*—' She began walking over to the hut by the security fence. This, at least, had windows, albeit smeared.

'It's not a shop,' said Liz, following her somewhat impatiently. She caught her up. 'And that door looks rotted through. Look, I know I keep saying it, but this is Marguerite McAllister we're talking about.'

'I know,' agreed Thelma. 'We might as well go back.' She looked over to where they'd come. 'Who's that Pat's talking to?'

* * *

Almost as soon as her friends had walked away Pat found herself suddenly feeling impatient to the point of irritation. Despite Thelma's dismissal of her story, her friends were in their own way being lovely and supportive coming here with her. However, the truth was that as soon as they'd got here, she'd been able to see the whole thing for what it had to be – a load of old hooey. A charity shop that suddenly vanished? What had Marguerite been on about? She thrust her hands deep into the pockets of her new maroon coat, one of a series of birthday-defying purchases she had made in the January sales.

'I hope you can see for yourself it's not suitable.' The rather shrill voice had a definite undertone of accusation and Pat turned to see a woman of about her own age, sporting a mustard-coloured cape and scarlet beret that infused in her a pang of smug superiority.

'Sorry?' said Pat.

'Tucked away down here, *no one's* going to see it, and when it's shut it's going to be a complete magnet for all the bored young people with their skateboards and vapes and what have you.' The woman sounded adamant as she picked her way across the puddles. As she approached Pat, Pat realized she was towing a rather reluctant-looking dog of indeterminate breed. 'It's just a shame it takes something as awful and tragic as what happened the other night to make you see.' Pat looked at her blankly. The woman shook her head in exasperation. 'Site,' she said, ticking the points off on the fingers of one scarlet glove. 'Access. Main road. Though I said all this in my many MANY letters to you people.'

'I'm sorry,' said Pat. 'I think there's some crossed wires going on here.'

'Aren't you from the council? About the site of the new Lidl Express?' Again, the woman sounded accusing.

18

Pat shook her head. 'I'm here with my friends, having a bit of a walk,' she said. What else was there to say? *We're here looking for a charity shop that's apparently vanished?*

'Oh.' The woman sounded as if she didn't entirely believe her. She peered at Pat through the gloom, grey curls framing a rather sharp-looking face. Now she was closer Pat could see that the mustard cape was lined in red. *Nay, love . . . not a good look!*

'I was told after what's happened that someone from the planning department would be coming,' said the woman. 'Why else would you be here? No one else comes down here unless they're fly-tipping.'

Despite everything, Pat decided it was rather wonderful to be taken for some sort of official figure; the new maroon coat was living up to expectations, albeit in an unexpected way. A thought struck her.

'Is this to do with the accident up on the main road?' she said. 'The car crash? Why would planning people come down here?'

'I keep on telling anyone who'll listen how *dangerous* that turning is. On a hill, a corner, just near the railway station. It's a complete and total death trap. Which is why it'd be complete madness to site any sort of shop down here.'

'So that car that crashed the other night, it drove out of *here*?' pursued Pat.

'Like a bat out of hell, according to Bob,' said Mrs Mustard Cape.

Pat realized Thelma and Liz had joined them.

'This lady was telling me about the accident,' she said to them, guessing correctly that Mrs Mustard Cape was someone who relished a good audience. 'The car that crashed was driving out of this track.'

'Shot straight out without even looking. Awful it was.' Mrs

Mustard Cape spoke with some relish. 'That poor lady. That road's bad enough, but on a foggy night . . .' She shook her head. 'She didn't stand a chance.'

'I wonder,' asked Thelma, 'about what time this was?'

'Are you *sure* you're not with the council?'

'No,' said Pat cheerfully. 'We're just nebbing in.'

'A minute after six.' The woman spoke promptly, sounding triumphant and definite, as if defiantly demonstrating what a good witness she would make. 'And I know that because a certain someone—' she looked fondly at the dog, which shiveringly ignored her '—a certain someone always makes a right fuss when the clock strikes six . . . because that's when a certain someone gets his din dins isn't it, Tofu? Up and nudging my foot as soon as *Pointless* finishes aren't you? Yes you are!! Anyway, I was just opening the tin when I heard the screech and the bang. Terrible it was.'

'And you say a lady was *killed*?' asked Liz, frowning in distress.

She nodded. 'They took her to the Friarage, but she died on the way. Mind you, it could have been much worse – the driver of the other car was only a young lad, coming back from college. Ever so upset he was. I took him out a cup of sweet tea. "They'll think it was me driving too fast," he kept saying, "but she shot straight out."'

'You said "like a bat out of hell",' said Pat.

The woman nodded. 'Whatever she was doing here . . . well, Bob reckons there was something fishy going on.'

'Bob?' asked Thelma.

'My neighbour. He was just back off shift and saw the whole thing. He got to the car, but of course didn't dare move her. All squashed in by the airbag she was, poor love. And in a terrible state. Talking some right weird nonsense.'

The three friends exchanged glances. 'What sort of weird nonsense?' asked Pat.

'Bob said she kept muttering the same thing again and again,' she said. '"St Michael protect me; St Michael protect me."' She looked at the three of them, eyes avid with tragedy. '"Carmen," he says to me, "Carmen, *I reckon that woman was in mortal fear.*"'

CHAPTER THREE

A spontaneous favour provokes speculation about the nature of saints.

Retracing their steps, the three lapsed into a sombre silence, which lasted all the way to the main road, with its growling line of traffic, exhaust curling and merging up into the fog. The workmen repairing the damage from the crash were in the last stages of packing up for the day; orange jackets bright against the murk as they hoisted their tools into the parked truck. Drawing level with the slim bunch of flowers, huddled in their cellophane wrapping, the three paused, all thinking much the same thing: that here was representation of a life abruptly ended. A line brutally and uncompromisingly drawn across all the plans great and small that buzz through people's minds: putting out wheelie bins, dieting, dreams of taking a lover or going on *Bargain Hunt*, of decluttering, travelling, connecting – all suddenly and inevitably stopped, made in one instant both irrelevant and trivial. As they regarded the flowers Liz and Pat knew that Thelma was saying a silent prayer, and in their own unsure way they both did something similar, before walking on by unspoken agreement.

'So,' said Pat eventually. 'The crash happened on the same

night that Marguerite saw—' here she paused slightly, glancing over at Thelma '—whatever it was she saw.'

'Not just the same night,' said Thelma, 'but practically the same time. Marguerite told you she caught the train just before six – and the woman said the crash happened just *after* six.'

'Do you think the two things may be connected?' asked Pat.

'Possibly,' said Thelma.

'Whether they are or not,' said Liz, 'I don't suppose we'll ever find out.' Her voice had a familiar finality about it, the tone she used to end unwanted phone calls, or lengthy chance encounters in Tesco. 'Anyway,' she added conclusively, 'I need to be getting back.' There was something in her voice that made Pat wonder again how things were at home, but just as she was about to ask, Thelma nudged her. Standing by the mussel-blue Corsair in the gathering foggy dusk was a young woman, talking volubly and tearfully into her phone; her gestures and body language conveying a sense of intense crisis.

'I keep on telling you,' she was saying, 'the train's been *cancelled*! There's no way I *can* get there for half past.' The eyes were staring and brimming with tears.

'Isn't that the girl who was putting down flowers?' asked Pat quietly. Thelma nodded.

'*Thirsk*!' the girl said. 'Thirsk station!' There was a pause, followed by a tearful shriek. 'I can't do that!' Now there was shrill panic in her voice. '*No way* can I afford a taxi!' She shivered violently; her jacket really was woefully inadequate for such a chilly day.

Pat regarded her with pity; the plump face was obviously built for smiling, not puckering with stress.

'Please forgive me for intruding.' Thelma's voice was calm and gentle. 'We couldn't help overhearing. Is everything all right?'

'My train's been cancelled!' The voice came out as a sort of

23

despairing wail. 'The train to Northallerton. And I need to pick my kids up from childcare before half past.'

Pat looked sideways at Liz; would she be wearing her 'let's not get involved' expression? But Liz was already stepping forward. 'Don't you worry, my love,' she said. 'We'll run you to Northallerton.'

Accepting lifts from strangers is something that most women would think twice about – unless, of course, the strangers happen to be three ladies of a certain age in a mussel-blue Corsair, with a boot full of tins for the foodbank. As the distance between Thirsk station and the Kids R Us after-school club decreased, the young woman – Brid – relaxed, and as she relaxed she chatted, and even smiled once or twice. Nature had intended her to be a jolly, plump thing surrounded by love and laughter; society unfortunately had other ideas. Finance – the fear of bills, and the crippling costs of childcare and heating – meant a life of dashing between no less than three jobs: care home, factory and the odd cash-in-hand stint at the local pub. What she would do without her bezzie Jade she honest to God did not know, she shared.

Fashion had her on a permanently low-carb, semi-fasting diet – 'But I dropped half a pound this week, God be praised!' – yet the necessity for quick and cheap food was at odds with this aim, giving her a sallow, jowly look. It was fashion too that dictated the skimpy top and the brief jacket that made all three ladies in their various layers privately shiver. Whatever star it was the young were following these days – social media, soaps, reality TV – it had given Brid dreams, dreams that lay stubbornly and intractably beyond the reach of Leeming Lodge, NY Plastics and occasional stints at the Moorland Gate – and had driven the father of Grace and Archie away to a hazy and not-to-be-relied-on distance.

At the Thornton-le-Street roundabout Thelma took advantage of a lull in the girl's breathless diatribe to speak. 'I wonder,' she said, 'but did you know the person involved in the car crash?'

'We couldn't help notice that you were laying flowers,' explained Liz.

'I did.' The voice had abruptly lost its cheer and energy, and once again the wide brown eyes started filling up. 'It was my sister.'

There was an embarrassed pause.

'Oh, lovey,' said Liz, instinctively rummaging in her handbag for the balsam tissues.

'No, it's okay,' said Brid somewhat hoarsely. 'It's not like we were close or owt like that. Like she were still my sister, but I didn't see that much of her.'

'Even so,' said Liz gently.

But by bit, snatch by breathless, teary snatch the story came out.

Our Terri had been a good few years older than Brid and they had different dads but the same mum – sadly no longer with us, God rest her soul. Brid and Terri, despite the age gap, had always got on, followed each other on Facebook and stuff like that, but what with one thing and another hadn't had time to meet up much in recent years. 'Though she'd always have been there for me,' said Brid. 'And she never ever forgot the kids' birthdays.' There was another trace of a wobble in her voice, and Liz hastily produced another balsam tissue. Terri had been with someone who was, in Brid's considered opinion, a right Nasty So-and-So.

Tate Bishop was supposedly some sort of businessman with a LinkedIn page and everything, but in Brid's eyes – and their mother's eyes – he'd always been no good. Dodgy. Terri had knocked around with him for years on and off, but then one day she'd ditched Tate and taken up with a bloke she was working for, and then married him. The first Brid had known of any of this was when Terri had messaged her and invited her over to this lush house out in the sticks where she and this Mal Stanley were living. Mal had been a good bit older than Terri and to be One Hundred Per Cent Truthful he had not, in Brid's opinion, been much of an improvement on Tate. In fact, if Brid were to be honest, Mal had creeped her out. But Terri had seemed happy enough, and it had been a lovely house, like something out of *The Only Way is Essex*.

Then, the next thing she heard was that Mal had died, and Terri were proper cut up and had put that huge house on the market without having anywhere to go. She wanted to move in with Brid for a bit, which was a non-starter due to the small nature of her flat. So, what does Terri go and do? Only moves back in with the No-Good Tate Bishop! And that had been the last Brid had heard . . . until the police had come knocking the day before yesterday. 'I never knew she had me down as her next of kin,' she said, voice trembling.

There was a pause as the three ladies assimilated this saga.

'I hope you don't mind me asking,' said Pat eventually, 'but do you know what she was actually doing in Thirsk? When she had the crash? I mean, was she visiting friends here or something?' She could sense Liz stiffening in disapproval on the back seat, and acknowledged to herself that it *was* a rather intrusive question. Of course, what she had *really* wanted to ask was what Terri had been doing belting out of a side road leading nowhere at a rate of knots, but she could think of no appropriate way of framing the question.

The point didn't seem to have occurred to Brid. 'I dunno,' she said. 'She must've been going somewhere – or seeing someone. Or—' her voice took on confidence '—or maybe she was picking something up she bought? She's a great one for eBay and she has this massive collection of shoes.' She stopped dead, her hand flying to her mouth. 'I mean,' she said shakily, '*had.*' Wordlessly, Liz passed over yet another tissue. Brid wiped her eyes. 'You need to be turning left at the next mini round-about,' she said in subdued tones.

Thelma obediently slowed. 'Forgive me for asking,' she said, 'and do please tell me to mind my own business, but were you and your sister raised Catholic?'

'Oh my God!' Brid sounded impressed and alarmed at the same time. 'Are you one of them psychics?'

Thelma shook her head. 'Not at all,' she said. 'Though I am married to a vicar. It's your names. I presume Terri might have been short for Theresa, and maybe you were christened Bridget?'

Brid nodded in the darkness. 'mum was a Catholic, not that she ever went to church that much. But her mum – Nanna Eileen – she looked after us a lot and it was all really important to her, all that religion stuff. And then when Mum got ill . . . well, Father Ryan from St Columbo's, he were there an awful lot. It's just on the right after the Tesco Express.'

Outside the Kids R Us nursery Brid leaned into the car. 'I can't thank you enough,' she said. 'You must let me give you something for petrol.'

'Not at all,' Liz said immediately and fulsomely. 'You're more than welcome.' If either Pat or Thelma thought that any rejection of this offer strictly speaking fell under Thelma's remit, neither said. As Thelma negotiated her way back through what passed for rush hour traffic in Northallerton the three once again lapsed into thoughtful silence.

It was Liz who spoke first. 'That poor lass,' she said, a distinct note of almost accusation in her voice. 'I do feel sorry for her.'

'All right,' said Pat defensively. 'All right, I'm sorry, I hold my hands up. I just wanted to know what she was doing there in the first place. You have to admit it's a bit odd, her driving to that bit of waste ground. And even odder belting away from it at ninety miles an hour.'

Liz compressed her lips. 'She must have made a wrong turn,' she said.

'Anyway, Thelma Cooper . . .' Now it was Pat's tone that sounded accusing. 'What was all that you were going on about?'

'What was all what about?' said Liz, still sounding disapproving.

'All that about Brid and her sister being Catholic. And don't say you were just being polite or anything like that.'

'She was asking about their names,' said Liz. 'What's wrong with that?'

'*And?*' said Pat.

Thelma said nothing for a moment as she slowed for the Thirsk Road turning. Then she gestured to Liz. 'On the back seat,' she said. 'My handbag. There's a sheet of paper. Be careful – it's a bit wet and fragile.'

'The one you found on the ground?' Liz opened the brown satchel with the respect women reserve for opening each other's handbags. Somewhat distastefully she extracted the soggy scrap and held the blurry writing up to where it caught the intermittent amber light of the passing streetlamps. 'It doesn't make much sense to me,' she said.

'Let me see,' said Pat, reaching behind her. She frowned as the rainbowed squiggles resolved themselves into words.

PAST AND PRESENT – BOTH THE SAME?

The last of the streetlights had been left behind; beyond the car windows the winter's night was looking very murky indeed. 'What does it mean?' said Pat.

'I don't know,' said Thelma shortly. 'You tell me.'

'But all that about her being Catholic?' persisted Pat. 'How does that come in? You might as well tell me.' She had no wish to reignite their earlier tension, but she knew there was something her friend wasn't saying.

Thelma sighed and Liz frowned, but both knew no amount of sighing and frowning could deflect their friend in her current bullish mood.

'It's what that poor woman was saying immediately after the crash,' said Thelma.

'Saints preserve us,' said Liz. 'Something like that, wasn't it?'

'Saint Michael,' said Thelma. 'Over and over again. *Saint Michael.*'

'So who's Saint Michael?' asked Pat.

'Saint Michael,' said Thelma. 'One of the Catholic saints.' She paused and then spoke almost unwillingly. 'It's probably nothing at all – and *please* don't go reading anything in this . . .'

'But?' prompted Pat.

'Well, traditionally *St Michael was the saint who guarded against evil spirits.*'

CHAPTER FOUR

The same tale is told three times plus an unexpected visitor arrives with a guitar.

It's notable that when people relate events to those they're close to, they invariably talk about those events in a way that reflects their own particular agendas at the time, whether they're aware of it or not. Thus it was with the three, when recalling the happenings of the day to their husbands.

Pat's narrative, when talking to Rod, was dominated by the more ghostly elements of the tale – the fog, the woman's fear, the deserted waste ground with no sign of any sort of shop, or shop-like building. 'But of course, Thelma won't admit it's *anything* out of the ordinary. She as good as told me to forget all about it.'

'Have you two fallen out?' asked Rod.

Pat shook her head as she chopped aubergines for an Angela Hartnett parmigiana. 'Of course not. But at the end of the day, *she* was the one going on about how the dead woman was invoking saintly protection from evil spirits. And then there was that paper she found—'

Rod looked up from the kitchen table where he was studying his iPad. 'What paper?'

'*Past and present — both the same?*' recited Pat while beginning to grate Parmesan. 'I mean what's *that* about?'

Rod frowned. 'And this is all to do with what that barmy carry-on Mad Margy was telling you about?' he said. 'Shops that vanish?'

Pat compressed her lips and continued slicing aubergines, clearly telling him he'd made the wrong response. 'The woman in that crash was *scared*,' said Pat. 'Apparently she looked *terrified*.'

'You'd look terrified if you'd just had a car smash into the side of you,' said Rod reasonably.

'What about the Catholic saint?' she said, sprinkling sea salt on the pale waxy lengths.

'What Catholic saint?' Rod was frowning distractedly at the iPad.

'I do wish you'd listen,' said Pat. 'Apparently the poor woman kept saying "*Saint Michael*", over and over again.'

'Maybe she was looking for the nearest M&S,' said Rod.

In spite of herself Pat smiled and took a reflective sip of her Merlot. Rod seized his chance.

'So, here's one I like the look of,' he said, angling the iPad round to her. With a feeling as chilling as any haunting, Pat looked. A series of images smiled up at her: sunsets over raked terraces, a picture-book walled town and elegant people of a certain age in pastel leisurewear exuding life and bonhomie as they sipped wine or excitedly pointed out the view to each other. Golden words strode tastefully above the images: 'Treasures of the Loire Valley'. She took another, somewhat larger, mouthful of the wine to dull the feelings she always had when Rod mentioned what he called their 'Joint-Birthday Jaunt'.

'Three vineyards, two chateaus and a medieval walled town,' he read. 'Where time really does stand still.'

'If only,' said Pat, blanching the aubergines.

'All the hotels are at least four stars on Tripadvisor,' said Rod.

'Great,' said Pat, taking another hefty sip of her wine.

'The coach has state-of-the-art toilet facilities,' he said.

'Has it?' said Pat. 'That's good.'

There was a pause.

'I really don't see what your problem is,' said Rod.

IT'S A COACH TOUR, she wanted to scream. A COACH TOUR FOR PEOPLE OF A CERTAIN AGE! And I'm NOT that certain age, not yet! In my head I'm twenty-three and a half. In my head I want to drink beer till midnight and go and see Florence and the Machine headline at Leeds fest, and I would like a shot if I thought my hip could stand it!

Aloud she said, 'No, honestly, it all looks lovely.'

Mollified, Rod took her hand. 'Our tour guides have been rated as top of their game,' he read. Pat varied her enthusiasm by making encouraging noises in her throat. Over his shoulder she read about gentle walks . . . qualified first aider on board . . . each coach has its own defibrillator . . .

'You never know what's around the corner,' said Rod, holding her hand tighter. 'And now I'm retired we need to be doing these things.' Pat smiled again, rather bleakly, inwardly wishing he felt a similar urge to decorate the downstairs cloakroom and clear out the garage.

As she loaded the dishwasher after supper she paused, sighed, trying (and failing) to picture herself in pastel leisurewear using a state-of-the-art toilet on a coach that was speeding towards a medieval walled town.

Her phone shrilled and for the second time in as many minutes she found herself gripping the work surface. Why was she jumpy? It was probably only Liam, ringing to confirm what time he would be coming home next weekend for Rod's birthday.

But it wasn't Liam. It was Marguerite. What could she want?

★ ★ ★

It was also the supernatural elements that were on Thelma's mind as she told Teddy. Not because she was especially unsettled by them as Pat was, but more because she wanted her husband to engage with her, rather than with his mobile phone.

'By all accounts that poor woman was really frightened, and part of me can't help wondering if it was maybe something more than just the car crash,' she said. She opened the Aga door, but it was not the bubbling brown and gold crust of the shepherd's pie she was seeing. 'The whole story's just so *fantastic*. And though I don't think for a moment there was such a thing as a vanishing shop, it's hard to imagine what it was Marguerite *could* have seen.'

Teddy made a noise that meant he was listening but didn't have anything particular to add. This was probably on account of the fact he was examining a great stack of parcels that were piled at the end of the kitchen table and entering their postcodes onto his mobile phone.

'And apparently the poor woman who died was invoking the protection of St Michael, guardian against evil spirits.' She put firm emphasis on the last sentence in an effort to get her husband's full attention. 'That bothers me. I know I probably upset Pat, but you have to be so *careful* with all that sort of thing.' She turned from the shepherd's pie, which was now cooling on the rack, and focused her gaze directly on her husband's blue eyes, now not so much to attract his attention as to *distract* her own from everything she was finding so very irritating about him: the parcels, the list, the clipboard. And the hat. Always that silly black beanie hat with its childish orange logo reading: *Hi! I'm your WAMMP Man!*

'It all feels very . . . disturbing,' she said, fighting to keep the annoyance from her voice as she saw that Teddy was still firmly focused on the WAMMP app. That grave attention he was giving to it and the stack of parcels was the same sort of attention that until recently he would have given to essays or tutorials that were part of his job as chaplain tutor at Ripon and St Bega Theological College – or 'vicar factory', as he referred to it. When it looked likely the college would close the previous year, Teddy had opted to step back from the job, finishing last summer.

When the college had been reprieved, he'd stuck by his decision, taking the chance to (in his words) 'see what's out there in the world'. Which was fine, but what seemed to be out there so far consisted of belting round North Yorkshire delivering parcels. The job for WAMMP – 'Wait A Minute Mr Postman!' – that had originally been a stopgap, was now in its fourth month. Over Christmas, deliveries had ramped up to a ferocious level, with Teddy leaving the house before eight and often not returning until well-gone six. Thelma had been promised that this state of affairs was only temporary, that after the festive period was over there'd be a slackening off. And though this had proved to be the case, a combination of staff shortages and flu bugs meant Teddy was still much busier than she was comfortable with.

Then, a few weeks previously, he'd been approached by the college, asking him if he'd be interested in some part-time work – nothing too onerous, just some marking and some lectures. With the income from that, plus his pension, he'd be markedly better off than he was working for WAMMP, whilst working fewer hours and avoiding hazardous driving round the foggy lanes of North Yorkshire. For Thelma the day when her husband returned safely to Ripon and St Bega's couldn't come soon enough.

'Have you heard anything from the college?' she asked. 'About when they want you to start?'

Teddy shook his head without looking up. 'Roxby, Maunby and Kirby Wiske,' he said. 'And that's the YO7s.' He spoke with the satisfied air of someone who had completed an arduous

'Someone needs to give that railway company a blumin' good rocket,' she said. 'Letting people down like that – *twice* in one week.' She unloaded the dishwasher with angry, forceful rattles. Like both Rod and Teddy, Derek regarded his wife from a kitchen table. 'That poor lass, she was at her wits end. And no wonder, what with losing her sister like that. The last thing she needed was a load of silly ideas putting into her head by people who should know better. I'm surprised at Thelma. Catholic saints indeed.' Liz thrust the spatula and wooden spoon in the utensils pot.

Derek looked at his watch and glanced instinctively at the back door. Picking his moment was the key thing he decided. Let her calm down a bit first.

'I still don't understand all that about a charity shop,' he said.

'You and me both,' said Liz tartly, slamming the last of the cutlery into a drawer. 'If it was anyone else but Marguerite McAllister . . . You remember all that business with the photocopier?'

Derek did, and if there was any danger of him forgetting the whole saga his wife was apt to remind him every year or so.

'And you say this shop disappeared?' he said doubtfully. 'How does that work?'

'You tell me.' She began dispatching plates into cupboards with sounds like pistol shots. 'There was nothing there, just some derelict ruins that obviously haven't been used for years. Someone should do something about them.' Shaking her head Liz shut the final cupboard door. 'And then *Pat* giving the poor girl the third degree about what her sister was up to didn't help.'

'So where do Catholic saints come in?' By now Derek was well and truly lost.

'Nowhere,' said Liz firmly. She hung her pinny on the back

37

of the door like a warrior dispatching their armour. 'Right: *Four in a Bed* or *Bake Off*?'

'Hang on,' said Derek, and there was something in his tone that stopped Liz dead in her tracks. 'I need a word.'

Her heart choked in her throat, as it generally did at such pronouncements. For a moment time stood still. 'What sort of word?' she heard herself saying as she sat down at the table.

'It's about our Tim,' he said.

'What about him?' What with getting tea and relating the story of the charity shop, Liz hadn't had the chance to ring her son as she'd planned. 'I thought that was all sorted,' she said, not because she thought it was but because she desperately wanted it to be.

'Not exactly,' said Derek.

The noise of a key in the back door made them both turn. And there in the doorway was their son, with two holdalls and a guitar.

'Thanks for letting me stay,' he said.

CHAPTER FIVE

Two friends don't fall out and a plan is hatched.

'Thelma won't be happy; she's always so funny about *anything* like this.' The following morning found Pat on the phone to Liz. She sounded defensive, Liz thought, which usually signified she was revving up to some sort of confession. Phone tucked awkwardly under her chin, she made an indeterminate noise to show she was listening as she simultaneously attempted to jiggle the spare room duvet into a clean cover.

'But remember *she* was the one who started on about Catholic saints. Protection against evil and all that. And she was dead right − I looked it up: Saint Michael, guardian angel against evil spirits, there in black and white. And whatever Thelma Cooper says, people *do* see things. She's always so adamant about this sort of stuff.'

'That's Thelma,' said Liz, remembering all the hoo-ha with the Witches' Kitchen.

'I mean, don't get me wrong, it's not like we've fallen out or anything,' said Pat. Wrestling with the duvet, Liz grimaced. Long experience had taught her that her friends 'not falling out' − with all its attendant undercurrents and tensions − caused a lot more stress than any actual row. And at the moment, the very last thing Liz needed was her friends 'not falling out'. No, scrub that; the very last thing she needed was her friends not falling out – and her being caught bang in the middle.

'The fact Marguerite wants to find out a bit more about what she saw . . . well, surely that makes sense? After all, it was an unsettling experience, supernatural or not.'

Yes, on the defensive, thought Liz. She was about to open her mouth and say something placatory, when the phone flew clean out from under her chin and despite her making a graceful (ish) dive across the bed it disappeared with a triumphant clatter down the gap between the bedhead and the wall. Retrieving it meant a scramble under the bed and by the time she was able to listen again (hair sticking up, cardigan floured with fluff) Pat was reaching the end of her confession.

'. . . At the end of the day, all we're doing is going to see some woman in Boroughbridge. It's not like we're sacrificing a chicken on Brimham Rocks.'

'I'm sorry,' said Liz, 'I dropped the phone; you'll have to tell me that again.'

In the deliberate tones Liz knew she used to use with her bottom phonics group, Pat explained again that because of her experience – or whatever it had been – Marguerite believed she was developing some sort of Second Sight and wanted to go and talk it through with someone who might be able to offer her some insight. According to a friend from the 'Single Let's Mingle' group there was a woman in Boroughbridge who was second to none and indeed had insights that were just Plain Uncanny.

'And she wants you to go with her?'

'Why? Do you think I shouldn't?' Pat's slightly defiant tone told Liz that she was having doubts.

'That's entirely up to you,' said Liz, resuming battle with the duvet. She wasn't sure what else she could say. Her own opinions on the whole subject were rather underdeveloped, to say the least. As a schoolgirl she and some friends had snuck in to see *The Exorcist*, which had scared her witless for weeks afterwards. And then, whilst at college, she'd been to Ripon Fair and had her fortune told and been assured she was about to meet a dark, athletic stranger with a yen for travel. A month later she'd met the sandy-haired Derek Newsome, diffident, asthmatic and with an engrained love of Bispham.

'If you want to go and support your friend,' she said, 'that's up to you.'

'Not that Thelma will see it like that.' Pat dropped her voice conspiratorially, as if their friend was hovering censoriously at her shoulder.

'Have you told her?'

'No. Do you think I should? I mean, she'd only get all het up.'

'It's up to you. You might want to say something before we meet next week. Get it all out in the open. But I'm sure she'll be fine.' Actually, Liz had no idea whether Thelma would be fine or not, but she wanted to get the bed made up so she could shut the door on this disrupted room with its holdalls and guitar and push it all out of her mind for a couple of hours at least. A *guitar*! What on earth was Tim doing with *that*? To the best of her knowledge, he hadn't touched one since his Venture Scout days. She sighed and forced her focus back on what Pat was saying.

'. . . Might well not make it to the garden centre this week, I've a few things on.' There was an evasive tone in her voice Liz recognized well.

'Listen, my love,' she said, 'I'm going to let you go. I need to get on.' Her voice was perhaps a bit firmer than she meant it to be, and she immediately felt a stab of guilt at her edgy tone.

41

'Is everything all right?' asked Pat.

'Everything's fine.' Liz sighed. 'It's just we've got our Timothy staying with us for a few days. But it's fine.'

Call ended, she resumed the making up of the bed with a frustrated, panicky energy. What on earth was going on with her son? On Derek's stern instructions she'd refrained from asking outright questions, but every look she gave, every sigh she failed to repress – even the way she'd handed him some cheese and chutney sandwiches to take to work – fairly screamed: *why have you walked out on your wife and child?*

'So, what did Pat's text actually *say*?' asked Liz, again gripping the phone under her chin.

'Going with M to see woman in Boroughbridge. *A medium.*' Thelma managed to imbue the two words with a particularly dark significance.

'I see.' Liz wasn't sure what else she could, or indeed even should, say. She felt a pang of annoyance at Pat for following her advice in such a way as to have Thelma immediately call her.

'Granted, I know she's been in a bit of state lately.' In Thelma's world, 'a state' was a broad term encompassing everything from menopause to bereavement. 'But you just have to be so careful with these things.'

Liz sighed; for the second time that day she had been forced to stop doing what she was doing to give a friend's call her full attention. This time she'd been peeling and chopping carrots for a mince casserole, a childhood favourite of her son's – as if some end-of-the-week Friday comfort food would prompt him to say exactly what the blazes was going on. There had even been some mention of estate agents, which she was trying hard not to think about. Once again, she reluctantly forced her mind away from her son to her friend. 'She probably wanted you to

42

hear it from her, rather than Marguerite.' Why must her friends choose *now* 'not to fall out'?

'And the whole thing just seems a bit, I don't know, *odd*,' said Thelma. 'Marguerite has some strange experience and we're supposed to believe there's a connection between that and some poor woman's car crash? Is that what Pat thinks?'

'I really have no idea,' said Liz, itching to return to the carrots.

'Is everything all right?' Thelma's voice was suddenly curious. There was never any hiding anything from Thelma.

Liz sighed again. 'Our Timothy's come home for a few days.' She tried with a light voice to play down the unplaydownable.

'I see,' said Thelma.

'Anyway,' said Liz, 'I must get on. I'll see you on Thursday.'

'Actually, that was one of the reasons I was calling,' said Thelma. 'I'm unlikely to make coffee o'clock.'

'Really?' The dismay was apparent in Liz's voice. This took 'not falling out' to a whole new level.

'I've something on,' said Thelma. 'I'll see you both the week after.'

Call ended, Liz looked in exasperation at the heap of half-chopped vegetables realizing the full extent of how dismayed she actually felt. Meeting with her friends was a very important part of her routine, and the thought of any disruption to that gave her a chill of insecurity. Not because she wanted to talk about Tim – in fact, until she knew more, she'd much rather keep quiet on the subject – but her friendship with Thelma and Pat was a reassuring constant in a world that could be very inconstant and sometimes downright distressing.

Pat and now Thelma both crying off! What if this 'not falling out' went on and on? It all seemed so *silly* – the whole thing … No, not silly; after all a woman had been killed. And whatever was going on with Marguerite's vision or the car crash Liz

43

instinctively didn't like it. And it seemed to be driving a wedge between her friends. But what could she *do* about it? A thought from earlier chimed in her mind.

Browning the mince, she felt the beginnings of an idea forming, and by the time she was mixing the stock it was more or less there. Its very boldness made her frown worriedly into the distance and it was only the smell of scorching food that brought her to herself. It *could* work. At any rate, it'd be worth a try.

CHAPTER SIX

In the ghost of a store where time stands still, there is talk of funerals and thoughts of what might have been.

The following Thursday was yet another mild, foggy day, coming after a week of mild foggy days. In Thirsk market place the last of the fronds from the Christmas tree were swept up, leaving the cobbles shiny, damp and bleak. Crossing from the car park, Thelma wrinkled her nose at the ongoing grey murk and thought worriedly of Teddy's chest; she was sure she'd heard the beginnings of a cough that morning. And navigating through all those foggy lanes, when people were apt to drive so recklessly!

Once again, she remembered that awful crash by the station and gave a shiver that wasn't altogether to do with the all-pervasive damp. For all her adamant protestations, there was something about the whole thing she found frankly disturbing ... And Pat going to see a medium! But even so, was it right to have ducked out of their coffee session like that? But then, she hadn't been entirely lying as she *did* have somewhere she wanted to go that morning. She wanted to pay a visit to the Busby's closing down sale.

For some weeks now the restrained shop frontage in Thirsk

market place had been plastered haphazardly with cherry red and white posters reading: 'Closing down sale' and 'Everything must go!'

For the people of the town, the store, with its rambling series of rooms and levels, its unevenly shaped departments with their discreet music and tartan carpets, had been an immovable fixture for all of their lives. To them, the closure of Busby's was yet another sign that the world in general was 'Going To The Dogs', but the hard truth was, and had been for some time, that the clothes, the appliances and the crockery were all things that could be found a good deal cheaper online.

Thelma had never been a regular shopper there but had made an annual visit each December when she would take her class to the famous Busby's Christmas Grotto. Every year one of the back storerooms on the first floor would be decked out as some festive location that children would progress through to reach Santa, who would be sitting waiting in a red-and-green-bedecked boardroom. The grotto had long been the passionately cared-for baby of Anne Lewis, head of kitchen appliances. For ten months of the year she was a grey-haired, rather short-sighted lady amiably supplying the people of Thirsk with spatulas and frying pans, but come November and December she was the undisputed Grotto Queen, acquiring a steely drive and purpose that transformed cardboard, papier-mâché and netting into a series of breath-taking scenarios generally held to be as good as anything Leeds had to offer. The Gingerbread Factory, the Teddy Bears' Workshop, Narnia (complete with lamppost and White Witch) . . . Year after year, one of the perennial topics of local conversation was what Anne Lewis would come up with next.

Of course, all this had stopped many moons ago, but nevertheless, looking round the denuded remnants of the store now, Thelma experienced a sharp, sweet sadness for times past. The space was a ghost of its former self, only a few display stands huddled together in the middle of the various rooms, covered willy-nilly in what disparate remains of the stock were still left – screwdrivers, coasters, handkerchief sets and lawn feed. High on the wall, looking sadly down, was the grand gold face of the Busby clock, once a respected guardian of time, now frozen forever at ten past six. A woman with two small children was industriously scouring the shelves and Thelma could tell the woman was as sad at the meagre selection as she was herself.

Whole areas of the store were now empty and cordoned off, stretching sadly and meanly away: ladies' apparel, perfumes and make-up, greeting cards and stationery. Without the stock it was just an uneven, empty space. Thelma frowned, then stopped. What was that sudden flicker of an idea? Something significant. But *what*?

Before she could pursue the thought, she realized that the woman with the children was looking at her with an uncertain recognition. Did she know her? She looked familiar but lacked a context. Not church or the church choir – an ex-pupil, maybe? The woman was plump, wearing a coat that was way too skimpy for such a damp, grey day. The older child was a solemn girl with dark, fat plaits; the younger one a boy of maybe six or seven who was casting around the store with a barely restrained energy.

'Come on, Archie.' The girl was talking to her brother with weary bossiness born of long practice. 'There's nothing here.'

'You said we might find summat nice,' said Archie, looking balefully at his mother.

At that second, recognition came to Thelma.

'It's Brid, isn't it?' she said. The young woman looked at her again and for a second Thelma felt that unnerving social panic that you get when you've spoken to someone by mistake. Then her face cleared.

47

'Mrs Cooper?' she said. 'Hello.' She turned to the children. 'This is the kind lady who gave Mummy a lift the other day.'

The children regarded Thelma dispassionately. 'Are there some more things somewhere else?' asked Archie.

'We heard they were selling things off cheap,' explained Brid. 'There's an INSET day at the kids' school, so we thought we'd have a trip out – see if there was anything we could get. But there's hardly owt left.'

'And how are things with you?' asked Thelma.

'You know.' She smiled. 'Getting there.'

'The jobs all going well?'

'Too well. I'm being offered extra shifts all over the place – the pub, the factory . . . If I could cut myself in half I'd be well away.'

This account of day-to-day living was cutting little ice with Archie. 'There's another lot of stuff up those steps,' he announced. 'Can I go and look?'

'You go with him, Grace,' said Brid. 'I can see you from here. You are NOT to touch and NOT to go off anywhere or it's no screen time for three days, d'you understand me?' They both nodded and jogged across to what had once been the kitchenware department.

'I've this mate, Jade, and we double up on childcare and stuff, otherwise everything'd be eaten up by daycare fees.' Barely taking a breath, Brid was back on the subject of day-to-day living. 'Jade has a girl who's Grace's age, so we do sleepovers when one of us has got evening work. I've got it better than many, but it's still relentless I don't mind saying, Mrs Cooper.' She was one of those people who are able to maintain a conversation whilst doing something else altogether, in this case keeping her eyes roving across to her children as they picked over the denuded display stand. Thelma's eyes, experienced with long years of playground duty, roved with them.

'I hope you don't mind me asking,' she said, 'but have you heard any more from the police about the accident?'

Abruptly, Brid's weary and watchful expression was replaced by one that was dark and bleak.

'Dangerous driving, that's what they're saying,' said Brid. 'I'm not being funny, but I could have told them that. Terri just pulling out of that side road at the wrong time on a foggy night – it's not rocket science! Archie, NO!'

Her voice snapped across the store, freezing Archie where he stood holding an enormous length of electric flex like a handler with a python. 'I said no touching!' She turned her attention back to Thelma. 'I'm on with the funeral now,' she said without drawing breath. 'I've all *that* to organize on my Jack Jones.'

'Surely her partner will be doing that?' said Thelma. 'This Tate? You did say she'd been living with him?'

'Him?!' Brid puffed out her cheeks expressively.

Thelma looked enquiringly at her.

'I don't want anything to do with him. I tell you, Mrs Cooper, I do not like that guy. There's something about him.' Brid shook her head. 'I mean, he practically forces her to go back to him . . . but now she's dead, he doesn't want to know a thing about her.'

'He actually said that?'

'He hasn't said anything because he won't talk to me. Just after she died he messaged me saying he was going to sort the funeral, and then suddenly I start getting all these calls from the undertaker saying I'm the next of kin, and what casket do I want?' Her voice sounded shrill, in the way it had when she was stranded by the station. 'They say her estate will pay for it, but what if it doesn't? I can't afford it.'

'And you've presumably called him?'

'Mrs Cooper, I've tried ringing, I've tried emailing – I even tried turning up at that Ghost Experience he's running over near Harrogate. But it's the same thing every time – he's unavailable. Voicemails, automated emails – "Tate Bishop is not available but will get back to you". Only he doesn't. If you ask me, now he's got her money he's not bothered.'

'She left her money to him?'

Brid nodded. 'That's what she told me the plan was. They both have wills leaving everything to each other. Grace! Keep an eye on your brother!' The solemn figure in plaits turned and nodded.

The treacherous thought hit Thelma like a sudden migraine. *If I'd had a little girl, I'd have put her hair in plaits . . .*

Biting down the painful moment, she forced herself back to the problem in hand. 'It's a big job organizing a funeral,' she said. If her voice was suddenly shaky Brid didn't notice it.

'I know,' she said wearily. 'I'm on with seeing the vicar next. Sorting out all the God side of it.'

'Have you anyone in mind?' asked Thelma.

'I'm going to go down the local church,' said Brid. 'Or maybe look online.'

'If you need any help . . .' said Thelma. Brid looked at her, puzzled. 'My husband is ordained,' she said. 'He works at Ripon College, in the theology department.' It wasn't such a lie – he was still a vicar and very soon he *would* be back at the college, even if only part-time. Brid looked at her uncertainly, not sure how to respond. She really looked very young.

'Or,' said Thelma, 'Did Terri's late husband have family who could help?'

Brid rolled her eyes and drew in breath in a way that promised a tirade of some description, but whatever she was about to say was interrupted by a small but significant crash and a shout of 'Archie!' She hurried over to the display stand where several objects were now rolling across the floor.

'Mummy, I did tell him,' said Grace.

'I just wanted to see,' said Archie defensively, the suspicion of a tremble appearing on his bottom lip.

'I said not to touch,' said Brid, frantically scooping objects off the floor.

Thelma frowned. So, Tate had offered to pay for Terri's funeral, but had then cut off all communication? And why that roll of the eyes at the mention of Mal's family? What had she been about to say? She forced herself back to the present where Brid and Grace were efficiently replacing items on the display stand whilst Archie looked sorrowfully on. There was something infinitely vulnerable about the little family group. Again, her gaze focused on the solemn figure in plaits patiently repairing the damage caused by her brother.

Walking hastily away she stepped out into the market place where the cold breeze slapped her cheeks. The shapes of the shops were blurred, but whether that was by the fog or by sudden tears she was unsure. 'Lord,' she said in an undertone, 'guide my steps.'

There was a buzz from her phone and she glanced at the incoming text.

ANY CHANCE YOU COULD COME
TO GARDEN CENTRE AFTER
ALL? I'VE HAD AN IDEA. LX

CHAPTER SEVEN

Strange thoughts and odd experiences are had in an Absolutely Gorgeous Family Home.

'Do we have any idea why Tim should be stopping with them?' asked Pat. 'Is it that Leoni's looking after her mother, or that they're having the bathroom remodelled – something like that?'

'I don't *think* it's anything like that,' said Thelma.

When she'd arrived at the garden centre in response to Liz's summons there had been no sign of her friend, just Pat sitting at the round table in the corner. In view of their 'not falling out' this could have been rather tricky; fortunately, in light of Liz's previous bombshell, a subject was ready to hand to cover any potential awkwardness.

'I mean her *Timothy*.' Pat shook her head. 'Do you know any more than me?'

Thelma shrugged. 'Just that he's moved out and is staying with her and Derek for the time being.'

'Poor Liz.' Pat sighed and took a bite of her Melmerby slice. 'Poor Jacob, come to that. How's *he* going to be coping with all this?'

They both took pensive sips of their coffee, thinking of Liz's grandson and his absolute need for everything around him to be Just So.

'Do you think there might be someone else?' asked Pat.

Thelma thought exactly that; in her experience, more often than not it was the presence of a third party that inevitably made the calmest of marital waters choppy. All she said however was: 'Liz didn't mention that.'

The two of them exchanged a significant glance.

There was another pause. As with all good friends, they had between them an unspoken agreement never to criticize each other's husbands and children. It was this that prevented Pat from mentioning the nickname she had for Liz's son: 'Brown Bread Tim'. Every aspect of his life – wife and child, job selling machine parts for Ormondroyds, the five-a-side league he was in, his passion for Hartlepool United – always seemed so steady and unspectacular. '*Her Timothy*,' said Pat again. 'Of all the people in the world.'

Thelma coughed discreetly. 'Of course, there was *that time*,' she said. It was all she needed to say and there was a pause as they both recalled Tim's affair with Rochelle the barmaid from Dishforth, some fifteen years his senior – a liaison that had torpedoed his relationship, A levels and membership of the Venture Scouts, to the immense distress of his mother.

'But that was when he was still at school,' said Pat eventually. '*Years* ago.'

'What was years ago?' Neither had heard Liz approaching, so involved had they been in their speculation. Both spoke simultaneously.

'Busby's Grotto,' said Thelma.

'My magenta hair,' said Pat.

Looking at her friends Liz allowed herself the briefest moment of satisfaction; she reckoned she'd timed her appearance just about right. Her plan to both get the pair of them talking

53

and have the subject of Tim broached in her absence seemed to have worked well.

Not that she was going to leave it at that.

'So,' she said, setting down coffee, two bags of seed potatoes and arranging her fleece on the back of her chair. 'I've been *thinking*.' Her voice was brisk and the tone one they both recognized – the one she used for planning class assemblies and celebration days. 'All this funny business with Marguerite McAllister.' Taking a cautious but firm step on what was proving to be pretty thin ice, she looked squarely at her friends.

Neither of them spoke.

'*Something* happened,' she continued. 'Exactly *what*, we don't know. And whether it's somehow connected to that poor lady in the crash . . . well, we don't know that either. But one thing we *could* do is what you always say we should do.' Here she nodded at Thelma. '*We find out more.*'

There was a silence.

'I don't see how we can,' said Pat eventually. 'That poor woman is dead, remember?'

Thelma nodded, trying to look disinterested and distant but even as she did so, she was aware of the memory of Brid's sad face and the conversation they'd just had in Busby's.

'Exactly,' said Liz. 'We know very little. But one thing we do know is that this Terri Doo-dah—'

'Stanley,' supplied Thelma.

'Terri Stanley,' said Liz, 'shot out of some side road, the same side road where Marguerite reckons she saw some charity shop.'

'A shop that wasn't there the next day,' pointed out Pat.

'So,' said Liz, 'the question we come back to is this: are these two things connected?'

Her friends looked at her expectantly.

Liz slapped a marked card folder onto the table. Thelma

54

looked surprised and Pat suppressed a smile. This was usually Thelma's party trick.

'From the *Thirsk Advertiser* web page.' Liz retrieved a printout from the folder. 'Businessman's widow killed in fatal car crash. Terri Stanley, thirty-three, widow of late businessman Malcolm Stanley from Marley on Swale, stepmother to Shaun and Michelle.'

'Brid said she lived in a village near here,' said Pat. Thelma said nothing, remembering again Brid's expression at the mention of Mal Stanley's family.

'It says he died eight weeks ago in tragic circumstances. Some sort of fall at home,' continued Liz. She looked at her friends who were both wondering where all this was leading. 'I know,' she said. 'You're wondering what all this has to do with the price of fish? The thing with looking is you have to have an idea *where* to look.'

'We've been to the waste ground,' said Pat. 'There was nothing there.'

'Well.' Liz reached for the folder. 'I had another little brain-wave, which you may or may not want to go along with.' Both her friends wondered if they, in fact, had any choice in the matter. Liz produced another sheet of paper, headed with the familiar logo of Spooner and Collins, the local estate agent. Beneath it was a picture of a large, stolid-looking Sixties detached house, which, despite all the photographer's skill, still managed to look rather sullen. 'Brid said her sister was selling her house, which was a big house. And there's only one big house for sale in Marley on Swale.'

Offers in the region of £875,000, the text carolled up gleefully at them. *This stunning six-bed house is in a breath-taking Yorkshire village with excellent access to a range of local facilities.*

'I wondered,' said Liz, 'whether we might not want to go and have a look round? See what we can find out?' She looked at her friends. 'Well?' she said, when they remained silent.

Pat smiled. '*CSI Thirsk*, starring Liz Newsome,' she said. 'Okay, I'm in.'

They looked at Thelma, who appeared to be rather breathless and railroaded – feelings her friends knew she was not at all familiar with. She paused, not seeing the other women but again Brid's sad eyes as she spoke about her sister and remembered her own words: *Lord, guide my steps*.

'I suppose it couldn't do any harm,' she said.

The words 'Yorkshire village' bring certain images to the minds of most people, images of dry-stone walls, crouched cottages, characterful pubs beside wide grassy greens. And to be fair, most villages in North Yorkshire have at least some of these elements.

And then there are places like Marley on Swale.

It was a bedraggled, lanky sort of place, where the road snaked and looped through as if trying to shake off the houses, which stood adjacent to it at odd, awkward angles. During World War Two, Marley had been at the edge of a large Canadian air force base; the legacy of this defined the village in the form of large tracts of weed-broken concrete fringed by vast tin sheds repurposed as factory units bordered by the A1. The houses of Marley were an unspectacular mix from the previous two centuries; the most recent being a blemish of early twenty-first-century shoeboxes optimistically named 'Kingfisher Reach'.

The pub – like so many rural pubs – was closed, fenced and boxed off with tin over the windows and flimsy builder's fencing, and the village shop looked shabby, half-hearted and barely stocked. Even on the brightest days Marley on Swale failed to look anything much, and later that Thursday afternoon when the thickening fog had smeared everything into anaemic shapes, it really did look to be, as Pat said, 'the Arsebone of Existence'.

If ever a house failed to live up to its name, it was Sunny View Lodge. The sullen Sixties structure had obviously never

56

been any sort of lodge, and the belt of dripping utilitarian fir trees that set it apart from the rest of the village stifled any views and would have effectively blocked out sunshine had there been any. As Thelma's mussel-blue Corsair and Liz's white Fiat turned down a tree-lined driveway, an anoraked woman in a headscarf looked on impassively from the garden of a neighbouring bungalow, putting Pat in mind of an extra from *The Wicker Man*.

The estate agent from Spooner and Collins was standing on the mossy gravel beneath the trees, watching out for them with the air of a disgruntled dogger. She was a large, untidy-looking woman, wearing a large, untidy-looking cape, with a rather cheap-looking clipboard shoved awkwardly under one arm. She seemed slightly surprised at the sight of two cars and the three ladies emerging from them.

'Mrs Cowper?' she said to Liz. 'You rang earlier today?'

'I'm Mrs Cooper,' Thelma corrected firmly. After making the bold suggestion they view the house, Liz had only been too happy for Thelma to make the viewing in her name. 'These are my two friends, come along to give me moral support.'

'Val Carpenter, Spooner and Collins. Call me Val.' She eyed them narrowly, as if suspecting them of planning to call her something else. 'I have to tell you from the get-go,' she said, door key poised, 'that the lady who owned the property very sadly died last week. A nasty car crash – all very sad and distressing.' She put the key into the door and gave the white plastic structure a bit of a lift and shove. 'So, of course, that throws everything up in the air somewhat, and though we are still doing showings, please bear in mind it's all a bit of a tangle.'

She opened the door and a damp, neglected smell wafted out. 'So,' she said, 'this is Sunny View Lodge – an Absolutely Gorgeous Family Home.'

Val Carpenter was one of those people who are incapable

of lying convincingly; from her opening words, through every subsequent enthusiastic comment, it was obvious she thought much the same as Thelma, Pat and Liz – that the place was a depressing dump. It wasn't that it was small – room opened on room opened on room – and neither was it neglected – despite the clammy atmosphere, it was clear from the carpets and the wallpaper that this was a place that had had money spent on it – it was *how* that money had been spent, the features that had been slapped on it over the years in blasts of fashion-driven whims. The round windows, like portholes, in the dining room walls. The plaster ornamental niches in the dining room (reminiscent of urinals, Pat thought), the zig-zags of rather rusty track lighting in the kitchen above granite work surfaces that were just the wrong shade of grey.

In the living room was a vast, sprawling fireplace with large, liver-and-corned-beef-coloured slabs of stone. In the right context of log fires and family teas it might have been all right, but in the shadowed living room it looked garish and at odds with the rest of the space, like botched plastic surgery. It wasn't helped by evidence of the last remnants of clearing out. A pile of paperback books leaned against a coffee table, piled with various lamps and a large box containing vast gold tassels from curtain ties; the whole collection huddled forlornly together like evacuees waiting to be billeted. 'You can see what a splendid room this is,' said Val Carpenter.

Liz frowned as something caught her attention but before she could pursue the thought Pat gave a loud exclamation. She was looking against the wall where bizarrely a large number of women's shoes were lined up. 'Who lived here?' said Pat. 'Imelda Marcos?'

Not a flicker of a smile impacted on Val Carpenter's features. 'The lady who lived here was fond of shoes, so I gather.' Though not apparently enough to take them with her.

Liz regarded the pairs of brown, white, black and blue, neatly and sadly arranged, each thinking of the feet that would never wear them again. It put her in mind of Derek's cousin Ruby and her collection of handbags. The vast majority would only be used once or twice before being summarily dispatched off to the charity shop. She sighed at the melancholy memory and looked over at her friends. Thelma seemed grave, almost sad, and Pat . . . Pat was now staring out of the window as if trying to remember something. All at once she felt a guilty flush – they were here because of her. The plan had been to find out more as a way to draw her friends together. She needed to do *something* to make sense of this depressing experience.

'So, this lady who died here—' Her voice was brisk and the estate agent tensed up.

'She didn't die *here*,' said Val emphatically. 'I said she died in a car crash.'

'So, what's the situation exactly?' persisted Liz. 'With the house?'

'What my friend means,' interjected Thelma, 'is who does the house technically belong to *now*?'

Val Carpenter shrugged. 'We haven't been informed about that yet,' she said. 'What I *can* tell you is this place is in top nick.' She patted the Regency stripe wallpaper protectively. 'The lady who died, she'd been widowed herself and had wanted to downsize. That's why she had the place on the market.'

'I understand,' said Thelma smoothly. The tone of her voice was clear to Liz; her friend was in 'finding out' mode. 'After a long marriage, it's only natural you'd want to move away from somewhere that has associations.'

'I don't think she'd been married that long,' said Val. 'I gather she was a bit younger than her late husband, and they'd only been married a year or so. Even so, it must have been upsetting.' She lowered the clipboard slightly in a way that was obviously meant to denote delicacy of feeling. 'Is that why you wish to relocate?' she said to Thelma.

'No, nothing like that,' said Thelma hastily 'I – we – just fancied a change.' By the flustered way she spoke, Liz could tell her friend was wincing at having to tell a lie.

The tug of suspicion returned to Val's face. 'If you'd like to come through to the main hall,' she said stiffly.

The hall, which was the main entrance, was a wide, cuboid void around which a polished open staircase ascended to the upper floor. Dominant on the side wall was an iron skeleton clock, black lines against the off-white expanse, hands stuck at ten to three.

'It really is a lovely, sunny space,' said Val Carpenter half-heartedly.

Sunny but distinctly chilly, thought Liz, shivering despite the fact she was wearing her thickest gardening fleece. On the floor by the front door was that spray of mail, common to empty houses. One thing stood out amongst the white envelopes though – a green flyer bearing the image of a startling dark silhouette. The text read: *Village Voices.* Some sort of protest meeting maybe? She frowned. She'd seen something else on the floor that had also caught her attention – something in the living room. What? Thinking to go back and see, she caught sight of Pat. And stopped.

Her friend was staring up at the stairs, her face set, her brow slightly furrowed, as if trying to bring something to mind. Something extremely unpleasant, Liz thought. She saw Thelma had noticed, and now Val Carpenter was also looking at her.

'Is everything all right?' she said.

Pat was looking at the stairs. 'It's just . . . the stairs,' she said uncertainly.

'What about them?' said Val. Her voice was all at once steely suspicion. 'They're not to everyone's taste, but they can be replaced, and I'm told they're compatible for fitting a stair lift.' At that moment a phone shrilled into life, somewhere deep within the shabby handbag on the agent's arm. 'Excuse me,' Val said, her voice still wary.

'What's the matter?' Liz turned to Pat as Val retreated through to the living room. Thelma waved a cautious hand at Liz, who realized she needed to lower her voice. 'What is it?' she said.

'I don't know.' Pat looked both upset and uncomfortable. 'Just a *feeling* . . .'

'What sort of feeling?' said Liz anxiously.

What sort indeed, thought Pat, trying vainly to weave the floating cobwebs in her mind into something more tangible. 'I don't know,' she said. 'Like there's *something* I should have done. I don't know. *Something.*'

Thelma looked at her friend seriously. 'You've been looking a bit odd since we got here,' she said.

Pat looked at the other two. 'It's the strangest thing,' she said. 'I keep getting the feeling I've been here before.'

'Have you?' asked Thelma.

Pat shook her head as if trying to clear it. 'No, of course not,' she said. 'But things feel somehow familiar – the garden, this clock, *these stairs* . . .' Her eyes followed them warily upwards, past the wall and the iron clock, as if afraid of what she might see at the top.

'Could Rod have maybe done some work here?' asked Liz, looking doubtfully at the polished treads.

'It's possible,' said Pat. 'But then why would I have been here?'

At that moment it was Thelma's turn to stiffen. Again, she waved a hand, indicating they should lower their voices, and nodded her head towards the door where Val had retreated. Wordlessly the three gathered by the door.

'. . . she *is* legit? Cowper . . . Thelma *Cowper*?' Val Carpenter's voice was grim. '. . . they don't look like journos, but you never know . . . Her number's on the booking.'

The three looked at each other. *Journalists?* 'Why does she think we might be journalists?' hissed Liz. Thelma flapped her hand to quieten her.

'Okay, thanks for calling, Casey . . .' said Val. 'Yes, I'm good for Sowerby; I'm nearly done here. Look, I've got to go—'

When Val Carpenter re-entered the hall the three women were looking nonchalantly round the space.

'There's no need to ask the time,' said Liz brightly, gesturing to the gaunt black iron outline of the clock.

'*Stands the church clock at ten to three, and is there honey still for tea?*' said Thelma.

Val looked at her blankly. 'It's just gone two,' she said.

'It's a poem,' said Thelma. 'Rupert Brooke. We learned it at school.'

Val looked unimpressed. 'Shall we take a look upstairs?' she said flatly.

Rather gingerly the three followed her. Liz, in particular, kept a firm grip on the banister. She didn't like the thought of trying to go up or down the polished wooden treads. Suddenly she was aware Pat in front of her wasn't moving. 'What is it now?' she said.

Her friend turned a worried face to her. 'I don't know,' she said. 'I had this sudden . . . I don't know, this sudden *thought* . . . *Somebody crying* . . .'

'What d'you mean? Who's crying?' Liz stared at her, but Pat was shaking her head as if trying to clear it while climbing the last few stairs.

If the downstairs was sprawling, the upstairs was just the opposite. Apart from a large, rather indeterminate space at the top of the stairs, the six bedrooms seemed rather plain, with wardrobes and bathroom fittings in the style beloved some thirty years ago, in shades of coffee brown, pale blue and avocado. The master bedroom was an ice palace of mirrored wardrobe doors.

'And this is the *second* en-suite bedroom!' Val Carpenter came to a stop in front of a door at the end of the corridor with the air of someone about to unveil the pièce de résistance. Pat clutched Liz's arm. 'On the wall,' she said. 'On the right as you go in . . . *it's tiger-print wallpaper!*'

Liz felt a shiver of fear. 'How can you possibly know?' she said. With chilly uncertainty the pair followed Thelma and Val through the door and with a thrill of horror Liz saw the vista of black with snarling tiger heads and red, green and blue foliage.

'The en suite is through here,' said Val grandly, throwing open the door and revealing yet more dull green fittings. But Pat wasn't looking at that. She was looking at a space where tell-tale indentations on the carpet indicated the bed had stood.

A bed . . . a woman sitting there, tense on the edge . . . silhouetted against the window . . . A thud of music from outside . . . and when the woman turned . . . tears shining on her face in the half-light.

'Come back,' she said. 'You will come back, won't you? PROMISE ME!'

CHAPTER EIGHT

A moment is taken in a neglected garden and rumours of ghosts are roundly dismissed.

Simultaneously locking the door of Sunny View Lodge and checking her phone, Val Carpenter said, 'As I say, there's been a lot of interest in this property.' She hadn't said, and in any case neither Pat, Thelma nor Liz believed her. The sensation felt by all three at leaving the house was one of overwhelming relief, akin to walking out into bright summer sunshine after a hospital visit.

'Have you any questions?' asked Val. Her voice was dismissive, the implication clear – she didn't think any questions were forthcoming.

'Just one,' said Thelma pleasantly. 'Why did you think we might be journalists?'

Val fumbled with the keys, dropping them on the gravel. 'Journalists?' she asked. 'I didn't think that. What made you ask that?' She began walking away. 'So sorry,' she said. 'I really have to dash. I'm late for another appointment. Also, don't forget, things are rather up in the air. But if you are interested then do, please, give me a bell.'

* * *

Liz watched her friends pulling off in the mussel-blue Corsair, following after Val Carpenter. She couldn't be sure, but they seemed to be getting on again, and if that had been achieved then at least some good would have come out of this frankly depressing afternoon. Ideally she'd have liked to be with them, then they could have repaired to the garden centre for what Pat termed 'a caffeine debrief' but she'd arranged with Tim that she'd collect Jacob from school and at the moment it was doubly, trebly important that there was as little disruption to his routine as possible.

But what a sad house! And what had been all that about them being *journalists*, of all things? And Pat. What had been going on there? Her funny do on the stairs . . . and then that tiger-print wallpaper. She shook her head perplexedly, not at all sorry to be leaving Sunny View Lodge behind.

Reaching in her bag for her car keys, she noticed her phone was flashing. Three missed calls from Leoni over the past seven minutes. With a dropping feeling of dread, she returned the call.

'Liz, thank God!' Leoni's habitually stressed tones now sounded positively operatic.

'Is everything all right?'

'Everything's fine.' (It obviously wasn't.) 'Liz, I was wondering, is there any way you could pick up Jacob tonight? Only there's training here at the surgery I really can't miss, and Tim isn't picking up.'

'Leoni, love, Tim already asked me. I'll be on my way to get him in a minute or two.'

'Thank God!' Leoni's voice sounded as though tears were not too far away.

'Did he not tell you?'

'He might have done. I don't know, I'm all over the place at the moment.'

65

'You've got a lot on your plate.'

'You can say that again.' Thankfully the voice was regaining some of its control.

'I'm only too happy to collect Jacob – you know that.' In fact, if she'd had her way, she'd have moved him in as soon as all this nonsense of Tim's started, but naturally, she left this thought unvoiced.

'I know, Liz, thank you.'

Liz wondered whether to speak, but before she could process the thought, she found the words tumbling out. 'Leoni, if it's any help, I've told our Tim in no uncertain terms he needs to go back and sort things out.'

A pause. 'Thanks, Liz.' Another pause. 'Don't be too hard on him.'

That was unexpected. Was the reason Tim had left to do with something Leoni had done? Plump, cheerful Leoni, with her WhatsApp groups and job at the surgery? Surely not?

'Don't get me wrong, Liz, I'd love him to come back. I hope to God he does. He's just . . . in a bad place.'

Liz frowned. What did she mean by *that*? Thoughts and fears of cancers, depressions and money problems surged through her mind in a tidal rush. 'Is he okay?'

'Liz, it's for him to tell you. Look, I really have to go. Thanks again.'

'What a hole,' was all that Pat said as they drove away from Sunny View Lodge, her voice rather shaky despite her best efforts. Thelma didn't reply as she negotiated the turn out of the drive but her slight nod implied she was in total agreement.

For a moment they were silent, as if unwilling to speak whilst in the confines of Marley on Swale. Pat realized that she was clutching the seatbelt tightly. The flat, foggy landscape felt like her mind: full of vaguely sinister shapes that she didn't care to dwell on. She sensed her friend was waiting for her to speak but she felt unwilling to say anything about the troubling experience she'd just had – not given Thelma's adamant views on such subjects. But eventually, she couldn't bear the silence anymore. 'I can't see we learned anything very much,' she said. 'Despite DI Newsome's best efforts.'

'Perhaps.' Thelma slowed for the Busby Stoop roundabout. By the tone of her voice Pat could tell that she didn't agree but wasn't going to say.

'Well, did we?'

'I was just wondering,' said Thelma. 'Exactly *why* Val Carpenter thought we might be journalists.'

'Because of the crash?' ventured Pat. 'Poor Terri Doo-dah getting killed.'

'Someone killed in a car crash who had been selling a house,' said Thelma. 'Tragic though it is, it's hardly something undercover journalists would bother about.'

'No.' Pat frowned out at the thickening fog.

'And then,' said Thelma, 'there was your reaction to the stairs. For some reason that made her rather suspicious.' Pat felt herself stiffen, tightening her grip on the seatbelt.

'Okay,' she said. 'Okay, you're going to think I'm crackers.' Her words came out in a defiant rush. 'But that feeling I'd been there before, it got stronger when I went upstairs.'

'As I say,' said Thelma, 'maybe you *had* been there before.'

'No.' Pat's voice was flat and defiant. 'No, I would have remembered. But things felt familiar – looking in through those round windows, and the bedroom . . . I *knew* it was going to be tiger print.' She wasn't going to mention that awful, hopeless sobbing, or that strange, dislocated feeling of familiarity.

Thelma said nothing, just slowed for the turning into the main road.

'It can happen. I don't care what you say.' It was suddenly

very important to Pat that she communicated something of the thoughts haunting her, even if Thelma couldn't – or wouldn't – understand. 'Premonitions and memories of previous lives. I know you don't agree but I know what I felt in there.'

'I'm not agreeing or disagreeing with you,' said Thelma in the mild tones she used to use in difficult staff meetings. 'I'm just saying the simple explanation is so often the more likely one: that you *have* been there before.' Her voice was sure, her certainty verging on the dismissive. Pat felt her own comments were challenging something rock solid in Thelma's mind, something so solid that there was no possibility of even attempting to communicate her viewpoint to her friend.

'*But I'd remember if I had.*' Her words felt like those of a stubborn little girl.

'Not necessarily,' said Thelma, her voice patient and kind. 'You might remember being there but not connect it to the actual place.' She paused. 'When we remember things,' she said after a moment, 'it's not always the *context* we remember. We might recall a conversation or an event, *but not necessarily remember the place where it happened*. How many times do you remember saying something to someone – say, Rod – but not remember exactly *where* you said that.'

'So you're saying what I felt back there – it might be nothing more than a memory?' Pat realized her voice sounded slightly on the sulky side.

'Val Carpenter did say they used to have parties in the garden, and you said you remembered looking *in through* the round windows, just as you would have done *if you were in the garden.*'

There was a silence.

'A party,' said Pat eventually.

'You and Rod did used to be regular partygoers.'

The past tense rankled but it wasn't just the implication her party days were in the past that irritated Pat. Thelma had given a considered, rational explanation to the sensations that had plagued her at Sunny View Lodge, but in doing so had cast a cold, forensic light over something important, something Pat was unsure whether she feared or craved during these bleak foggy days.

Now the silence was very definitely verging on the awkward. Passing the racecourse, the first houses of Thirsk began appearing, one still had its Christmas tree up, winking blue, yellow and red in the bay window.

'Oh please!' said Pat to break the silence more than anything else.

'Twelfth night was two weeks ago,' observed Thelma.

But Pat didn't respond. Another sudden stab of memory had taken her by surprise. One moment she'd been looking at the tree and its gaudy lights – and then she was seeing more lights. Coloured lights reflected in the round windows of Sunny View Lodge. And . . . *music playing*.

A party?

Call ended, Liz didn't feel like driving off immediately. There are times in life when one needs space to stand still and breathe; unpromising as it was, the garden of Sunny View Lodge would just have to do. She got out of the car and made her way across to the unkempt lawns, inhaling the damp air, trying to calm herself after such an unsettling phone call.

The garden was squeezed round to the side and stretched away at the back in an oblong shape. Liz, a seasoned horticulturalist, found the garden way more depressing than the house. The grass was faded and shaggy, such borders and beds as there had been were way beyond neglected with tangled, choked blotches on and around the grass. Fir trees policed the space on all sides, giving the whole place the air of a prison compound; beyond she could catch glimpses of the old airfield and hear the soft roar of the A1. And yet . . . as odd fingers of watery sunlight pierced the trees and illuminated the mist, there *was* a kind of beauty there . . . certainly a peace that had been singularly lacking in the house itself.

She looked about with her seasoned gardener's eye. If those trees were trimmed right down, if the slabs of wet grass were broken with anemones and maybe heliotrope – plants suited to shade – to give a bit of colour, some character . . . maybe some ferns . . . Maybe this garden could be a place of quiet beauty. Unlike the house. *The house*. She stopped dead recalling that snag of memory. *There'd been something she'd seen without seeing it* – something that puzzled her. She'd been meaning to look again, before all that palaver with Pat had driven it out of her mind. What was it she'd seen in the house?

'Hello there!' The cheerful voice romped through the stillness with a burst of laughter, making Liz spin round in fright, almost coming to grief on the wet grass. 'So sorry!' Another burst of laughter. 'I didn't mean to startle you!'

The woman walking towards her was slight and cheerful, one of those people who pass unnoticed in photographs, but in reality, dominate any setting through their sheer vitality and energy. Now that energy cut through the damp, tangled vegetation making the garden suddenly seem a place that *could* be okay if people would pull out their collective fingers. She smiled at Liz from under an iron-grey fringe, fronting short iron-grey hair, the sort one washed and ran a comb through, because hey, there was *far* too much to be getting on with to spend time faffing with such things.

'So sorry, didn't mean to startle you,' she said again. 'Only I was passing and couldn't help noticing the car and I thought, "Hey up – someone's looking round Sunny View Lodge!"' She stretched out a purposeful hand and as she did so Liz noticed the dog collar visible under the puffer jacket and purple jumper.

70

'Reverend Marian Hargreaves, or the Reverend Mare, or just Mare—'

Slightly taken aback, Liz smiled, finding her hand squeezed and pumped in a no-nonsense energetic way.

'I'm so sorry, it's really appallingly nosy of me,' she said, 'but this poor old house standing empty . . . I know everyone hereabouts just wants to see it come back to life.'

'Actually,' said Liz, 'it was my friend looking round. I just came to look with her.' She smiled uneasily at the slight deception; just how much of a sin was it to lie to a vicar?

'I see. Well, do pass on my warmest wishes and crossed fingers to your friend,' she said. 'And you're both very welcome at St Jude's if any of you happen to be passing.'

'I was just looking at the garden,' said Liz. 'Thinking how it could do with some TLC.'

The Reverend Mare sighed. 'I know,' she said sadly. '"*I passed by the field of the sluggard and by the vineyard of the man lacking sense; behold, it was completely overgrown with thistles and its surface was covered with nettles*." Only you wouldn't get a vineyard growing in Marley on Swale, not even in these days of climate emergency. And of course, by all accounts, Mal Stanley was anything but a sluggard!'

'Mal Stanley? He was the man who used to live here? Whose wife just died?'

'That's right.' Was it Liz's imagination or was the smile gently fixed? And was that a slight air of restraint in the cheerful voice?

Still, it was a definite plus to be talking about a subject that *wasn't* connected with her son. And now she had a chance to find out something that might make this whole depressing afternoon worthwhile. 'Did you know the family here?' she said.

'As well as I know most people in the parishes.' Mare sighed again with the sense of a mighty task that always needed doing,

71

day in and day out. 'That is to wave and smile in passing. Anyway ...' She smiled with the determination of one changing the subject and produced a creased green flyer; Liz realized it was the same as the one she'd seen in the hallway. '*Village Voices*. Our community play, which is on in just a couple of weeks' time. Big village fundraiser. Come one, come all, bring family and friends,' she said. 'Apparently it's going to be really something.'

Liz nodded, smiling a faint, distancing smile, as you do when invited to things you have no desire to attend. How to get the conversation back on track? 'My friend did like the house,' she said, mentally wincing at the deception – or more accurately, the flat-out lie. 'But of course everything's up in the air with the lady who owned it dying.'

'Yes, indeed.' Mare smiled uneasily. 'Poor Terri.'

'By coincidence, I know her sister,' said Liz. 'She said how Terri had it tough.'

Mare paused, suddenly preoccupied with the bright green flyers. 'Well, I suppose it's common knowledge,' she said, 'that Mal Stanley was someone on a bit of a dark path.'

'It was some sort of accident, wasn't it?' Liz persisted.

'It's common enough knowledge,' said Mare. 'He had a fall, one afternoon when Terri was out.' She looked at Liz, face clouded. 'She found him when she got back, poor love, at the bottom of the stairs.'

Liz thought of those polished treads and shuddered.

'Anyway,' said the Reverend Mare, obviously keen to change the subject, 'I must be away. I've the architect looking at St Jude's – the QI report. Every five years someone has a good prod and poke around so they can tell you everything that's wrong with the building. And when you've four buildings totalling well over a thousand years these prods invariably turn up something nasty! Do tell your friend I really hope she takes the place on, and just to give me a shout any time! Oh, and don't forget – *Village Voices*! Spread the word!'

At the gate, she stopped and turned, suddenly awkward. 'Look,' she said, 'I don't know if you or your friend have heard any of the stories flying round about this place.'

'Stories?' said Liz.

'Saying the place is, well . . . haunted?'

'No,' said Liz. *Haunted?* But looking back at the house in the fading afternoon light she could all too readily imagine such a thing.

'Well, take it from me, it's all utter tosh.' Mare spoke robustly, nodding across towards the bungalow where earlier the woman had been standing sentinel. 'Jean Bickle – she lives in the bungalow yonder – she's never seen a peep, and believe you me, nary a sparrow beats its wings without Jean noticing it.' Mare gave a final, reflective look at Sunny View Lodge. 'Not that the place doesn't have its ghosts – everywhere does – but at the end of the day it's the living we have to worry about.'

Liz looked after her. The Reverend Mare had known more than she'd said, and that she'd stopped herself from saying more was obvious, but what? And what was all that about ghosts?

It was easy to dismiss the notion when the woman was there – her sheer energy would make any self-respecting phantom think twice – but now the house and the garden both seemed that bit mistier and darker, the melancholy that shade deeper. Liz hurriedly retraced her steps to the car; she'd need to get her skates on if she was going to get to the school in time to pick up Jacob. She took a last uneasy look at the house.

The house.

Once again, she stopped. What *was* it she'd seen? Frowning, she stopped, trying to remember. It had been all that palaver in the hall that had put it out of her mind, so it must have been before that, whatever it was. The hall, with those tacky

73

niches? Or the dining room with the round windows? The sitting room with *the objects* . . .

She hurried over to the lounge window. Shading her eyes, she could just make out the pile of paperback books, and the top one, with its lurid cover, blood-red writing and a swastika in flames. If she wasn't very much mistaken it was exactly the same type of book she'd seen lying in the bushes on the waste ground by the station.

CHAPTER NINE

In Borrowby there are vistas of vineyards and disturbing recollections.

That evening found Pat sitting on her son Liam's bed. His bedroom was a place where she retreated when she needed some time alone, and when the weather (or the number of glasses of Merlot she'd had) made her usual place, the lay-by on Borrowby Hill, impractical. The long, low space was lit by a soft halo from Liam's Harry Potter lamp; on the wide window-sill lay Larson the dog, as he often did when Pat retreated here. With Liam away at university he generally avoided the room, although from time to time Pat would find him lying recumbent outside the door as though awaiting her son's return.

Outside the window, mist blurred the edges of the winter darkness. Pat sighed, picking her way through the disturbing events of the afternoon. Those strange feelings of déjà vu – the stairs, the wallpaper, that woman on the bed – it had all been so unsettling. Supernatural vision or just a memory? She couldn't be sure either way. And to have it all logically explained away like that by Thelma – was that a relief, or a disappointment? She wasn't sure of that either, but one thing she did know was that it had been a definite irritation. Another irritation.

Stop! This was not helping; she had not come in here to get worked up about Thelma, she'd come to try and make sense of her thoughts. And if what she'd experienced *had* been memories . . . well, when and where had they been created? She took a deep breath and tried to focus on those hazy ghosts of images like Thelma had suggested – not thinking of dates or names, but events. *Think* . . .

Coloured lights on round windows . . . and then fading up in her mind, like the image on an old television, other images, sensations: a smell of cut grass . . . a warm night . . . something light round her shoulders . . . something she was *holding* in place . . . *A shawl!*

She had it! With sudden certainty she knew she had been wearing her St Honoré shawl, that gorgeous wisp of vibrant colour. Now *that* dated it. The shawl had finally ended its days at some Young Farmers' shindig, wrapped round the head of her eldest son, Justin. He'd been dressed up, shrieking and shouting his way through some skit or sketch. So that must have been around the time of his A levels – and he was now approaching thirty – (*Don't go there Pat!*) – which meant at least twelve years ago, or perhaps more as she wouldn't have allowed such use of the St Honoré shawl unless it had been way beyond the first flush of youth.

And a smell of grass . . . So it *had* been some outside event, just as Thelma had suggested. (*Right yet again* . . . She felt her jaw clenching.)

She seemed to be seeing blobs of light from lanterns and hearing the thump of music. So, a party of some description. She must have gone inside to use the loo . . . and that must have been when she saw the crying woman . . . She frowned, for there the memory abruptly faded into a tangle of foggy uncertainty.

'Here you are!' Rod was standing over her, open laptop in

hand as if there was some game of hide-and-seek in process and finally he'd tracked her down. Larson opened an eye and surveyed them both sleepily, then resumed his slumbers. 'What are you doing in here?'

She wanted to say: *Trying to work out if I've had a supernatural vision or just a memory,* but that would definitely have been a bit 'out there' for her oh-so-practical husband, so instead she made some vague comment about getting Liam's room ready.

'He's not coming back now, remember,' said Rod, plonking himself down beside her. 'He's off to Bern's.' As if she could have forgotten! The plan had been for him to come home this coming weekend but late that afternoon he'd rung to postpone and although she was glad he was finally going to meet his boyfriend's parents in Ireland, she couldn't help a chilly sense of sadness at the thought she'd not see him for another month. She forced her mind back to Rod who was swivelling the laptop round towards her in a business-like manner. With a resigned feeling Pat realized they were back off to the South of France.

Sure enough there were dreaded golden vistas of vineyards and chateaus, only this time it was a different website. 'Harry Fisher at shooting,' he said enthusiastically, 'he recommended this company. Not so well known but top notch, apparently. All sorts of deals with local suppliers: wine and pâté and what have you. One long party, Harry reckons.'

But still a coach tour for people of a certain age . . . The bleak thought pressed against Pat's thoughts like the mist outside as her husband rattled on about truffle tastings and something called a Cheese-a-Thon. Rod had always been like this. It was one of his defining characteristics, finding out every last detail about something and then passing it all on to Pat in an enthused monologue. Starting up the business, describing various jobs over the years, outlining his cancer treatment . . .

'So, what do you think?'

She looked at her husband, and then turned away. Now was the moment. Now was the moment when she knew she *had* to say . . . had to say: *I would sooner have rocks dropped on my chest than go on some old fogeys coach tour for our birthdays*. But then, as she looked at his face lit softly by the warm glow of the computer-generated image of some French hillside, she saw the wrinkles that never used to be there, and she remembered the fear, the weariness, the unremitting *grind* of his illness . . . and she knew she could say no such thing. And anyway, if she had, he'd only say, *So what do you want to do?* And she didn't have an answer. She just knew it was *something else*. Something to do with *excitement* and duty-free scent on the backs of her wrists and *parties* . . .

Parties . . .

'Changing the subject a minute,' she said, 'I was wondering, do you remember ever going to Marley on Swale?'

'*Marley*?' Rod looked at her as he always did when she went off at a tangent. 'What's that got to do with anything?'

'I was there this afternoon. I went to this house with Thelma and Liz, and I thought I'd been there before.'

With great effort Rod relocated himself from the South of France to the north-west of Thirsk. 'I go there all the time,' he said. 'That's where Grewlthorpes are, remember? On the old airfield.'

'I'm not talking about joists,' she said. 'I mean a party.'

'A *party*?' His tone was growing more and more incredulous. 'What sort of party?'

'This would be a while back. At least ten or twelve years back.'

He frowned. 'You don't mean that do at Mal Stanley's place?'

Pat stiffened at the use of the name. 'Yes,' she said, 'yes, that's *exactly* what I mean. How did you know him?'

'We both do. Well, did. He died the back end of last year.'

'And we went to parties at his house?'

'Party. It was just the one. We never liked him, if you remember. He was a bit of a git.'

'In what way? What did he do?'

'I don't know. Gitty things . . .' Rob realized this wouldn't be enough and frowned in an effort of remembrance. 'He ran that machine supply company next to Grewlthorpes. Always falling out with people. Kicked off big time if he didn't get his own way. One time he made a whole load of people out of work and refused to give them any sort of pay-off.'

'Was he married?'

'*Married?*' Rod was looking at her as if she'd made reference to some obscure Eastern cult. 'Of course he was married; gave Christine a right shitty time by all accounts—'

Christine!

A thin, reedy voice . . . 'I'm Christine, lady of the house, for what it's worth . . .'

It had been *there*. It wasn't so much that the memories stirred but they aligned themselves.

A floral dress with a vast lace collar. A hairstyle plainly meant to look like the Princess of Wales . . .

'I'm so sorry! I was looking for the toilet. I heard you . . . Is everything all right?'

'I'm just trying to work out how much longer I can stand this . . .'

NOT sadness in the voice but NEED – irritating need . . .

And that had been the start. Some people have no problem in unburdening themselves to complete strangers, regardless of whether that stranger was in need of the loo or not; Christine Stanley had been one such person. What was the term? *Oversharing.*

A thin voice, slightly slurred, droning on and on . . .

'Is she still alive?' she asked, bringing herself back into the present.

Rod shook his head. 'She died a while back,' he said. 'Some sort of car crash or something?' He frowned, trying to remember. 'I think I heard he'd married again.'

'So what was this party?' asked Pat.

'You remember!' Another character trait of Rod's was his insistence that memory of events was a mere matter of choice. 'It was when he got his driving licence back.'

Of course. A garden thronged with people – lights, tick; music, tick – and that heady sound of conversation outside at night. A rather nasty sweet-tasting wine, bright summery clothes – gaudy T-shirts, floaty skirts, sandals – a swelling cheer at the sound of an insistently sounded horn as a car nosed down the driveway. Behind the wheel a man dressed as some superhero – *Batman* . . .

Thrumming cheers . . .

'Way to go, Mal!'

'He's back behind the wheel . . . Be afraid – be very afraid!'

She remembered thinking the whole thing was rather childish. The man took off the Batman mask – she remembered a proud expression, smug – revealing rather bad yellow teeth, the sort of smile that felt like a snarl. And then there'd been another comment, the voice hushed: '*Now Christine'll have no way of knowing where he is . . .*'

How or when she'd gone inside she no longer remembered, but she vaguely recalled the sound of distant sobbing and gingerly climbing those slippy stairs, and the woman sitting on the bed, tears catching the red and blue and yellow of the lights outside.

'*Some people just chip away at you bit by bit by bit . . .*'

Pat had glanced surreptitiously at her watch and realized half an hour had passed. '*I'm sorry, I just need to use the bathroom . . .*'

'*You will come back, won't you? You will come and talk to me?*' There had been need – oppressive need – in the slurred, thin tones.

'Yes, of course I will . . .'

But she hadn't. And then at some point . . . Christine Stanley had died.

'Look, Pat, this coach tour – you do still want to go, right?' Rod's voice dragged her forcibly back to the Dordogne. 'You don't have to.'

'Yes,' she said. 'Yes, I *do* want to go on this coach tour.' He looked at her, unconvinced. 'Because if you don't,' he said, 'that's fine. But we have to get something else sorted. Time's ticking on.'

As he left the room he didn't see the frowning expression on his wife's face.

Time's ticking on . . .

What did that make her think of? Something significant . . . something that had happened today . . . *Of course!* That skeleton clock by the stairs at SunnyView Lodge. She could hear Thelma's voice saying, *'Stands the church clock at ten to three . . .'*

And Marguerite, leaning forward in the café, face excited . . .

'It said it was two fifty.'

Two clocks in two different places, *but both showing exactly the same time . . .*

CHAPTER TEN

*Treasured times are missed, research done
and an unexpected warning received.*

Thelma was sitting by the unlit gas fire in the front room, shivering slightly, despite her thick cardigan. The heating wasn't due on for another ten minutes and in these days of fuel bill insanity she was making a point of not putting it on early. She glanced balefully at the pile of boxes and packages in the corner of the room: tonight was not turning out how she'd planned. She sighed and turned her attention to the old green teacher's mark book open on her lap, the one she used when trying to order her thoughts. The first few pages of tight squares were a monument to her last ever class; a neat list of the children's names, the pages charting their weekly progress in reading, and in spelling and maths tests, but beyond that were the pages where she worked out some of life's knottier problems – organizing the redecoration of the hall, planning the Advent group – things that defied simple and straightforward lists.

Now she looked at a new page of squares. Written at the top were the words 'Sunny View Lodge' – and the rest of the page was, as yet, blank.

She checked the clock. Twenty past seven. Even if Teddy

came home in the next five minutes it'd be too late for them to catch up on that Scandi-noir thriller; neither of them were any good with subtitles after eight o'clock. She sighed, a deep regretful sigh. In the old days, this time of day had always been a time to treasure, Teddy back from college, her back from school, him sitting at the kitchen table as she prepared supper, both dissecting the events of their respective days. And even after she'd retired and he'd left college, there'd always been *something* to talk about. Now, since he'd become a delivery driver the general rule was he'd be in late and straight upstairs into a lukewarm bath in an effort to heat his bones.

Tonight, on arriving back from Sunny View Lodge, she'd felt determined to claw back some time together – a hot, stodgy supper; maybe spag bol – and some Scandi-noir escapism. Something to dispel the chilly bleak mood that had descended on her at Sunny View Lodge and clung even now like the tendrils of fog outside. She'd been taking off her coat and wondering if they had a jar of pesto, when the doorbell had rung, a firm, business-like double chime. Opening the door, she'd seen a veritable heap of Wait A Minute Mr Postman delivery boxes and with the uncompromising figure of Big Cyn, the WAMMP delivery coordinator sprinting back from the van with yet more parcels wedged firmly under her ample chin.

'But we've had today's delivery.' Thelma had surveyed the heap aghast as Big Cyn lowered the parcels, purple highlights glinting in the security light.

'It's extra for Ted.' Big Cyn had sounded gloomy as she'd taken a photo of the stack with her iPad. 'THREE off sick. Thank you and goodnight.'

There'd been nothing for it but for Thelma to heft them all inside, which had taken her four trips. She hadn't liked to put them all in Teddy's study, where she knew he had an intricate system of what went where, so the only alternative without lugging them all upstairs, seemed to be the corner of the living room. Looking at them she knew he'd be at least an hour entering them onto his delivery app.

She'd felt weary beyond words and had settled in her favourite wing chair, angled subtly away from the chaos in the corner – now being eyed with predatory suspicion by Snaffles. After a moment she'd stirred herself enough to place a certain green cardboard folder on the coffee table, all ready for when Teddy came in.

And then had come calls.

First Liz telling her what this Reverend Mare had to say, and about this book she'd seen. Shortly after that, Pat had rung saying in an offhand way how it *had* been a memory – albeit one that had felt like a vision – and that strange thing about the time of the clock in the hallway. Everything they'd said left her frowning – frowning and reaching for her beloved green mark book. She looked at the blank page. Should she not in fact be making a start on supper? But at that moment with a beneficent click the central heating turned on and she felt a pulse of warmth break the chill grip of the room.

Still frowning, she began to write.

Reverend Mare (Mair?) says SVL NOT haunted.

Book at SVL – maybe the same as found on waste ground?

Clock on wall at SVL – maybe stopped at the same time as the one MM maybe saw? (This latter 'maybe' she underlined three times.)

Pat been before – met first Mrs Stanley – unhappy.

She reached for her laptop. Time to see what the internet had to tell her about the late Mr Mal Stanley.

Twenty minutes later she felt little further on. What she'd been able to glean from the archives of the *Thirsk Gazette* had tallied with Rod's summation: Mal Stanley had indeed been a bit of a git. Of course, local papers as a whole tend not to say that someone *isn't* nice (aside from the usual doleful litanies from Northallerton magistrates' court), but they do tend to comment when local people – especially wealthy local people – perform good deeds for their fellow man. And Mal Stanley, for all his wealth, seemed to have done no such thing.

Thelma had been able to find only two articles concerning him: one about a dispute with a local farmer, which had resulted in a pile of manure being dumped on Mr Stanley's driveway, and another about twelve people getting the sack with no notice in the run-up to Christmas. Plus, a very brief story about the drink-driving ban. None of it very bad on its own, but put together ... well, it seemed there was some truth in the opinion of this Reverend Mare that Mal Stanley had been someone on a Dark Path.

There had been a short paragraph about the death of his wife from eleven years ago – '*Tragic Death of Woman Motorist*' – giving scant details of a collision with a lorry, which might or might not have been caused by ice on the roads, and then a final brief story dated just over eight weeks previously – '*Death by Misadventure for Local Businessman*' – telling how a fall at his home had been judged to be accidental, and partially a result of the illness he was suffering from.

She had typed 'Marley on Swale' into the search bar, wondering if there was anything else to be found, but there was only an article about this forthcoming village production, *Village Voices*, made possible by a Rural Jump-Start grant, whatever that was.

She turned off the laptop and reached again for the green mark book. At that moment there was a rattle in the door and a cheery cry of 'Your WAMMP delivery man has landed!' Both Thelma and Snaffles stiffened. Snaffles because he always did and Thelma because until quite recently her husband would announce his arrival with a shout of 'Vicar in the building'.

85

'Living room,' she called, lacking the energy to make her voice equally cheerful.

Teddy's eyes were bright and his cheeks glowing, the picture of good health. His face when he lowered in to bump against Thelma's was cold. Straightening he caught sight of the parcels. 'Aha,' he said almost gleefully. 'Big Cyn said she'd left off a batch. I didn't know there'd be so many.'

He rubbed his hands together as if relishing the challenge.

'I didn't want to put them in your study and spoil your system,' said Thelma.

'Thank you.' He nodded approvingly and sat opposite her. 'How's it all going? How was the great trip to Marley on Swale?'

She was surprised he'd remembered; she'd only mentioned it briefly over the phone that lunchtime. But that was the thing with Teddy – he was just as genuinely interested in her doings as he ever was, never mind what else needed doing (or in this case, removing from the corner of the living room). It was just that now he had so much less time to show that interest. 'I don't exactly know what it was I was looking for,' she said, 'so it's impossible to say if we found it.'

He nodded gravely. 'And what did you find?'

Thelma considered. 'A sad house. A sad, empty house where there had obviously been more money than love.' She gestured to the laptop. 'From all that I can gather, it seems this Mal Stanley who lived there wasn't a very nice man. His wife died some eleven years ago in a car crash. He seems to have been ill and had some sort of fall, and died. and then two months later his second wife dies . . . also in a car crash.'

'At exactly the same time and in exactly the same place a woman claims to have seen a phantom shop,' said Teddy. Thelma found herself remembering the sad shell of Busby's. There certainly was a phantom shop. She wondered if Brid and the children had managed to find anything to buy.

'One sees all sorts of odd things I'd never come across in the dear old vicar factory when out delivering.' Teddy's words broke into her thoughts. This was an increasingly recurrent theme of his these days: the many sights encountered on his delivery round. The funny, the bizarre and the tragic – from the variety of what he termed 'Hell's smells', to the elderly but vigorous couple he'd named 'The Shaggers of Sharow'. He shook his head. 'Today I took a parcel to a woman – this was two in the afternoon – and she opened the door in a onesie and dressing gown; she'd obviously not bothered getting dressed.'

Biting back a spasm of irritation, Thelma reached for the coffee table and handed over the holly green folder. Teddy as a social anthropologist observing the folk of North Yorkshire was something that for whatever reason got well and truly on her wires. 'From Brummie Maureen,' she said firmly. 'For job at college.' She spoke as if the lady herself had been round instead of just sending Thelma an email, which she had printed out and put in a folder to give it more weight. 'It's nothing much, just your details, NI number, that sort of thing.'

'Ah,' said Teddy. It was a tone she recognized only too well, one he used when he was about to put off a task. 'Excellent. And I really must get those boxes out from under your feet.' He stood up and left the room. Thelma half shut her eyes and sent up a quick prayer – though for what she wasn't quite sure.

It was then her mobile rang. Number withheld. 'Hello?' she said, on red alert for any would-be telephone fraudsters.

'Mrs Thelma Cowper?' The voice had a tone Thelma instinctively didn't like, a sort of whiney self-entitlement.

'Who is this?' she said, prepared to ring off if the words 'insurance' or 'broadband' were mentioned.

'Is this Mrs Thelma Cowper?' said the voice insistently.

Thelma frowned. 'Yes,' she said after a slight pause.

'You don't know me, Mrs Cowper, but I'm going to tell you something that you need to hear.'

Thelma was about to say, *What's that?* but something stopped her.

A little uncertainly now, the voice continued. 'I understand that you viewed a property today in Marley on Swale.' Thelma stayed silent. 'Are you there, Mrs Cowper?' Now there was an unmistakable tinge of irritation in the thin voice. 'I'm telling you something you're going to want to hear. *You don't want to be buying that property.*'

Finally, Thelma spoke. 'May I ask why?' she said.

'It's a bad place. You need to know that. *Bad things have happened there.* And there's a lot wrong with it.'

'I see.' Thelma knew she was expected to say more, ask questions – however, she resisted. It was a trick she'd learned from several encounters over the years with didactic Ofsted inspectors and Primary Advisors. Be quiet, and let *them* do the talking; don't question, justify or defend. Now it was the only power she had in this strange situation and from the irritation and uncertainty in the reedy voice she could tell this strategy was working.

'So, I'm just saying . . . stay away from that house,' said the voice. There was a finality in the tone and Thelma knew the conversation was coming to an end.

'Before you go,' she said firmly, 'there's something *you* probably need to know.'

'Oh?' The voice wavered, sounding surprised and cautious.

'I fully intend to put in an offer as soon as the property becomes available,' said Thelma. 'A cash offer,' she added, and rang off.

CHAPTER ELEVEN

An enquiry is rebuffed, a trip undertaken and an accusation levelled.

'You said *what?*' Liz sat down in her conservatory with a bump, almost dropping the phone.

'I said I was interested in the property and fully intended to make a cash offer for the place.'

'What on earth made you say that?' Liz had a sudden grim vision of Thelma and Teddy relocating to that awful sad house and her feeling compelled to go and help them with that sad, shadowed garden.

'Whoever it was who rang me wanted to put me off buying that place.' Liz noted Thelma was using what Pat called her 'tens-and-units explaining voice', the one she'd used to use with her class. 'And the only thing I could do was let them know they hadn't been successful.'

'Why?'

'Because I want to know *why* they – whoever they are – want to put me off.'

'I see,' said Liz dubiously, looking out at her garden, pearly with mist and frost. 'But we don't know who *they* are.'

'I have a pretty good idea.' When Thelma spoke as if

something was glaringly apparent Liz always felt slightly miffed. 'But I need your help to find out ... if you're free this morning?'

'This morning?' A catalogue of tasks and chores rose up in Liz's mind.

And of course there was the question of Tim . . . Going through his room to try and find out some clue as to what was going on was, she knew, both wrong and a betrayal of trust on a very fundamental level, but . . .

'It has to be this morning. I want to catch them on the back foot.' Thelma broke into her thoughts, her voice gently insistent.

'Could Pat not go?'

There was a slight, repressive pause. 'I believe today is the day Pat and Marguerite intend to make their trip to Boroughbridge,' said Thelma darkly.

Call finished, Liz returned to the breakfast table. The silent breakfast table. Tim at one end, Derek at the other, Jacob in between – all regarding their various devices intently. It was a silence that deeply bothered Liz. Normally, silence at the Newsome breakfast table wasn't a problem; it was a pause before the events of the day, a companionable thing that rested lightly between her and Derek as he perused the online *Yorkshire Post* and she wrestled with that day's Wordle. This silence, however, felt altogether different.

'Who was that?' said Derek without looking up.

'Just Thelma,' said Liz. 'I'm going to meet her in Ripon today.'

The three people at the breakfast table sat silent; as her late father would have said 'answer came there none'. She looked at her son staring moodily at his phone, as he'd done these past few mornings, barely touching his coffee. Offers of muesli, toast – even a bacon sandwich! – had all been refused but she knew now, from a couple of fact-finding sessions in the wheelie bin, that any breakfast he'd eaten had been purchased from that new drive-through Greggs. Jacob was solemnly working his way through porridge (made, of course, with oat milk), eyes never leaving the screen of his iPad. Was *he* okay? With Jacob you never could tell.

'So, what are you doing in Ripon?' asked Derek without looking up. For a moment she felt tempted to say that she and Thelma were planning a flash mob fan dance across the market place. 'We're going into Spooner and Collins,' she said instead.

That did get a response, both Derek and Tim looking up at her with the beginnings of puzzlement on their faces, but Jacob interrupted the moment before it got going. 'What's that word when you're doing something, but you can't keep on doing it because there isn't enough stuff left?' he said.

The other three spoke in unison: 'Unsustainable.'

'That's a big word for a Friday morning,' said Derek.

'Grandpa,' said Jacob, infinitely patient, 'I told you, I'm writing to Greta Thunberg.'

'Well, give her my love.' This joke from Tim fell as flat as it could as, when it came to his passions, Jacob had little or no sense of humour. With a bone-weary sigh Tim stood. 'Come on then, champ, get ready to hit the road.' Eyes still on his iPad, Jacob went to clean his teeth.

'Is he all right?' Liz asked. Tim nodded, engrossed again in his phone. Annoyed, Liz went right up to her son; as she did she caught a glimpse of the screen, the distinct blue and white flash of a Facebook page. Reflexively Tim killed the screen, almost convulsively stuffing the phone into his inside pocket.

'For God's sake!' His voice was exasperated, even angry.

'I asked you a question,' said Liz her face close to his, eyeballing him so he was forced to look at her.

'Mum, he's fine.' In his voice was a long-suffering 'for the nine millionth time' tone. It was a tone that was obviously meant to deflect and for most people it would have worked but not with a concerned mother who had been starved of facts for three days.

'And Leoni?' she said.

'What about her?' Although Tim was in his late thirties his tone was very much late teens. She felt a growing, destabilizing prickle of anger.

'Is she fine? Because she sounded anything but when I spoke to her yesterday.'

'Mum, I *told* you, we're working stuff out.' Actually, he'd done no such thing, all he'd done was shut down the subject every time she brought it up. Now he headed for the door, obviously eager to leave the room, the house, the situation. Liz stood in his path, barring his way to the door.

'I need to know what's going on,' she said. 'And please don't say you have to go and you'll be late because even if you are I still need to know what's happening.'

Tim rolled his eyes in a bored way that again recalled his eighteen-year-old self.

'Timothy,' she said warningly.

He simply stepped round her and walked into the hall where he could be heard shouting: 'Jacob, I'm walking out the door in three minutes.'

Liz became aware Derek was looking at her. 'Don't tell me to leave him alone,' she said.

He came and put his arms round her, something unheard of at breakfast time. 'I was just going to ask why you and Thelma were going to Spooner and Collins,' he said, chin resting on her head.

'Just so Thelma can find something out.' She was aware of a guilty reticence creeping into her voice.

Derek's views on Thelma and herself and Pat 'finding things out' were well known. But now he merely nodded. 'Maybe that's a good idea,' he said. 'Take your mind off things.'

Something else unheard of at this time of the morning – and any other time, come to that.

It was never straightforward picking up Marguerite. Unlike Thelma or Liz, who would be waiting on the pavement at the best possible place for a car to stop, Marguerite would wait inside and it was only when Pat actually arrived that she would put on her coat and shoes, have a final wee and lock up. Plus, her flat was a particularly awkward place to stop with no pull-in parking, near a roundabout on the main road into Northallerton, necessitating Pat to bump up onto the pavement, hazards flashing whilst sending text messages plus a quick blast of the horn. By the time Marguerite had ambled outside the traffic was already starting to build, and by the time she'd settled herself in the Yeti and fannied about with the seatbelt there was a tailback stretching almost as far back as the station.

'So, are you ready for this?' Marguerite spoke with the air of someone about to go on a white-knuckle ride. Judging by her outfit, she obviously was. A jumper of vibrant orange was offset by blue beads and a blue scarf twisted purposefully through her greying hair. 'Remember,' said Marguerite, 'we're doing this because I need to *know*.'

'Anyway . . .' Pulling out into the Friday morning traffic, Pat said what had been on her mind ever since the previous day. 'This clock you saw in that charity shop—'

'There wasn't a clock,' Marguerite interrupted with smooth superiority.

'I thought you said you saw a clock that had stopped at ten to three.'

Marguerite smiled, slightly smugly Pat thought.

'That's what my mind *told* me it was.'

'But it wasn't?' Pat frowned at the steamy windscreen.

'No.' Marguerite pulled out her phone and opened WhatsApp.

'It was—' she frowned down at the screen '—a manifestation of the passage of time.' She smiled at Pat from the height of her knowledge. 'I've joined this WhatsApp group,' she said, 'It's called "Beyond the Now". It's brilliant; there's so much people don't understand about this sort of stuff.'

'And you think this woman in Boroughbridge does?'

'She has Sight.' Marguerite spoke solemnly. 'She sees spirits, and is afforded a perspective most of us don't have. What I want to do is explain to her exactly what I saw, so she can help me interpret it.'

Pat sighed. She could imagine that any spirits were going to be hard pushed to get a word in edgeways once Marguerite started banging on about Gary the photocopier man. This all felt rather murky, and worlds away from the mental scenarios she'd created of Marguerite joining a walking group or maybe a choral society.

'The clock I saw,' continued Marguerite. 'Is what it all comes back to. A timepiece is such a powerful symbol; it represents the past and present and future.'

Negotiating the roundabout onto the A168, Pat felt a twitch of memory. *Past and present* . . . what did that make her think of? Of course – that paper Thelma found on the waste ground. What had it said?

PAST AND PRESENT – BOTH THE SAME?

Could there be something in what Marguerite was saying?

As far as estate agents went, Spooner and Collins tended to be the default, safe pair of hands in Ripon and Thirsk. Other companies with their flashy logos came and went, but the sober green signage of Spooner and Collins had been a steady fixture on Westgate in Ripon and Kirkgate in Thirsk ever since Ian Spooner and Jon Collins had returned from national service and decided the chicken factory wasn't for them.

Walking towards the Ripon branch, Thelma fully expected at least some traces of a wobble from Liz about her plan, but her friend seemed remarkably resolute, even slightly grim. 'You're quite clear about what you're saying?' said Thelma again.

'I am,' said Liz. Yes, definitely grim, and more than slightly.

'Give it five minutes after I've left, and then we'll rendezvous in Oliver's Pantry.'

Liz nodded, crossed the road and went in. Thelma lingered a few minutes, looking at the January Reads display in the window of the Little Ripon Bookshop, before following her friend. After a cursory glance at the estate agent's window (feeling appalled as ever at the way house prices were rocketing up and up) she went inside.

The office was long and narrow, desks arranged crossways; it always put Thelma slightly in mind of a railway carriage. The first desk, with the name 'Val Carpenter' on a Toblerone-shaped block, was empty. (Just as a judicial call by Thelma had established it would be.) The middle desk – that of Colin Patterson – was occupied by an uneasy-looking youth who was talking to Liz. Thelma could hear him peppering every other sentence with the word 'basically'. And at the back of the office, a girl sat alternately blowing her nose and half-heartedly tapping at a keyboard.

'It's Casey, isn't it?' said Thelma. The girl looked up, face a bland, heavily made-up mask. On her desk was a mug bearing the legend: 'Keep Calm and Trust the Estate Agent'; strewn around were packs of tissues and throat lozenges (both opened). 'I'm just admin,' said the girl somewhat hoarsely. 'I can show you some stuff, take your deets, but you're best off talking to Col. He'll be free in two mins.' She sniffed heavily.

'Actually, it was you I was wanting to talk to,' said Thelma pleasantly, sitting down. Casey's face – as far as Thelma could tell under the make-up – looked wary.

95

'Like I say, you're better off waiting for Col.'

'I viewed a property out in Marley on Swale yesterday. My name's Thelma Cooper. *Not* Cowper.'

Now the face was very definitely wary, and something else besides. The words came out in a tumble. 'That's Val Carpenter's listing,' she said. 'She's out at the moment but it's definitely her you need to talk to. I can tell her you called.'

'No,' said Thelma still just as pleasant. 'It's you I want to speak to. I want to know why you gave my number to a stranger — *and just who exactly that stranger is.*'

CHAPTER TWELVE

Vehement denials are made and abnormal things happen in a very normal room.

Napier Road, Boroughbridge was, thought Pat, the epitome of British normality: twin rows of Thirties semis that could have been anywhere from Wick to Aberystwyth to Portsmouth to Surbiton. She had wondered, as she parked up in front of number ten, if she might feel *something* – some frisson, some sense of impending otherness – but the only thing she felt was a mental nudge that it was bin day tomorrow, a thought prompted by the ranks of grey wheelie bins flanking the privet hedges and stucco walls.

'Oh my God!' Marguerite convulsively clutched at Pat's arm, indicating a bay window displaying an airer draped with T-shirts. 'Did you feel that? I got a definite sense of something!'

'That's not number ten,' said Pat.

Jen Barlow, appearing behind the frosted glass of number ten's front door, was also in her own way normality made manifest. She was a dumpy, cheery woman in a floral blouse with scraped-back hair – the sort of person you wouldn't look at twice in a queue or a car park or walking a dog. 'Come through,' she said brightly, as if they were there for any number of reasons other than ones of looking beyond the confines of this present world. As they followed her through a hall smelling of Pledge and cooking, Marguerite again clutched at Pat's arm.

It was, thought Pat, going to be a long hour.

In the sitting room – once again the word 'normal' sang out in Pat's mind – the grey IKEA sofa, a slightly out-of-perspective painting of Bolton Abbey, the *TV Quick* lying sprawled face down on the coffee table. Even the obligatory conversation about the ongoing fog and damp was exactly the sort of exchange you'd expect to have in such a room.

'Anyway,' said Jen with an air of getting down to business, 'as I said on the phone, I don't normally do pairs.'

'I can wait outside,' said Pat, suddenly thinking that actually there was nothing she'd like better.

'Oh, no!' Jen held up a staying hand. 'No, it's totally fine, I just wanted to flag up in advance that things might get a bit confusing.' Marguerite nodded enthusiastically. 'It's mainly for me why we're here,' she said eagerly, fingers straying to the tantric crystals. 'As I said on the phone, I've recently experienced a vision. And it's made me aware I'm a bit psychic.' She smiled shyly as if confiding great news. From the carefully controlled nod of Jen's head, Pat guessed this wasn't the first time she had heard this.

'Just to make it clear,' said Jen, 'I don't charge but I do accept donations. And any money given, it all goes to Yorkshire Air Ambulance.' She appeared to feel more explanation was needed. 'I've always had a bit of a gift,' she said. 'This way I get to put it to good use. And it's so much less clart than running a raffle.'

'Shall I tell you a bit about the charity shop I saw?' said Marguerite eagerly. 'At least, I realize it wasn't actually a charity shop *as such*—'

'Actually no, if that's okay,' said Jen. 'And if it's all the same to you I'd prefer silence.' Her voice was firm and confident.

She straightened herself in her chair and fixed them both with a gaze.

And suddenly . . . the ordinariness was overwhelming.

In a voice low enough not to attract Col's attention, Casey denied Thelma's charge completely, adamantly and frequently. Here, however, she was at a disadvantage; if there was one thing Thelma had plenty of experience of, it was guilty people denying any sort of wrongdoing. The fact that in this case it was a twenty-something as opposed to a seven- or eight-year-old mattered not a jot.

'I could lose my job, doing something like that,' said Casey, nervously clutching the coaster. 'I absolutely did *not* give your number to *anyone*, Mrs Cowper.'

'Cooper,' said Thelma. She was saying very little, in her experience by far and away the best thing to do. The trick was to let the guilty speak. *And speak.* Watching all these Scandi-noir crime dramas she often felt all concerned were missing a trick, with their grim rooms and barked-out questions. How much more effective would it be sitting them down somewhere unthreatening, with a middle-aged lady primary school teacher to hand.

At first Casey fired out her defence willy-nilly, like a child lobbing snowballs until she sniffed herself to a teary-eyed halt. Then, gently but firmly, Thelma spoke. She was careful not to accuse Casey head on; instead, she calmly presented the facts. Only Val Carpenter and the Spooner and Collins office knew of her visit to Sunny View Lodge, and Thelma knew Casey had her number after listening to the call Val had taken. Casey ducked her head at all this, shaking it furiously as if this could erase the reality being set before her. The denials came faster and faster, until finally Casey stopped abruptly and said, 'There's nothing more I can say, Mrs Cowper.'

'Cooper.' Thelma stood up. 'Thank you for your time.'

'So, is that it?' asked Casey uneasily.

'You'll appreciate that I have to pass on my concerns,' said Thelma gravely. '*Someone* gave my number to this stranger. I find it very hard to believe it was Val Carpenter, but you never know.'

'Val knows I'd never do anything like that,' said Casey a trifle smugly. 'You can talk to her, of course, but she'll say the same thing as me.'

'Actually, I thought I'd talk to Mr Spooner,' said Thelma.

'He's retired.' Casey spoke with the air of presenting a fait accompli.

'I know,' said Thelma. 'He goes to our church; we sing together in the choir.'

Casey's collapse came swiftly, and as is usual in these cases, with more than a touch of the shambolic, the words rapidly stuttering out.

Now she came to think about it, when she'd been taking down the details someone *had* come in . . . and then the phone had rung . . . and there was no one to answer, so maybe, just *maybe* this lady had somehow, *somehow* seen Thelma's number on her pad and maybe this was the same lady as had called Thelma.

'Maybe that was it,' said Thelma reasonably. 'Perhaps if that lady gets in touch again you could ask her? I really don't like to bother Mr Spooner, or even the police.' (At this, Casey's eyes widened in horror.) 'If whoever she was, was able to ring again, I'm sure we could sort this whole thing out.' Thelma stood up, presenting her trump card. 'And I really don't know how you knew it was a lady who called me,' she said with a pleasant smile.

Casey looked miserably down at the mug of Lemsip in front of her.

Thelma thanked her for her time, recommended lemon and honey in boiling water, and left the office. Liz, she noticed, was still in full flight with Col. She really was playing her part well.

Taking one last glance back she could see Casey frantically stabbing her mobile phone, eyes sliding uneasily round the room.

Jen Barlow must have been sitting in her armchair for a good five minutes, eyes half closed as if she were asleep. Marguerite nudged Pat, the meaning of the nudge clear: *what's going on d'you think?* She was fingering the tantric crystals almost as if she were considering chucking them over the silent woman.

'Should I start telling her what happened to me?' she whispered. 'Give her a bit of something to focus on?'

'Let her do it her way,' whispered back Pat.

Marguerite nudged her again, sudden, urgent and Pat realized that Jen Barlow's eyes were wide open and for the first time she noticed what a vivid shade of green-grey they were.

'I'm sorry,' she said. 'Sometimes you slip between the cracks. That's the best way I can put it.' Her voice was quiet and there was a quality to it that hadn't been there before. 'You're both part of the same story,' she said.

Leaning forward, Marguerite exhaled in excitement. 'We both knew Gary,' she said, 'This person I know.'

'It's not about love, this story,' said Jen. 'I'm not seeing much love at all.' Her voice was sad and infinitely bleak. 'You're on the edge,' she said, but it was Marguerite she was looking at. She turned those vivid eyes to Pat. 'You,' she said, 'you're in closer. But, lovey, I'd advise you to walk away. Really – *walk away*. There's nothing but darkness. And you're surrounded by so much light and love. Stay with that.'

As she was speaking, the queerest sensation stole over Pat. It was as if every object in the room took on unfathomable detail – the lines of the cornice, the folds of the curtain, the patterns of the electric fire. Suddenly that ordinary, normal room with its IKEA furniture and *TV Quick* magazine was as sinister and terrible as any Gothic castle in a thunderstorm.

'There's someone wants to see you,' said Jen Barlow, as conversationally as she might announce the arrival of the window cleaner.

'Is it someone who wants to tell me about a man who collects clocks?' Marguerite sounded almost plaintive.

Jen shook her head. 'This person here . . .' Her eyes fastened on Pat. 'She's here to see *you*.'

'To see *me*?' Pat's thoughts flashed frantically round the roll call of people she knew who had died and might possibly want a word. Her Nana Pat? Rosemary from grammar school? Surely not her one-time colleague and Nursery Nurse Topsy Joy?

'She's upset,' said Jen. 'Are you all right, love? Don't cry . . .' She frowned, looked at Pat, concerned. 'She's saying . . . she's saying . . . *Why didn't you come back to me?*'

Afterwards, Pat didn't remember running to the toilet, a sloping cubicle under the stairs. The vomiting felt emotional as well as physical, painful, wrenching sensations that left her weak and spent as she tried to free the toilet roll from its crocheted doll's crinoline. Kneeling down again in front of the toilet her eyes fell on a neat Blu-Tacked sign above the cistern: *If you sprinkle when you tinkle, be a sweetie and wipe the seatie.*

There was something very cheering about the mismatched chairs and green and orange walls of Oliver's Pantry on such a dreary day. Two coffees and two slices of lemon meringue pie ordered, Thelma took a seat upstairs and stared thoughtfully out of the window. In the mist the shops on North Street had acquired the grainy air of a black and white film showing on an old television set. Her thoughts felt similarly murky as she went through her conversation with Casey, and once again she wondered just *why* someone should have rung her up to warn her away from Sunny View Lodge. A movement at the door revealed the familiar turquoise mac of Liz, who walked towards the table, a veritable sheaf of Spooner and Collins rental properties under her arm.

'Were you successful?' she said, unwinding her scarf and dropping into the seat across from her.

'That remains to be seen,' said Thelma.

'I mean it *was* her who gave out your number, this Casey person?'

'Oh yes,' said Thelma. 'Without a shadow of a doubt.'

'I just can't see how you can be so certain.'

'It's a question of name,' said Thelma. 'Mrs *Cowper*. That's what Val called me when we met. *It's also the name the caller used*, which showed there was in all probability a link between them. It was unlikely to be Val Carpenter – there were a hundred ways she could have put us off the property when showing us round – which just left Casey.'

'I see.' Liz took a pensive sip of her coffee. 'But I don't see where that gets you.'

'Further on than before,' said Thelma cryptically. 'Thank you for all your sterling work by the way.' She looked at the properties on the table. 'I can see you played your part really well.'

'Who said I was playing a part?' said Liz and there it was again, that grim note. 'If our Timothy wants space, space he can have.'

Thelma was about to say more (much more) but at that moment the shrill of her phone cut across the half-full café.

'Who's that?' said Liz.

'Unless I'm very much mistaken my mystery caller,' said Thelma.

CHAPTER THIRTEEN

There are excuses, fibs and rather nasty coffees.

Their waitress had a heavy cold. 'FYI,' she said. 'The Vegan Eggs Benedict is off. The tofu man doesn't come on a Saturday.' She put their coffees down. They looked to be on the muddy side with a coagulating cloud of yellowy milk.

'Excuse me!' said Pat.

'The milk appears to be off,' said Thelma.

'Oh no,' said the waitress with the air of someone enlightening the unenlightened. 'That's how it comes. It's all plant-based. And soya milk does that.' The sleeve of her shapeless grey cardigan flew up swiftly to stifle a sneeze.

Pat and Thelma exchanged a look, an expressive look that said everything that needed to be said about their current surroundings.

Bygone Daze (funk not junk!) was situated on the Helmsley Road, just along from the top of Sutton Bank, in what had been until recently The Hambleton Arms. To lease a one-time pub on a busy tourist road and repurpose it as an antique shop cum tea room must have seemed an inspired idea. However, like so many things, the reality had not matched up to the initial promise. This was partly to do with the nature of the funk not junk, that particular type of artefact known as 'retro', which trod that perilously thin line between objet d'art and dusty old tat. The Quality Street tins, the spindly coffee tables, the Hornsea pottery plates; these were all things both Pat and Thelma clearly remembered in use. To sell it all as retro antiques needed some careful showcasing of the objects – not dumping willy-nilly across the bars and tables and surfaces of the former bar. On a watery Saturday, with uncertain girders of chilly sunlight ruthlessly spotlighting the various artefacts, the effect created was more akin to Miss Havisham than Mary Quant.

Pat took a reluctant sip of her coffee. 'So,' she said, 'this mystery lady who rang you, trying to put you off buying Terri Doo-dah's old house—'

'She's called Michelle—'

'She asked you to meet her here?' She cast a disparaging glance round Bygone Daze.

Thelma nodded. 'Thank you for coming along,' she said.

'It's fine,' said Pat brightly, though it wasn't, not really. The truth was that after her experience in Boroughbridge the previous day, the last thing she wanted was to see Thelma. But Liz had sounded so worried when she'd rung, saying how Thelma had an assignation with a strange woman, and how she – Liz – absolutely had to take Jacob to a Paper Not Plastic seminar at the library so could Pat *possibly* go along to make sure Thelma was All Right? These last two words had been imbued with such a dark emphasis, implying there was at least some risk of their friend ending up coshed in a ditch.

'But what I don't get,' said Pat 'is *why* this Michelle person wants to see you. Surely she'd want to avoid you, having been rumbled?'

Thelma shrugged. 'For some reason she wanted to put me off buying the house in Marley. And I'm *guessing* if she wants to put me off, *she's been doing the same to other people*. She must

105

be worried I'm going to expose what she's been doing. So it's in her interests to meet me and keep me onside.'

Pat took another sip and pulled another face. 'Why do you reckon she wanted to put you off in the first place?'

Thelma shrugged. 'That,' she said, 'is the forty-million-dollar question.' She looked at her friend. 'Never mind that,' she said. 'Are you all right?' It was the question she'd been wanting to ask since meeting her, but ever since she'd arrived, Pat had kept up a stream of chat – bright, distancing chat about nothing very much – a tactic Thelma recognized all too well. There was something about her friend this morning . . . It wasn't that Pat was pale – Pat didn't 'do' pale, what with her hair, her make-up, the accessories (that scarf really was lovely) – but today . . . today, all three elements looked as if they had had their work cut out for them.

'I'm fine,' said Pat brightly, with more than an undertone of *Why shouldn't I be?*

With some fortitude Thelma gave the elephant in the room a hearty slap.

'Yesterday was your trip to Boroughbridge?'

Pat nodded. 'I went with Marguerite.' Her voice was light and casual enough to let Thelma know exactly how much of a big deal this had been.

'And this lady was some sort of spiritualist?'

'I don't know if she'd call herself that,' said Pat. There was a pause. From the defensive look on Pat's face it was clear to Thelma she *wasn't* all right and equally clear she was trying very hard to look as if she was.

She chose her next words carefully. 'Did Marguerite find anything out?' she asked.

There was another awkward pause, but as Pat was opening her mouth to speak, they were interrupted.

'Mrs Cooper?' Pat felt a stab of shock at the thin, reedy

voice. The *familiar* voice. Its owner was a rather striking woman with pale make-up, a dark bob of hair, a smart jacket and shoes.

'Michelle?' asked Thelma.

Michelle nodded. 'Thank you for coming,' she said graciously. 'Can I get either of you anything?'

'No, thanks,' said Pat and Thelma simultaneously and firmly.

'Something to eat? They do a rather good beetroot and banana loaf.' Pat found herself trying not to stare. That *voice*. That memory from all those years ago . . . that thin, reedy voice—

You will come back, won't you? You will come back and talk to me?

'I wonder—' The words were out of her mouth before she had time to think. 'I hope you don't mind me asking. Are you by any chance related to Mal Stanley?'

The woman shot Pat a sudden, startled look. Her eyes darted across the room, as if deciding whether to speak.

'He was my father,' she said reluctantly.

Michelle Stanley didn't have any problems with the coffee; indeed, she termed it 'perfection' in casually arrogant tones as if it was the tastiest beverage ever to come her way. Pat found herself studying her, seeing if anything about this woman tallied with those hazy memories she had in her mind's eye of the woman in the floral dress and the man in the Batman mask – Michelle's parents.

'So.' Michelle smiled at them in a faux self-deprecating way, as if sharing a wry joke. 'I really must apologize to you, Thelma. I was thinking coming here – whatever must she be thinking of me? Calling her up out of the blue like that!' She spoke quickly, her words cascading out. 'You know that terrible cliché of your phone being about to die? Well, it really was! Plus, the reception where I live, it's shocking, a complete joke in this day and age.'

Thelma could have challenged all of these assertions, but she merely smiled politely and said, 'Oh, where's that then?'

'Over Harrogate way.' The comment was pitched at a level that Pat termed 'throwaway vague' – a tone she was an expert at detecting in her sons when they attempted to hide things from her. 'I was over this way with work,' said Michelle, 'and I thought, probably best to set the record straight.'

'What is it you do?' asked Thelma.

'Oh, a bit of this, a bit of that. Local government. And I had a couple of parcels to pick up from the depot in Thirsk.' She smiled fondly round at the torn knitting patterns, rusty biscuit tins and chunky mugs. 'It's like time's stood still here. I can never resist coming in when I'm in this neck of the woods. They always have such super stuff!'

Close to, she wasn't cutting quite such a striking figure; a sudden shift of the chilly winter sunlight was showing an altogether tattier picture: marks of wear on the shoes, shiny patches on the jacket and rather frayed cuffs. Yet there was a confidence about her, an arrogance even, and Pat realized she had little or no self-knowledge of these sartorial defects.

'So,' said Thelma pleasantly but firmly, 'Sunny View Lodge.'

Michelle laughed, in that way people do when trying to explain away something they've done. 'As I say, I don't know *what* you must be thinking of me,' she said again. 'But I happened to hear you were seeing it from someone online. Not that I have anything to do with the village these days. A friend WhatsApped me. I knew it had been on the market, of course I did . . . Anyway, I thought, "Michelle, do you say anything, or do you keep shtum?"'

'About what?' asked Pat.

Michelle shrugged. 'Where to start?' she said. 'There's all sorts of issues with the place – well, there always were. I remember growing up there, leak after crack after leak! It was one thing after another! Drove my poor old mum mad.' It was, Pat thought, when she was speaking that the resemblance to that hazy memory was most noticeable.

The things I've had to put up with . . .

'You grew up there?' she asked, pushing back the memory.

Now there was a slight waver in Michelle Stanley's smile. 'Oh yes,' she said. 'We moved there when I was a babby boo.' She shook her head. 'And it was still going on, even when Mum died, and then when Dad and Terri were living there. And I thought to myself, you really need to make sure whoever does buy the place knows *exactly* what they're taking on.'

'It didn't look like there were any problems,' said Thelma.

'Then that's fine!' said Michelle. 'Phew! Reliefski and all that! But you might just want to have a few cheeky little surveys done. Cover your backs.' She smiled at them beneficently. 'Oh, and please,' she said, almost as an afterthought, '*please* don't land the lovely Casey in it. If she lost her job because of her looking out for a pal, well, I couldn't live with myself.' She nodded dismiss-ively, signalling that as far as she was concerned the conversation was at an end. Thelma, however, was not nearly done.

'You said when you called me,' said Thelma, stirring her coffee in a further futile attempt to blend in the soya milk, 'you said that it was a *bad* house.'

'Did I?' Yet again, that 'throwaway vague' tone.

'A bad house where bad things happen,' said Thelma doggedly.

'I was referring to the roof most probably.' Michelle laughed. 'Believe you me, water dripping into that conservatory is enough to qualify as bad in anyone's books!'

'And you lived there with your mum and your dad?' asked Pat.

'And my kid brother, Shaun. One big, not-so-happy family.' The smile flickered on, but now an undertone of something else, something darker, had entered her voice.

'Can I just ask?' said Thelma. 'I presume the house is – was – owned by your stepmother? The lady who died the other week?'

Michelle gave another bark of laughter, this one rather harsh in tone. 'Well, it wasn't owned by me,' she said. 'Thank God! No, Dad left it to Terri, God rest her soul.'

'So,' continued Thelma, 'if I were to go ahead with purchasing it who would I be buying it from?'

Michelle shrugged. 'Whoever poor Terri left it to. Tate Bishop most likely.' Her mouth tightened in something approaching a sneer and now Pat saw a clear resemblance to the man in the Batman mask.

'Tate?' she said, thinking it wiser not to reveal the fact they had already heard about Terri's ne'er-do-well partner. She could tell from Thelma's slight nod she'd made the right call.

'Her ex.' Michelle's mouth made a moue of distaste. 'Well, sort of ex. She'd left him when she met Dad but even after they got married, Tate was always sniffing around, him and his flash cars. Me and Shaun think he'd had money off her on more than one occasion.' She twisted her handkerchief. 'No one can say Terri had an easy time of it.'

'Because of this Tate?' asked Thelma.

Michelle looked round conspiratorially, as if suspecting a listening device to be concealed in a nearby fondue set. 'Because of being married to my dad,' she said. 'God rest his soul. I don't know if you know, he was suffering from multiple sclerosis and his mobility wasn't good. And towards the end . . . well, he was becoming downright impossible to live with. Terri usually got the rough end of whatever mood he was in. Though his accident, well, it knocked me for six—'

Her tone was bleak, and Thelma got a sense of actually how much she missed her father, however difficult he might have been.

'I heard he fell down the stairs,' she said.

Michelle nodded. Her voice was curiously neutral. 'Terri had gone out for the afternoon, and when she came back there he was.' There was a dark pause. 'She was terribly upset – and maybe she shouldn't have left him all on his own – but as I say, Dad could be an absolute pain in the bum when he was that way out. Who can blame her for wanting an afternoon to herself? I know I would've. And *afterwards*—' Her voice came to a sudden stop and she appeared to be deciding whether to speak more. 'Well, put it this way,' she said carefully, 'I can see why she did what she did.'

'Which was?' asked Pat.

'Going back to Tate so quickly,' said Michelle. 'Dad was only dead two weeks before she'd moved out and gone back to him.'

Again, Pat and Thelma exchanged one of those unobvious but significant looks that lady primary school teachers are so good at.

'I think she was lonely,' Michelle continued. 'I mean, she'd already left the guy once, so it can't have been exactly love's young dream. And—' again she dropped her voice, scanning the bar '—I know she was rather scared of him. I remember talking to her at the funeral and she mentioned she was having security cameras fitted, and I said, "Why on earth are you doing that?" and she said, "One word, Michelle: *Tate*."'

'I wasn't aware of there being any security cameras at the property,' said Thelma.

'Well, it was soon after that she went back to him,' said Michelle. 'So she didn't need to.'

'And she was living with Tate when she had the accident?' asked Pat.

Michelle nodded. 'Up near Middlesborough.'

'Does he work, this Tate?' said Thelma.

'Ah,' said Michelle significantly 'Now *there's* a question. Shall

111

we just say he's someone with a number of irons in a number of fires. What you call a "Mover and a Shaker".' The tone of her voice implied Tate was mixed up in at least two international crime syndicates. 'Is everything he does legal? *He'd* say it was, *I* couldn't possibly comment. There's always some carry-on or other. His latest scheme is this big ghost walk thing at some derelict hotel somewhere.' She shook her head. 'All I can say is God help the ghosts.' She smiled and stretched as an obvious precursor to moving. 'Anyway—' she said.

'If you'd excuse me for one moment.' Thelma spoke quickly.

'Yes, I'd better be making tracks.' Michelle stuffed the stained hanky in her pocket and made as if to stand.

'If you could wait just two minutes,' said Thelma. 'I just need to ring the charity shop where I work. Check what time they want me.'

Michelle looked uneasy. 'I really do need to be making a move,' she said, frowning.

'I'll be as quick as I can,' said Thelma firmly, edging out of her seat.

Although Pat knew Thelma was doing an extra shift at the shop, there was no doubt in her mind that her friend's retreat had been for some other, strategic reason. What it was exactly she wasn't sure.

'Listen,' said Michelle, frowning after the retreating figure. 'I do hope you and your friend know I was only doing what I thought was for the best.'

'Of course,' said Pat. 'Thelma was naturally curious.'

'Can I just ask you something?' Michelle looked at her and there was more than a note of challenge in her voice. 'How did you know who I was? Are you from the Marley? Do you know people there?'

'No,' said Pat. 'Nothing like that. I knew your mum. At least

I met her once – a long time ago.' She was conscious of her heart thudding.

Without any obvious change of expression Michelle's demeanour changed; the eyes grew sadder, new shadows cast sombre lines across her face. But all she said was, 'She'll have been dead eleven years this month.'

Just a few months after she'd met her at the party, Pat realized.

'I'm sorry,' she said. 'I heard it was a car accident?'

'Yes.' In that one word was something as bleak as the sunlight in that cold, dusty room. 'It's no secret that she'd had a row with Dad. *Another* row, I might say.' She shrugged uneasily, as if trying to normalize what never could be normal. 'She left the house in a bit of a state . . . and she drove straight into a lorry coming from Grewlthorpes.' The words were weary, devoid of emotion and yet at the same time infinitely sad. There was something very practised about the way she spoke; for her what had happened was as engrained and unconscious as the faded clothes and scuffed shoes.

Why didn't you come back and see me? You said you would!

The need in that reedy voice . . . And if Pat *had* come back . . . if she *hadn't* snuck back downstairs to the summery party in her St Honoré shawl? What then?

Come back to me . . .

She remembered that odd, cold feeling she'd had on the stairs. What had that vicar woman said to Liz? The house *wasn't* haunted, which meant people obviously thought it *was*.

If she'd thought about it she very probably wouldn't have spoken. 'I wonder . . . did Terri ever say anything . . . about something *strange*?'

Suddenly Michelle was tense, guarded even. 'In what way strange?' she asked.

'Something . . . I don't know . . . something you'd find hard to explain.' Something . . . *odd*.' She wanted to say, *Do you think your mother is present in your old house?* but her tongue felt suddenly thick and it was an effort to marshal her speech.

Now Michelle Stanley was staring at her, a frightened look on her face. 'I don't know what you mean,' she said in a faint voice.

'You see someone told my friend—' Pat was about to explain about the possibility of Sunny View Lodge being haunted but suddenly Michelle was speaking, almost *gabbling*.

'Tate,' she said. 'Tate was pestering Terri. I'm sure that's why she went back to him. I think – *I'm sure* – Terri was frightened of *him* – terrified.'

'I'm so sorry,' said Thelma. Both women started, not having heard her approach. 'I got waylaid. You're right: there really is some wonderful stuff here.'

'I have to go.' Michelle sounded scared. 'I said I needed to go. Now I'm going to be really late.' She stood, almost stumbling, and retreated across the room.

Through the dusty window Thelma and Pat watched Michelle Stanley get into a tan-coloured Maestro and almost roar out of the car park.

'She wasn't lying when she said she was in a hurry,' said Pat.

'She certainly seemed bothered about something,' said Thelma thoughtfully. 'When she first came in, how did you know who she was?'

Pat took a deep breath. 'It was her voice,' she said. As she explained about her memorable encounter with Christine Stanley all those years ago, she was aware of sounding defensive, even though it had been Thelma's suggestion it was a memory as opposed to a vision. But Christine's car crash – her loneliness; the words spoken at Boroughbridge – she didn't mention.

Thelma listened gravely. 'So Mal Stanley's daughter wanted

to scupper the sale of her father's house,' she said. 'I wonder *why.*'

'When we were talking just now,' said Pat, 'she suddenly seemed frightened.'

Thelma looked at her. 'Have you any idea why?'

Pat looked at her squarely. 'I mentioned feeling there was something *strange* at the house. Okay, it may have just been my memories but it felt like something more than that to me. And then Michelle suddenly started going off on one about this Tate . . . almost gabbling about how Terri was scared.'

'Scared of Tate?' asked Thelma.

'Yes . . .' Pat paused, frowning. 'Yes, but it felt like there was something *more* to it than that. I'm sure it was something to do with the house—'

Why didn't you come back to me?

Pat shivered and not just because of the chilly bar. She was aware Thelma was looking at her intently but she wasn't going to say any more.

'Whatever it was she was scared of,' said Thelma, 'what you have to bear in mind is that Michelle Stanley is a woman who tells lies.'

Pat looked at her. 'All that claptrap about her phone being out of juice?' she said.

'That and other things,' said Thelma, making a final effort to stir the coagulated remains of her coffee. 'I didn't just go to the facilities. I also took the opportunity to nip into the car park and have a little look-see into Ms Stanley's car.'

'And?'

'You remember her saying she didn't have much to do with Marley?' said Thelma. 'Well there's a whole stack of those flyers for that village play that's being put on there.'

Pat frowned. 'She *definitely* said she had little contact with the place anymore.'

'And,' said Thelma, 'on the back seat were the parcels she'd been to collect. *With her address on.* Where did she tell us she lived?'

'Over Harrogate way,' said Pat, mimicking 'throwaway vague'.

'Well she doesn't. Not unless Rievaulx Gardens, Northallerton, classes as Harrogate.'

CHAPTER FOURTEEN

Answers are demanded, fun rejected and talk of neck cushions is unexpectedly interrupted.

'*Village Voices* is *such* an exciting project, Thelma! The way it's *energizing* the whole community – it's so brilliant and inspiring!' Mairead Hope-Hamilton from Open Fist Arts addressed Thelma with energetic familiarity, as if she'd known her well for many years. She hadn't, they'd barely been speaking on the phone for three minutes. 'We've a superb writer on board who has collated and written up these stories – Kez Maleski. Did you catch *Love Letter to my Ovaries*?'

Thelma had not caught *Love Letter to my Ovaries*, nor did she feel inclined to. 'So is *Village Voices* a project run by the church?' she asked.

'No. They're only *using* the church to rehearse and stage the piece in, which is brilliant as it's such a focal point of the community! But the whole project is overseen by Open Fist Arts, funded by the National Rural Hardship Fund.'

Thelma supposed she could see the point of this – her own involvement in amateur theatre over the years had given her a deep faith in the beneficial power of drama but she did rather wonder whether any rural hardship might not have been better addressed by investment in foodbanks or maybe the local bus service.

'Can anyone be involved?' she asked.

'Are you a budding thesp? How brilliant!'

Thelma looked at the tally she had started keeping in the margin of the charity shop rota list; it was Mairead's seventh use of the word.

'I was thinking more the publicity side of things. Leaflets.' *Such as the pile she'd seen on the back seat of Michelle Stanley's car.*

'Jamie Adams,' Mairead said. 'He's the man on the ground. Brilliant actor, done all sorts of stuff, and we're so lucky to have him on board. He's the director and general man on the front line pulling all those strands together.'

'So he's in charge of publicity?' Thelma persisted.

'Everything like that.' Mairead sounded vague, confirming Thelma's suspicions. She had met many, many Mairead Hope-Hamiltons over the years – big on enthusiasm but less committed when it came to the actual nitty-gritty of jobs that needed doing. 'Tell you what.' Mairead spoke as if bestowing a huge favour. 'I'll take your number and tell him you're keen on getting involved!'

Call ended, Thelma felt buffeted by Mairead's energy. Knowing arts organizations the way she did, she had no faith that either Mairead or this Jamie Adams would ever get back to her, and she'd have to think of another way of finding out more about Michelle and the leaflets – if that was what she *wanted* to do. She yawned, feeling suddenly tired, her energy sapped by Mairead's enthusiasm. Ideally she would have liked a five-minute sit-down; this, however, was not possible in the back room of the Hospice Charity shop. Yesterday had obviously seen a hefty number of donations – not at all unusual for the post-Christmas period when people were decluttering – and every last chair and flat surface was obscured by numerous bin bags stuffed to bursting.

The sudden, sharp intake of breath next to Thelma's left ear seemed to indicate at the very least a moderately bad accident of some description. Verna, the charity shop manager, was clearly unimpressed by the state of the back room.

'Everything's been left everywhere!' she stated in tones of flat horror. 'Does Polly not KNOW shop protocol for storing donations?' One of Verna's signature characteristics was throwing out accusatory rhetorical questions like javelins, which had the effect of reducing complex situations to a black or white simplicity. The truth would invariably be something much greyer – being in this instance that on busy days, with donations coming in thick and fast, no matter what protocols were in place there was often little time to do more than move the bags out the main shop and put them just anywhere. Surveying the scene with a carefully applied look of sorrowful horror, Verna shook her head. Thelma knew it was pointless to say anything given the ongoing feud between the manager of the charity shop and Polly, her deputy, which was now in its third week. The origins of the row were hazy to say the least – something to do with Polly's erratic time-keeping coupled with Verna's autocratic style of management. There was one version to be had from Verna, another from Polly and at least half a dozen other variants from the other volunteers.

'I'll make a start on sorting these,' said Thelma, calmly reaching for the latex gloves.

'What if I need help in the shop?' snapped Verna. 'What if more donations come in?' Rhetorical javelins flung she looked angrily round the space, but fortunately at that moment the shop bell rang and she retreated darkly, shaking her lacquered head.

As Thelma snapped on the gloves, she went over what little she'd gleaned from Mairead Hope-Hamilton about *Village Voices*.

Not a lot. Certainly nothing indicating how Michelle Stanley came to have a stack of flyers on the back seat of her car whilst claiming only scant connection with Marley on Swale. Opening the first bag – crammed with an assortment of towels, pillow-cases and knitted cardigans – Thelma sighed. To her seasoned eye this looked like a bit more than a mere January declutter. The quantity of items crammed in together betrayed the haste of a house clearance, a home turned, cupboard by drawer, into a series of empty rooms.

She frowned. What did that make her think of? *Of course!* Marguerite McAllister's fantastical story. Seeing the growing piles of linen it seemed doubly, trebly impossible that a charity shop of all places, with its every last tea towel and bin bag, could just *vanish* overnight. What could the *facts* possibly be? She remembered many times over the years when children had come to her with emotional, breathless convoluted stories, which had sounded utterly preposterous. Underneath them there had always been something very mundane, but what on earth could lie under this particular story? Nothing in all her years of teaching – in all the excuses, subterfuges, deceptions amongst children and adults – offered any parallel whatsoever.

The shrill of her phone broke into her reflections. Teddy? Squashing down thoughts of the car in a ditch with him coughing feebly over the airbag, she answered.

However it was not Teddy.

'Is that Thelma Cooper?' The voice – slightly breathless, slightly nasal – was unfamiliar to her.

'It is,' she said carefully, reminded of the other night and Michelle Stanley's cryptic warning.

'Mairead Hope-Hamilton gave me your number. It's Jamie Adams from *Village Voices*. She says you're maybe interested in getting involved?'

★   ★   ★

As Thelma laboured in the back room of the charity shop, Liz was surveying her lounge critically. Were all the plastic pumpkins maybe a bit much? They were so indelibly *Halloween*, and yet with the main lights off, they undoubtedly created an atmosphere, especially considering the fog outside, which was yet again thickening to decidedly supernatural proportions. She looked round again, checking everything was in place – lamps, vegan flapjacks, *Ghostbusters* 1 and 2 both ready by the DVD player.

It had been some time since they'd had a Saturday film afternoon with Jacob and *Ghostbusters*, a perennial favourite of his, had seemed the obvious choice. Ever since that awful breakfast the other day, a conviction had been growing in her that she needed to do *something* for her grandson – something to distract him from whatever was going on with his parents, and something to divert his mind away from its current obsessions about the climate and all things environmental, which although worthy, were hardly uplifting.

Was it, Liz wondered, all maybe a bit childish for her serious-minded grandson? But what else could she arrange for him that would both appeal and distract? Her mind fastened idly onto something Thelma had said, something about something being run by Terri Stanley's partner . . . some ghost walk somewhere? Something like that? Would a ghost walk maybe be something Jacob would enjoy? Mind you, she had to be careful not to do anything that might be construed as getting further involved with that ridiculous story of Marguerite McAllister's. Since Thelma's ominous warning from Michelle, and then the trip to meet with her, Liz had been ever more regretting her rash decision to corral the others into viewing the house in Marley. Having her two friends 'not falling out' was, she decided, much the preferred option.

The noise of Derek's car pulling up made her look round

the room one last time. The shirts! Five of them hanging from the picture rail, the product of that day's ironing – four white work shirts of Derek's and a blue collarless one belonging to Tim. Taking the latter down to carry upstairs, she frowned at the garment – it wasn't really her son's style at all. For as long as she could remember he'd worn either nondescript grey shirts for work and equally nondescript polo shirts at home. This collarless jobbie . . . he'd not worn anything like this for years. *Not since . . .*

The memory hit her with the force of an electric shock. Sitting in this very lounge trying to think of things to say to Tim's then-girlfriend Lucy as Lucy had smiled and equally obviously tried to think of things to say back. She'd been such a nice lass, Lucy – an ideal first girlfriend who was polite, friendly, suitably chaste and not too demanding of Tim's time. And in turn Tim had treated her with the same grave consideration he'd approached his A levels and various Scout badges.

That afternoon they had arranged to go out to the Toby Carvery to celebrate Tim's eighteenth birthday, only he hadn't appeared at the appointed time, just sent a text saying he was held up. She knew he'd been out with some friends, for someone else's birthday, and she guessed they'd been at some pub or other, but more than that she didn't know. Annoyance had been fading into concern when she'd heard the rattle of a key in the front door. 'We're in here,' she'd called, cross and relieved all in one, as you are when someone shows up over an hour late.

'Sorry.' Tim had appeared in the conservatory door flushed, blue collarless shirt dishevelled, buttoned up the wrong way . . . and a wild look in his eye. And suddenly Liz *knew*. Knew without a shadow of a doubt he'd been with someone and her little boy was her little boy no more and was lost forever to her.

And now, back in the present, there was a similar rattle of

the key in the same lock, just as there had been all those years ago.

'Hello,' she called, forcing a welcoming 'everything's as it should be' smile onto her face. And there was Jacob standing in the doorway, eyes impassive behind their thick spectacles regarding the lamps and flapjack with his usual deadpan stare. Behind him stood Derek with his 'I need to tell you something' look on his face.

'Who ya gonna call?' cried Liz, waving the *Ghostbusters* DVD, as if this could force the scenario into cheerful life.

There was a pause.

'Actually, Grandma,' said Jacob, glasses winking as they reflected the pumpkin lights, 'Actually, I need to FaceTime Jordan.'

'Jordan?' she heard herself saying weakly.

'Anti-frackers,' said Derek, cheer forced into his voice too. 'His environmental group. We can do all this later, can't we?'

'Of course,' she said, more brightly than she intended. 'Maybe after tea.'

Jacob nodded and turned to go. In the doorway he stopped and turned. 'Grandma,' he said in sombre tones, 'you do know that single-use plastics in things like pumpkin lamps are causing the oceans to clog up?'

Derek came and put his arm round her for the second time in a week. 'He's growing up,' he said. 'It doesn't mean he doesn't think it's all lovely.'

She nodded, horrified to find herself blinking back sudden tears. Maybe Jacob was growing up, but some instinct told her that no matter how much he grew there was still something inside him that *needed* a bit of fun and excitement.

In was in the kitchen, as the vegan fish fingers were browning under the grill, that she had time to think and various things clicked into place in her mind.

The blue collarless shirt . . .

That Facebook page closed by Tim so abruptly and angrily . . .

What if . . .

The thought seized her with the strength that the memory had. What if *she* – Rochelle Bamford, the barmaid from Dishforth – was *back on the scene . . . ?*

'So come on then, Pat, what do you want for your birthday?' Simone was more than slightly flushed from her second glass of sparkling rosé. Pat looked at her son's girlfriend, so pink, so happy, so *young . . .*

To be like you! she wanted to scream.

'She has no idea,' said Rod, also flushed and also smiling. 'And if you do find out please let me know, otherwise it'll be a Whistles voucher.'

Pat began clearing away the remains of the Angela Hartnett lamb and aubergine with gremolata. The others – Rod, Simone and her son Andrew – were all happy smiles in the aftermath of an undoubtedly delicious meal, only she felt disconnected from the cheerful scene. She was glad – *of course* she was glad – that her middle son had found love with her favourite nail technician and everything about their relationship was lovely, from the rented mobile home in Dishforth to the confidence and purpose it had given her rather shambling and shambolic son. But tonight, with the conversation so firmly fixed on her impending sixtieth birthday, it felt rather as though she was observing everything through a thick pane of glass.

'So what about you, Rod?' asked Simone. 'What do you want?'

'That's easy,' said Andrew. 'Craft beer and a bottle of Old Spice.'

'Actually, no,' said Rod. 'What I want for my big birthday is a neck pillow.'

Big birthday . . . Like it was something to be proud of!

'You what?' said Andrew, his face a puzzled frown. 'A neck pillow? What's that when it's at home?'

'It's a pillow. For your neck,' said Rod. 'Inflatable. It goes round your neck.'

'What, like a noose?' Andrew put his hands on Simone's neck and she gave a shriek and a hiccup and told him to give over.

'It's for the coach,' said Rod, refilling glasses. 'Those long hours speeding through France. Keeps you comfy.'

Pat thought of that time too many years ago when they'd hitchhiked to the Isle of Wight festival, that hour's snatched sleep on a freezing garage forecourt.

'I'd give owt to go to a vineyard, me,' said Simone. 'I reckon it must be lush.'

A sudden, sharp bark broke into the moment. Larson, who had been tolerantly watching proceedings from the settee, had stiffened and was staring at the kitchen door. He gave another short bark and charged quickly (for him) towards the wooden panels.

'What's up with him?' said Andrew.

Larson barked again, and then coming through the back door was Liam, muffled up, his Leeds United scarf twined round his neck and the beginnings of one of his chesty coughs.

'Greetings, fam,' he said.

There was a surprised pause and then each of them was, in their own way, all over him, following the lead of Larson who was on his hind legs, head thrust firmly into Liam's neither regions. Andrew was all 'hey, bro'; Rod was asking about train times, and *why* hadn't Liam said he was coming; Simone, who knew him from school, grew even more pink-cheeked at this sudden joyfully unexpected addition to the party.

Only Pat knew something was wrong.

125

Later, as a second bottle of rosé was opened and a winter berry crumble with vanilla-pod custard dispatched, Pat climbed the stairs to her son's room where he had gone 'to dump his things'. The door was firmly shut, Larson stretched outside like Cerberus guarding the underworld.

Music thudded.

'Liam,' she said, 'can I come in?' In her mind were the beginnings of sentences about bacon sandwiches and maybe getting a load of washing started.

'I'll be down with you in five.' The voice was cheerful, but firm. Very firm.

'What's up with our boy?' she said to Larson who regarded her solemnly whilst scratching an ear.

At that moment her phone buzzed with a musical chime. Her first thought was that it was a text from maybe Thelma or Liz, but drawing it out she saw the semi-familiar pink and yellow Instagram icon. Instagram wasn't something she used over-much – there were one or two ladies with impossibly wonderful house interiors she followed, plus her son Justin's incessant motivation videos. But it was none of these; it was someone she wasn't familiar with, a Chris369 wishing to send her a message. Some bot no doubt. Periodically these would appear on her feed, impossibly handsome men with dogs and waterfalls, looking for soulmates.

But neither did the message appear to be from some bot with a waterfall.

The words were clear and stark and yet it took a second for them to come into focus, and a further second for the sense to emerge. When it did, Pat felt a cold clutch on the back of her neck.

YOU NEED TO KNOW THAT EVERYONE
THINKS TERRI STANLEY WAS A MURDERER.

CHAPTER FIFTEEN

In a cold space a dark story is told, and Pat has an unwelcome blast from the past.

'*Ghost stories?*' Thelma looked doubtfully round the stacked plastic chairs that fringed the space that had been cleared at the front of St Jude's church, Marley. The pale young man – Jamie Adams – nodded. 'Originally, the idea was it was going to be any local stories, but they quickly realized that no one was going to be that fussed about the great turnip blight of 1954, so they hit on using local ghost stories.' He regarded the three of them steadily with earnest blue eyes with a hint of mocking humour. 'The Grey Waif of Pickhill, some crashed Canadian airman from nineteen-forty-something and the ghost of Mad Jack Farr, Dick Turpin's sidekick shot by Sweet Polly Thwaite, barmaid of the Cock and Bottle.' His voice held a fine sense of the dramatic and with his high cheekbones and slightly soulful face he looked, thought Pat, not unlike a member of a boy band – albeit a rather aged member.

She, Thelma and Liz were sitting on three plastic chairs arranged in a rough semi-circle in the space where *Village Voices* was to be performed in a couple of weeks and where a Sunday afternoon rehearsal would soon be starting. In front of them was a black stage block; on this Jamie was perched, one foot on the top, the other dangling. If he hadn't already announced himself as actor and director, Thelma could have guessed it from this pose alone.

'According to Mairead Hamilton-Hope,' he said, 'it's verbatim theatre at its finest.' He paused, raising those wide blue eyes heavenward as if seeking divine guidance on what to say and how to say it. In this pose he put Thelma in mind of a medieval saint, the sort painted on woodwork in European cathedrals. A slightly sardonic grin flitted across his face. 'It's either that or a load of overblown tosh. It's up to you to decide! So—' he rubbed his hands and sat up with an infectious spasm of energy '—you want to get involved with the production, ladies?'

'It certainly all sounds very interesting,' said Liz.

'The thing is,' said Jamie, 'we've been rehearsing since October, so we're all pretty much cast up. But we can always use a few more yokels to stamp in the background and generally go *ee bah gum*.' Pat looked at Thelma and Liz, and found herself smiling at the image. Looking back at Jamie she realized he was smiling directly at her.

'We're more interested in the publicity side of things,' said Thelma firmly.

'Yes,' said Liz, equally firmly.

'Facebook? Twitter?' said Jamie. 'We always need a re-tweeter, Thelma.'

Pat found herself biting her lip.

'I was thinking more . . . leaflets,' said Thelma.

'Things we can take round,' said Liz.

Jamie Adams looked at them for a long moment. 'I'll not say no,' he said. 'I've over a thousand buggers *someone* ordered in a fit of exuberance. Meesh took a load to distribute round the council offices, but there's still a stack left.'

128

'Michelle Stanley?' said Pat, trying to keep her voice casual.

Jamie nodded. 'Sister to Shaun, my other half.' He looked at them, the sardonic smile playing round his mouth. 'So I hope you don't mind me asking,' he said, 'but would you be the same three ladies who were looking round Sunny View Lodge last week?'

There was an uneasy moment and Liz looked as guilty as if she'd been caught torching the place. 'We did look round the property,' said Thelma carefully.

Jamie nodded. 'So,' he said, 'do you just want to talk about leaflets? Or do you want to know about Terri Stanley?'

'What you have to remember about Mal Stanley,' said Jamie, 'was that he was not a nice man – not in any way, shape or form. In fact—' again, a sardonic smile lit those features '—he could be a right ess-aitch-eye-tee.'

It was ten minutes later. What might have been quite an awkward situation seemed to have been passed over easily enough. Now, as he made them coffee (in an incongruously good machine), Jamie told them how the woman watching their visit to Sunny View Lodge from her bungalow – Old Ma Bickle, as he called her – had wasted no time in spreading the word round Marley that there was interest in the property. This had been corroborated by the Reverend Mare, and from there the Marley jungle telegraph had done what it did best. Jamie had also talked to his sister-in-law who was, according to him, absolutely gutted at what a tit she had made of herself.

'Should be here in the play,' he'd said. 'She's a right drama queen.'

Was it, Pat wondered, Michelle who had sent that disturbing Instagram message? She had intended to show Liz and Thelma, but when she'd reopened the app, she found it had been deleted, and as she'd omitted to screenshot it she had no proof it had

129

ever been there. From what Jamie was saying about the Marley network, it could have been anyone who sent it.

'Made enemies left, right and centre, did our Mal. Deals, backhanders – nothing *illegal* – but he was never one to let human feelings get in the way of business.' Liz remembered those press articles Thelma had found. All those people dismissed at Christmas and that pile of manure dumped on his car . . .

'It was much the same in his personal life,' continued Jamie. 'According to Shaun and Meesh, he and Christine – his first wife – enjoyed a rather turbulent relationship, the general consensus being that he made her life a living hell.'

Pat stirred uneasily in her chair, in her mind that reedy voice once again whimpering in her ears.

'Then, when his son had the brass neck to tell him he was in fact *gay*, Mal demanded – with threat of legal action – every last penny he'd given him for a house deposit.' He shook his head. 'I don't think Shaun's ever got over that. Not that he'd ever say.'

He shifted position, crossing one leg over another, as outside the church the wind murmured drowsily, freeing a sudden drench of sunlight to illuminate the toddlers' corner with its assorted rainbow plastic bricks and trucks.

'And then Christine up and dies on him,' he continued. 'The one person who actually *wanted* to be with him, trashed by a lorry. His mistress – his latest mistress – exited stage left as fast as her waxed legs would carry her and old Mally Boy found himself facing the one thing even he couldn't blag his way out of: a life alone on the wrong side of sixty-five. And it's fair to say he hated the prospect.' He paused and Thelma found herself admiring the voice, the poise, the timbres of emotion. With proper direction he would, she thought, be excellent in a Tennessee Williams play. Maybe as Brick in *Cat on a Hot Tin Roof*.

'There were other ladies but nothing lasted long. Plus, his lifestyle was starting to catch up with him. You don't treat your liver like a ball pool for forty years without *some* consequences. And then a couple of years ago he asks Meesh to move back in. Now when I say "ask", I'm putting it mildly – it was more a case of he chucked every guilt-laden card in the pack at her. And Meesh, who'd been especially close to her mum through all Mal's dalliances, said words to the effect of "on your bike, chummy".'

Once again the wind stirred and each of the three ladies drew their coats more tightly round themselves; St Jude's was undeniably on the chilly side that Sunday afternoon despite a poster outside advertising it as a designated 'warm space'.

'It was around that time Shaun and I got together,' said Jamie. 'And that was my introduction to the Stanleys – Meesh coming round at all hours in floods of tears because of some emotional hand grenade Mal had chucked at her.'

'So, he didn't approach Shaun?' asked Thelma. 'To ask him to move back in?'

Jamie gave a short bark of laughter. 'He did not! Because not only was his son a homosexual, but he was a homosexual who was living with an *actor*. Shock Horror.'

Once again the sun shifted, not unfortunately onto the four but rather onto the foodbank bin and the notice advocating putting nothing down the toilet other than that which God intended.

'And that,' said Jamie, 'was the point at which Mal decided to engage a paid companion. 'There's this agency in Thirsk called "Charlotte's Aunts" which provides carers, home helps and people living in. We're talking paying through the nose here, but that didn't bother Mal. It all got off to a slightly shaky start as the first woman disappeared off into Thirsk after three days, tottering back some eight hours later, wig askew, reeking

131

of Malibu. She was rapidly followed by a woman who lasted a further three days before departing in floods of tears calling Mal every name under the sun. And *she* was succeeded by our Terri – Terri Matheson, as she was then.'

'Terri was his *carer?*' Thelma was surprised. She remembered Brid saying her sister worked for the man she later married, but she assumed it was as a secretary of some description.

Jamie nodded. 'And to answer your unspoken question ladies: thirty-seven years. As in, "there was an age gap of". It could be that she was genuinely in love with the guy.' He paused and regarded them. 'It could also be that I'm Dame Shirley Bassey, complete with sequins.' Jamie sat back, smiling and puffing out his cheeks in a rather endearing way, with the air of someone who has arrived at the end of act one.

Elliott Harvey to a tee, thought Liz. It had taken her a bit longer than her friends to mentally pigeonhole Jamie, but now she had it: *Elliott Harvey*, a small blond scrap of a lad who had been virtually silent for the first half of the year in her class, and then overnight had found a flamboyant self-confidence that had the rest of Year Two eating out of his hand. The last she'd heard he was running a highly successful restaurant in Soho.

'So Terri was working for Mal as a live-in help?' asked Thelma.

Jamie nodded. 'Cook, cleaner, companion, et cetera, et cetera. Not that any of us twigged about the "et cetera". Me and Shaun, we hardly ever saw them, for all us just living across the village—'

'You live in Marley?' asked Liz, surprised. With the relationship between father and son so strained, surely Marley on Swale was an odd choice of a place to live?

Jamie nodded. 'We've a place on the other side of the village, on the Pickhill Road. About five minutes from Shaun's garage.' He seemed to know what was in Liz's mind, as he again flashed that smile. 'Shaun isn't that different from his dad. If Mal had a problem with him, so what? Why should *he* be the one who had to move away? There was definitely a big element of two fingers up to Daddy in all this, which is why we're living in the middle of a potato field instead of somewhere like Harrogate.

'Anyway . . .' As he spoke, the three had the distinct sense of act two starting. 'The first we all knew of any *wedding* was on Facebook. A picture of the happy couple outside Northallerton registry office, with the caption: "She's going to TRY and make an honest man of me".'

'You mean . . .' Liz was shocked. 'He didn't even tell his own children he was planning to remarry?'

'Didn't tell his children, didn't tell his family . . . He did inform one or two chums at the golf club who drank his health before seeing them off for two weeks in PortAventura. And so Mr and Mrs Mal Stanley landed up back at SunnyView Lodge.'

The noise of the door opening, accompanied by a cheery 'knock knock' made them look round as the Reverend Mare appeared. 'Sorry to butt in on your little conflab,' she said, 'but your cast are starting to gather and it is rather chilly. Shall I tell them to come in?' Today the sweater was burgundy rather than green but everything else – the hair, the jacket, the energy – were pretty much the same, Liz noted.

'I'll be two secs, Mare, I'm just finishing up,' said Jamie. 'And talking of chilly, I'm not being funny, but I don't suppose you can bung the heat up? It's *Village Voices* we're doing, love, not *Frozen*.'

Mare laughed and shook her head. 'It comes on one till three,' she said firmly. 'At seventeen degrees. Until then it's winter woollies time!' It was then she caught sight of Liz. 'Hello again,' she said in surprise. 'Don't tell me you *are* going to buy the house?'

'These are my two friends,' said Liz. 'The ones I looked round the house with.'

Pat and Thelma smiled politely, and Thelma wondered how big a lie she'd have to tell about her intentions towards Sunny View Lodge.

'This,' said Liz, 'is the Reverend Mare, the one I told you about.'

'She's also,' said Jamie, 'a bossy old baggage who keeps this village and at least four others ticking over.'

'Ignore him,' said Mare, heading to the doors. 'Artistic geniuses are rather thin on the ground round these parts, so we have to show them *certain* leniencies. And if you could remember to put the chairs back for Wednesday communion that'd be splendid.'

'Thy will be done,' said Jamie. He was, realized Pat, one of these people with whom it's hard to tell if they're being sarcastic or just teasing. 'Oh, FYI I moved some bags of manky carrots. Someone had dumped them right here on the stage.'

'Brilliant!' Mare smiled brightly. 'Wonky veg,' she said to Liz, Pat and Thelma. 'Cheap bags from Morrisons much needed for our "Cordon Bleu on a Budget" classes. All donations welcome!' The door banged behind her and cheerful greetings and supplications to people to wipe their feet could be heard.

Jamie smiled sardonically. 'We've got about five minutes,' he said. 'Where was I?'

'Mrs Stanley number two,' supplied Pat. She liked this Jamie, she decided.

'You never met Terri, I take it?' He fixed each of them in turn with that soulful, pale blue gaze. All three shook their heads and he nodded, satisfied. 'Nice as pie. Big brown eyes, ready smile, bit on the plump side, but hey, aren't we all!' He sucked in his own stomach, which under the Argyle sweater looked trim, verging on the washboard. 'The sort of person who always remembers your name, always knows the right questions to ask you, looks directly at you . . .'

He paused and Thelma, veteran am-dram actress, sensed an impending denouement. 'She was also a scheming madam with an eye for the main chance. The main chance in this instance being Mal Stanley.' He shook his head. 'Part of me admires her. Part of me's like, yes, you go, lady. But a couple of months after they got back from PortAventura there were very definite cracks appearing in love's not-so-young dream. Mal, as I said, was not the easiest person to love. And his body was starting to pack up at a rate of knots. Plus—' another dramatic pause '—by then there was *another* face on the scene—'

'Tate Bishop?' said Pat.

Jamie looked at her. 'I thought maybe Meesh would have brought you up to speed,' he said. 'What did she have to say about Middlesborough's answer to Del Boy?'

'Bit of a dodgy so-and-so,' said Liz.

Jamie nodded. 'I'd put it a bit stronger than that,' he said. 'A nasty git. He's the only person I know who could give Mal Stanley a run for his money in terms of shifty dealings. Someone who made things happen, not all of them good. What Tate wanted, Tate got. From what she said to Meesh, that included Terri.'

'So Terri and Meesh got on all right?' asked Thelma.

'Maybe "got on" is putting it a tad strongly,' said Jamie. 'But Meesh worried about her dad, and Terri was there for him. For Terri, well . . . what with Mal and Tate, life wasn't exactly a bed of roses. More than once I saw the second Mrs Stanley driving through the village in tears.' He paused, casting his eyes heavenward, once more the renaissance angel. 'And then came Mal's accident.'

The three looked at him expectantly.

'Once again, the first we knew about anything happening was via social media. It didn't bother me, but to get a WhatsApp saying your dad's dead . . . Shaun and Meesh didn't deserve that.'

'It was a fall, was it not?' asked Thelma.

Jamie nodded. 'A fall down the stairs. Headlong. Broken neck.'

There was something very stark in the careful way in which he spoke, almost as though he could have been reading from a script. Or a police report. Thelma noticed Pat's soft shoes instinctively gripping at the floor and knew her friend was remembering those slippery open treads at Sunny View Lodge.

'And do you think it *was* an accident?' ventured Thelma.

Jamie looked solemnly at them. 'I'm repeating what I was told,' he said. 'Terri goes out, leaving Mal alive, and when she came back . . .' He made a discreet chopping gesture against his neck. He shook his head. Suddenly he was no longer the renaissance angel but something darker and sadder. Not so much Tennessee Williams, thought Thelma, but a character from a Jacobean tragedy.

'There's no denying Terri was very cut up. You should have seen her at the funeral – weeping, wailing, the whole nine yards. But then, of course, less than three weeks later . . . back she goes to Tate. Exits stage left leaving, incidentally, me and Meesh to clear all Mal's stuff out of Sunny View Lodge. Goodbye, Mrs Stanley, don't forget your coat.'

He looked like he was about to say more when the door opened and the cast of *Village Voices* began to troop in, led by the Reverend Mare. 'You have heat for exactly two hours, thespians!' she announced.

Jamie stood with a resigned shrug and a smile. 'Okay, you lovely people,' he said, retrieving a page that had fluttered from his notebook, 'today's the day we're going to sort once and for all the banishing of the Grey Waif of Pickhill. Can I have the mob ready to stone and hurl abuse at the pesky so-and-so! Get in a circle and be ready to warm up in five – and I mean that literally!'

136

Liz took Thelma to introduce her properly to the Reverend Mare and Pat found herself next to Jamie. 'Thanks,' she said, 'for your time. Because, really, this is none of our business. It was just after Meesh ringing Thelma like that.'

'Like I say,' he said, 'a drama queen. She's a bit weird about the place.' He looked around the hall. 'I'm sorry you got involved,' he said.

Pat nodded. There were about fifteen people in the church now, an assortment of young and old chatting, laughing and frowning over their lines. Had one of them sent that Instagram message to her?

'You didn't answer Thelma's question,' she said suddenly. 'About whether you thought Mal's death was an accident.'

Jamie was silent for a moment. Then he looked directly at her. 'I know,' he said. He seemed to guess something of what she was thinking as he took a flyer and scribbled a phone number on the back. 'In case there's any more you want to know,' he said. At that moment a soft voice spoke.

'Jamie, I've brought them lights and stuff from Shaun.' The voice belonged to a dark-haired, sharp-faced young man carrying a great box of electronic equipment. 'Where d'you want it?'

'Just down there, Luke,' said Jamie. There was something suddenly stiff, even formal in his tone. He turned back to Pat but she was staring at the sharp-featured man with a hostile glint in her eye.

'Hello, Luke,' she said coldly.

The young man shot her a startled, guilty glance.

'Do you two know each other then?' asked Jamie.

'Oh yes,' said Pat. 'Luke and I have a bit of a history, don't we, Luke?'

CHAPTER SIXTEEN

Harsh words are said, and a shared resolution is set to be broken three times.

'So,' said Liz in the flustered but determined tones of someone trying to get a conversation back on track. 'Jamie Adams's story. What do we think?'

'I know what I think,' said Pat indignantly. 'I think anyone involved with that weasel Luke Atkinson needs a jolly strong warning!' Her indignant voice cut clean across the Sunday afternoon hubbub of the Thirsk Garden Centre Café. Liz and Thelma glanced round, but it was so crowded no one noticed. They had repaired here to collect their thoughts and have what Pat had termed 'a post-Marley debrief', though in actuality it was proving to be more of a Luke Atkinson debrief. The way Pat was talking made it clear she held him responsible for all recent events, from car crashes to disappearing charity shops.

'We don't actually know he's *involved* as such,' said Liz.

'He's working for Jamie, isn't he?' Pat sounded as if that was all the proof that was needed.

'Strictly speaking, he's working for *Shaun*,' said Thelma mildly. A trawl on her phone as Pat had driven them back to the garden centre had filled her in on Shaun Stanley Motor repairs,

Busby Stoop. She wondered how it had co-existed in such close proximity to Mal Stanley's machine supplies company given the animosity between father and son.

'Whoever he's working for they need to be watching out,' said Pat darkly. 'You remember what he did to our Liam.'

Both Liz and Thelma did, vividly. It had been around the time of the untimely death of their friend and former colleague, Topsy. Luke had been Liam's first tentative relationship. At that time his sexuality had still been a secret – a secret Luke had blown wide open when the relationship had gone sour, trumpeting the fact across social media. Fortunately, friends, family and school had been consistently and overwhelmingly supportive to Liam; indeed, both Liz and Thelma privately thought in some ways Luke might almost have been said to have done Liam a favour. However, this was a thought they'd never shared with Pat, and looking at her now, they both recognized it was a thought they never would share. This was one of those times during a long friendship where unvoiced support was by far the best strategy.

'Look,' said Liz, 'your Liam's well away from him now. He's doing really well at Durham, seeing that nice lad off his course and you've got him home for a few days.' As she spoke she couldn't help feeling a slight chill of sadness at the contrast with her own family situation.

Pat nodded. 'I know,' she said. The long hours Liam was spending alone in his room was something she didn't have the energy to think about, not just now.

'Anyway,' said Liz with a certain dogged determination. 'That story Jamie told us. *What do we all think?*'

There was a brief pause filled by a waitress calling out 'Two Melmerby slices!' in hopeful tones.

'Because,' Liz continued in her organizing voice, 'I'm going to say what *I* think, and you're not going to like it, but I'm still going to say it anyway.'

The other two nodded and Pat took a fortifying sip of cappuccino.

'I think,' said Liz, 'that all this with Marguerite seeing a charity shop is some big mistake. Yes, I'm sure she did go into some sort of charity shop, or even, knowing Marguerite McAllister, wandered into some person's garage . . . *but she did it somewhere else*. Not where she thought and *not where we went*. I think she must have got confused in the fog or something. And as for the rest of this—' a dismissive hand shooed away family rifts, sinister exes and lethal staircases '—I can't see it's anything to do with us. This Terri Doo-dah may or may not have killed her husband, and whether she did, well . . . I can't see it matters very much.' The other two did a slight double take at this rather cavalier dismissal of possible murder. 'I mean, he's dead and she's dead,' she hastily qualified. 'Let the dead bury their dead.' This rather ghoulish statement took even her by surprise, but as she said it, it felt *right*.

There was a pause whilst the other two considered her words.

'Well,' said Pat, 'for what it's worth, I also think Marguerite saw something – something that can't easily be explained. What it was exactly I've no idea, but there was what the Spirit Lady in Boroughbridge said—' here she looked defiantly at Thelma '—and also the fact Terri seemed so scared. Though what Marguerite saw, and how it connects with Terri Doo-dah, I don't see how we can ever find out. And if Luke Atkinson is involved in *any* way shape or form, then I certainly don't want to be. And as Nostradamus here says—' she nodded at Liz '—let the dead bury their own dead.'

They both looked at Thelma.

'Well?' said Liz.

'I don't know,' said Thelma, stirring her coffee in a gesture they both recognized well. 'I just don't *know*.' Her mind felt as crammed as one of the bin bags full of donations she'd wrestled with the day before. The sheer improbability of a charity shop vanishing . . . The whole strange story of Terri Stanley, Mal, Michelle . . . She thought of that small family unit she'd seen in Busby's – Brid, Archie and Grace. They'd not seemed bothered in any way, so why should she be? 'I suppose,' she said slowly, 'I suppose I can't really see any point in trying to find out more.'

They looked at each other, feeling a certain amount of relief in their hearts as though they'd been let off some sort of hook.

They little knew, however, that for each one their viewpoint was about to be changed.

Arriving home around two o'clock, Liz felt a strong sense of purpose, of something she needed to be getting on with now that disappearing charity shops and people falling down stairs had more or less been satisfactorily laid to rest.

Now was the time to find out, once and for all, what was going on with Tim. More pressingly: was Rochelle Bamford once more on the scene? After his previous moody, ill-tempered refusal to talk, Liz's first instinct had been to present him with some sort of ultimatum – a sheaf of Spooner and Collins rentals, accompanied by something along the lines of 'fess up or sling your hook'. This idea, however, had been challenged by Derek the previous night. Like all important exchanges in their marriage, it had been initiated by her husband whilst she was in the middle of doing something else; in this instance, kneeling in front of the washing machine sorting her son's dirty clothes. Here Derek had approached her, asking in calm tones exactly why she was so intent on confrontation with their son.

'Because I need to know what's going on,' she'd said testily, extracting a number of coloured socks from amongst his white shirts. (Why could men never grasp the idea of colours running?)

'All you're going to do is drive him away.'

'Good.' She spoke firmly and tartly. '*Good.* I am sick to death of pussyfooting round the place not daring to speak. Let him go and see how he gets on in some bedsit up Topcliffe Road.'

'You're not thinking this through,' said Derek. She'd bristled at this. As far as she was concerned that's exactly what she *had* been doing, mostly at three o'clock in the morning. 'Think about it.' His voice had been calm and reasonable. 'Whatever's going on in our Tim's life, *he's under our roof.* Where we've a much better chance of talking sense to him than if he was off in some bedsit.'

Liz had looked rather bleakly at her son's Wayne Rooney football shirt, the one he used for sleeping in. 'I thought,' she said, 'that all this sort of carry-on was behind us.'

Derek put out a hand. 'Up you get, old lady,' he said. 'We need to get up to date with *The Apprentice.*'

But now, with everyone out, it was time for a fact-finding mission.

'Hello,' she carolled, deliberately loud and cheerful as she let herself in, though she was almost certain there'd be no response. Derek was at some Sunday running event, Jacob was with Leoni and Tim had announced that morning he was off to see 'a mate'. A mate – or maybe a predatory ex-barmaid? Involuntarily her lips tightened.

'Hello?' she called again, double-checking the coast was clear. Heart thudding, she climbed the stairs (knees creaking somewhat) and approached her son's room with a sense of dread, both at the chance of being caught and more pressingly with what she might find there. 'Get a grip,' she said to herself and opened the door.

And took an immediate, instinctive step back.

It was the first time she'd really looked in the room since Tim had properly moved back the other day – and it was uncanny. Once again, the room that had been the spare room for the past sixteen years was her son's room. Box files where his homework files used to be, paperbacks on the shelf – not the thumbed Stephen King and James Herbert but smart, glossy paperbacks like *The Art of Success* and *Seven Habits of Highly Effective People*. Instead of rugby shirts, hanging from the wardrobe door were his suits and shirts; on the chest of drawers was a rack of CDs. It wasn't that the things were the same, but that it was all *arranged* the same, just as it had been twenty years ago. When he had been seeing Rochelle Bamford.

She looked more closely at the CDs ... *Hang on*. She frowned as she peered at the cramped print. As far as she could remember these *were* largely the same – Black Sabbath, Eminem ...

Memories sprung up fresh and sharp – Tim locked away in his room, music furiously thudding as she fretted downstairs. Thankfully now there was an expensive-looking pair of headphones next to the CDs.

The same music ... *The same barmaid?*

Stifling any pangs of guilt she began rifling through the drawers in the bedside cabinet. Quite what she expected to find she was unsure. Maybe a picture of Rochelle pouting out at the world with '*I'm back*' scrawled across it in carmine lipstick? But search as she might there was nothing that gave any proof one way or another. (And no sign of any condoms, thank God.)

At a loss, she stood in the middle of the room, casting her eyes round, not sure whether she felt relieved or disappointed. As she did, she noticed something white on the floor – a receipt. Another Greggs receipt she noticed, lips pursing at the thought of those rejected breakfasts. What had he been eating now? She looked. Looked closer. Frowned. Looked again.

Why on earth had he been visiting a Greggs in *Preston*? She knew he travelled with Ormondroyds, but to the best of her knowledge Leyburn was the limit of his patch.

A rattle from the front door made her start guiltily.

'Grandma?' The gruff shout came through the letterbox. *Jacob*. But he wasn't due for ages!

She hastily gave the room the final expert glance of a fact-finding mother, checking all was as she'd found it, and hurried downstairs as fast as her knees allowed her, to where Jacob's distorted face could be seen pressed up owlishly against the glass.

'I'm sorry,' she said, opening the door. 'I thought you said four.'

'I did say four.' Jacob arranged his shoes precisely on the shoe rack in their customary place. 'But Mum got all weepy again and wanted to go to Millandra's.'

That sounded ominous. And here she was snooping round her son's room when she was so patently needed elsewhere. She followed Jacob into the kitchen.

'Is she here, your mum?'

'No, I walked on from the mini roundabout,' he said, taking a glass of water. (One of his eight a day.)

She looked at him gulping down the drink, frowning and preoccupied.

'Tell you what,' she said brightly. 'How about I make some popcorn and we watch *Ghostbusters*?' She felt a sudden glow at the unexpected prospect of this deferred treat.

For a moment a light flickered uncertainly in Jacob's face. Just the merest moment, before it was quickly frowned away. 'Actually,' he said, 'I'm need to write to Leo Lloyd.' Leo Lloyd was their local MP. 'Me and the anti-frackers are going to bombard him with protest mail.'

He cut such a forlorn figure, trudging upstairs with his iPad, and Liz watched him, feeling that familiar swelling desire to protect him from the world and all the awful things it could throw at him. She thought of that brief, tantalizing flicker on Jacob's face. She *had* to give him *something* diverting.

The sudden thought lit up in her mind like a shaft of sun on a gloomy day. Taking her iPad she launched Google and it only took her a moment to find what she wanted – somewhere thrilling and uncomplicated.

Dare you face the secrets of Yorkshire's most haunted hotel? Flaxby Hall is waiting for YOU!

CHAPTER SEVENTEEN

A funeral is planned, a nudge perceived and a depressing task interrupted with a welcome invitation.

Arriving back at 32 College Gardens, Thelma was aware of a certain feeling of relief. But it was an uneasy relief, as if an easy path had been taken at the expense of a right one. Impatiently she shook her head. She'd more than enough to be worrying about without adding vanishing charity shops. Teddy was, she noted, out on his deliveries again. The idea had been that there would be fewer drops to make on a Sunday – 'a mopping day' – but this term proved to be over-optimistic. By her reckoning he'd now worked something like ten days without any sort of meaningful break.

She thought of the application. It had lain untouched on the coffee table for a couple of days until she had laid it gently but firmly on his desk where he was planning his WAMMP deliveries. (Either that or watching clips from *Dad's Army* on YouTube.) Checking the form this morning she'd seen he'd filled it in – in his open, bold handwriting – but it had not been put in an envelope and he'd made no mention of posting it. Only that morning she'd had a text from Brummie Maureen asking when he was going to drop it in.

She looked at the folder now. Surely he intended to post it, so what would be the harm in saving him a job by posting it herself? Or even . . . dropping it round at the college? Without giving herself time to think she put the form into an envelope.

'I'm saving him a job,' she said aloud to Snaffles who was watching her unblinkingly from Teddy's leather armchair.

As she approached, Thelma could hear the Sunday afternoon shouts and cheers from the playing fields beyond the long, low Victorian college. The lights of the building were coming on, offering the prospect of warmth and shelter from the darkening January afternoon; she imagined behind each one the weekend business of student life going on: laundry, essay writing and phone calls home. With sadness, she remembered the days when she had been a part of this, albeit only on the fringes – the various functions and services, the fuddles and of course the college am drams . . . *And,* she thought with a sudden resolve, *I will be again*.

She posted the form almost furtively in the big mahogany box in the tiled entrance lobby, and headed back up the main path between the college lawns, head ducked down. Thus it was she didn't properly notice the two approaching figures in skimpy, unsuitable jackets, one short, one taller, until she was nearly face to face with them. One of them registered as familiar and indeed was slowing, peering closely at Thelma, nudging her companion.

'Is it Mrs Cooper?' The face of the shorter one was lit with relief. 'It is Mrs Cooper, isn't it? It's me – Brid Matheson.'

Of course!

'Good afternoon, Brid,' she said. 'How are Grace and Archie?'

'Oh, full of it.' The eyes rolled good-humouredly. 'Grace is bossing us all about left, right and centre and Archie's on with taking the plugs off everything to see what fuses they have.'

'God love him.' This came from Brid's companion, a stocky lass with cheerful mauve hair.

'This is my friend Jade,' said Brid. 'The one I share childcare with.'

'Childcare, chocolate and prosecco,' said Jade with a wide smile. 'Lots of each.'

Thelma smiled back. 'So, what brings you both here?' she asked.

Brid looked awkward. 'It was actually you I was looking for, or rather your husband. Only you said as how your husband was a sort of vicar here at the college.'

Now a sort of delivery driver, thought Thelma – but not for much longer!

'Yes,' she said, 'I did.'

'Only I'm getting on with our Terri's funeral and I'm wanting to talk to someone about all the God side of things and was wondering if he could maybe help me.'

'She loved horses, did our Terri. Always down the stables when she was a kid; our mum used to have a right go at her. Said she should be focusing on her schoolwork. So, our Terri used to leg it out the back window.' Brid smiled wistfully at the memory.

She was sitting side by side with Jade on the sofa, holding a mug of tea. In front of them was the remains of a plate of garden centre Dishforth Thins. Snaffles was curled up contentedly in Jade's lap, having taken an uncharacteristic shine to this bright-haired stranger (who kept telling him he was a Beautiful Mog). With Teddy off God knows where on his delivery rounds, Thelma had offered her own help with planning the service, an offer that had been eagerly accepted.

They had pretty much agreed on the hymns – 'All Things Bright and Beautiful' and 'The Lord's My Shepherd' – and now they were trying to decide on suitable Bible readings. Keeping the animal theme, Thelma had suggested the parable of the lost sheep, but Brid was adamant she wanted the story of Noah's ark because of the animals, and because Terri had used to read it to her when she was a little girl. Thelma wasn't sure exactly how appropriate it was for a funeral, but it was what Brid wanted and that had to be what counted.

'She always said she wanted to be a vet, and I reckon she were bright enough but once she took up with Tate that were pretty much it for school.' Brid's voice was sad, prompting Jade to put her non-cat-stroking arm round her shoulders.

Listening to Terri's sister, Thelma was forming a picture of a girl who loved well, but none too wisely. It put her in mind of a former pupil, Janine Humphries – always so talented with her maths – and how her place at a top university had been thrown over in favour of a small-time drug dealer in Pickering.

'It's ever so good of you to help me, Thelma,' said Brid, not for the first time.

'I'm only too pleased to help,' said Thelma, also not for the first time. The truth was slightly more complicated than that. Yes, she was pleased to help the girl, of course she was, but she was also aware of some slight pangs of guilt. Guilt because her mind was racing, persistently playing the same thought, over and over again: here was a golden opportunity to find out more about Terri Stanley. Could she be the murderer all Marley on Swale believed her to be? But was it the right thing to do, to find out more? Especially in light of their group resolution?

'I'd be happy to pay of course,' said Brid.

'She said how you don't need to,' reminded Jade, rubbing Snaffle's neck. Snaffles gave a rasping purr of agreement.

'Exactly,' said Thelma. 'There's absolutely *no* question of any sort of payment.' Brid nodded, suddenly overcome, doing that thing of flapping her hands in front of her eyes instead of using a tissue.

'Come on, lovey,' said Jade, providing a tissue.

'I'm so sorry,' said Brid. 'I just want to do right by our Terri.'

And it was these words from the forlorn figure that that made something click into place in Thelma's mind. She was a great believer in nudges from the Almighty, and if this meeting wasn't such a nudge then she didn't know what was. She could almost hear a voice saying: *Get cracking, Thelma!*

Her mind raced through various facts and events with the cool precision that comes as first nature to so many lady primary school teachers.

'You say you saw Terri after her husband died?' she asked.

'Just that one time,' said Brid. 'We met up in town.'

'She must have been very upset.'

Brid frowned slightly. 'I wouldn't say *very* upset,' she said. 'I said that to you at the time, didn't I, Jade?'

Jade nodded. 'Not *very* upset,' she echoed obediently.

'But you said she was wanting to move in with you? It sounded like she needed support.'

Brid frowned. 'I think it was the company she was after. It's a big old barn of a place – where she was living – for just one person,' she said.

Thelma nodded, thinking of the chilly expanses of Sunny View Lodge.

'I wish I had let her move in,' said Brid wistfully. 'Then none of this would have happened.'

'Babe,' said Jade. 'There's barely room for the three of you in that flat, let alone anyone else.'

Brid half closed her eyes. 'Maybe,' she said. 'Anyway, then she started saying how Tate was on at her to move back in with him. I told her right out not to be so bloody stupid. It wasn't like she were badly off or owt like that, she could easily have rented somewhere. The way she were talking, it was like she didn't have a choice. "You don't understand," she kept saying.

"No," I says, "I don't."' Brid sighed. In the light of the lamps, she looked very young and very sad. 'You know, I reckon our mum were right, God rest her soul. She always used to say our Terri *could* have gone on and been a vet if it weren't for that Tate.' She shook her head, her eyes dark. 'He's bad news, Mrs Cooper. I'm sure he got our Terri to do bad stuff for him.'

'Bad stuff?' said Thelma.

Brid nodded. 'Steal and things. Cover things up for him. There was this one time all these boxes appeared in Terri's room. Mum went mad. "Get that stuff out of my house," she said.' She sighed again, a deep, sad sigh. 'I tell you, it's my belief if she'd not gone back to him, well . . . she'd be here today.'

After she'd gone Thelma jotted down her thoughts in the green mark book.

Jamie said Terri was upset about Mal – but Brid says NOT.

She frowned. Of course grief was inconsistent and unpredictable but even so there was a contradiction here.

Brid says Tate made Terri do bad stuff – WHAT bad stuff?

With its habitual rattle, the front door opened. Teddy.

Teddy.

But no cry of 'WAMMP delivery driver'.

'Front room,' she said, concerned at the silence. And then there he was, standing in the doorway regarding her.

'More parcels came,' she said cautiously. 'I put them in your room.'

'Of course,' he said.

Thelma steeled herself. 'Oh, before I forget,' she said casually, 'I was passing the college so I dropped your application form in to save you a job.'

There was a silence.

'About that,' he said and suddenly he was looking searchingly at her. If only he'd take that ridiculous hat off.

151

'What is it?' she said, her mark book suddenly gripped painfully in her hands.

'I don't want to go back to the college', he said, 'I don't want to stop this job. *I want to keep on driving.*'

Like Thelma, Pat was also aware of a sense of relief at having turned her back on Sunny View Lodge and everything that went with it – those unsettling memories, the trip to Boroughbridge and of course Luke Atkinson. She gave herself a shake. No, she was not going to start dwelling on *him*. Maybe she had overreacted a tad, but it had been such a surprise. Of course the wonder was that she *hadn't* bumped into him before, with them both living in a small town like Thirsk. Especially, she reflected (with no small degree of smugness), when you considered he hadn't gone off to university, unlike Liam. In that Liz had been spot on – Pat's son did have so much more going for him than that weasel.

Except.

There was *some* upset going on with her youngest son – the silences and the long sojourns in his room signalled that as surely as it was foggy outside. She was certain it was something to do with that cancelled trip to meet Bern's parents, though hints, questions and forays into coat pockets neither affirmed nor contradicted this notion. But then surely he was bound to encounter many such bumps along love's highway? She remembered the multiple times she'd been called on to intervene with Justin's numerous emotional car crashes. Whatever was up with Liam, he was just going to have to sort it out for himself.

As though she'd summoned him with her thoughts, he appeared.

'Greetings, parentage.' She looked up as Liam walked in the back door, followed by a swirl of fog and, at some distance, Larson.

'Boots,' she said automatically.

'I know.' His voice was pained, as if he somehow hadn't planned to tread half North Yorkshire across the flags.

'And watch Larson – I don't want mud everywhere.'

'There isn't any mud on him.' Liam nodded at Larson who had retired straight to his basket. 'He barely left the path.'

'Really?' Pat looked at the dog. For him not to nose in every hedgerow going was completely untypical. He looked back at her. He seemed all right. Probably just tired and fed up with the never-ending murk. Like she was. Tired and fed up and fit only for a coach trip to the South of France.

'I'm off upstairs,' said Liam.

'Is everything okay?' She tried not to sound too interrogative.

'Tickety-boo, Ma, just tickety-bloody-boo!' His voice was light and airy, as though he was making fun of whatever situation this was. Another sure sign that things were wrong. And that whatever the matter was, he had no wish to talk about it.

'I saw Luke Atkinson today.' The words came out before she was entirely sure she was going to say them.

Liam froze, framed in the doorway to the stairs. 'Oh?' he said. 'How come?'

'Apparently, he's working for that guy I went to see in Marley. Well, his partner – his husband, I suppose.'

'I know,' said Liam. 'Well, I know he has a job round here.'

'How?' Her tone was sharp.

'We're in touch on Facebook.' He laughed at her expression. 'Ma, I'm in touch with lots of people on Facebook. It's hardly the darknet.' He peered closely at her. 'You didn't *say* anything?' he said suspiciously.

'No.' She spoke defiantly as though the mere possibility was a fantastic idea – not mentioning how both Thelma and Liz had firmly ushered her out of the church before she could in fact utter a sound.

Satisfied, Liam turned and went upstairs, leaving Pat with the sense of a conversation over but by no means finished. Why did so many conversations have to conclude with her various sons (and husband for that matter) walking out of the room? She sank into a kitchen chair, her mind processing their exchange. *In touch*? What did that mean? And on *Facebook*! She felt a surge of anger as she yet again pictured that insinuating post that had outed her son. Surely Liam wasn't friends with Luke? Or . . . more? The images of the past few days slammed into her mind – his sudden return, his reluctance to talk about Bern – those long periods in his bedroom? Surely *not*? Without giving herself time to think she rummaged in her handbag, trembling fingers finding the glossy edge of the folded flyer with the phone number scrawled on it.

Jamie picked up on the second ring.

'Hello,' she said suddenly floundering. 'It's Pat . . . Pat Taylor. We met today at the church—'

'Pat!' The warmth of his tone took her by pleasant surprise. 'Hello! I was going to ring you!'

Her thoughts swirled. Ring her? *Why*? She had a sudden nasty feeling a stack of leaflets might well be heading her way. And how to get onto the subject of Luke Atkinson? To give herself time to think she said. 'How did the rehearsal go?'

'A bloody nightmare.' Jamie's voice was dramatic. 'Don't even ask. Honest to God, Pat, I nearly twatted that Voice of the Past. Seriously, I should've gone with my first plan of having all the Voices played by the same person. But never mind me, how are you and your mates?'

'We're fine,' said Pat, puzzled.

'I mean after—' he dropped his voice to a rich baritone '—"Mal Stanley: the mini-series". I hope I didn't freak you all out.'

Pat smiled, thinking of the various things she and her friends had faced in the past. 'Not at all,' she said.

154

'Not your mate Liz? She were looking a bit fuddled by the whole thing.'

'That,' said Pat, 'is her default expression.' Jamie gave an appreciative snort of laughter and Pat felt a glow. 'Listen,' she said, emboldened, 'I wonder if we could maybe meet? There's a couple of things I'd like to ask you.'

'Sure.' The reply was warm and immediate and gave Pat a further glow.

'We could maybe meet for coffee,' she said tentatively. 'There's the garden centre – or a place in the market place – Mrs Hall's Larder.'

Jamie gave a bark of laughter. 'I think,' he said, 'we can do a bit better than that.'

CHAPTER EIGHTEEN

Information is shared, plus a near-death experience provokes an angry outburst in College Gardens.

'Where is she?' Down the phone Verna spoke in stressed tones of the utmost crisis. 'She's not here! And I've somewhere I need to be!'

'She could just be parking up,' suggested Thelma tentatively.

'Do we *know* that?' Verna seized on the statement. 'Does she even know what time she's on? Has she *read* the rota? Does she even realize it's Monday?'

Thelma did not even try to answer these questions, In her experience, when Verna was going off on one, trying to answer her point for point only extended the crisis.

'Can Mary maybe manage on her own for five minutes?' she asked tentatively.

'If it IS five minutes,' said Verna. 'What a nightmare!' There was a pause. 'I'll just have to cancel my appointment,' she said. She spoke as if said appointment was a much-needed hip replacement, when in fact Thelma suspected it was an all-day brunch at Oliver's Pantry with her sister.

'I can come over,' she said. 'But I'll be an hour.'

'No. You've got things to do.' The comment was expertly

pitched to make a lesser person than Thelma feel guilty about leaving the manageress of the charity shop to do what she was paid to do. 'Hang on, she's here!' Verna abruptly rang off.

'Problems?' said Detective Sergeant Donna Dolby.

'Just colleagues,' said Thelma.

'I thought you were retired?' DS Donna never let any questionable fact slip past, not ever.

'The charity shop,' said Thelma.

'Ah.' DS Donna rolled her eyes. '*Shops.*' The dark tone in her voice sounded as though she were referring to some inner-city drugs den. Her eyes roved across to the Edinburgh Woollen Mill where Jeanette and Moira were chatting brightly behind the counter. 'Why there aren't more homicides in shops I do not know!'

There was obviously some anecdote behind all this but Thelma didn't like to ask exactly what. After all, it wasn't as if she knew the detective sergeant particularly well. In her mind she always referred to her as 'DS Dolby' and this was only the third or fourth time they'd ever actually met for coffee. Their paths had first crossed back during those awful days following the demise of Thelma's friend Topsy; DS Dolby had been the one she went to regarding some other wrongdoing, and who had subsequently kept her up to speed about the prosecution of Topsy's murderer.

Then, about a year later, she'd happened to bump into her in the garden centre. Donna Dolby owned a new build in Richmond and was assiduously cultivating a garden for the first time in her life. A conversation about shrubs had evolved into a coffee, and this had been followed periodically by more coffees.

On what basis their relationship operated, Thelma was never entirely sure. They were certainly not close enough to be called friends, and there was always a certain formality that was never far from Donna's tones as though she was constantly self-checking what she was saying. Thelma admired her practical, no-nonsense approach to her job, and she liked to think Donna valued her instincts and judgements. This was, however, the first time Thelma had contacted DS Dolby asking her for information.

'Anyway.' Donna laced her stubby fingers together and eyed Thelma. 'What's this all about? And should we be in more formal surroundings?'

'I don't think so,' said Thelma. 'At least, I hope not.' In plain, unfussy terms she related the whole story, about Marguerite, the charity shop, about Terri Stanley and the car crash, and about Mal Stanley and his fall down the stairs. Donna was a good listener. She looked intently at Thelma, asked the occasional question, scribbled down the odd note, but otherwise was still and silent.

After Thelma had finished, she shook her head and closed her book. 'There's nothing there we could get involved with.' Was it Thelma's imagination or did she detect a slight note of relief?

'So, no alarm bells?' she said.

'I wouldn't go so far as to say *that.*' Donna smiled grimly. 'You'd be amazed how many grey areas there are between right and wrong.'

In fact, Thelma rather thought she wouldn't, but merely nodded.

'This Marguerite,' said Donna. 'Bit of a fruit loop, is she?'

Thelma considered. 'Marguerite is usually right about what she *sees*, but she always seems to come up with the wrong explanation.'

Donna frowned. 'I'm wondering what you mean by that,' she said.

'To give you an example,' said Thelma, 'there was this one time at school when a puddle kept appearing in the corner of

158

the practical area. Marguerite was adamant it was one of the children; she felt they'd developed a phobia about using the toilets and needed counselling.'

'And it wasn't?'

Thelma shook her head. 'It was a leaky radiator valve,' she said.

'So she's someone who gets the wrong end of the stick?'

Thelma nodded.

'Is she someone who likes a drink?' asked Donna.

'I don't know her that well, and of course I haven't seen her since she dropped to part-time,' said Thelma. 'But I wouldn't have said so. There are no signs.'

Again, Donna puffed out her cheeks. 'You'd be surprised,' she said.

(Once again Thelma caught herself thinking that in fact she wouldn't.)

'But she's obviously got the wrong end of the stick *somewhere* along the line. Charity shops don't just disappear.'

Thelma nodded, aware of a certain amount of relief. Everything had been feeling so murky and uncertain lately, especially with Pat's flirtation with spiritualism and the painful memories it was in danger of stirring up for Thelma. But if DS Donna Dolby with her notebook and bag of seed potatoes said that charity shops couldn't just disappear, Thelma felt pretty confident that they couldn't, and that Marguerite had indeed in some fundamental way got the wrong end of the stick.

'Anyway.' With a brisk gesture Donna whipped a sheet of A4 paper from a folder in her bag. 'I found out what you asked. And—' Thelma was again aware of the formal tone to her voice '—there is nothing here that isn't in the public domain. However, I would appreciate it if you weren't to broadcast the fact you've been getting info directly from the police.'

Thelma nodded. 'Of course,' she said. 'You have my word.' One of the benefits of being a lady of a certain age was that as a rule people didn't tend to doubt you when you made this statement.

'It all looks fairly straightforward.' Donna indicated the print that filled maybe three-quarters of the page. 'Malcolm Henry Stanley was a bit of a so-and-so and his name cropped up a few times for bits of this and bits of that, nothing substantial. Nothing you couldn't find for yourself in the papers.'

Thelma nodded, thinking of the file she'd begun compiling.

'He wasn't in the best of health – problems with his legs. One afternoon his wife – his second wife – goes out, leaving him with the district nurse who was dressing his legs. The nurse leaves maybe ten minutes later. Meanwhile, Mrs Stanley comes here to Thirsk where she has an appointment with a local company called—' she consulted her notebook '—Charlotte's Aunts. I believe it's the company she used to work for. While she was there, she gets a call from her husband saying he couldn't find his medication, or something of that ilk, so she rings a neighbour, asks her to go round, and heads off home at a rate of knots. Neighbour goes round only to see him through the front door lying at the foot of the stairs, with, it turns out, a broken neck. Mrs Stanley arrives home then, calls for an ambulance and the rest, as they say, is history.'

'I wonder,' said Thelma, 'would this have been around ten to three?'

DS Donna looked at her. 'What makes you say that I wonder?' She consulted her notes. 'Terri called her neighbour at 2.47, the neighbour dialled 999 at 2.52.'

She looked at Thelma. 'So, there's no way Mrs Stanley could have shoved hubby down the stairs, not unless she could magically transport herself over from Thirsk.'

'No,' said Thelma thoughtfully. 'I wonder why everyone in the village thought she *did*.'

Donna shrugged. 'People have a way of adding two and two

and making fifty-six. In my experience, at the end of the day the simplest explanation is usually the right one. Anyway, as to your second question.' She whipped out a second sheet, this one with considerably more print on it. 'Tate Bishop.' She paused and looked at Thelma. 'A scrote,' she announced.

'I see,' said Thelma.

'One of these bits of pond life who crop up doing this, that and the other. Nothing major, nothing you can put your finger on. But nevertheless, a scrote.'

'He sounds quite sinister,' said Thelma.

Donna rolled her eyes. 'I'm sure that's how he'd *like* to be described. And don't get me wrong, he has a lot of fingers in a lot of pies. And my advice to you and your friends would be to stay all the way away from every single one of them.'

Sitting at home in her favourite wing chair, a mug of hot, strong Yorkshire tea at hand, Thelma considered what she'd learned. Terri Stanley *hadn't* murdered her husband. Only lots of people seemed to think she *had*. And if she hadn't . . . had someone else? And why was she considering maybe clearing Terri's name? For the sake of Brid?

At that moment there was a rattle from the front door, but once again there was no cheery cry of 'Your WAMMP delivery man has landed!'

'Living room,' she called.

Teddy opened the door and came in still wearing his jacket and hat. He smiled a greeting but it wasn't a smile that reached his eyes. He sank down heavily opposite her.

'Is everything all right?' she asked. She was aware of a sudden lifting of the heart – *maybe he'd been sacked*.

'Is everything all right?' Teddy repeated her words. He nodded slowly. 'The answer would have to be "yes". But it could well have not been.'

'Whatever do you mean?'

He cast his eyes to the ceiling, and she knew he was gathering himself to tell a story – and that she might as well get comfortable because she was going to hear it whether she wanted to or not.

He'd been doing a delivery in Rainton – the village where Topsy had lived – in one of the bungalows down Carr Lane; he'd knocked, and there'd been no reply. There'd been no delivery instructions, which was a real bugbear, as just one redelivery could throw the whole of the following day's schedule out.

'So I went round the side,' he said. 'I gathered from the handrail, and so forth, that this was an elderly person's house. And sure enough, going round the back, there was an old lady, who *looked* asleep, bless her – head back in her chair, mouth wide open. I tried braying on the door a few times – no response. And I'm thinking, *This Does Not Look Good* when I think to try the side door. And this opens. And that's when it hit me.'

'Hell's smells?' said Thelma. Teddy nodded. 'Gas,' he said. 'Like a wall. *Gas.*'

He looked at his outstretched feet. 'I become aware then that the old lady has stirred, not only has stirred, but has gone through to the kitchen. It's one of those old-fashioned cookers with a gas grill. She's left it on and forgotten about it. And she is holding up the wand, ready to ignite the place.' He shut his eyes, leaving Thelma to conjure up the image of him hurling himself across the kitchen and wresting the wand from the startled woman's hand.

'Another five seconds . . .' He sombrely let the words trail into ominous silence. He shook his head and seemed to recover somewhat. 'Still, I stopped her. That's the main thing. We even ended up laughing about it, once I'd made her realize I *wasn't*

162

some intruder.' He looked at his wife who was regarding him soberly. 'All's well,' he said cheerfully.

'No,' said Thelma. 'All is *not* well.' He looked at her, startled. 'It's *not* all right,' she said. 'I *hate* this. I hate you being out all hours, I hate you being tired and I hate the thought of you being blown up in a gas explosion in Rainton. And ... ' She took a deep breath. 'And I hate the thought of you not going back to the college.'

There, she'd said it. Suddenly aware she was trembling, she met his gaze.

His eyes, sad and concerned and loving, met hers. 'But Thelma,' he said gently, 'when I'm out on the round, I feel *free*. Free in a way I never used to feel free in college. I feel,' he said earnestly, 'real peace.'

'Well bully for you,' she snapped. 'I wish *I* did!' And to both their horror she burst into hot, angry tears and left the room.

CHAPTER NINETEEN

At the dark heart of Yorkshire there is dissatisfaction and a surprise revelation.

By Wednesday afternoon, after a couple of relatively clear days, the fog had come creeping back, welling up across the drab countryside like an recurring rash. On the A1, despite the amber speed restrictions, there had been a collision just south of Leeming Bar and crawling northwards Liz began to worry they'd be late for the six p.m. start of 'Beyond Darkness with Gareth Ap-Glyndwr'. Any hopes of conversation with Jacob – one of their lengthy 'sort out the world' chats that they hadn't had in such a long time – had not been realized. On being collected from school, he'd promptly plugged himself into one of the 'Burning Planet' podcasts he was so obsessed with and aside from some gloomy observations on car exhaust had remained silent.

Without that distraction and to keep her mind off the ever-growing number of mental rabbit holes concerning Rochelle Bamford, Liz had tried to focus on Jacob's forthcoming treat. Would he like it? In her mind she pictured the excited words on the Flaxby Hall Experience website: *Tate Bishop presents Beyond Darkness – with Gareth Ap-Glyndwr, one of the world's leading parapsychologists! Thrilling experience for all – plus pie'n'pea supper!* She kept on glancing at the solemn figure on the back seat gazing out at the smoky darkness and fuzzing lights of traffic. Was what she'd booked entirely appropriate? Would travelling through *'the dark secrets of Yorkshire's most haunted building'* give him a welcome jolt of cheerful distraction? Or would the *'chilling glimpse of the dark world beyond this one'* be too much for her grandson?

When she'd booked the tickets, she'd been reassured by the lad on the phone that loads of families were coming, plus a party of Scouts from Yarm. Surely anything that included a pie'n'pea supper couldn't be that bad? And no two ways about it, in her opinion it'd do Jacob the world of good to be chilled by something that *wasn't* connected with carbon emissions. Or the problems of his parents.

Negotiating the way through a grey, dripping wood, however, down the potholed, weedy drive that was the approach to the Flaxby Hall Hotel, she felt those faint misgivings recur. It really was a gloomy place. In the thickening darkness the ranks of tree trunks brought to mind stories she used to read to her class about magic forests where wolves roamed to trap the unwary traveller.

Get a grip, Liz!

She glanced at the dashboard. Ten to six. Just in nice time.

Flaxby Hall Hotel wasn't a hall, it was a wide, flat-roofed building in the style of architecture that screamed out 1960s and indeed was rather reminiscent of something out of *Thunderbirds*. It was a place that Liz knew *of* – one of those places that had hosted weddings and conferences but for whatever reason had been nobody's first choice of venue. She herself had been there some years back on a primary English conference and her abiding memory had been of weak coffee and unpleasantly pungent toilet disinfectant. Like many such places, it had folded sometime in the past ten years, though from time to time she had heard of various proposals for the place – luxury apartments, a shopping outlet, even an eco-resort, whatever such a thing was. However, in death, as in life, it had been nobody's first choice and Flaxby Hall had been left to moulder peacefully in the woods, growing steadily more dilapidated and engendering the occasional scandalized letter in the *Thirsk Advertiser*. Until now.

Getting out of the car and seeing the place close up in the gloom, Liz felt even more uneasy – the building really was in a sorry old state. She wasn't sure what she'd expected; somewhere (as the website promised) *'eerily spooky'*, but this wasn't eerily spooky, it was dirty and grim and depressing. The expanse of wide picture windows were plated with dull steel sheets, and the once white walls were stamped with spreading patches of brown and green mould, and bright with red and blue graffiti. On the wide patio where brides had once tossed bouquets and conference-goers flirted on summer evenings were cracked slabs, tangles of brambles and a burnt-out sofa. 'Behold the Tory economic recovery,' shouted out one bit of rounded lettering. It was hard to disagree.

Other cars were pulled up and people could be seen looking uncertainly at the sad façade of the building. There were mostly couples, well wrapped up, presumably in anticipation of the promised *'pervasive chills of fear'*, and a bright and loud party of four giggling girls who were holding a bottle of prosecco and sporting pink sashes that read: 'Middlesborough Girls on the Lash!'

'Does anyone still need to pay for their parking?'

Liz recognized the voice as the one on the phone she'd spoken to when booking the tickets. It belonged to a rather spotty young man – the sort of person her father would have referred to as a 'Callow Youth'. On his lapel a badge proclaimed him to be Bailey Bairstow – Events Coordinator.

'Pay for parking?' The largest of the Girls on the Lash looked indignant. 'You are having a giraffe! We've already shelled out forty quid each on tickets!'

'Parking's on top,' said Bailey Bairstow with a certain air of bracing himself. Obviously, this wasn't the first time he'd had this exchange. 'You have to pay – it's for the parking insurance.' He nervously shook a Tupperware box to emphasize his point.

'What insurance?' The Girl on the Lash looked puzzled. 'I work for Aviva and I've never heard of no parking insurance.'

Bailey Bairstow's eyes slid fearfully to the hotel. 'Sorry, but that's what I've been told to say.' Something about his obvious nervousness sounded a chord of pity amongst the ghost hunters and there began a resigned fumbling about in bags and pockets for cash. Only Liz had followed his nervous glance towards the building. Told by whom? What was he so afraid of?

An answer of sorts presented itself in the form of another splurge of stark red graffiti, which suddenly caught Liz's eye. It read: *TATE BISHOP IS AN EVIL BASTARD.*

The dank lobby of the hotel was as sad and shabby as the outside. Gone were the plush sofas and low coffee tables leaving scuffed, muddy tiles in a gloomy, damp void. Everywhere was a pervasive smell of damp. At one side were a number of fold-up tables that looked like they'd come from a school dining hall and behind one stood a blank-faced woman well padded up in jumpers and a fleece.

'Sandwiches,' announced the woman in disinterested tones. 'Sandwiches and drinks.'

'What's happened to the pie'n'peas?' asked one of the Girls on the Lash.

'Off,' said the woman. 'Caterer's blobbed.'

The bad feeling amongst the ghost hunters grew as it transpired that not only were there no pie'n'peas but they were expected to pay for the substitute sandwiches.

'I've got ham; I've got cheese,' said the woman in 'take-it-or-leave-it' tones. 'Five pounds per sandwich.' Most of the ghost hunters took one look at the anaemic display, obviously sourced from the nearest garage, and decided to leave it.

'Bloody hell,' said one of the Girls on the Lash. 'It'd have been cheaper to have a spa day.'

Liz looked round the lobby, unhappy for quite different reasons.

Tate Bishop.

In her eagerness to arrange this diversion for Jacob she'd not thought this through at all – completely failing to consider the implications of bringing Jacob into the proximity of the man she'd heard nothing but bad about. Was he actually in the building, this nefarious Mover and Shaker? The nervousness of Bailey Bairstow argued he was . . . *A nasty git* – that was how Jamie Adams had described him. But in what form was his nastiness made manifest?

She scanned the lobby as if he might suddenly materialize, arms akimbo, staring at them all with undisguised malice. Not that she had any idea what this man looked like. Black hair, she imagined. Black, thick hair and a piercing gaze – like that man off *Poldark*. She realized with a start that Jacob was no longer standing mutely by her side, and with a stab of panic she cast around. But there he was, looking at the table opposite the sandwich woman – the one with the books and sweatshirts. The latter looked both cheap and tacky – a rather lurid green with an orange logo saying: *I survived Flaxby Hall!*

Joining him, Liz looked at the price and winced. They may have looked cheap but that certainly wasn't reflected in the price. Jacob was looking at one of the stacks of books – *Voices From Beyond*, by Gareth Ap-Glyndwr, who smouldered out from the cover in black and white elegance. Again, the price was anything but reasonable. Nevertheless, she felt for her purse. At least Jacob was taking an interest in something. 'Would you like one?' she said to him. He rolled his eyes at her. 'Grandma, you can get these off Amazon Marketplace for one pound eighty-seven plus postage.'

She tried again. 'Are you hungry?' she said. 'I could maybe get you a sandwich?' She tried as hard as possible to make the rather sad offerings sound attractive. Again, the roll of the eyes. 'I asked that lady what the vegan option was,' he said in scandalized tones, 'and she said "*cheese*"!'

'Ladies and gentlemen!' It was Bailey Bairstow, standing by the inner door. 'If you'd like to follow me, we'll now go into the dark heart of Flaxby Hall.'

'Be afraid,' said one of the Girls on the Lash, 'be very afraid!'

'I don't know why they say it's so haunted,' said Jacob in an undertone that was far from an undertone. 'It was only built in 1967.'

The dark heart of Flaxby Hall Hotel turned out to be the old ballroom, a large damp void with rows of folded-up chairs facing a raised stage. Above the centre of the floor hung a tarnished mirror ball, missing a large number of its mirrors.

Seated on a decidedly rickety chair some three rows back, Liz looked at Bailey Bairstow standing on the stage like an unconfident head teacher about to deliver an assembly to a rowdy school. He really did look ill at ease, glancing repeatedly off the stage. Was Tate lurking in the shadows behind him, maybe? The atmosphere felt very far from '*pleasantly spooky*'; it felt cold and dirty and sad. What had she been thinking of bringing Jacob here? She wanted to put a protective arm around him but knew exactly the reaction such a gesture would provoke.

Behind them the Girls on the Lash were not impressed either.

'I wish they'd get a move on,' said the largest one. 'I'm freezing my tits off here!'

Liz, although privately agreeing, was nevertheless glad Jacob was once again plugged into 'Burning Planet'.

Bailey Bairstow turned on a microphone, which obligingly screeched and whistled. 'Ladies and gentlemen,' he said, 'I'm so sorry for the delay. There's been a very slight technical hitch and we're just going to be two more seconds—'

There was a general groan. Liz sighed; in her book, 'two seconds' could last anything from twenty minutes to a day and a half.

But just then the lights plunged abruptly, surprising everyone including Bailey Bairstow who could be heard giving a distinct squeak of surprise.

From the darkness came a recorded voice, one that Liz recognized as belonging to that man who did the weather on *Look North*.

'For centuries, the name of Flaxby Hall has sent a shiver down the spines of locals,' it intoned. Next to her Liz could feel Jacob stiffen, and she readied herself to shush him if he called out to dispute this version of history.

'There has been human activity on this site since the dawn of time when the Pagans made human sacrifices to their Roman gods,' continued the voice.

'The Pagans didn't make sacrifices to Roman gods,' said Jacob indignantly and one of the Girls on the Lash gave an explosive giggle.

'Shhh!' said someone.

'The dark legacy of those times have persisted to this very day.'

Was it Liz's imagination or did the *Look North* weatherman sound slightly bored?

'And now Tate Bishop has dared bring word-famous parapsychologist Gareth Ap-Glyndwr to probe the dark heart of Flaxby Hall. *Dare you experience what he finds?*'

There was a discordant crescendo of music and on the darkened stage area a figure emerged from the gloom, strikingly lit from behind. In the dark Liz felt Jacob's fingers seek out and grip her own.

'Here he is,' said someone as the lights faded up to an eerie twilight.

It became clear as the man appeared that he bore scant resemblance to the man on the cover of the book. Either that or the world-famous parapsychologist had let himself go in a major way. Before them was a stocky, stooped figure, sporting long, lank hair. His face was rather puffy and in need of a shave, and even in the dim light it was apparent his eyes were red-rimmed.

'Bloody hell,' one of the Girls on the Lash could be heard to say. 'Is he the ghost or what?'

'Okay . . .' The man's voice was rather uncertain, with a guttural heavy-smoker quality. 'Okay. Are we all excited to be here at Flaxby Hall?'

There was an uncertain pause. 'Yes,' said someone half-heartedly.

'So.' The man looked over to the left. 'We've a great show for you tonight.' He also kept peering away off the edge of the stage – was he too looking at Tate Bishop? 'But before we get started, has anyone ever seen a ghost?' There was another pause. 'Go on—' Liz was sure she could detect a slight slur '—has anyone ever seen a ghost?'

There was a distinct murmur in the audience, and no wonder, Liz thought. She'd never been to any sort of ghost-hunting event but was pretty certain it shouldn't be run like this, which came across as some sort of fifth-rate pantomime. Even her Year Two assemblies had been way better than this.

Jacob nudged her. 'Grandma,' he said. 'That isn't Gareth Ap-Glyndwr.'

'Are you sure?'

In the darkness she could sense the roll of the eyes. 'He has his own YouTube channel, Grandma!'

Liz looked at the shambolic figure onstage. Of course he wasn't Gareth Ap-Glyndwr – he was just another helpless lacky of Tate Bishop.

'So . . .' The figure onstage sounded desperate. 'So, before we get started, has anyone in the audience got any questions?'

For the third time there was an uncomfortable pause.

'I've got one.' The voice from the side of the stage was ringing and melodic and definitely pissed off. The figure that strode on stage was wearing a black rollneck sweater under a leather trench coat and what looked like seven-league boots.

'*That's* Gareth Ap-Glyndwr,' said Jacob firmly.

'Gareth,' said the man on stage, suddenly looking trapped and not a little sly. 'Gareth, mate, brilliant you could join us here at Flaxby Hall.'

'My question for you, Tate Bishop,' said Gareth Ap-Glyndwr, pointing a finger at his chest, 'is where's the fifteen hundred pounds you assured me would be in my bank account first thing this morning?' He looked round at the crowd. 'Sorry, ladies and gentlemen,' he said. 'If I were you, I'd be asking for your money back.'

'First sensible thing I've heard all evening,' said the largest of the Girls on the Lash as Gareth Ap-Glyndwr strode off stage.

There was a general mutter amongst the crowd who looked on as the shambolic man made a rapid retreat from the ballroom after the parapsychologist.

'Sorry, folks,' said Bailey Bairstow. 'I just . . . Sorry.' Obviously lost for words, the Flaxby Hall Events Coordinator fairly legged it after the other two men.

It began to dawn on the assembled ghost hunters that that was it for Beyond Darkness. With a grumbling they began standing and gathering their things.

Only Liz sat still, her mind racing furiously.

Tate Bishop? *That* shambolic figure? *Tate Bishop?*

CHAPTER TWENTY

Fashion choices are enthusiastically received and there is a graphic demonstration of the hazards of a crowded wine bar.

At about the same time Liz was leaving Flaxby Hall, Pat was waiting to meet Jamie Adams.

There was, she reflected, one thing that didn't change as she grew older: she never liked waiting for someone in a pub or a wine bar. She could remember herself in that cheesecloth top, waiting in the Accrington Arden for Andrew Collier, anxious – not just because of being under-age, but plagued with thoughts of how it looked . . . A girl on her *own*! Had she been stood up? How sad was that! And tonight, she realized she was having similar thoughts, though she decided ruefully that now she was of an age where few people would give her any more than the briefest of glances, and despite her sparkly, cherry red top, she was largely invisible to the customers of Pals of Pinot.

Tonight the wine bar was about half full – a marked contrast to how it had been on the few occasions she'd been in before. Tonight, there was lively noise and laughter, courtesy of a group of people Pat recognized from the Skipton Building Society. They were celebrating one of the group's birthday; in their midst a rather pallid-looking woman was smiling uncertainly next to two huge slowly revolving shiny lilac balloons in the shape of a three and a zero. Present-giving was in progress; a strident woman, her mouth a challenging slash of scarlet with a lot of overconfident teeth, was handing her various gifts. She was wearing a lurid pink T-shirt bearing the legend: *Celebrate your birthday the way you came into the world: naked and screaming!*

'Go on, Court,' she ordered. 'Hold it up!'

Looking even more uncertain, the birthday girl held up a bright magenta thong with black furry edging.

There was a cheer.

Pat sighed. *Thirty*. Half her age. When she was thirty Justin was a toddler, Andrew was on the way and they were managing – God knows how – in that caravan outside the semi-derelict shell that was now their house. Happy, if chaotic times. And now she was very nearly sixty.

The group fizzed up with great gusts of laughter and watching them Pat felt very alone. Very alone, very sober and decidedly old. She looked critically down at her top, the subject of much deliberation. Did this meeting warrant the glittery red? And also, her Moroccan earrings, the ones Rod called her 'wind chimes'?

Of course, there was always the possibility that Jamie had forgotten their meeting – but given his enthusiasm on the phone, surely not? She remembered his enthusiastic suggestion, savouring his warm tones in the same way her mind savoured the cheerful atmosphere of the wine bar, the cocktail menus and the sepia pictures of Paris that adorned the stripped brick walls of what had once been Thirsk post office.

'Pat, *oh my God*, you look fabulous! I love that top! How *fab* is that!' Lost in her gloomy thoughts, she hadn't seen Jamie come in (or more accurately, judging by the turned heads, made his entrance). He looked pretty amazing himself in a sky blue sweater, which perfectly complemented his blond boy-band good looks. Pat could see T-Shirt Lady nudging her friends and felt an escalating thrill that this glamorous man who was adding such wattage to the energy in the bar was coming to sit with *her*. Plus, there was the knowledge that the cherry red top was obviously spot on. Smiling, she stood, wondering how best to greet him – a question he solved by giving her a firm, Paco-Rabanne-scented hug. 'How *are* you?' he said. The pale eyes fixed on her reassuringly, and she knew with glowing certainty she was the most important person in the room.

She sternly checked herself. She was here for a purpose, to find out about the doings of Luke Atkinson. 'Oh, you know,' she said, 'getting there.'

He picked up her glass and sniffed. 'Mineral water?' He shook his head. 'We need some prosecco, NOW.'

Two glasses of prosecco later, Pat was well and truly warmed up and any doubts she might have had about the meeting were evaporating along with the bubbles of her drink. Jamie was good company – no, he was *great* company. His stories of the rehearsals for *Village Voices* were infinitely more entertaining than the real thing could possibly be. His current woes surrounded the lad playing the Grey Waif of Pickhill – the one Pat had noticed doing Peter Kay impressions.

'I swear to God, he's bigger than I am!' Though the lad had learned his lines and been on time for every rehearsal, starving village waif he was *not*. 'I tell you, Pat, he's broken his bloody crutch twice already!'

Pat was vaguely aware she needed to broach the subject of Luke, but surely there was no hurry? From *Village Voices* they had moved on to the subject of Liam and his current problems. The cough had worsened and he was spending a few more days at home on what was termed 'Remote Study'.

'So you think he's had some sort of falling-out with this Bern person?' Jamie frowned in concentration; he really was an excellent listener. 'With all due respect, Pat, how can you be sure, if he hasn't actually said?' Pat sighed, marshalling her troubled thoughts and as she did so he did that lovely thing of topping up her glass without being asked.

'He was sleepwalking,' she said.

'My God.' Jamie frowned, puzzled. 'Is that even a thing these days?'

'Oh yes,' she said. 'It certainly is.' For all Liam having left home to study engineering, his sudden appearance at the end of their bed, glassy-eyed and coughing slightly, had been exactly as it had been during his childhood and stressful adolescence. 'It happened a lot when he was younger,' she said. 'The last time was during his first relationship.'

'And would this be with Luke Atkinson?' said Jamie. Pat nodded, eyes suddenly blurring. This was why she had come, so why didn't she trust herself to speak? Was it the prosecco making the emotion surge up like this?

'Excuse me,' she said. 'I just need to pay a visit.'

In the ladies' she regarded herself in the mirror. 'Get a grip, Patricia,' she said. Was she *really* going to let that weasel Luke Atkinson spoil a night that was turning out so unexpectedly lovely? She took a deep breath and looked more closely at herself in the mirror. The taps of the sink seemed to be rather a long, misty distance away. How many proseccos had she had?

Leaving the ladies', Pat saw more people had joined the birthday party and the bar was now some two-thirds full. Suddenly she felt vulnerable, panicky even, as she carefully navigated her way round and between people not even slightly aware they might be in the way. She was just, with many apologies, dodging a group of girls bright and sparkly as Disney fairies, when a sudden, violent shove made her stumble. At the same moment a cold splash down her back and shoulder made her gasp loudly. 'You want to watch where you're going, love.' The voice was strident and sour, belonging to Mrs T-Shirt. She'd cannoned into Pat and in doing so emptied a glass of something with ice all down her left side.

'I'm so sorry!' said Pat with a yelp. *Why* did people invariably apologize when accused of doing something, regardless of whether they'd actually been doing it? She was pretty certain she hadn't been in the wrong, yet here she was saying sorry and even offering to buy another drink.

T-Shirt Lady didn't even acknowledge her, she just turned back to the bar shouting: 'Abi darling, we need another marmalade gin. This one's been spilt by *someone*.'

There was a horrid, scornful emphasis on the last word.

Pat sat back down, feeling rather shaky and ashamed. Jamie stared at her in concern.

'What was she saying?' he demanded.

'I offered to buy her another drink,' she said.

'Pat, why? *She* went into you – I saw it.'

'It's fine,' said Pat. '*Please*, don't worry.'

He shook his head. 'She's pissed – you only have to look at her to see that.'

'She's not the only one,' said Pat ruefully.

'Here,' said Jamie, handing her another glass of prosecco. 'Get this down you.' He gave her a long searching look. 'So,' he said, 'Luke Atkinson.'

'Are you having problems with him?' asked Pat.

Jamie shrugged. 'It's Shaun he works with. But from what I gather he turns up, does the job, says all the right things in all the right places. He certainly sorted out the mess left by the last office manager. Look,' he said. 'None of my business and all that. Tell me to back off. I just couldn't notice a bit of an atmosphere between you two.'

'Has Luke told you about Liam?' asked Pat.

'He's told me something.' Those blue eyes met hers. 'Not the truth, I'm guessing, knowing Lukey boy.'

Pat felt cold, like her shoulder. 'It depends on what he said.'

'That he and Liam were a thing, and then it stopped being a thing and Liam got upset.'

Once again, Pat's feelings were like the prosecco bubbles, frothing and forcing their way into her mouth, choking her speech and blurring her thoughts.

'That's not exactly what happened,' she said.

'So, tell me what *did* happen.' The pale eyes were firmly on her, and she knew she couldn't fob him off with anything less than the truth. 'I don't want to get him into trouble at work,' she said, realizing that actually she wanted to do exactly that.

'Like I say, he works for Shaun, not me. And I don't think Shaun'll care one way or the other, as long as the invoices go out on time.'

Telling Jamie didn't feel at all like the sort of triumphal denouement she'd imagined so many times over the years. Maybe it was the emotion, maybe the prosecco, maybe her sticky shoulder, but it all felt somewhat incoherent and tawdry, a bit like tales of woe related to her by children in years gone by.

'Anyway,' she concluded, 'it's all a long time ago.'

'DON'T whatever you do, say "water under the bridge",' said Jamie. 'I bloody hate that phrase. Sometimes that bridge just isn't ready for that water to go under it. But the fact is, well, your Liam's doing all right now, isn't he? He's got his course – his life in Durham. A mum who looks a dead ringer for Julia Roberts, which incidentally is every gay man's dream.'

'Now I know you're pissed,' she said. He smiled and they clinked glasses. 'I'm afraid,' she said suddenly with the clear-eyed honesty that alcohol affords. 'I'm afraid Liam might get back with him. He might already *be* back with him as far as I know.'

'Listen.' Jamie took her hand. 'Listen,' he said again. 'As far as I'm aware Luke is not seeing any ex. As far as I know.' There was a quality in his voice she didn't quite understand, but before she could register it, he was clinking her glass again. 'I'll try and find out,' he said.

Another bottle of prosecco magically appeared then, and Pat suddenly found herself launching into the subject of coach trips to the South of France. 'Oh my God,' he said, 'will you just stop? You are killing me!'

'It's just the fact it's for *seniors*,' she said.

'Seriously, stop,' he said again. 'Pat Taylor, if you are a senior, I will show my arse in the bloody market place. Look, this is what you're going to say.' He put a hand over hers and again she caught an intoxicating whiff of his Paco Rabanne. 'You're going to say: "Roddy, sweetheart, it's fucking fantastic you've gone and organized us jolly-bobs, but please can you do it somewhere that *doesn't* involve driving round the countryside in a travelling morgue complete with its own defib?"'

Pat laughed so much she began to wish she'd put one of her 'just in case' pads in, the ones she normally wore to Mums, Bums and Tums with her friend Olga.

'No,' he said. 'I've a better idea. Listen to this. You and Rod, you're going to come over to dinner and me and his lordship are going to tell you all about *Key West*. We went there when we got together and Pat, it is literally *the* best place in the world.'

As they finished the next bottle – *surely* not their third? – she looked at photos on Jamie's phone, feeling herself falling in love with Key West. It was all so simple – they'd forget the coach tour and go there with Jamie and Shaun and sit there night after night in Mallory Square watching the sunset while sipping cocktails.

Her and her new bezzie mate.

What was Jamie saying now? Something about Tate . . . Not the art gallery, presumably . . . Who was Tate again? With some effort she forced her mind back from the Florida Keys to a wine bar in Thirsk.

'Tate who used to be with Terri Doo-dah?' she said, feeling her words slurring slightly. She needed some water.

'Someone crossed him,' Jamie said patiently. 'Someone crossed Tate Bishop – and I heard he's ended up in James Cook Hospital, in intensive care.'

'Oh my God,' she said. 'This fellow did something to Tate?'

'And Tate did something back to him.' Jamie looked grim and then smiled – a sudden, bright smile. 'I think it's high time we switched to shots.'

'No!' said Pat 'No . . .' She felt a sudden weary desire to curl up there and then on the floor of Pals of Pinot.

A violent crash shocked her into semi-sobriety and she turned – as did everyone else in Pals of Pinot. 'Oh my God, Bev,' someone was saying, sounding unsure whether to laugh.

Just in front of their table T-Shirt Lady was sitting dazedly, hat askew, legs unbecomingly open, amidst the debris of a tray of drinks. As she tried to move it became glaringly apparent she was not just a little pissed. 'Bev,' said someone else. 'Are you okay, Babes?'

In spite of everything, Pat felt a swell of pity. The woman had lost all semblance of dignity and her face was crumpling as if she was going to cry. Part of Pat wanted to go and help, but another, more sensible part, knew she'd probably end up on the floor next to her. Besides, friends and bar staff were swooping down with dustpans, floor wipes and glasses of water.

All at once she was aware Jamie was staring at her.

'Can I ask you something?' he said, and Pat realized with

faint surprise he was a lot more sober than she was – either that or he could hold his drink really really well.

'Go on,' she said. She realized a certain amount of effort and concentration was needed to enunciate every word clearly.

'Okay,' he said. 'So exactly *why* were you and your pals going round seeing Sunny View Lodge?' He raised up a warning hand. 'And *don't* tell me that Thelma wants to relocate there. She is one classy lady and if she wants to relocate to Marley on Swale then I'm Dame Judi complete with Oscar.'

'Okay.' Pat took another mouthful of water. Her ears were ringing, and the music in the bar was throbbing in her ears. 'Okay. Here's the thing.'

'Deep breath and spill, girlfriend,' he said.

Just like it had been with the story about Luke, this tale was hard to tell – again because of the prosecco. Even with a straightforward story it would have been difficult, and this story was far from being straightforward (and not made any easier by the group of beautiful girls who were now singing along to Katy Perry). Jamie seemed to be having an equally hard time following this tale; just as she got herself into some sort of flow, he'd interrupt, asking her to repeat what she'd just said. Either that or a question invariably framed with, 'I know I'm being really thick here but . . .'

'So,' said Jamie at the end, 'can I just ask – why is this Marguerite so sure it's a vision?'

'She's on this Facebook group,' said Pat. 'Yorkshire Paranormal something or other.'

She poured herself another glass of water. 'I know,' she said. 'Crazy.' And indeed, under Jamie's clear questions that's how the whole thing felt.

'Not *crazy*,' he said thoughtfully. 'Random definitely, but somehow not crazy.' He was frowning and took one of her hands in his. 'Pat, my love,' he said. 'Has it occurred to any of you that this Marguerite has got it all, well . . . arse over tit?'

Pat nodded vigorously. (A huge mistake.) 'Absolutely,' she started, feeling her tongue suddenly grown unmanageable. 'Absolutely,' she said again. 'That's what Liz says.'

'And is Liz Mrs Specs or Mrs Fleece?'

Pat felt a bubble of laughter rising up and out of her. 'Mrs Fleecey,' she said.

'It sounds,' said Jamie, 'like she knows what she's talking about. And anyway, I can't see how any of this connects with Terri, God bless her, nor this whole shop thing. Knowing Terri, she'd just have taken a wrong turn in the fog.'

'We've all decided to let it drop,' she said in exaggeratedly clear tones. She was feeling more than a little woozy and knew only too well how she'd feel tomorrow. (Would she even make coffee at the garden centre?) 'Let the dead bury their own dead. I'm sorry, that's not meant to sound as brutal as it sounds.'

There was a pause and Jamie nodded. 'Very wise I'd say,' he said. He appeared to be wondering whether to speak, before frowning and talking rapidly. 'The thing about Terri,' he said. 'I reckon she *was* a scared lady, bless her, but I don't think it was anything to do with any weird shops. She was scared in her *house* – in Sunny View Lodge.'

That house. In a dark corner of Pat's mind, the figure on the bed stirred.

'And you think it was because of Tate?' she asked tentatively.

Again he looked at her, that blue, troubled stare. 'I think,' he said, 'she was undergoing some sort of mental stress. That's the explanation I think.'

'The explanation for what?'

He took a deep breath. 'A week before she died, a package was delivered to the house. She must have ordered it and forgotten to have it redirected. And Meesh was there clearing out, and being a right nosy beggar she opens it. And *inside* . . .'

'Yes?'

'Tarot cards.' He looked at her, his eyes worried.

'*Tarot cards*?' she repeated.

Jamie nodded. 'There's something else,' he said. 'Something I haven't said . . . Something Terri told me and Meesh before she left Sunny View Lodge. She asked Mare over—'

'The vicar?'

Jamie nodded. 'She asked her to come to the house, and . . .'

'And what?'

'She wanted her to bless the house. *She wanted her to rid the house of evil spirits.*'

Pat felt prosecco replaced in her stomach by something infinitely colder and a reedy voice sounded clear in her head.

Why didn't you come back to me?

CHAPTER TWENTY-ONE

Beer Fears are followed by real fear, and a
one-time Blackbird gives food for thought
about the moral obligations of parasites.

Charlotte's Aunts was tucked discreetly away up Kirkgate, just beyond the James Herriot Museum. It's single pristine but unadorned bay window spoke of somewhere that didn't feel any great need to self-advertise. Inside, oatmeal carpets and Classic FM gave much the same impression, putting Thelma in mind of some high-end boutiques, or that Botox place favoured by the rural Dean's wife. Behind the reception desk, an elegant lady with sculpted lilac hair was talking on the phone in fruity higher-end Yorkshire tones. 'Is there a lock on the bathroom door?' she was saying. 'Most bathrooms have *some* sort of lock.' With an abstracted smile at Thelma, she gestured a beringed hand of plum-coloured nails over towards a taupe-coloured sofa. 'Of course, Daphne,' she continued. 'It might well have been a misunderstanding. Maybe Mr Gerrard genuinely *didn't* know you were in the shower.' She dropped her voice and turned her back discreetly.

As she waited, Thelma offered up a quick prayer asking for guidance. After all, was it the right thing for her to be doing, finding out more about Terri Stanley like this? Would it not be the best thing to let Brid bury her sister and all the rumours of scheming and murder with her, as she and her friends had agreed?

Her phone buzzed. She felt a guilty flush. Liz or Pat? She was due to meet them at the garden centre at eleven for their customary coffee. But it was Teddy. No message, just a view of Ripon from Sharow Hill, presumably taken as he was out and about on his rounds. She sighed. Since her outburst the other night, the two had said very little to each other. Not because of any animosity, but because as usual they'd spent very little time together. The past couple of days he had been out of the house before eight, and not back until gone six. By the time he was home, he was pretty much done in and by mutual unspoken agreement conversations had been superficial – the fog, that skip on Blossomgate, the latest saga in the feud between Verna and Polly.

Thelma's outburst loomed large between them, like one of Big Cyn's parcel drops. She looked again at the image of muted trees and distant cathedral. How on earth to respond in any meaningful way? Some comment . . . But her tired brain refused to supply any. She sent a smiley emoji and stuffed her phone back in her handbag.

'I'm so sorry!' The receptionist turned, call finished, bringing a rather startling set of improbably white teeth to bare on Thelma. 'Is it Mrs Cooper?'

Thelma nodded.

'Mrs Cooper, I wonder, could I trouble you to jot down one or two little details for me about your relative?' she said. 'We find it helps to have a wee bit of background.'

Smiling politely, Thelma took the rose-coloured document, shrinking somewhat at the request. A wee bit of background? It looked more like a full-blown medical history to her. It was one thing to tell a few airy half-truths in order to get into a conversation about Terri Stanley; it was quite another to enter into detailed fictions about what the rose-coloured form delicately referred to as 'continence needs'.

What she would have done, she wasn't quite sure, but at that moment the ivory door opened wider, and a couple marched purposefully across the waiting room looking rather disgruntled. Both had the engrained tan of expatriates and even considering the general chill of the day they were heavily swathed in expensive-looking coats and scarves. Behind them walked another woman with short hair and a smart trouser suit and with, Thelma thought, a rather fixed smile.

'We fly back out on the seventeenth,' said Tanned Woman in an assertive voice, 'but we are on hand till then.'

'And just to be clear, you're happy for your mum to be hospitalized in the event of another attack?' said the short-haired woman.

'Like I said,' said the man, 'do what you need to do. Payment isn't a problem.'

They both wasted no time in exiting the premises, as if hurrying away from some impending obligation. The receptionist smiled sympathetically at the short-haired woman. 'I take it you did spell things out?' she said.

'In words of one syllable, Veronica,' said the woman. She seemed about to say a lot more when she caught sight of Thelma. Her calm, professional demeanour was suddenly replaced by a slacker look, one of surprised recognition.

'*Mrs Cooper*?' said the woman. 'Mrs Cooper from St Barney's?'

Thelma looked at the woman again. 'Charlotte Sykes,' she said to her one-time pupil.

Bending down to empty the dishwasher was, Pat realized, a mistake. Standing up, she felt a nauseous throb behind her eyeballs and had to steady herself against the worktop. What had she been thinking, allowing herself to get into such a state? What had she said? Nothing too terrible hopefully. There had been that upset with T-Shirt Lady, of course, but that hadn't been her fault, and she must have been in quite a state herself to fall over like that. Still, she felt uneasy. Normally she was quite good at shaking off the paranoia that comes with a hang-over – 'Beer Fears', as Andrew called it. She tried to remember exactly what she'd told Jamie about Luke. What if he were to speak to Luke, and it all got back to Liam? She shot a guilty look towards the stairs. But, she realized, there was more to worry about than any discretion about Luke, there was Jamie himself. She liked him, and was very much afraid she'd spoilt any friendship by making a drunken tit of herself.

When she was with him she felt like *herself* – that beer-drinking, incense-burning self who strode round the real ale pubs of Bradford in those purple Doc Martens and dirndl skirts, in love with the Housemartins, Saltaire Blonde Beer and sunrises over Lister Park. Not some nearly sixty-year-old getting into a shameful state on what she still thought of, despite being retired, as a school night. She contrasted Jamie and being with him, with her two friends who she was due to meet later that morning. Even though Liz and Thelma were roughly the same age as her she felt much much younger, and suddenly knew she'd say very little if anything about the previous night.

A cough from Liam's room brought her to herself. Said cough had, over the past day, deepened and entrenched itself on a par with the many other coughs that had dogged his childhood and adolescence. He'd been given a few days' leave by the university on the proviso he kept up with lectures via Zoom and had ensconced himself in his room. Pat was torn between being glad he was where she could keep an eye on him, and wishing there were two counties and sixty miles

188

between her son and Luke Atkinson. There was another cough. Soon it would be time to venture upstairs with a mug of tea and gentle offers of porridge, cough mixture and, if needed, a listening ear.

'Come on, old woman, get moving,' she said aloud but somehow, despite her mind's call to action, her body stayed where it was, gazing out of the window at the bird table where a few ghostly sparrows were hopping in the January murk. Yesterday's fog had thinned, but it was still a dark old day. She found herself closing her eyes and thinking of – where was it? – Key West! That sunset Jamie had described. He hadn't been serious though. Surely it was one of those things you say after a few drinks. Like that invite over to dinner! She felt a sudden impulse to text Jamie, to say: *It's all right, I know you were just being polite!*

And then there were those darker memories from the evening, as murky as the fields outside . . . Something about Tate putting someone in hospital? And Terri being mentally unstable . . . Something about tarot cards and an exorcism? She suddenly heard Jen Barlow's words – *walk away. There's nothing but darkness.* She shuddered.

How glad she was they'd decided to let the whole Terri Stanley business drop.

At the end of the drive a car was slowing. A delivery? But there was something about the tan-coloured Maestro that registered as familiar . . . Her fuddled brain was still groping for the answer when Michelle Stanley got out and began walking purposefully towards the house. Immediately she felt convinced of the fact she knew of the night out with her brother-in-law and had come to berate her for some obscure but completely justified reason. But when she opened the door, Michelle was smiling, albeit a bit worriedly.

She flashed the card Pat had given her like a warrant card.

'I hope it's all right, me just poling up here,' she said in tones that obviously entertained no such doubts. 'Only you did say, if I ever wanted to talk . . .' There was a self-entitled tone in her voice that brought to mind the figure on the bed all those years ago.

'Of course,' said Pat.

'The thing is—' Michelle looked doubtfully over her shoulder '—the thing is . . . *I'm scared.*'

The word that came into Thelma's mind in her memories of Charlotte Sykes was 'determined'. Not bright, not up there on the giddy heights of the Kingfishers table, but firmly entrenched with the Blackbirds, where she delivered a steady 2B for Maths and English, and progressed up the school reading scheme at a steady hike as opposed to a spectacular dash. Seldom absent, always on time, second descant on the recorders, armband group at swimming and the third shepherd in the nativity play with the one line reliably delivered. And yet . . . there had been something about that steadiness that had stuck in Thelma's mind and kept Charlotte Sykes alive in her memories in a way that some of those flashier Kingfishers had not.

'The army?' Thelma regarded Charlotte across her polished wooden desk. (Rosewood, it looked like.)

'Four years. Mostly in Afghanistan.'

Regarding the square jaw, the steady gaze, Thelma could believe it.

Charlotte smiled faintly. 'I know what you're thinking,' she said. 'It's something of a leap from serving in Helmand Province to working with the elderly in Thirsk. Well, I can tell you, Mrs Cooper, it's not such a leap as you'd think. In fact, the Taliban were a doddle compared to some of our clients.'

Thelma smiled. 'I can imagine.'

Charlotte smiled back. 'Anyway, Mrs Cooper, what can I do

to help you? I understand from Veronica that you have a relative in need of companionship?'

'Actually no.' Thelma sounded apologetic. 'I'm afraid I haven't.'

Charlotte frowned, puzzled. 'Oh?'

'I can't bring myself to lie to you,' said Thelma. 'I have a young friend. Her sister used to work for you as one of your carers. She died – the sister – just the other week in rather strange circumstances and I was wondering if there was anything you could tell me about her.'

Charlotte gave her a long, searching look. 'I'm intrigued,' she said eventually. 'Of course, there are certain confidentiality issues I can't and won't break. But tell me more.'

'The name of the woman is Terri Stanley,' said Thelma. She was about to say that she wouldn't have been called that when she worked for Charlotte but her former pupil's face had darkened.

'Just one moment,' she said and picked up the phone. 'Vee,' she said. 'Two coffees, love. My usual, and white, no sugar for Mrs Cooper; two spoons of milk.'

'How did you know?' said Thelma.

'If you remember,' said Charlotte, 'it was my job to bring your coffee out to you when you were on playground duty.'

Thelma hadn't.

'So,' said Pat. Her words sounded maybe a little more meaningful than was strictly polite, but Michelle had been here a good twenty minutes and was showing no signs of coming to any sort of a point. If it hadn't been for that initial dramatic statement her appearance could easily have been just a social visit.

On walking into Pat's kitchen she had erupted into a series of gasps and squeals about the various fixtures and fittings: the Aga and the settle, the creel and the scrubbed table – even the obscure wooden paddle that graced the beam above the fire

191

nook. All Pat knew about its origins was that Rod had found it on some tip somewhere, and it came in very handy to prop open the utility room window on hot days. Michelle, however, had pronounced it to be a butter paddle and had stood rapt in front of it for a good two and a half minutes.

'Yes, of course.' Michelle drained the remainder of her coffee. 'You said to get in touch if I ever wanted to talk.' She sounded almost accusing, and once again her mother's reedy tones echoed in Pat's mind. Today she was wearing a powder blue suit, which Pat identified as Hugo Boss – albeit faded Hugo Boss, well past its sell-by date.

'The thing is . . .' Michelle glanced nervously at the window. 'I think someone's been watching me. *And I think it might be Tate Bishop.*'

Pat remembered Jamie's tale from the night before. And felt a little thrill of fear. 'Why do you think that?' she said. 'What's happened?'

'Three times now there's been someone in the street outside. Parked up, looking right at the house.'

'And you think it's Tate Bishop?'

'I can't be sure. I mean, the first time I didn't think anything of it. I just thought it must be a delivery as I get a lot of parcels delivered. But then the next night it was there again – and then when it was there last night, I went up to the front window, and hid behind the curtain and got a good look at the driver. And I'm almost sure it was Tate Bishop. It was definitely a man. Just staring at the house.' She shuddered.

'Did you tell the police?'

She shook her head, dismissively, almost scornfully. 'What could they do? They wouldn't believe me, and besides, it's not as if he actually did anything.' She sighed. 'I just wanted to tell someone . . . I don't know, just in case something happened to me. And you . . . you seemed to understand how I might be feeling.'

Pat focused on making her voice calm and reassuring, the voice she'd used on so many occasions over the years sorting out various spats between children in her class. 'Michelle, you have got to tell the police. You say they can't do anything – well, they certainly can't if you don't tell them. At the very least they'll give you a number you can call. And—' she took a deep mental breath '—and if it happens again, you can call me.' She emphasized the words by taking Michelle's hands in hers, hoping her reticence was undetectable. She'd been feeling lately that she'd let Michelle's mother down all those years ago and this was something she could do that would go some way to putting things right. Michelle nodded. Were those tears in her eyes? It suddenly occurred to Pat with a stab of pity that for whatever reason Michelle likely hadn't got many people she could turn to with this sort of worry. Why else come to her – a virtual stranger?

'Why do you think it might be Tate?' she said. '*Why* would he be watching you?'

Michelle sighed. 'I told Terri in no uncertain terms to stay away from him. When she told me about the CCTV, I said, "Darling, the man is Bad News with a capital B!"'

'But she didn't.'

'No, she didn't. And I don't know what she said to him. She could've said anything, she was all over the place, God Bless her. You see, in my opinion, Terri wasn't a well woman.'

'Oh?'

'After my father died she was very nervous – weepy, driving very erratically, that sort of thing. If you ask me, it's no wonder she had a car crash. I know Jamie told you she had the vicar over to bless the house, but I think at the root of it all *she was afraid of Tate*.'

'Terri Matheson,' said Charlotte. 'I always thought I'd not heard the last of her. Though of course I'm sorry she's dead.' She looked out at Kirkgate, where for the first time in days a watery sun was glinting off the pavement. 'She came to see me, you know, the day Mr Stanley died. I have to admit I was a bit surprised to see her walk in here, bearing in mind what she'd done.'

'Which was?'

'Marrying the man she was employed to care for. The first thing we knew of any wedding had been when Mal Stanley's daughter came marching in demanding to know exactly what sort of knocking shop we were running. I don't know what she expected me to do; the pair were both adults and no one had done anything wrong.' She held up one hand 'Not *technically* wrong. But it didn't sit right, if you know what I mean.'

Thelma did. She'd seen many instances over the years of people doing things that were *technically* not wrong – going on a night out when off work sick, parking in front of a neighbour's house – not technically wrong – but not *right* either.

'But then Terri was someone I couldn't be doing with from the get-go,' said Charlotte. 'Oh, she came across as pleasant enough – our clients thought she was the bees' knees – but I saw a different side.'

'What side was that?' asked Thelma.

'The side that could and would phone in sick at the last possible moment. The side that fed me a pack of lies about why she hadn't done this, that or the other.'

The side that pushed her husband down the stairs? wondered Thelma.

'And then there were other things – things that went missing from the places she was working. Nothing major, just the odd bit of money, maybe some valuables . . . You have to remember, some of these people are very muddled, bless them, and these things could so easily have been mislaid.'

'Mislaid or taken?'

194

'After a while you start to wonder. But I have to stress that I've no proof for any of this,' Charlotte said. 'No proof whatsoever. But she just always struck me as someone who wouldn't hesitate to help herself to whatever it was she wanted. A parasite.' She looked at Thelma. 'What you have to remember, Mrs Cooper, is in this game we're *all* parasites to an extent, cashing in on a big problem: what to do with our elderly. In Afghanistan it didn't even register as an issue: the elderly were absorbed into the family unit without a whisper. Here, it's a rather different story. Most families don't want Mum, Dad or Auntie cluttering up their homes – but neither, if they can possibly help it, do they want them burning through the family inheritance in care homes. Which is where we come in.'

She sighed. 'I hold my hands up. We're cashing in. But if we didn't, someone else would – and at least I can do my level best to see these people get the dignity and respect they're owed. Which is why I don't have a good word to say about Terri Matheson. Or rather *didn't*.' She took a sip of her coffee, looking pensively into the past.

'Do you think Terri married him for his money?' asked Thelma.

'I'm sure of it.' Charlotte spoke immediately and decisively. 'It's that old joke: *"What did you first see in the millionaire Mal Stanley?"* But that doesn't mean she didn't care for him after a fashion. Okay, at first I thought, like everyone did, that Terri was just out for herself, but then I saw how she was when she came in that day.'

'This was the day he died?'

Charlotte nodded. 'She showed up here – all smiles, butter wouldn't melt – asking about respite care. You had to admire her brass neck. But then, whilst she was here, he rang, and he seemed to be in quite a state. I have to say that she was lovely with him – calming, comforting—' Thelma thought of the little girl who had wanted to be a vet '—and I remember thinking, *maybe you do care after all*. Immediately after she rang off, she was onto some neighbour asking her to go and check up on him, and then she dashed off home – only to find he'd had a fall and was dead. I had to tell all this to the police.'

'I wonder,' said Thelma, 'was there anything about that call that struck you as *odd* in any way?'

'I don't think so.' Charlotte wrinkled her nose reflectively. 'I mean, I couldn't hear him. She kept telling him to calm down, and that she was coming right home.'

'She didn't say what the matter was with him?'

Charlotte shook her head. 'She just apologized, said she had to go, and immediately rang the neighbour. She was talking to her as she left the office. That was what made me realize that in spite of everything, she was quite worried about him.'

'Because of what she said?'

'The fact she took the call in the first place. Whenever I'd spoken to her in the past, she'd always made a point of having her phone turned *off* – I always used to think she was dodging calls. I remember thinking, she must be worried about him to be leaving it on.'

Crossing the market place Thelma reflected on the conversation with Charlotte. It had been good luck for Terri that Mal had rung her just as she'd been in the office with a witness. She frowned as a thought suddenly occurred to her – *why* had Mal called her, exactly? She'd assumed – as indeed everyone seemed to have – that it was for some medical-related emergency . . . but what if it *wasn't*? What if Mal had been anxious for some *other* reason. What had he said to Terri? Something that made her immediately call the neighbour. Why get the neighbour to call in and check on him?

''Scuse me, love.' The man was carrying a large box of what

seemed to be coat hangers and Thelma realized she was standing outside Busby's, the man one of a few people carrying out the last of the stock and fittings. Through the main doors could be seen a cavernous empty space where there had once been the ordered world of the department store. She frowned as there was a sudden elusive flicker of thought. Something important.

But what?

CHAPTER TWENTY-TWO

At the round table in the corner tensions rise, a minor bombshell dropped and a pastry fork brandished.

To other customers at the Thirsk Garden Centre Café that Thursday morning the three ladies sitting at the round table in the corner looked like a thousand other such ladies sitting at a thousand similar tables. They might have noticed the worried frown on the face of one. Maybe, if they'd looked closely, they could have detected a rather bleary expression on the face of another, but really there could have been so many reasons for these looks. An energy bill maybe, or the problems of getting a doctor's appointment perhaps.

However the conversation currently running between the three friends covered much darker territory.

'So Terri Stanley *couldn't* have pushed her husband down the stairs,' said Liz with a frown of concentration.

Thelma shook her head. 'Not according to DS Donna and Charlotte Sykes.'

'And there was me thinking,' said Pat rather tightly, 'that we had agreed to let this all drop.' Her hangover headache, which had faded, was thudding back with a vengeance.

Liz, however, busy pursuing her own conjectures, didn't

notice the growing tension in her friend's face. 'The thing about Tate Bishop,' she said, 'is that for all that nasty graffiti, and that young lad looking so nervous, when you actually saw the man standing there, well . . . he just looked rather pathetic. I almost felt a bit sorry for him.'

'This is the same Tate Bishop who put someone in hospital and is stalking Michelle Stanley?' said Pat sourly. Her hangover wasn't the only source of discomfort coming from her head. There was a tight twitch somewhere to the left of her jaw, which had started as a faint tingle as Thelma had recounted her meeting with DS Donna. This tingle had ramped up to a distinct tension during the account of the visit to Charlotte's Aunts and by the time Liz had poured out the story of her trip to Flaxby Hall it was a full-blown clench of the jaw accompanied by a tight grip in her pastry fork.

Plus, Thelma apparently had two carrier bags of wonky veg in the car she was all set to donate to the Reverend Mare. Was this what they termed 'letting things drop'? Okay, she had asked to see Jamie but that was about Luke – and Michelle had turned up unbidden. Thelma's actions in particular were in a whole different league.

'Of course, we've only Michelle Stanley's word that Tate *is* stalking her,' Thelma was saying. 'Don't forget, she is someone who tells lies.'

Pat was aware of the pastry fork digging painfully into her fingers as she pictured the woman in her kitchen, the woman whose mother she had failed all those years ago.

'Liar or not,' she said firmly, 'I know a frightened woman when I see one.'

Liz was still reliving the dark heart of Flaxby Hall. 'The whole set-up was a total shambles from start to finish,' she said, shaking her head. 'You should have seen what people were saying on Tripadvisor.'

'Is Jacob all right?' Thelma's tone was again mild, but it left Pat in no doubt about her feelings on the subject of a ghost-hunting night. Again, she felt that irritated clench in her jaw.

'Why shouldn't he be all right?' she said before Liz could reply. 'He wasn't the one who lost eighty quid on tickets.'

'Jacob's fine,' said Liz. 'Actually, I was quite proud of him. You should have seen the review he wrote for TripAdvisor. But you're right about the money. I don't know what I was thinking of, taking him there.'

'You were trying to give him a good time,' said Pat combatively. 'There's nothing wrong with that.'

'Like you say, it does all sound a mess, the whole thing,' said Thelma. She took a thoughtful bite of her toastie.

'One person on TripAdvisor was talking about suing,' said Liz.

'It all rather gives pause for thought,' said Thelma. Her friends both looked at her, recognizing that tone in her voice.

Why doesn't she just come out and say whatever it is she's thinking of? thought Pat irritably. She very much needed another strong coffee but completely lacked the energy to get one.

'Pause for thought about what?' asked Liz, eyes wide.

'Tate Bishop,' said Thelma. 'Everyone's been telling us how he's this arch manipulator, a man of many talents with fingers in many different pies according to DS Donna.'

'That's what Jamie said,' agreed Liz. The casual use of his first name added another notch to the tightness in Pat's jaw.

'Brid said much the same thing,' said Thelma.

'So *what*?' said Pat. She perhaps needed to take some more aspirin. How long had it been since she'd taken the last lot?

'*So,*' said Thelma, 'in my experience, ruthless, manipulative entrepreneurs tend to be pretty organized. And this whole Flaxby Hall carry-on—' she spoke in a way that made her distaste quite clear '—well, it seems to be anything but.' She nodded at Liz. 'A total lulu from what you're saying.'

'So, it's a lulu,' said Pat. 'And maybe this Tate Bishop isn't exactly the Elon Musk of Leeming Bar. I repeat: *so what?*'

'It just makes you wonder,' said Thelma, 'what else might we be thinking wrongly about in all this?'

'Such as?' Pat gripped her pastry fork tighter. She sensed somehow that this conversation was about to charge off in a direction she didn't care for at all.

'I'm wondering,' said Thelma, 'how Terri Stanley actually got on with her stepchildren.'

'Fine,' said Pat firmly. 'That's what Michelle told both of us. She said it again today.'

'We do know that Michelle tells lies,' said Thelma in her 'difficult staff meeting' voice. 'And Charlotte did say Michelle came in very angry, when she heard about the wedding.'

'What *I'm* wondering,' said Liz, 'is do we believe that Jamie?'

Pat's tension was replaced by a calm that felt wide and cold and glacial. 'What do you mean?' she said. '*That* Jamie?'

'Well,' said Liz, 'we don't know him, so why should we believe him?'

'*I* know him,' said Pat. Her friends looked at her.

'We only met him once,' said Liz.

'Actually I talked to him last night,' said Pat. 'We went out together. To Pals of Pinot.'

As soon as she said the words, she realized by dropping in the information like this, she had irreversibly made a Thing out of it. The muted reaction of her friends told her everything she needed to know about her midweek trip to Pals of Pinot. Looking at them trying – and failing – to look casual and unsurprised gave her something of a 'what the hell' moment. 'I wanted to find out more about what Luke Atkinson was up to,' she said. 'And it's no good looking at me like that. Not when you're off chasing Tate Bishop—' she pointed the pastry fork accusingly at Liz '—and you've been talking to the police and chasing up care companies.' Thelma looked worriedly at the fork that was now pointing at her. 'What is this? *CSI Thirsk*?'

There was a ghastly pause. 'Okay,' she said. 'Here's how it is. No one's been dosed with poison; no one's been sent anonymous letters. Mal Stanley fell down the stairs – whether he was pushed or not I can't see as we'll ever know. And then Terri Stanley had a car crash.' She looked defiantly at her friends, Liz worriedly twisting her napkin, Thelma gazing steadily from behind those large glasses. 'Something Jamie *did* tell me,' she said, 'is that *Terri was scared*. And I *don't* mean just because of Tate. Jamie said she didn't like being on her own in the house. Okay, she might have been in a state because of Mal's death, but I think it goes deeper than that. She'd been buying tarot cards. I don't know what she'd been doing with them, but according to Jamie she asked the Reverend Mare to come and bless the place.'

'Like *The Exorcist*?' said Liz, eyes fearful.

'I don't know,' said Pat. 'And—' she waved the pastry fork again at Thelma '—and you can stop looking like that. Things *do* happen – things that can't be explained. And you making me feel small every time I raise the subject isn't going to change that fact. *Something happened that night*. We know Marguerite saw *something*. A charity shop – maybe some vision – something. And when Terri drove out of that side road that night, *she was scared*. Scared of *something*. But she's dead. And whatever she did or didn't do died with her. And I for one am not going to get involved anymore.' She stood up.

'Your Baldersby slice,' said Liz.

'You have it,' said Pat. 'I have to go to the Wine 'n' Dine. I need to buy some wine,' she added redundantly. 'Rod and I are going over to Jamie's for dinner.'

And she walked off.

Liz looked in horror after their friend, who was purposefully navigating her way past the growing numbers queuing for the café. 'Should I go after her d'you think?' she said doubtfully.

'I don't know.' Thelma looked uncharacteristically tired, dejected even. 'Probably best to leave it.'

Liz sighed unhappily. 'I feel like I put my foot in it,' she said.

'Neither of us knew she'd met up with Jamie,' said Thelma. Her voice sounded so flat, so tired, that Liz felt an impulse to take her friend's hand. If it had been Pat she would have, but then there were some things you just didn't do with Thelma.

She looked sadly at the abandoned Baldersby slice and sighed. 'All this because of Marguerite McAllister and some blumin' charity shop,' she said.

Thelma stirred her almost empty coffee cup. Paused. And stirred.

'What?' said Liz.

'I don't know,' said Thelma slowly. 'I just wonder *how* Marguerite knew it was a *charity shop* she saw.'

CHAPTER TWENTY-THREE

A psychological theory is shared and a call partially overheard.

Walking round Wine 'n' dine, Pat was in a turmoil of feeling.

Typical! Typical of those two . . . Making sweeping great pronouncements about Not Getting Involved and Leaving Well Alone – and *then* going off and doing the *exact* opposite! And then when *she* said about going out with Jamie . . . that disapproving reaction. Like she'd made a huge and silly mistake.

Angrily she forced herself to focus on the array of bottles. The last thing she felt like today was any sort of alcoholic drink whatsoever, but nevertheless wine had to be bought for Friday night. If it was her and Rod the answer would be easy: a bottle of that French Merlot they sold at Tesco's, either that or some Barefoot Chardonnay. But this wasn't her and Rod. It was her new best friend. Coming here to Wine 'n' dine with its shelves and racks of bottles and faint smell of wood added an automatically classy element not afforded by a supermarket. But what to buy? It felt almost like this meal with Jamie wouldn't happen if the wrong wine was selected.

She forced herself to stop, take a deep calming breath, aware of a bigger truth emerging. How long had she known Liz and

Thelma? For the best part of twenty-five years? Maybe nearer thirty. Perhaps what she needed to realize was that, like most workplace relationships, once that common thing that had drawn them together had gone – the work itself – there was nothing very much left. She thought of the two figures she'd left behind at the round table in the corner. Liz in that fleece the colour of Brussels sprouts, Thelma with those wide glasses and greying bob of hair. Maybe the truth was they were all growing apart?

And maybe it had taken her new friendship with Jamie to make her see this. How long had she known him? Less than a week. But she knew instinctively that her friendship with him was important to her. Yes, there was all that invigorating buzz where someone bright and clever and funny finds you bright and clever and funny, but it went further than that. There was in his blond, irreverent presence an antidote to the gloom she'd been feeling lately about pensioners' coach trips, Marguerite's vision or whatever it was, and of course those wild frightening thoughts in Boroughbridge. Jamie somehow seemed an *answer* to all of that.

And yet . . . was that how Jamie saw *her*? She checked her phone – no message. Her mind morbidly went back to the previous night. No two ways about it, she'd been in one heck of a state. There was some comment she remembered making as they were waiting for their taxis – something about boy bands – and all at once she remembered how forced his laugh had seemed. She briefly closed her eyes in embarrassment. Was he even now thinking how inappropriate she'd been, and hoping she'd forget his invitation?

She suddenly realized she'd walked twice round Wine 'n' dine without actually selecting anything. From behind the counter the woman serving smiled encouragingly but Pat was feeling way too fragile to enter into any conversation about the best wine.

Come on, Patricia, for God's sake get a grip.

She looked again at the ranks of bottles. The sage green glass ones felt in some way classier than the clear ones, or the bottle-green ones. Those labels – the ones that were parchment-coloured, with the monotone print – they looked quite refined. She peered more closely at the various fonts and designs – one depicted a vineyard of some description – and before she knew it her mind had made a leap over to the Dordogne to a luxury coach with its own toilet and defibrillator. She shrugged almost angrily and grabbed two bottles: one red, one white.

The woman behind the counter smiled approvingly and told Pat she'd made a great choice! As she wrapped each bottle in tissue paper Pat impulsively sent Jamie a WhatsApp: LOOKING FORWARD TO TOMORROW! She added a bottle of champagne emoji and then deleted it, but even so, she still felt embarrassed and overeager.

'Thelma! What a gorgeous surprise!' There was no trace of irony or accusation in Marguerite's voice, despite the fact that Thelma hadn't called in on her, or indeed had any meaningful contact with her beyond Christmas cards for at least five years.

'I just happened to be passing,' said Thelma, feeling a slight pang at the lie. But then, Marguerite was always so wrapped up in herself and her affairs it was highly unlikely she'd notice. Sure enough, as Thelma followed her through into the living room, Marguerite plunged into an involved and lengthy account of a row with her energy supplier with no question at all about how Thelma was, or why she was visiting after such a long time.

'I said, there simply has to be *some* sort of boo-boo,' she said, leading Thelma into the living room where on the coffee table stood a clock, swathed in what looked like an inordinate amount of bubble wrap.

'I know energy costs are skyrocketing up and up,' Marguerite was saying, 'but even so! Come on, guys! What a load of nump-ties! So until they get their acts together, it's heating all the way down.' That would explain the enormous fluffy pink hoody and pale lemon leggings; she put Thelma in mind of a large Easter egg.

Thelma sent up a quick prayer for guidance, and that she might find out something of what she was looking for – though what that was exactly, she really wasn't sure. She just felt very strongly that after that awful upset with Pat, it was vitally important to talk with Marguerite face to face about what had happened to her. She was just considering how best to switch onto this rather bizarre line of conversation she needed to pursue when Marguerite did the work for her.

'Do you like my clock?' she asked, rather coyly, Thelma thought.

'I do,' said Thelma. It was, she saw, what was known as a Napoleon clock – the sort that would sit on a mantelpiece, the case all graceful wooden curves.

'It's a gift for someone,' said Marguerite and stopped herself as a smile played round her lips. Thelma was pretty sure who that someone probably was. What interested her was the choice of gift.

'It's a lovely clock,' said Thelma. 'Why are the hands at ten to three?'

'To make it the same as the one I saw in my vision,' said Marguerite with no trace of embarrassment. 'You heard about that?'

'Pat did say something,' said Thelma. 'You saw a charity shop?'

'No,' said Marguerite. '*Not* a charity shop.' She looked at Thelma for a moment, a smile playing round her lips. 'I *thought* it was a charity shop.'

'What was it?' asked Thelma.

'A mental projection,' said Marguerite, not without a trace

of pride. 'My mind making sense of various images. Sometimes the psyche is like that, sometimes it needs to give you a jolly big kick up the backside and say "oy!"'

Thelma, whose psyche had never shown any such aggressive qualities, merely nodded.

'It's a very common phenomenon apparently,' said Marguerite. 'Me seeing a "charity shop" was just my mind *interpreting* what I saw. I got a research paper about it through just today – apparently someone had read about my vision on the Yorkshire Paranormals website, and sent it across! Some professor in an American university. I couldn't believe it! Someone in America interested in what little old me saw!'

'And what did you see?' asked Thelma. 'Exactly?'

'A light in the fog. That was the first sign. That represents a search for clarity apparently. And then inside . . . all the objects . . . a whole mishmash of images representing different things. All that male clothing, that was my *perception* of masculinity. And the pictures, they stood for my past life. But the clock—' here she gestured at the swathed object on the coffee table '—that's the key one. Showing me how superficial our concept of time is—'

A scrappy piece of paper . . .

Past and present – both the same?

Thelma recalled herself back to the present. 'And was there any women's clothing? Blouses, shoes, coats?'

Marguerite shook her head. 'Why would there be? If it's my perception of masculinity?'

Thelma nodded. 'And were there any signs?' she asked.

'There were lots of signs,' said Marguerite, puzzled. 'I just told you.'

'I mean physical *signs* – like you'd find in a charity shop,' interrupted Thelma. '"RSPCA", "All donations welcome" . . . anything like that?'

'How could there be?' said Marguerite. 'It wasn't a charity shop.'

'No, I'm sorry, of course.' Thelma nodded gravely.

Driving home her mind was racing round and round – it was like there was something, some truth starting to emerge like shapes from a winter fog . . . What this truth was she didn't know; all she knew was it was there. Driving into College Gardens just as the day was fading, she became aware of another, bigger reality that lay behind all her investigating – one she'd not admitted even to herself, and one that was infinitely more self-interested than any high-minded notions of helping Brid Matheson. The commonplace truth was that speculating on what had happened with Terri Stanley was proving very effective at taking her mind off the ongoing situation with Teddy. Teddy and something else . . . that once so-familiar sadness, which she'd felt brewing inside her ever since she'd seen that solemn little girl with the plaits.

The reason why she was so prickly about any mention of mediums. Should she have said something to Pat about how she felt? But then, it was something she could barely explain to herself. She sighed. Now, just when she needed friends more than ever, she'd succeeded in driving one of them away.

When Pat walked in the door, bottles discreetly clinking in their purple tissue paper jackets, the first thing she heard was Liam's cough coming from the living room. The Benylin! She'd completely forgotten! What sort of an appalling, terrible mother was she? Then she became aware of the tone in Liam's voice – loud but at the same time pacifying. 'Calm down,' he was saying, 'just calm down and tell me it from the beginning.' Was this Bern he was talking to? Intrigued, she carefully put the carrier bag on the table and moved to the living room door.

From his basket Larson regarded her sleepily; normally when she walked in carrying a bag he'd be sniffing trustingly round her ankles, fixing her with a direct, soulful gaze. She smiled at him, held her finger to her lips.

Liam was standing with his back to the living room door, framed in the window.

'He said what? Random! How's that your job?' Here he broke into a cough. 'And that's why he got so angry with you? I just can't see why *he* didn't get rid of them—' Another cough. 'Just calm down, I can't hear you.' On the table the bag from Wine 'n' dine settled with a tell-tale clink, and Liam turned and saw her in the doorway. His face twisted with annoyance.

'Look,' he said, 'I'll call you straight back. Two seconds.' Everything about him warned her not to speak, but she spoke anyway. 'Was that Bern?' she said.

'No,' he said, retreating to the stairs.

'He can always come and stay here,' she said to his retreating back. There was no response.

Another less than satisfactory conclusion to a conversation with her son. And how could she have forgotten the Benylin?

Her phone buzzed. It was Jamie replying to her earlier text. YOU BET, SISTER. GET A TAXI

And emojis of three bottles of champagne.

CHAPTER TWENTY-FOUR

In the dark heart of Yorkshire career choices are discussed and there is yet more anger.

No matter how worried she was, how stressed, how preoccupied, there were some things Liz never hurried; one of those things was her driving. However, retracing her steps to Flaxby Hall, having left her friends on such a dreadful note of discord, there was more than one red-faced slow-down sign she triggered in the villages between Thirsk and Leeming Bar.

What an awful scene! Pat storming off like that! With Liz, 'scenes' were one of her number-one all-time black dreads – and now, now she'd provoked an almighty one between her two best friends. It'd been all her fault – blundering on in that stupid, clumsy way about Jamie Adams . . . Of course, there was no way she could have known that Pat had gone gallivanting off to Pals of Pinot with him, but she should have noticed how upset her friend was getting.

She wasn't sure exactly *what* dashing back to Flaxby Hall and finding Tate Bishop would achieve . . . She just hoped he'd be able to tell her *something* about Terri Stanley – what she might or might not have said that would somehow smooth things over – something to show Pat she had listened to her and had taken her seriously. The thought of facing up to someone who had apparently hospitalized one person and was stalking another was, in her current state of agitation, the merest technicality.

There was a man in a hi-vis jacket at the entrance to the puddled car park, talking to the driver of a rather battered silver van bearing the legend 'Yarm Sound Systems'. What was being said Liz didn't know, but the van suddenly shot forward, causing the hi-vis-bedecked man to leap back and yell angrily after it.

The man snatched out his phone, and as he did so Liz recognized him as one of the lurking figures from the other night. 'Bailey, Mick here, car park.' His voice was laconic, as if he'd had a very very long day already. 'FYI. A complete tool is heading your way at a rate of knots, wanting a word with Tate.'

Call done, he leaned in towards Liz's window. 'It's all closed here, love. Any enquiries you're best to phone that lot.' He gestured with a thumb to a white A4 notice on a fence behind him. It was in a plastic sleeve but obviously damp had got in at some point, blurring the words. Thankfully, Liz could still more or less make them out: *AS OF JANUARY 18TH FLAXBY HALL GHOST TOURS INC LTD. HAS CEASED TRADING. ALL ENQUIRIES INCLUDING INVOICES PLEASE SUBMIT TO* . . . There followed the name and number of a Newcastle solicitor. So, the dark heart of Yorkshire had folded. Liz couldn't say she was surprised.

'Actually,' she said, 'I was hoping for a quick word with Tate Bishop if he's about.'

The man rolled his eyes. 'You and half North Yorkshire, love,' he said. 'I'll tell you what I told that Knob Brain before you – if Tate owes you money, you're just going to have to get into the queue with everyone else, me included.'

'This isn't actually to do with money,' she said. 'It's personal.' She was about to say more, but at that moment the man's phone rang and he stepped back, seemingly indifferent as to whether she went looking for Tate or not. One of the advantages of being a grey-haired lady of a certain age, Liz reflected, was that people tended not to notice whether you slipped into places where others – such as aggressive van drivers – were warned off.

The lobby of Flaxby Hall felt even sadder, if that was possible. The trestle tables were stacked at the side, flanked by a load of plastic – presumably containing the sweatshirts and books. The smell of damp was much stronger today and without any sort of trappings, be it hotel fittings or trestle tables, it was just a space – an empty, meaningless space. Walking in, Liz was instantly aware of a repeated hammering and thumping, accompanied by angry words, coming from a corridor leading off the lobby. Following the commotion Liz could see the stocky bald man slamming his hands against an office door; on his arms, neck and head were a truly kaleidoscopic array of tattoos.

'You're going to have to face me some time, Tate, you thieving bastard!' he shouted.

'I'm telling you, he's not in there.' Liz heard a familiar voice, and there was Bailey Bairstow Venue Coordinator looking as uneasy as ever.

'Yeah, and I know he is,' said Tattoo Man. 'He's in there and he's got five hundred and sixty-nine pounds ninety-nine of my money. Five hundred and sixty-nine pounds ninety-nine he's going to give back.'

'Seriously, mate.' Bailey spoke earnestly and sincerely, in a rather high voice. 'Seriously he's *not*. He went out about an hour since. You're welcome to carry on waiting but to be fair he could be gone some time.'

Tattoo Man sighed with resigned disgust. 'You can tell that thieving bastard from me he needn't think he's going to get away with it. He owes me money,' he said and with a final slap on the door strode off past Liz. Tate's bodyguard exhaled a long, shuddering breath and leaned back against the wall.

'Are you okay?' said Liz.

Unwillingly he snapped back into professional mode. 'I'm so sorry,' he said formally. 'My name is Bailey Bairstow and I'm the Venue Coordinator. The company's ceased trading. We will be contacting people regarding refunds but obviously there's a lot of sorting out that needs to be done first. But I promise, we will be in touch.'

'Never mind that,' said Liz. 'Are *you* all right? I couldn't help noticing you've been rather in the thick of things.'

'I'm fine.' The words were bright and brittle and put Liz in mind of Pat in one of her bury-my-head-in-the-sand moods. 'Just busy! Anyway . . .' Bailey Bairstow cast his head uneasily around, reminding Liz of so many children from over the years, caught up in the middle of something that had spiralled way out of their control. 'Anyway, it is what it is.'

'So, when you close up here,' said Liz, 'what are you going to do?'

'I've a few options,' he said in what was clearly meant to be a slick way. 'A few possibilities I'm going to follow up.' He looked at Liz and obviously realized she wasn't fooled. 'I don't know,' he said worriedly. 'I don't know. Something will turn up, fingers crossed.'

'What did you do before this?' asked Liz. 'Did you work for Tate Bishop then?'

Bailey shook his head. 'I was at college. I was at college but managing a band in the evenings. Have you heard of a band called Septic?'

Liz had not.

'It was brilliant,' he said, face looking relaxed – animated, even – for the first time since Liz had seen him. 'And then one night we were playing at this gig and Tate saw me and said I had just the right skill set he was looking for, and I was wasted in college.' Even knowing as he evidently did how wrong it had all gone, there was a tinge of pride in Bailey's voice as he remembered the night that he'd been headhunted. 'And at first it was brilliant. It was so exciting setting the whole thing up and meeting Gareth Ap-Glyndwr . . .'

'So what happened?'

'Tate's partner . . .' He shook his head sadly. 'She was killed in a car crash a couple of weeks back. All this ghost-hunting stuff – it was her idea. And ever since she's not been around it's all just fallen apart. Tate seems to have lost it. You can't blame him though.'

Liz considered all the money that was owed and the general levels of disorganization and thought that actually you probably could.

'It's so sad,' said Bailey. 'But I can't go back to college.'

'Why not?' asked Liz.

Baily shook his head vehemently. 'I just can't. I realized *this* is what I want to do.'

'Not *this* exactly,' suggested Liz in a gentle tone that encompassed the lobby, the stacked tables, the smell of damp.

Bailey looked at her sadly.

'Okay,' he said, dropping his voice. 'I didn't tell you this, but Tate *is* in the office. He told me not to say to anyone, and he may well not answer if you knock.'

'I know he is,' said Liz, moving towards the door. 'I heard your colleague outside.' She smiled at Bailey Bairstow in a kindly way.

'Just be careful,' he said after her. 'He's not in a good place.'

Liz knocked tentatively at the door of the office. 'Mr Bishop,' she said. 'Mr Bishop, I wonder, could I have a quick word? I'm not here about money.' No response. 'I'm here to talk about Terri,' she said.

There was a pause, and then a stir from within. With a tinny rattle the door opened and looking out at her was Tate Bishop.

He was dressed in the manner of an executive on vacation, soft linen suit and baggy blue T-shirt. It was an outfit that would have worked in a traditional office workplace; however, here in the middle of an abandoned building, it looked unsuitable and out of place. Plus, Tate Bishop was a good fifteen years too old and twenty kilograms too heavy to really carry it off. He wasn't looking quite as flushed and bleary as he had the other night, but it was easy to see he was, as Bailey had said, not in a good place.

'I'm very sorry to intrude,' she said. 'I do realize this is a difficult time for you, and I don't really want to take up much of your time.'

Tate Bishop regarded her for a long moment through appraising grey eyes. Then he stepped wordlessly back to allow Liz into the office. As she passed him, she caught a distinct tang, either of aftershave or booze or possibly both.

Like his outfit, the office had aspirations beyond a derelict hotel just off the A1. A spartan wide table – slightly too big for the space – dominated one side of the room; the chairs around it were spindly, steel things that didn't look at all comfortable. There was evidence of disarray on the laminated white desks and shelves – jumbled folders, opened ring binders – spaces where PCs had obviously once stood. On a varnished beer barrel an orphaned printer blinked sadly. On the wall was a large black poster bearing the words: 'Take no shit' in stark white letters; next to it was a yearly planner. On January 6th, someone had drawn a large red star and written the words 'we have lift-off'; a week previously, someone else had written 'we have crash-down'.

Tate Bishop was still staring steadily at her in a way that transcended the shambolic figure she'd mentally dismissed the other night, and to her faint surprise gave her a prickle of discomfort. Moreover, he put Liz in mind of someone whom she couldn't quite place but she instinctively felt the association was not a good one. What had DS Donna said to Thelma? *Stay well away . . .*

'Thank you for seeing me,' she said. Her voice was suddenly a lot less confident than she'd have liked.

'So, what's this about Terri?' he asked. His voice was curiously soft and low.

'I wanted to ask a couple of questions,' she said.

There was a silence. He sat on one of the chairs, the fight seemingly gone out of him, and all at once it occurred to Liz that whatever he may or may not have done, Tate Bishop was a man stricken with grief.

'And just who are you?' he said finally.

'My name is Liz Newsome; I'm a friend of Terri's sister.'

'Brid?' His voice came sharp; his body tensed. '*Brid* sent you?'

'Not exactly,' said Liz.

'Then what exactly? Is this about the funeral? Because if it is I've already said I'm having nothing to do with it.'

'It's not about the funeral, it's about Terri's late husband's family.'

'That lot?' His voice was harsh and Liz felt a frisson of something like fear. 'That bunch of toxic no-hopers put you up to coming?'

Liz tried not to look shocked at the vehemence behind the words. 'No,' she said. 'I wanted to ask about the house really.'

But Tate was not for listening.

'You can tell Brid from me, Missus whoever you are, to steer well clear of that son and daughter – and in fact I shouldn't be surprised if they were the ones who did for her.' The stare was now openly hostile.

'You mean one of them *killed* her?' she said. 'But it was an accident, surely?'

Again, another silence, during which Tate knotted his fingers

217

together and stared at them. Eventually, he looked up at her, as if surprised she was still there. 'The police told me,' he said, 'that Terri was a reckless driver. Reckless my arse. Shite driver yes, reckless no way! She'd *never* pulled out of a road without looking – not Terri.'

'Do you know *why* she was there, in that side road?' she said. 'It leads nowhere.'

'God knows.' His voice was angry. 'Probably got lost, knowing her. She just told me she was going out to collect something.' Tate looked morosely at the wall planner and Liz noticed tears bright in those bleary eyes. Who was it he reminded her of?

'She'd have been distracted when driving,' he continued, voice bitter. 'No, I'll tell you what I think, I think one of that lot messaged or called her and she took a wrong turn and crashed, the daft cow.' He looked at her. 'Is that it?' he said. 'Does that answer your question?'

'Thank you,' said Liz. She didn't think it did, but she definitely wanted to go. She moved as if to leave but Tate stood in one sudden, fluid motion, so he was directly between her and the door.

'One moment, Liz Newsome,' he said. 'Maybe I've got some questions of my own.'

'Please get out of the way,' said Liz, fighting to keep the panic out of her voice.

He looked at her as if suddenly amused, and stepped back. 'You see this furniture? It's worth probably more than Terri's precious sister makes in six months. Those PCs that were taken away were two and a half grand apiece. The iPad was Which? recommended. Yes, it might have gone belly-up, but it's the biggest ghost walk in the north that's gone belly-up – not some shitty pub or some low-life warehouse. I've lost more than Brid will ever have, and I don't want *any* money from her.'

218

What on earth was he going on about? *What money?* Brid had next to nothing, Thelma had said. 'I'm going now,' said Liz firmly.

'Tell that sister of hers I don't want any of that bloody money,' he said and suddenly, angrily kicked the table, which skittered back, knocking two of the chairs sideways. Too rattled to try and make sense of this, Liz shrank back in shock and in that moment, it came to her who Tate Bishop reminded her of. Her former student, Wayne Linsel. Him, and his boasting, his tantrums and that collection of Top Trumps cards.

Liz moved for the door, and animal-like, Tate sprang to stand with his back to it, hand on the handle. 'You can tell Brid whatever Terri might have told her, *my* conscience is clear and I can prove it—'

'Please move away,' she said, her voice icy and authoritative. Shady businessmen were one thing; boastful, angry little boys were quite another matter.

At that moment there was a rattle and the door opened violently inwards, causing Tate to stumble.

'What the fuck?' he said angrily as Bailey Bairstow looked in.

'Sorry to interrupt, Tate,' said Bailey, his voice high and shaky. 'I thought you should know that some people have just pulled in the car park, and I reckon they might be police.'

'That's all I fucking need,' said Tate, and snatching his coat was gone.

Standing on the steps of Flaxby Hall Liz took a great gulp of damp woodland air as a large four-by-four roared off up the drive. There were no new cars in the car park.

'Are you okay, missus?' It was Bailey Bairstow.

'I'm fine,' she said. 'But thank you for coming in like you did. I'm guessing all that about the police was made up?'

Bailey looked at his feet. 'Like I said, he's not in a good place.'

'No,' said Liz. 'I can see that. And I'm very grateful to you.'

'Anyway.' Bailey sighed sadly and turned to go back inside.

'Bailey,' said Liz. He stopped and looked at her. 'My advice to you,' she said, 'is to have nothing more to do with this place or Tate Bishop.'

Bailey shrugged hopelessly. 'Maybe,' he said.

'Go back to college.' Liz's voice was quiet and firm. 'Get your qualifications. Then you'll find it so much easier to do what you want to do. You could even take up with your Septic friends again.'

'I don't know.' Bailey looked awkward and undecided.

'I do.' Liz smiled at him. Bailey smiled back and standing there on the cracked steps of Flaxby Hall hotel Liz had a sudden memory of Friday spelling tests, and the hopeful pride on the faces of children who'd achieved full marks for the first time.

CHAPTER TWENTY-FIVE

*There is discussion of darkness, a figure is spied in
the gloom and cheer is found in the lights of HG4.*

'So – peel!' The Reverend Mare brandished a battered vegetable
peeler in one hand. 'And chop!' In the other she held a rather
sinister-looking knife. 'A terrific way to get the old angst out
of the system!' Over her bottle-green sweater, she was wearing
a plastic apron, one of those made to look like a saucy maid
with fishnet stockings and swelling cleavage. Standing there,
knife in hand, Thelma thought the image rather bizarre and
terrifying.

The group regarded Mare with frowning concentration from
behind the various trestle tables set up at the back of St Jude's
Church. There were seven or eight of them, all with their piles
of wonky veg and assorted plastic bowls, knives and peelers,
and to Thelma they all looked barely out of school.

'Okay,' said the Reverend Mare. 'So, this is where I get to
do my Noel Fielding bit!' She smiled round encouragingly.
'Bakers, you have forty minutes to make a delicious, nourishing
vegetable hot pot. On your marks! Get set! *Bake!*' Her energy
and humour reminded Thelma of Pat showing her class how
to make toilet roll angels, so very long ago. Instinctively she

checked her phone. Nothing from her friend. Not that she had really expected there to be. Not after the way she'd walked out the day before.

As the peeling and chopping started, Mare came over to Thelma, drawing the back of her hand across her forehead and looking suddenly tired. 'Wowee,' she said. 'Give me a sermon any day of the week. Though I suppose all that *was* a sermon of sorts. Anyway, thanks so much—' she indicated two carrier bags full of wonky veg that were sitting by the altar table '—you've no idea how helpful that is.'

'That's no trouble at all,' said Thelma.

Mare smiled wearily. 'We were talking on Diocesan Zoom the other day and someone made the very valid point that whereas people can do all manner of extraordinary things on TikTok and YouTube, so many of them don't actually know how to peel a carrot.'

Thelma nodded, hit with a sudden memory of Home Economics lessons with Miss Hockley Milk jellies and cauliflower cheese . . .

'Though it fundamentally pains and appals me to say it,' continued Mare, 'I do find myself *a teeny tiny bit* in agreement with Leo Lloyd.' Their local MP had recently sparked national outrage by claiming that all people needed to get through the current economic crisis were some basic cookery skills. She shook her head. 'People think a place like North Yorkshire is all barm cakes and dry-stone walls. They don't realize how much real poverty there is in places like this. One gets so very *angry*.' Her face darkened and suddenly Thelma was put in mind of Jesus overturning the tables of money lenders in the temple.

'How is the play going?' asked Thelma with a gesture towards the various stacked scenery flats.

Mare smiled wearily. 'We're getting there,' she said, but there was an undercurrent of something in her voice. 'It's jolly lovely the church is being used for these community events, but at the end of the day it is first and foremost a church and I do find myself having to de-theatre the place for the actual services.' She nodded to the side wall where a stack of flats was leaning precarious against a stack of chairs.

'You've presumably asked them to clear up when they've finished?' asked Thelma.

Mare nodded. 'I've spoken to Jamie,' she said carefully. 'More than once.'

'Can I just ask,' said Thelma, 'what do you think of the play itself?'

Mare shrugged. 'I was sorry to lose the turnip blight bit,' she said. 'I thought that was jolly interesting.'

'I mean the ghost stories,' said Thelma. 'In a church.'

Again, Mare shrugged. 'There has been a bit of muttering,' she said. 'But then there's a whole chunk of the New Testament that is essentially a ghost story. It's the sadness of the stories I find difficult.'

'Oh?' Thelma frowned; she hadn't considered this.

'The Grey Waif of Pickhill – that's essentially about child neglect,' said Mare. 'And then that poor Canadian airman wandering the lanes trying to get back home – what was he? Just twenty-two? Maybe twenty-three? But people are fascinated by the old ghosties apparently; at least that's what I'm told by Rural Arts. And Lord knows we need the money.' She raised her eyes heavenward but Thelma suspected it was the church roof in her thoughts, not the Holy Father.

'I wonder,' said Thelma, 'if I could ask you a question? About Terri Stanley.'

'Fire away,' said Mare. Was it Thelma's imagination or had a sudden restraint entered the cheerful voice?

'You said you saw her after Mal died.'

'I did.' Now there was definitely a guarded quality to her voice.

'I wonder, did she say anything about Mal's death? I know he rang her when she was out – did she say *why* he rang?'

Mare shook her head. 'I can truthfully say that all she said was she should never have left him that afternoon. That's all she said – several times. She should not have left him alone.' Her voice still held the same cautious note but Thelma felt instinctively she was telling the truth.

'One other question,' she said. 'And please tell me to mind my own business if I'm overstepping, but did Terri Stanley ever ask you to *bless* the house in any way?'

The Reverend Mare said nothing, but frowned and fingered the vegetable peeler. 'I suppose Jamie told you this?' she said guardedly.

'Yes,' said Thelma.

'It was confidential,' said Mare. 'But if Terri told Jamie . . .' She paused, considering. 'Terri Stanley did ask me to come and perform a blessing. This was soon after Mal fell down the stairs, and before you ask, she didn't say exactly why.'

'One imagines,' said Thelma, 'she was afraid for some reason.'

'Maybe.' Mare looked across the church to the altar, her eyes sad. Thelma had a sudden insight that here was someone who had seen a lot of the darkness the human soul had to offer. 'Of course,' she said, her voice suddenly serious, 'there are times when people become aware of the world beyond this one. Thin times, I call them. And then there are times when the darkness people carry threatens to overwhelm them.'

Despite all the activity and chat St Jude's Church suddenly felt like a place of shadows.

'And you think Terri Stanley was someone who carried a lot of darkness?'

'I think we all do.' Mare stood up, once again brisk and energetic and Thelma realized the conversation was over. 'Do excuse me.' Mare turned to the assembled cooks. 'Bakers!' she said jovially. 'You have half an hour left! And then I'm going to go all Jamie Oliver on you with a pinch of herbs!'

Driving away from St Jude's, Thelma considered. The Reverend Mare knew something more than she was saying – that was certain. Something about Terri Stanley, something to do with her blessing of the house. *But what?* Had Terri thought the house was in some way haunted? That was generally why people sought such things. If so, by whom? Mal? Mal's first wife? She thought too of Mare's words – *the darkness people carry*. What exactly had been the nature of the darkness carried by Terri Stanley?

Beyond the village the fog was much worse, everything reduced to sinister shapes and shades; in places she had difficulty even making out the lines of the road.

Thus it was that the tall figure who appeared by the side of the road took her completely by surprise. The shock was cold and primal, her first thought: *the lost Canadian airman!* Slowing further she realized the figure emerging from one of the many old airfield tracks that characterized this side of Marley was no ghost but a young man. As the mussel-blue Corsair crawled past, she momentarily but clearly caught the pinched features of Luke Atkinson hunched up against the cold; in each hand was gripped an empty bag for life.

What was he doing out here? And where was he heading, carrying those bags? What had been in them? *And why did he look as though he'd been crying?*

Instinctively she found herself slowing, turning in a handy driveway and heading back. What she would say to Luke she wasn't exactly sure but as she neared the corner, she saw a grey Mini pull out from the side and drive past her, away from the village. She stopped and parked where the Mini had been a minute previously. Getting out of the car she peered down the murky track.

Without really knowing what she was doing, she began retracing Luke's steps down the foggy track. It was one of those tracks that typified the fringes of Marley – cracked concrete, some rusty wisps of fencing and thick tangles of rampant, thorny undergrowth. In the bleak, freezing fog it felt literally like the ends of the earth. How far should she go?

A sudden lift in the murk, like a hand twitching aside a curtain, gave her a view across to a house that looked familiar. Of course! Sunny View Lodge! The tree-sheltered bulk lay some hundred yards across a ploughed field. The path must have looped round more than she thought – this fog was so disorientating. She looked over to the house. From this direction it looked like it'd be perfectly possible to approach the house without being seen by anyone, like that ever-present neighbour in the anorak. Had Luke, for some reason, been spying on the house?

She was about to head back to the car when an acrid tang caught at her nostrils and the back of her throat. Somewhere, something was burning. She moved cautiously round the back of a particularly thick clump of hedges following the smell. There she found the glowing remains of a fire, smoking, shuddering embers of vibrant orange. What on earth was being burnt in this forlorn spot?

She walked closer until she could make out the charring remains of shaped wood.

Coat hangers?

Driving back through the darkening afternoon, Thelma's mind was full of questions about what she'd seen. Why was Luke burning *coat hangers*, if indeed it had been him responsible? Thelma could think of many different, easier ways to dispose of coat hangers that didn't involve trailing out into the fog and starting a bonfire, but why get rid of them in the first place? Luke struck her as someone to whom clothes mattered. You'd have thought someone like him would want more coat hangers, not fewer. And why had he looked so upset?

Walking up the path of 32 College Gardens she realized how cold it was getting. Approaching the door, she stopped dead, registering the huddle of shapes in the porch. She felt a clench of irritation; obviously Big Cyn had paid them yet another visit.

The front door opened just as she was hefting the last of the parcels into Teddy's study and had trapped her finger between a parcel and the table. 'Hello! It's your friendly WAMMP delivery driver!' The cheery greeting dissolved into a wet wheeze Thelma didn't like the sound of.

'In the dining room,' she said.

Teddy came in and surveyed the scene. 'Oh Lawks,' he said, 'I didn't know about this.' He began checking his app with a frown of concentration, letting all the warm air out of the dining room in the process.

'Know or not, they're here,' said Thelma, trying hard to keep the irritation from her voice.

'Drat, drat and double drat,' he said in his Dick Dastardly voice, the one he used when trying to make light of something that annoyed him. 'It's here – the app's just updated.'

'You can sort them after supper,' said Thelma firmly. 'Pasta or curry-in-a-hurry?'

He looked at her apologetically. 'Actually,' he said, 'I think if it's okay with you I'll just do my HG4s.' Another wave of annoyance swept over her. HG4? That postcode covered Ripon and a large swathe of surrounding countryside. '*Now?*' she said tightly.

He nodded and coughed; no two ways about it, the cough was on the verge of meaning business. 'Otherwise, I'm thrown out for tomorrow,' he said. 'I'll be half an hour, tops.' Through their marriage Thelma had learned 'half an hour tops' was more an optimistic statement of hope than an actual accurate assessment of time.

The obvious response was surely something along the lines of 'it'll keep'.

Instead, she picked up her fleecy scarf from the chair. 'In that case I'm coming with you,' she said.

It was one of the bigger houses on Studley Hill. Teddy was engaged in marking 'delivered' on the app as Thelma re-entered the car. 'I need,' she said, 'an extra strong mint.'

He looked up, concerned. 'Oh dear,' he said. 'Hell's smells?'

She nodded. 'Cat wee,' she said. Even at two paces (hastily made four), the smell had slapped her roundly across the face. And yet the lady in her Jaeger skirt and lamb's wool cardie had looked perfectly respectable, the house from what she could see perfectly neat and tidy.

'I better do the next one,' he said, suppressing yet another cough. She shook her head. 'We have our system,' she said. 'You do the app; I do the drop. It's fine.' And the strange thing was . . . it was. Actually, she was rather enjoying herself. She wasn't exactly sure why. Partly the people who were in the main cheerful and grateful. (Cat Wee lady had given an especially warm smile.) And there was something about seeing the different houses, something about the glimpses of all those other lives – the bookcases, the TVs, the pictures on the wall – that gave a sense of a world beyond the sad dark one she seemed to have been living in just lately.

And there had been that . . . *sharing* with Teddy – that sense of working together on a common purpose. She couldn't remember the last time she'd felt such a feeling.

'Just the one more,' pronounced Teddy as she trotted back from a house on Dallamires Lane. The man who had answered the door had been almost scarily tattooed yet had greeted her with such a lovely smile. 'Then why don't we treat ourselves to a fish supper?'

Sitting in the car outside Northgate fisheries, Thelma said a quick prayer of thanks. For what she wasn't exactly sure, but she had been feeling low, and now she wasn't and sometimes that was enough. Sometimes it didn't do to look too closely into these things. Sometimes it's best just to think 'I'm happy' and leave it at that. Of course, there was still that unresolved upset with Pat, but tonight she was happy to let it drop. Tonight, she was content to sit in the car and look at the lights of HG4.

Almost idly she took the opportunity to examine the WAMMP app. It looked fairly straightforward: a list of addresses that somehow linked to the satnav, the addresses colour coded green for Whenever, amber for Tomorrow at the very least and red for Now, if not sooner. She flicked through the addresses; there seemed to be a lot in Thirsk.

Hang on . . .

Her thumb paused. There *was* a name she recognized, and an address. Michelle Stanley, who had no less than *three* parcels due her.

Interesting.

CHAPTER TWENTY-SIX

Laughter during dinner is followed by revelations, bitterness and a story of near-death.

'I said, lovey, you are the Grey Waif of Pickhill – a malnourished, chronically ill product of an uncaring society – you are not Billy Bloody Bunter!' Jamie took a mighty sip of wine from his glass – his Waterford crystal glass. 'CUT all the cheesy grins!'

No two ways about it, Jamie was on fine form. Even Rod – to whom amateur dramatics were as remote a concept as Hadron colliders – was laughing. As for Pat, midriff aching, she was again beginning to wish she'd had the foresight to wear one of her 'just in case' pads. Shaun, the fourth person at the table, didn't smile but continued looking moodily down at his plate.

'How's the Voice of the Present getting on?' she said. 'Has she started turning up?'

'Don't!' Jamie grimaced expressively as he topped her glass up. 'Voice of bloody *not* present! *Another* rehearsal missed! And I'm sorry but I don't care if Sheba the Cockerpoo is throwing up. Not my problem, missus! Honest to God, it'd have been easier going with my first idea of having both voices played by moi. I'm already having to be the voice of the past, one more won't make much difference.'

'Has the vicar been allowing you to put the heat on?' asked Pat.

'The Reverend Knitwear? Don't get me started on *her*!'

Pat could feel a laugh bubbling up again. 'What's she said now?' she said.

'Okay, I get that it's a church and one has to do churchy things, but she only ever gets three in the audience – four tops, at that midweek service. It's taking us a full twenty minutes plus to set all our stuff up. Just for once can't she do all her churchy stuff at the side somewhere? I said, "Look, darling, there's all this wonky veg underfoot, Lego bricks coming out of every orifice, I can't see what difference our set is going to make one way or another." Now—' He indicated the remains of the pheasant casserole in front of them. 'Any more for any more?'

Both Rod and Pat made 'it's lovely but I'm full gestures'. And indeed it had been lovely, the casserole seasoned to perfection, the potatoes crisply roasted, the broccoli and carrots exactly hitting that fine line between hardness and mush.

Jamie began stacking plates and dishes. 'The thing about the Rev,' he said, 'is that for all her "this is a community space, folks", I don't actually think she likes us being there. If she's not one hundred per cent in charge it's real "toys out of the pram" time . . .' He picked up the tray. 'I know I wouldn't like to get on the wrong side of her. Still, I'm used to being Mr Unpopular!' He smiled at Shaun and touched him lightly on the shoulder in a careless but caressing way.

Pat stole another glance at the man sitting across the table. Moody – that was the word that kept coming into her mind. Mr Moody. Unlike his sister, he reminded her of neither Mal nor Christine Stanley. He had a rather beaky nose, and thin lips that gave him a somewhat cruel, almost Roman-emperor look. Pale eyes that had a way of fastening themselves disconcertingly on you when you spoke. A rather thickening stomach but you could tell in the past he'd been what people term 'lean and mean'. Heathcliff, Pat decided. An ageing, rather gone-to-seed Heathcliff. He made no effort to help his husband with the dishes, rather shifted in his chair and stared at the taupe linen tablecloth.

'So how are your ticket sales doing?' asked Rod. Pat glanced across at her husband. At least he was making an effort, though she still felt annoyed about what he'd said in the car on the way over.

'A total nightmare, Rod.' Jamie's voice was grim as he stacked the Denby ware on a tray. There's only seventeen the first night and *ten* on the second. This is a *community play*. Like, "hello, community! Are you actually out there?"' So saying, he lifted the tray and exited the room, leaving the sudden hush of an empty stage.

'So,' said Rod cheerfully. 'Have you heard about this business with that waste incinerator by Baldersby?'

Shaun nodded. 'Not good,' he said. It wasn't that Shaun didn't speak, just that when he did, his answers were economical. Considered, not a word wasted. Without the prattling distractions of Jamie everything felt rather forced. Stilted and forced.

We're like three actors sitting on a stage who don't know their lines, Pat thought.

She looked round the dining room they were sitting in. Three actors on a very opulent stage. Because the house – Mallory Square – was gorgeous. The driving rain outside had only afforded the briefest view of a long, rather spartan two-storey building fronted by a bricked forecourt, but inside was an altogether different story. Every room she'd seen was gorgeously, expensively and tastefully furnished with soft sofas, glass tables and spindly chairs, all discreetly lit. Apparently somewhere there was even a newly fitted hot tub and sauna. And yet for all the obvious money, the house had a curiously sterile air. It was something Pat struggled to put her finger on, until it came to her all at once.

There was no clutter.

No car keys on the side, no empty Amazon packets under chairs, no books or opened bills or haphazardly left shoes anywhere. A stage set.

The only sign of anything remotely personal was a picture above the stone fireplace in the opulent living room. It was one of those enlarged photographs reproduced onto canvas. It showed Shaun and Jamie posed together, barefooted on a sheepskin rug. Shaun was clasping Jamie from behind and they were both laughing those natural, unforced laughs that expensive photographers are so gifted in capturing. The happy look on Jamie's face was so – Pat searched for the right word – so *vivid* that there was almost a heart-breaking quality about it.

'The thing is—' Rod's voice brought her back into the present moment '—a waste incinerator's something everyone needs but nobody wants.'

'True enough.' Shaun nodded.

Not for the first time Pat marvelled at her husband's ability to coax conversational waters from the toughest of stones. Shaun was definitely looking a bit more relaxed, although it had to be said, a thousand light years away from that laughing man on the sheepskin rug.

The buzz from her handbag sounded penetrating. Smiling apologetically, Pat stole a glance at her mobile phone. Surely not *another* text from Liz? That would make it six at least. As yet she'd not replied because she didn't give a stuff about whatever it was Tate Bishop had said or hadn't said – she didn't want to think of Liz or Thelma. Definitely not Thelma, not tonight. But the text wasn't from Liz, it was from Liam, saying: WHAT TIME ARE THE OAPS RETURNING? Was he okay?

Thankfully Rod, deep in conversation about waste incinerators, hadn't noticed.

'Just nipping to the you know where,' she said.

The downstairs cloakroom made her exclaim out loud. This wasn't a stage set, it was more of a shrine. A shrine to the theatre. Or rather Jamie's career in theatre. All over the lavender walls were framed programmes and posters, presumably of plays Jamie had been in. The Bush, the Donmar Warehouse, the Royal Exchange. And the photos, black and white photos showing Jamie – a younger, leaner Jamie – in a grubby vest, sitting on a beer keg staring moodily into space or staring earnestly into the eyes of a black girl who held him by the elbows. Jamie had barely talked at all about his acting career the other night but it was obviously important to him. Nevertheless, the display struck an odd note – if you were proud enough of something to create a shrine, why give over a toilet to express that admiration?

She texted Liam: 11.00 AT EARLIEST. YOU OK? Although his cough was improving she'd argued against him going back to Durham for a few more days. She remembered that tetchy exchange with Rod on the way over. All she'd done was say she'd need to ring him to remind him to take his cough medicine. Which wasn't fussing and certainly wasn't wrapping him up in cotton wool, as Rod had suggested. At that she'd relapsed into a frosty silence, speaking only in clipped monotones to navigate the way to Mallory Square.

There was another buzz from her phone. Not Liam, but Jamie. IN KITCHEN. GET YOURSELF IN HERE GIRLFRIEND and an emoji of a champagne bottle.

He was standing alone in the vast grey and steel space that didn't look as if any sort of meal had ever been prepared there. For a second, just a second, as she walked through the door, his face was set – blank, empty – and Pat found herself making a contrast between a person and their smiling counterpart on a sheepskin rug.

'Hey, girlfriend.' The smile and voice were snapped smartly back into place. 'Are they okay out there?'

'They're onto waste incinerators,' said Pat.

'Excellentay!' Jamie reached into the fridge and grabbed a bottle of prosecco by the neck, wielding it like a club. 'Let's you and me get this party started.'

Pat looked at the bottle cautiously. Really, she mustn't have anything approaching the amount she'd had to drink the other night. 'Is there anything I can do to help?' she said. 'With the meal?'

'It's all in hand,' said Jamie, wrestling with the cork. 'God bless Scarborough Fayre.' He nodded to a stack of cartons sitting by the recycling and Pat recognized the logo of the upmarket meal delivery service she and Rod very very occasionally used. No wonder the kitchen looked so clean.

Watching the mercury-coloured bubbles clamouring up the sides of a glass she suddenly said, 'Are you okay?'

'Why?'

'No reason,' said Pat. 'You just looked—' She stopped, unsure what words to say, how to express the feeling that here was an actor who for whatever reason was suddenly unsure of their lines.

'If you must know,' said Jamie, handing her a glass, 'I'm knackered. This blumin' play. God knows why I took it on; my agent went apeshit. He wanted me to go for a National Tour of *The Full Monty.*'

Pat thought of those black and white photos in the cloak-room. 'Why didn't you?' she said.

'Me and a load of ex-soap stars flashing our bits in Bradford, Bath and Stevenage?' He grimaced. 'I don't think so.'

'I was looking at all your photos in the other room,' she said. 'It's really impressive.'

'Was,' he said. 'Past tense.' He sighed. 'Now I'm lucky to get a three-line medic in *Emmerdale* and I'm directing some community play in back of Beyondsville. Which is going pear-shaped at a rate of knots.' He raised his glass. 'Cheers!' He gazed out at the black night visible through the rain-streaked window. 'You work and work at something and it's not working so you work harder . . . and there comes a time when you wonder what the hell you've been playing at.' His voice sounded small, curiously lost. Was he still talking about the play?

A ping from the microwave broke the moment.

'Eee bah gum,' said Jamie, affecting a thick accent. 'It seems t'Yorkshire tart and Crem Harrogate is reet ready.'

'I had a visitor,' said Pat. 'Michelle.'

'Oh?' His face was curiously guarded. 'What did she want?'

'She thinks she's being stalked. Or rather someone's looking in the house. And she thinks it might be Tate Bishop.'

Jamie's reaction took her by surprise. Instead of looking concerned or shocked or worried he merely rolled his eyes and shook his head. 'Right,' he said. '*Right*.' He took a thoughtful swig of his prosecco. 'What did you say to her?'

'I told her to tell the police,' she said. 'But I've been wondering if I shouldn't say something myself.'

'No.' His voice was sharp and sudden and insistent. 'No.'

'What about Shaun? Should we not at least be telling him?'

'No.' His voice was low now, low and bitter. 'I don't think his lordship will be interested.'

Pat looked at him. 'Jamie,' she asked, 'have you two had a row?' That would explain Shaun's moody silence.

Jamie paused, and looked again outside. He seemed to be making his mind up about something. Finally he turned to her. 'Sort of.' He sighed. 'It was stupid really . . . Shaun had been looking at my car – I'd been on at him to for weeks now. There was something up; the steering was dragging a bit. Anyway, finally he gets round to it this week and today I'm collecting the dinner, and driving down Sutton Bank, and suddenly *the brakes stopped working*.'

'*What?*' Pat's eyes were wide as she pictured the one-in-four hill with its hairpin bends.

'I swear to God, Pat, I'm stamping down on my brakes and fuck all's happening. And all I can think is, if the car crashes there's going to be fucking crème Harrogate everywhere.' He tried to laugh but failed.

Pat, thinking of Sutton Bank, didn't even try. 'So, what happened?'

'Fortunately God heard me screaming at the top of my voice and somehow – *somehow* – the bloody brakes kicked in just as I got to the bottom. I managed to get round the corner, park in that pull-in and phone him.'

'And Shaun came and got you?'

'Eventually. Gets the car into the garage and has a look at it himself.'

'And what was it?'

'Nothing. That's what he said.'

'He looked at it himself?' Pat frowned. This whole thing was feeling a bit odd.

'Made a big point of it. Wanted, I think, to show me how daft I'd been. The hysterical husband. But Pat, I swear to God – *I thought my time had come*.'

'Jamie!' She put her arm round him. He was, she noted, shaking.

'Now of course he's in a mood because he thinks I'm making a fuss over nothing. He can be just like his dad, I swear.'

Pat mentally winced; that was not a good comparison. 'Well it's all okay now,' she said.

237

He stared fixedly at the Le Creuset oven gloves. 'Pat, don't mention this will you?'

'I won't if you don't want me to.'

'And that other stuff with Meesh. Don't mention that. I'll speak to her.'

'If you're sure.'

He nodded. 'Honestly, Pat, I know this sounds awful but sometimes . . .' His voice dropped almost to a whisper. '*Sometimes I'm scared of him.*'

When they went back into the dining room, it was as if someone had flicked a switch on Jamie. Now he was all cheerful prattle, talking about the new hot tub and the steel and glass fittings, the only issue being it was like having a soak on the set of *Silent Witness.* A lot of the comments he made were addressed to Shaun – light, conversational hooks like 'd'you remember when?' and 'what was the name of that builder we used, babe?' – but these Shaun largely brushed off with polite, barely adequate responses. Bearing in mind what Jamie had been through that day, Pat found this rather insensitive.

'Okay then,' said Rod as the coffees were being poured. 'So how's about we see this famous hot tub then.'

'Rod,' Jamie stood up, 'I thought you'd never ask.'

'You go,' said Shaun with sudden energy. 'Let Pat and I drink our coffee.' And before Pat quite realized what was happening, she found herself on her own with Shaun. She looked at him with the beginnings of a panicky flutter: silence within a group of three people could be largely concealed, not so with two. But barely had the door closed than Shaun fixed her with those pale, unsettling eyes.

'So,' he said, 'you were looking round my dad's house.' All at once Pat sensed he'd been waiting for just such an opportunity to talk to her.

'My friend was,' she said, feeling somewhat on the spot.

'And you went with her,' he pressed.

'For moral support,' she said. He looked at her and nodded to himself as though he were mentally assessing her.

'But your friend isn't interested.'

'I don't know.' She and the prosecco were beginning to resent this interrogation. 'And if she isn't, it's hardly surprising after your sister rang her.'

'Meesh?' He looked at her in what seemed like genuine surprise. 'Saying what?'

Did he really not know?

'Warning her. *"Things are wrong with this house – bad things have happened in this house"* . . .'

He briefly shut his eyes, much like Jamie had when she'd told him about the stalking. '*Right,*' he said.

A sudden thought occurred to Pat. 'If my friend *was* interested in buying,' she said, 'I'm presuming that the house has been split between you and your sister and your dad's widow?'

Shaun gave a short laugh and took a mouthful of wine. 'Dad left everything to Terri,' he said. 'Every last little thing.' The way he said the words was cold and bitter, and she found herself remembering Jamie's words: *sometimes I'm scared of him* . . .

She looked at Shaun; he was staring off into some dark, remote place.

Finally, he spoke. 'Terri Matheson,' he said, 'was a conniving, manipulative bitch.'

Driving carefully through the curtains of rain, Rod said, 'Don't ask me to go there again.'

Pat looked at her watch – barely ten thirty, and yet when they'd come back from seeing the hot tub Rod had made it clear to her through frowns and nudges he wanted to go. After her awkward conversation with Shaun, Pat was only too happy to comply, yawning and brushing off Jamie's protestations and offers of nightcaps. The evening had not gone at all how she'd hoped and there'd not been a mention of Key West, but she realized she was actually quite glad for that.

She looked out at the driving winter rain; she couldn't escape the feeling she'd abandoned her friend somehow. But to what? Her mind again went over everything she'd seen and heard that night – Shaun's angry words about Terri, Jamie's haunted look, his strange reaction to what she'd said about Michelle, and that frightening tale about the car brakes – over and over, back and forth rhythmically, like the windscreen wipers that were barely keeping up with the downpouring rain.

All at once she realized she wanted very much to talk things through with Thelma and Liz. With a pang she envisaged their favourite table at the café, the round one in the corner. She sighed. That ship, she feared, had very much sailed.

As they drove into the yard, she was surprised to see lights on in the kitchen. As Rod stopped the car, the rain intensified, drumming on the roof. Coat over her head, she dashed into the house, bursting open the back door.

The two figures standing in the kitchen, arms round each other, sprung apart as if detonated.

'You said eleven,' said Liam, accusingly.

However it was not her son who had her attention but the man whom he'd been holding: Luke Atkinson.

CHAPTER TWENTY-SEVEN

A busier than normal day leads to two unplanned errands.

It wasn't until lunchtime on that Saturday that the crowds of customers scouring the racks and shelves of the charity shop began to thin. As fast as they could get new stock out on the shelves it had flown out – or at least the better-quality items had.

'People just haven't got the money, that's why we're so busy,' said Polly. 'We got our energy bill last week – nearly five hundred pounds, can you believe it.'

The door shut and for the first time that day the shop was free of customers.

'Right.' The deputy manager of the Hospice Charity Shop flicked back her long red hair and bent over a couple of black bags brought in earlier. In all the rush they'd had little chance to do more than stash them behind the counter. 'I better get these shifted,' she said, 'before She Who Must Be Obeyed goes off on one. What time is she in again?'

'She and Harriet are due at one thirty,' said Thelma, checking her watch.

'If it's all right with you I'll head off *before* Madame graces us with her presence,' said Polly, fumbling one of the bags. 'And I'll make a start on these. One thing I can't face is another pigging Post-it Note making some snarky comment. I'm sure she has this place wired for sound.' She scowled at the Artex ceiling as if seeking out some listening device.

The hostilities between the manager and her deputy had not abated – far from it. Indeed, things had reached a situation where a cold-war-style solution had been adopted, with the pair of them working different shifts so that never the twain shall meet. Verna, however, was not helping matters, having taken to leaving a series of Post-it Notes pointing out things she felt were not being done right – spiky comments about the state of the stock, the back kitchen and people's timekeeping in general. Polly had (rightly) taken these crisply worded missives to be aimed directly at her and had begun making a point of leaving bags on the side, mugs in the sink and turning up five or even ten minutes late for her shift. The other day she'd arrived at ten to two, a full twenty minutes late – a fact Thelma had not nearly heard the last of from Verna.

'Oh yuck!' Polly was bending over one of the bin bags. 'Cigarette smoke. Oh pooh, that's disgusting! This'll all have to go through the washer.'

Cigarette smoke? Left alone in the empty shop Thelma frowned. That rang a bell . . . But what bell, where? She sighed. Her mind felt as cluttered and disordered as the back room of the shop. So much had happened, event following event.

Teddy. At least there was a peace of sorts between them. An accord because yes, she did understand why he liked the delivery driving . . . But had that changed what she *thought* about his job? Him charging about in all weathers for hours at a time? That cough was obviously digging in for the long haul, the mild, damp not helping, and there was still the worst of the winter to come. 'Protect him, Father,' she said, making a mental note to pick up some more Benylin. 'Protect him, and thank you for delivering Liz . . .'

Liz . . . She thought of what Liz had told her about her meeting with Tate. She thought of her brave, worried friend with a pang of guilt. She knew why she'd gone – to try and patch things up with Pat – but even so, she shouldn't have gone to see him like that on her own. And Tate had been so angry towards Brid of all people. *Why*? And what had he meant by the words '*my conscience is clear*'? And then there was his antipathy towards Mal's family and his stalking of Michelle – what did he hope to achieve by that? If, of course, he *was* stalking her. She knew Michelle told lies, but Pat seemed convinced . . .

Pat.

It was two days now since their confrontation in the garden centre and she'd not heard from her at all. (Though, to be fair, she'd not contacted her either.) The three of them were supposed to be going to see *Village Voices* in a few days' time – would Pat even turn up? And her friend's interest in the supernatural . . . *Should* she have been so dogmatic about it? That vanishing charity shop? That trip to Boroughbridge? But she'd felt so very strongly that her friend was walking towards something she should be walking away from; she *couldn't* just stand by and say nothing.

She realized that her mind was taking her somewhere she very much did not want to go – that awful time all those years ago . . . *that darkness*. Suddenly her heart was bounding, her breath quickening . . . She needed to *do* something – anything. She cast around the shop. Those paperbacks – they needed sorting for a start. She pulled the pile towards her and glanced at the lurid cover of the one on top . . . and stopped. That book Liz had found on the waste ground all those days ago.

What was it she'd said? That it was *by the same author as one of the books left in Sunny View Lodge.* Thelma frowned thinking of that sad pile of books and all those other things huddled together in the living room. Terri Stanley's discarded shoes . . .

Again her eyes roamed around the shop, the teapots and the cruet sets, the cardigans and DVDs, the only common factor being that they were unwanted.

'*Bring light to my darkness,*' she said.

A disappearing charity shop. Standing there, surrounded by so much stuff – books and china and knitwear – disparate, disconnected items, the idea it could all just vanish seemed laughable. She sighed and resumed sorting through the paperbacks.

Father, if it be your will, give me guidance, she said to herself.

'That sea oh double-you!' Polly's indignant voice cut brutally into Thelma's musings. 'I SWEAR she has this place wired for sound!' She marched up to the counter waving a raspberry pink Post-it Note.

Thelma sighed, mentally kicking herself. In the interests of general peace and her sanity, she had got into the habit of intercepting Verna's missives, but today had been so busy the thought had gone right out of her mind.

The note was typical.

> Hi! I know it's busy busy but please can ALL
> staff ensure donations are stored appropriately and
> SAFELY. A little thought saves a lot of time
> and trouble! V

'She means me,' said Polly. 'But she can go do one. What she doesn't seem to get in that perm of hers is that this place wasn't built to store loads of stock like this. Really, the space isn't fit for purpose.'

Here Thelma agreed; she could just remember when these cramped rooms housed Marshalls Button Shop, where presumably the stock consisted of small boxes of buttons, not great stacks of bin bags. She always thought of this as 'the charity shop' – but really it was a collection of rooms used by the charity shop.

Her hands sorting the books stilled. *What did that make her think of?* Oh yes, Busby's – the once well-ordered store that was now a series of sad, empty rooms . . .

Polly was still in full flow. 'If you're listening in, Verna,' she said to the ceiling, 'I'm going to leave all these bags on the side. See how YOU like the stink of smoke.'

'I can do them if you want,' said Thelma.

'No, it's okay.' Polly's spleen seemed to have been vented – at least for now. 'I've put the first load in. But we're just desperately short of coat hangers.'

Thelma grimaced. 'I saw someone burning a load of them yesterday,' she said.

And stopped.

It was as if various switches clicked over in her mind . . . *Something Polly had just said* . . . and the books . . . the smoke . . . the coat hangers . . .

A charity shop . . . a charity shop with only men's clothes.

She frowned.

Could it be?

After her shift Thelma undertook two errands; neither of which were ones she'd had planned at the start of the day.

The first errand led her to a discreet cul-de-sac on the Romanby side of Northallerton.

Number 6 Rievaulx Gardens was a large 1930s bungalow, white stucco gables with shabby green paintwork. The colours put Thelma in mind of something to be found in a public park.

Saying a quick prayer, she walked up the path, parcels clutched in her hand, giving herself no time to change her mind. Exactly what she'd say to Michelle beyond 'here's your parcels' she wasn't exactly sure. This was one of those occasions when she'd open her mouth and pray the words be put there. She hoped Teddy would forgive her for removing them from the stack in the study, and that it didn't throw his system into disarray too much. Had it been, she mused, divine providence that three WAMMP parcels for Michelle Stanley had been there in tomorrow's pile, or was it rather that there were parcels for the woman almost every day?

The bell didn't seem to work, so she knocked on the door. No response. She knocked again, feeling that rush of relief mixed with disappointment when an important but dreaded task is suddenly removed. But how to find out what she wanted to know now?

She made her way to one of the front bay windows. What was it Michelle had said to Pat? She'd looked out from the front window and seen the man in the street. She turned. Sure enough there was the road visible, but only just between two laurel bushes. You'd have to be right up at the window to see it. She looked at the window itself. It was obscured by nets – rather grubby nets, it had to be said. One was slightly tucked back, affording a triangle of vision into the room. Thelma peered in.

Her first fleeting thought was that she must have made some mistake and was looking in the garage – but no, there were picture rails and pictures on the wall. *Just* visible on the wall. For the room was rammed. Boxes and crates were packed and stacked everywhere – on the sides, on chairs, in great sullen piles – dominating and obscuring what furnishings there were. An exercise bike was hung liberally with dresses and tops, and watching disdainfully over everything was a dressmaker's dummy. It was impossible to tell whether this was a bedroom, living room or study. And it wasn't just the crates – round them were ranged bulging bags for life, crammed bin bags and other things, piled right up to the front window.

Thelma found herself remembering Jean Montgomery at church – how after her stroke the succession of visitors bearing casseroles and cakes all had the same tale to tell: a house crammed beyond habitation and even sanitation. But any suggestion of clearance was met with plaintive cries of 'but it's all going on eBay!'

'Can I help you, love?' The voice was both challenging and authoritative. Turning, Thelma saw standing by the laurels that perennial friend of investigators: the inquisitive neighbour.

'Are you from the council?' The man was young – couldn't have been more than thirty-five – yet there was an aggression and frustration about him.

'No,' she said. 'I was just delivering these parcels.' She held up the two WAMMP packages.

The man sighed in disgust. 'Why am I not surprised?' he said. 'You better leave them in the porch; every other bugger does.'

'If you don't mind me asking,' said Thelma, 'why did you think I might be from the council?'

'The state of this place!' He grimaced at the green and white bungalow as though pointing out the glaringly obvious. 'You should see inside – it's disgusting. Every room. And the stink . . . Not that it's any of my business how she chooses to live, but when it comes to *rats*—'

'Rats?' Thelma took a hasty step away from the house.

He nodded. 'It's only a matter of time before they come over to us. Parcels left with us all hours of the day and night, and then she's blocking the road with some van. There's not the room to double park, I told her.' He shook his head. 'Three times I've complained to the council. It's a complete joke.'

'I hope you get it sorted,' said Thelma. With twin prayers, one of thanks for what she'd found out and one for protection against vermin, she gingerly opened the porch and left the WAMMP parcels on top of the three Amazon packets already there.

'Professor Jonathan Sutherland from Mid-Florida University,' said Marguerite promptly and proudly.

'How interesting,' said Thelma. 'And he sent you this paper out of the blue? Having read your post on WhatsApp?'

'Facebook,' corrected Marguerite. 'The Yorkshire Paranormals.'

'And this professor, he knew of other instances?'

'It's a common phenomenon apparently,' said Marguerite. 'There's a man in Louisiana who had a vision of an Orange Plantation, and that prompted him to run for senator.'

'Goodness,' said Thelma.

Marguerite smiled. 'He wants to write a paper about me,' she said shyly, as if confiding some great secret. She was looking very upbeat today, almost . . . glowing.

'You seem very well,' Thelma observed.

'How clever of you to notice.' Marguerite smiled as if Thelma had just solved a particularly knotty crossword clue. 'There *is* a reason. But my lips are sealed.' She smiled again, looking like a plump version of the *Mona Lisa*.

Thelma wanted to say, *Is it a man?* but of course she didn't. Besides, Marguerite's shining eyes and the copper highlights glinting in her hair said it for her. It recalled to Thelma those febrile days all those years ago when love and deception had bloomed by the photocopier. Who could it be? Hardly likely to be Gary back on the scene. Maybe someone from the

Yorkshire Paranormals? But she wasn't here to talk about Marguerite's love life.

'It sounds so vivid, this vision you had. I keep on thinking about it,' she said. 'You say this clock you saw was ticking?'

Marguerite nodded vigorously. 'A really powerful tick,' she said.

'And can I ask,' said Thelma, 'this tick . . . *did it come from the clock?*'

Marguerite positively beamed. 'How clever of you,' she said. 'No, it came from all round me – like tinnitus – as it would, coming directly from my subconscious.'

Thelma nodded. 'And you say there were books?'

'Stacks of them. That represents wisdom, according to Doctor Sutherland.'

'I wonder,' said Thelma, 'did any of them look like this?' She showed Marguerite a picture on her phone – the cover of *SS Vengeance* – and Marguerite looked for the first time, uncertain. 'I don't know,' she said. 'I don't see how it can be because I was being afforded a vision – a premonition of change – and sure enough . . .' She smiled, confident and serene once more. 'Sure enough, things have changed!'

Sitting in the car outside Marguerite's flat, Thelma's mind was racing. Where before it had been tired and sluggish, now it was sharp and active, and her pen was barely able to keep pace with it as she scribbled words in her green teacher's notebook, squinting in the dim glare of the streetlights on Malpas Road.

Charity shop.

Busby's.

Smoke. Sound.

Paperback books.

A van.

Coat hangers.

She nodded, satisfied. Finally, things were fitting together, like the elements of a sudoku. There were just a few components missing.

Past and present — both the same?

How did *that* fit in?

CHAPTER TWENTY-EIGHT

Uncanny things are found in two deserted buildings.

'It's official, folks!' Sarah Unwin on the Radio York Sunday teatime show sounded gleefully chirpy. 'It is officially the mildest January for seventeen years! Climate change in action! What are *your* experiences of this fog? Are you missing the snow? Give us a call!'

'Piss off,' said Pat. She was squatting on her haunches by Larson's basket, looking down at him. Larson yawned and looked uninterestedly away. He'd barely touched his evening meal of minced morsels, which was unheard of. 'What's up, boy?' she said. He half-heartedly licked her hand and yawned again. It wasn't that he looked *ill*, just . . . off. She gave the top of his head a rub and stood up; if he was still looking peaky in the morning, she'd give the vet's a ring. Which was always a bit of a trial these days, ever since Jim Dudman had retired and the practice had been absorbed by some large outfit based in Richmond. Ages on hold to the most irritating muzak possible, punctuated regularly by claims that 'your call *is* important to us', and then some impossibly young-sounding person firing off questions at you in an alarmingly efficient manner. Not at all the same as Jim Dudman.

Sighing, she returned to the kitchen table and the iPad with its offending Amazon page. The words carolled out at her: *TravelEeze Inflatable! Travel with ease!* NEXT DAY DELIVERY! The inflatable cushion looked like some pale pink bloated organ.

She pressed 'order' feeling as if she was ordering her own dotage. Still, at least Rod knew what he wanted for his birthday; she herself had no idea. *Not* a travel cushion. She took out her phone and messaged Jamie. THE DEED IS DONE, she typed, adding a screaming-face emoji.

After a second the message came back: YOU GO GIRL! And an emoji of a champagne glass.

HOW ARE YOU? she typed back. After the worries he'd shared on Friday it seemed such an inadequate question.

The answer flashed up almost instantaneously. REHEARSAL – and a grim-faced emoji. N E JOY WITH LIAM?

Pat sighed as she messaged back: STILL IN HIS ROOM. There wasn't an emoji for a crap mother, so she sent another screaming one.

Involuntarily she raised her eyes to the ceiling. No coughing – that was something. And for the umpteenth weary time her mind trudged back to that scene the night before last when they'd arrived home. Though 'scene' wasn't exactly the right word to adequately describe the awkward ninety seconds that had transpired between herself and Rod entering the house and Luke Atkinson leaving it. Certainly, it had been nothing like the countless mental encounters she had had over the past couple of years where she'd told Luke calmly, cuttingly and coldly exactly what she thought of the way he'd treated her son. She'd said something like 'oh', Liam had said something like 'Luke's just off', and Rod had said words to the effect of 'watch the corner at the bottom of the hill, as it seemed to be flooding'.

And that had been it.

Afterwards, however, there'd been plenty said, though unfortunately shock and prosecco had combined to make most of her comments come flopping out as soggy clichés. What was going on? What was Luke Atkinson doing here? Had Liam forgotten the way that weasel had treated him? All these comments Liam had effortlessly (and soberly) fielded with calm, sardonic rebuffs. Luke was having relationship problems, problems he'd wanted to talk through with a friend. Which was what Liam was – a friend, nothing more. Luke had been seeing someone who was in the process of splitting up with his partner, and the partner's ex was having trouble moving on even though the relationship had run its course.

The other day there'd been a scene – a confrontation – and Luke had naturally been upset and wanting to talk. Pat had made some comment along the lines of how the relationship's course had more likely been cut short because of Luke Atkinson – at which point Liam had got angry and said if he could let bygones be bygones, surely his mother could do the same?

'What about Bern?' she'd said.

'What about him?' He looked at her, his face suddenly sad. 'As you'd say, Mother, that ship has probably sailed.'

'Probably? What does that mean? Shouldn't you ask him?'

'Okay, I'd say being found in the arms of someone else would up "probably" to "definitely".'

The news had come as a shock comparable to the shock of finding Luke Atkinson sitting at her kitchen table. *Bern?* In the arms of someone else? She felt almost foolish, realizing that in spite of never meeting him she'd set him up in her mind as someone special. Someone worthy of her precious, fragile youngest son's affection.

She wasn't helped in any of this by Rod who had quietly supported Liam and counselled everyone to Let It Drop and

Sleep On It. This course of action, was, she was sure partly motivated by the fact he wanted to catch up with the snooker highlights. 'Don't you care about our son?' she'd fired at him when he at last came to bed. Rod had sighed, told her they'd solve nothing at this hour and (again) that they should sleep on it. Which was all very well for him, off in a raspy slumber virtually the second his head hit the pillow.

Well, now she *had* slept on it (or more accurately *hadn't* slept on it) and a day later she was still in a state of turmoil. She desperately wanted to take Liam's words at face value, but how could she allow herself the potentially disastrous luxury of believing that weasel Luke Atkinson was involved with someone else when she'd found him in her own kitchen?

With a burst of Gloria Gaynor her phone vibrated into life. Jamie? Wasn't he in rehearsals?

'Everything okay?' she asked. 'Have they all walked out on you?'

'The rehearsal's over,' he said. 'Thank God.' The words were flippant, but his voice was distracted, uneasy. What was wrong?

'What is it?' she said.

'I'm probably completely mad. I'm sitting outside Sunny View Lodge. I was driving past on the way back from rehearsals . . . *and there's a light on.*'

'Perhaps someone left one on?' she said. 'Maybe there's been a viewing?'

'On a Sunday?' he said. 'Anyway, it just looks . . . I don't know . . . *weird* somehow.'

She shut the iPad. 'Do you want me to come over and have a look with you?' she said. 'I can be there in fifteen minutes.'

As the twilight deepened, the mussel-blue Corsair turned off Carlton Road and nosed its way gingerly down the cinder track adjacent to the station, the headlights' illumination making great floodlit arcs of the curtains of falling smoky drizzle. Thelma parked the car near the derelict lock-ups and turned off the engine and headlights, allowing herself a few moments to adjust to the gloom. Despite the lights from the station and the backs of the houses, it was very very dark. How she wished she'd thought to bring her hefty, rubberised torch!

The sudden rap on the window, from the figure that had materialized out of the murk, made her squeak with fright, hand instinctively clutching the rape alarm in her left pocket. 'It's me,' said Liz through the glass.

Thelma opened the car door. 'I said I'd ring you when I got here,' she said testily.

'I wasn't having you waiting in the dark,' said Liz adamantly.

Thelma felt a sudden and uncharacteristic impulse to hug her friend. 'It's very good of you to turn up on such a miserable night,' she said, putting up her umbrella. 'And of course, this may all be a colossal waste of time.'

'Why did we have to come at this time?' asked Liz.

'Because,' said Thelma, 'this is the same time that Marguerite saw what she saw. Or what she didn't see.' Car locked, she scanned round the darkness.

'I bobbed by the allotment on my way here,' said Liz, turning on a torch just like the one Thelma wished she'd brought. 'I thought we might need this.' As they began picking their way across the puddles she said, 'What is all this about anyway?'

'I've had an idea,' said Thelma. 'I want to try and see things as Marguerite saw them.'

'You'll have a job,' said Liz. 'There's nothing there.' Thelma didn't reply, just turned her footsteps towards the three derelict lock-ups.

'I thought we decided those were out,' said Liz, trotting after her. 'All the windows are covered and Marguerite said she saw light shining from a *window*, remember?'

'Exactly,' said Thelma, not slowing her pace. In the light of the torch her friend's face looked strange – was it the half-light or were her eyes actually half closed?

'Watch out where you're going,' she said.

'It was foggy that night,' said Thelma, 'so Marguerite would have seen less than we can see now.'

Liz sighed and followed, knowing there was no point in asking her friend any more at this point. Arriving at the low buildings Thelma let the torch play across the fronts, plastered with posters. The light illuminated a bright jumble of images and words. *The Grand Europa animal-friendly circus . . . A charity auction in Masham Institute . . . Steeleye Span playing at the Winter Spa Gardens, Ripon.* Liz frowned and looked closer – there was something about the posters that struck her as odd.

Thelma, meanwhile, was trying the door. 'Still padlocked,' she said.

'Here.' Liz turned away from the posters 'Hold the torch.' She produced something from her pocket and began working on the lock. 'This might not work,' she said warningly, but even as she spoke the lock clicked and snapped open.

'A lock pick?' asked Thelma.

'Paper clip,' said Liz. 'I usually carry one about with me, for the shed door at the allotment.'

'Well done,' said Thelma and Liz felt a little lantern glow of pride, quickly followed by a thrill of apprehension as the reality of entering an unlit lock-up on a rainy night hit home. She pushed opened the door carefully, fully expecting to find the figure of Tate Bishop lounging against the doorframe, but all they found was the cold waft of an empty building. Thelma shone the torch around, showing a bare room, about nine foot square with a single door on the back wall. She sniffed and grimaced. 'Can you smell something?' she said. The two ladies stood, sniffing the air like bloodhounds.

'Smoke,' pronounced Liz. 'Very faintly. But I'm almost sure that's smoke. Cigar smoke?'

But Thelma was not listening. She was standing in the middle of the space, eyes half closed and . . . was she muttering to herself?

Liz wanted to feel irritated but there was definitely something *odd* about her friend, almost as if she were *possessed* . . . No sooner had the disturbing thought come, than she impatiently stamped it down. What was it Pat would say? *Get a grip!* Think of something practical . . . The posters – what was it she'd noticed? She returned outside and again shone her torch over the bright patchwork of images on the three frontages. On two of them the posters were stuck directly onto the glass, but on the third – the unit they were in – they were stuck on a wooden board that neatly covered the windows.

She looked closer. The board looked to have been recently fixed and the screwheads glinted silver in the torch light. Excitedly she hurried back inside to tell Thelma – but the room was empty. 'Thelma?' she called uncertainly. There was no reply, and for a moment everything was still and dark. Then the back door opened . . . A dark shape appeared in the doorway, semi-lit from below by the torch.

'*Why did you do it?*' The voice was harsh, unearthly.

Liz screamed.

CHAPTER TWENTY-NINE

Uncanny experiences are had in two deserted buildings.

A similar waft of cold, stale air greeted Jamie and Pat as he unlocked the side door to Sunny View Lodge. Neither of them had thought to bring torches so they had to navigate their way through the empty house by the wan lights from their phones, which cast unnerving shadows. The plaster recesses resembled grotesque death heads in the wavering beams.

'God, what a morgue,' said Jamie. 'It's no wonder old Mally boy pitched himself down the stairs. I'd have done the same meself if I had to live here.'

Pat smiled uneasily. Jokes of this sort took on quite a different complexion when made in a dark, empty house. Dark apart from that faint, ethereal flicker they'd seen coming from one of the upstairs windows. At the foot of the stairs, she looked up uneasily at the looming frame of shadows cast by the open treads. The black outline of the iron clock looked grim and sinister in the light from Jamie's phone.

'What if there's someone up there?' she said. She realized she was clutching Jamie's arm and had no intention of letting it go.

'That, girlfriend, is what we're going to find out,' said Jamie.

He seemed almost to be enjoying himself. No, enjoyment wasn't the right word; it was as if he was relishing the situation they found themselves in, in a way that felt grim, almost feverish.

'I know,' said Pat. 'But I mean, it could be anyone – drug addicts or burglars . . .' The words faltered as she realized that, actually, she could think of no category of person who'd realistically be in an unheated, unpowered, empty house for the best part of two hours. 'Maybe,' she said, 'we better call the police?'

Jamie looked at her, a grin of mischief forming on his face. 'Good plan.' Suddenly he shouted up the stairs, 'This is the police. We know you're up there, so come down and stop playing silly beggars.' His voice was laconic, world-weary – unrecognizable and totally convincing.

'That was good,' Pat whispered. He grinned again.

'*Hollyoaks*. I was an unscrupulous constable,' he whispered. 'For my sins.' He shone his phone up the stairs again. 'Okay,' he said in the same laconic voice, 'we know you're up there.'

Pat stared nervously up at the gloom, fully expecting a pale, frightened face to appear. But there was nothing.

'Sod this for a game of soldiers,' said Jamie. 'Come on.' He started up the stairs and Pat timidly followed him, their feet making an echoing clamour in the dark. At the top Jamie covered the beam from his torch and Pat did the same, feeling a static crackle of fear as a faint glow became apparent from one of the doorways, the one on their left – the master bedroom with the mirrored doors.

Carefully Jamie pushed open the door, revealing what was within.

Pat clutched his arm, an instinctive scream lodging in her throat.

* * *

'I'm fine,' said Liz, though her voice was still shaky. 'Really, I am. You just gave me a bit of a fright.'

'I'm so sorry,' said Thelma 'I just—'

'—wanted to see how it was for Marguerite,' said Liz. 'You said. Anyway, come and look at these posters.'

Outside Thelma looked closely at the screwheads. 'So, someone could have removed this board without disturbing the posters, and put it back when they were done,' she said. Stepping back, she let her gaze rove over the posters. 'Have you noticed what the posters are saying?'

'All different things,' said Liz. 'Are Steeleye Span still even going?'

'The *dates*,' said Thelma. 'Look at the *dates*.'

Frowning, Liz peered closer. 'October 29th, November 4th, October 30th . . . And?' she said.

'*They all fall within a one week period*: October 29th to November 4th.'

Liz looked blank. 'So?' she said.

'Posters are usually slapped up a few at a time,' explained Thelma. 'I know that from when I was doing publicity for the college players. A couple of posters here, a couple there – all put up at different times. But these appear to have all been put up *at the same time*. And fairly recently, judging by their condition.'

'There's something else,' said Liz. 'Why put posters up here in the first place? It's not as though anyone would see them, apart from the odd dog walker.'

Thelma nodded and turned to go back inside. 'So that's the window Marguerite claimed she saw the light through,' she said. 'Now we need the ticking clock.'

Inside she shone the torch at the walls. 'Here,' she said.

'What?' Liz joined her and stared. Thelma's gloved hand pointed out a series of small holes.

'If you wanted to rig up speakers for sound,' she said, 'you need those pin things to hold the wires in place.'

'The ticking clock,' said Liz grimly.

By unspoken consent they walked through the door at the back to a smaller room, which was empty apart from another door in the back wall.

'It's open,' said Liz, trying it. 'We needn't have picked the lock out front.'

Thelma looked outside, shining the torch up and down.

'What's there?' asked Liz.

'A track,' said Thelma. 'Big enough for a car. Or even a van.'

'There were vans at Flaxby Hall,' said Liz. 'Three of them just parked up.' She glanced apprehensively over her shoulder, again imagining Tate Bishop materializing out of the gloom. 'Let's not linger here too long.'

Thelma was still looking at the track. 'I'm sure there's tyre tracks,' she said. 'Looking at it, I think this track might run up to Carlton Road.' They stepped back inside and she shut the door and shone the torch round the empty room. Here was a sink that looked long disused, and again, nothing. Except . . .

'On the floor – there in the corner,' said Liz, her voice sharp. 'Shine the torch there.'

In the corner was a rectangle. It was brightly coloured in yellow, red and blue with some sort of picture of a man sitting on a throne.

'Is it a postcard?' asked Liz.

'No,' said Thelma, 'it's not. *It's a tarot card.*'

It was the strangest thing. On the floor before the vast mirrored door a single candle was dancing, nearly out, in a vast sticky pool of wax that was spreading across a piece of old wood.

'Oh my God,' said Jamie slowly. 'This is seriously weird shit – this is Christine's old room.' His voice was hushed, almost shocked.

Pat's voice, however, was not. 'Only,' she said, 'this *wasn't* Christine's room.'

Jamie frowned at her. 'Of course, it was,' he said. 'It's the master bedroom. Where Mal and Christine slept.'

'It might have been once,' she said, 'but latterly Christine slept in another room altogether. That's where I saw her the night of the party. The one across the hall with the tiger wallpaper.'

'Okay,' said Jamie. 'Okay, but how do you know the room you saw her in was *her* room.'

'Trust me,' said Pat. 'If there's one thing a woman recognizes, it's another woman's bedroom.'

'Then I don't get it,' said Jamie, staring transfixed at the candle. 'What's going on?' He looked closer, made an exclamation under his breath and bent down, picking up what Pat had taken to be a patch of shadow. 'What have you got there?' she said.

Wordlessly he held it up.

'A hat?' she said. 'A beanie hat?'

'Not just any hat.' Jamie stretched the object, revealing a Nike logo. 'I'm sure this belongs to Luke Atkinson.'

Thelma dropped Liz off outside her door. After getting out of the car Liz turned and looked back at her friend. The short journey back from the waste ground had been spent in an abstracted silence Liz knew better than to break.

Thelma looked at her steadily. 'Thank you,' she said, 'for coming with me. I'm so very sorry if I scared you.'

'You think you know what's been happening,' said Liz.

Thelma nodded, but she looked troubled. 'I think I know the "*what*",' she said. 'But the "who" I'm still not *exactly* sure of. And as to the "why", I really have no idea – and without that the whole thing's impossible.' She shook her head, almost crossly, as if trying to clear it.

'You can ring me,' said Liz. 'Or we'll talk at *Village Voices*.'

'Have you heard from Pat?' asked Thelma.

Liz frowned. 'We're meant to be meeting her and Rod there, but she's not replying to any of my messages.'

She watched as the mussel-blue Corsair drove up the road, and then walked up her pathway; it really was terribly clammy and damp. She knew Derek was out seeing his auntie, so she might throw caution to the wind and knock the thermostat onto twenty-five for half an hour while she thawed out.

But she was not alone. To her surprise and faint alarm, the kitchen light was on, and she remembered turning it off. Derek was back already?

But it was not Derek.

Instead it was Tim who was sitting at the kitchen table, head supported by one hand, the other hand splayed out on the laminated surface.

'Lovey,' she said, 'whatever is the matter?'

'Hello,' he said without looking at her. His voice was weary beyond utterance, as though even saying that one word had cost him an effort barely worth making.

She was about to say more, ask again what was wrong, when she stopped herself. There was something puzzlingly *familiar* about his whole stance, his whole aura – the voice, the body language, the hopelessness. Something she'd seen in Tate Bishop in his sad, denuded office in that derelict hotel.

Grief.

'Tim,' she said tentatively, fearfully. 'Tim, love, Rochelle . . . is she *dead*?'

CHAPTER THIRTY

The contents of shoeboxes are bemoaned and out of darkness emerges a story of betrayal.

In her handbag Pat's phone buzzed; taking it out she saw it was a message from Jamie: HEY! HOW R U, GHOSTBUSTER? and an emoji of a sheeted phantom. She looked at the message for a long, nervous moment, thumbs poised, though she'd no idea what she was going to say; there was no emoji that could even begin to describe the thoughts that had been flitting round her mind. She was about to settle on a thumbs up, when she stopped. Hadn't she heard somewhere that these days people could tell where messages had been sent from? She put the phone back in her bag; she very much *didn't* want Jamie to know where she was.

She took a swift guilty glance round the bar of Swainby Golf Club, round the tables, stacks of chairs and intermittent trophy cabinets, colder and more sterile than it had appeared on the website at four a.m. that morning. It had been one of those nights when everything crashing and barging round her mind had transmuted into a series of uneasy dreams: Marguerite and Michelle Stanley looking out of her kitchen window to where Shaun was working under the bonnet of the Yeti, helped by the Reverend Mare ... only the pair of them were dressed as ghosts ... Around three a.m. the thoughts had abruptly juddered into a sort of order, falling into place with what she thought must have been an audible click, leaving her wide awake and wondering how to find out more.

Her phone buzzed again, and again. She gave a fearful look round the bar but the only signs of life this Monday morning were two staff spraying and wiping tables. Nervously she glanced at her phone, but it was only Amazon telling her that Rod's TravelEeze inflatable cushion was Out For Delivery. She turned off her phone and put it back in her bag.

'So, I turns around and I tells her straight.' One of the cleaners was in the middle of some tale. 'I says, you cannot go on like this.' She was making whatever drama it was sound simple and straightforward, and Pat was half-tempted to applaud. She felt a sudden impulse to go up to her and ask her: what should *I* do? Should I too be telling someone straight – and if so, who? My new friend? Or my son? Or this Bern who cheated on him? Or indeed the person Liam was showing every sign of going back to, even though they'd betrayed him in quite a different way? And who it seemed was lighting candles in the bedroom of an empty house? She grimly thinned her lips. Luke Atkinson was causing trouble yet again if she wasn't mistaken.

But that's just it – you don't know exactly what's going on. It was almost as if Thelma was sitting right there next to her. *He's a sensible lad, your Liam.* And there was Liz. Once again Pat felt that she wanted nothing so much as to be sitting with the two of them at the round table in the corner at the garden centre.

'It's Mrs Rod, isn't it? Good God, woman! How the devil are you?' The stocky man who hailed her from the doorway was laden down with four bags for life, handles bunched in each hand.

'Let me help you,' said Pat, darting forward.

'I'll not say no,' said the man cheerfully. 'Never let it be said that women don't have their uses!' This comment he punctuated with a loud laugh. With a familiar surge of irritation, Pat took two of the bags from him. Just how old was Roy Horton these days? He looked just the same as when she'd last seen him and Joan (whom he referred to as the GLW – Good Lady Wife). That had been at some golfing do four or five years ago, but then, the Roy Hortons of this world never seemed to age, seemingly stuck at a cheerful sixty-something for at least two decades.

'Come through to my office, Mrs Rod,' he said, setting off behind the bar. Pat followed. Roy was someone she only knew superficially through the fact Rod had once done some work for him. But when she'd been googling Swainby Golf Club in the wee small hours of that morning, his name had come up as the contact person for the Foodbank appeal the golf club was masterminding. It seemed to Pat almost like some sort of sign – and if not a sign, potentially an answer to her question of how to find out more about certain golf course clientele.

'How's Rod doing?' he said, simultaneously fumbling for his keys whilst attempting to prevent one of the bags spilling its contents. 'I heard he had a bit of a tussle with something nasty down below.'

Pat adroitly saved the bag. 'He's fine,' she said pleasantly. 'Thanks for asking.' If the man meant testicular cancer, why not come out and say it?

She followed him into a small room, which was obviously some sort of store, stacked as it was with boxes of crisps and those rolls of blue wiping paper. 'I'd say "grab a pew",' he said, setting down his load, 'but as you can see, we're somewhat inundated.' And indeed, every surface, every chair, table and even the floor were stacked high with packets of cornflakes and tinned food.

'Here's my contribution,' said Pat, proffering her bag, picked up from Booths on her way over.

'Bless you, my dear,' he said. 'Very much appreciated.' Somewhat to Pat's discomfort he took tins out of her bag, looking at them critically. 'I'm glad to see you've in no way stinted,' he added.

Pat frowned. Wordlessly Roy held up a couple of tins bearing labels saying 'Starbuyz', 'KostCutter' and then gestured to others bearing Polish writing she couldn't read.

'Right,' she said uncertainly.

'The word you're looking for,' said Roy, 'is cheap. Cheap and nasty.' He produced a tin of something pronouncing itself to be Starbuyz Bangers and Beans. 'This,' he continued, 'I happen to know was donated by someone who's in the process of having a million-plus-pound swimming pool added onto his already palatial pad near Richmond.'

Pat tutted sympathetically, inwardly thankful that all the contents of her box were from Booths. 'Still,' she said, 'you're doing a terrific job.'

'Are we?' Roy frowned. 'At the end of the day, we're a golf club, not a charity. I spoke out against it, but some of the younger members . . .' He shook his head. 'There was even some crazy talk of us being a designated warm space. But I spoke out.' He shook his head. 'You see the thing with all this—' he waved an airy hand at the assembled tins '—is that it doesn't do people favours, not in the long run.'

'Surely it helps though?' said Pat.

Roy shook his head eagerly. 'That's just it – *it doesn't*. All it does is make people reliant on handouts.'

'I don't think people choose to go to a foodbank,' said Pat, feeling a twitch of anger growing in her jaw. But Roy wasn't listening, he was looking at a tin labelled '*Wiejska zabawa*'.

'So what's that when it's at home?' he said.

267

He seemed set to go through the contents of each and every bag, so Pat decided it was high time to get onto the matter in hand. 'It's so nice being back here,' she said brightly. 'I'd forgotten how lovely the golf club was; it must be two or three years since we were last here. I was talking to someone the other day and she told me her sister got married here.'

'We do have a fair few splicings,' said Roy. 'Getting to be quite a thing.'

'This was actually rather a sad story,' said Pat. 'They got married back in April, then a couple months ago he died. And then would you believe, the other week *she* died in a car crash!'

'Ah,' said Roy. 'Would you be referring to Mal Stanley by any chance?'

'That's them,' said Pat. 'It all sounds so tragic.'

'Not so much tragic as turbulent,' said Roy knowingly. 'But then, I don't do gossip; I leave all that to the GLW. But yes, the Stanleys were always a rather, shall we say . . . colourful addition to our membership. Mal and his first wife were forever sounding off at each other for the world and his wife to see.'

Come back and talk to me! The reedy voice sounded petulant in her memory. Yes, thought Pat, she could imagine a public barney or two. 'I heard things weren't always smooth,' she said.

'As I say,' said Roy. 'I don't do gossip. But Mal was someone who had what the GLW would term a severe case of "Not-keeping-it-in-his-pants-itis". So, when he turns up sporting, shall we say, a younger model, no one was very surprised. Then of course there was the son.'

'Shaun?' said Pat. 'I met him.'

'Shaun Stanley,' said Roy, 'is what's popularly known as a Chip Off the Old Block.' He began emptying the bags for life of their contents as Pat looked on, wondering in what ways exactly Shaun took after his father. 'He worked behind the bar here, which lasted all of ten minutes, until he got into a rather heated disagreement with a customer, which he chose to resolve with two fists and a beer bottle. All quite nasty, but I gather his father – or rather his father's money – sorted that one. And then there was some lad he was at school with – some private establishment over Harrogate way. '

'What happened there?' asked Pat.

'Another spot of bother. Only the lad came off rather the worse for wear. Lost the sight of one eye so the story goes.' Pat frowned, remembering those pale eyes and intense stare, Jamie's voice saying '*sometimes I'm scared of him*'.

'And of course, there was the second Mrs Stanley.' Roy began arranging sets of gloves and mittens on the table.

'I gather she was a bit younger than him,' said Pat. Roy nodded, a serious, reflective look in his eyes. 'What was she like?' she asked.

Roy paused a moment before answering. Suddenly and uncharacteristically, he looked rather wistful. 'Were you to ask the GLW, she would say Terri was the sort of person more usually found *behind* the bar not in front.'

'But you wouldn't?' she said.

'I always felt rather sorry for the lass,' said Roy. 'Admittedly, I was in something of a minority, especially among our lady members. No two ways about it, she had her hands full with Mal Stanley, who by this time wasn't in the best of health.' He sighed. 'I remember their wedding. She looked so bonny in this peachy-coloured dress. I remember thinking then, *I wonder if you know what you're taking on*. Of course, when he died people said all the usual gubbins, but she was very cut up about it. Came here wanting to talk about setting something up in his name – a trophy or something. She was all over the place, poor lass.'

'He fell down the stairs, didn't he?' said Pat.

Roy nodded. 'Bless her heart, she kept going on and on

about how she should never have left him that day. I don't care what people said about her, I know a broken heart when I see it.'

'So, what *did* people say?' asked Pat.

'She married him for his money, that's all she was interested in, didn't look after him properly, et cetera et cetera. And of course, Mal's children weren't best pleased at being cut out of the will. There was that scene at the wake here; she didn't deserve that.'

'Scene?' said Pat.

'The lass was understandably upset. She's just buried her husband. And there's Mal's daughter doing a fair Medusa impression with her evil eye and whatnot – and then the other one comes up and has a right go at her. Personally, I don't blame her for throwing her drink in his face.'

'Terri threw her drink over *Shaun*?' said Pat.

'No, not Shaun. He didn't even put in an appearance. T'other one. Blond fella he's shacked up with.'

The interior of St Jude's had been comprehensively transformed. When Pat walked in, she saw the altar table and lectern had been moved and the space cleared. Lights glowed ethereally, illuminating what looked like black and grey pillars, creating a space that looked to Pat's startled eyes like something beyond this immediate world, a portal to some other place.

A figure materialized from the gloom, face lit eerily from below, casting ghoulish death's head shadows on the pale face.

'Why have you called me on this dark night?' The voice was low, deep and resonant, and despite knowing this was all an illusion, Pat felt fear itching her temples and the back of her neck; here was a reality beyond her immediate comprehension.

'Shit.' The voice was real and peevish now, and abruptly impartial cold lights snapped on revealing canvas flats and Jamie

270

fiddling crossly with a torch. 'Bloody thing,' he said. 'A right load of cheap crap. I said we need to buy *quality*. But hey, shut up, Jamie, you're only the director.'

'That all looks amazing,' said Pat.

Jamie looked up. 'The Reverend Mare hates it.'

'I'm sure she doesn't.'

'You know what she said to me?' He affected a high, fruity voice. '"I thought it might be a wee bit more *period*."' Jamie shook his head. 'I kid you not, those were her actual words. I know what's she's after.' He sat wearily on a stage block and opened his notebook. 'Everyone in crinolines and mob caps. I'm going to say to her: "Sweetie, this is a story of human darkness not 'effin *Bridgerton*."'

Now that Pat was closer to him, she realized that the lighting had only emphasized the truth as opposed to creating it; he looked terribly tired and pale, big purple smudges under his eyes. *And . . .* She leaned forward, looking closer.

'Jamie,' she said soberly, 'how did you get that bruise on your head?' This was not the question she had come here to ask, but nevertheless it was one that needed asking.

'Oh, that?' He laughed in a brittle way, fingers automatically straying to the pink and purple blotch on his forehead. 'You know that old cliché – a man walks into a door. Well, I did, I walked into a door. Or rather a stage flat. It's blacker than a celeb's bank balance in here when the lights are down.' He stood up. 'Listen, Pat, I'm so not being funny but everyone's due to pole up here in precisely seven and a half minutes.'

Pat took a deep breath. 'I've just been at the golf club,' she said.

'Swainby?' His voice was sharp.

She nodded. 'I was dropping something off there. And I got talking to someone I know.' She took another deep. How to ask this very difficult question? But before she could speak he abruptly sat back down on the block, his head drooping. A fat tear plopped on the floor between his feet.

She sat next to him. 'Jamie, what's the matter?'

Wordlessly he shook his head. Roy's voice sounded in her mind: '*A chip off the old block . . . a severe case of "Not-keeping-it-in-his-pants-itis".*'

'Is it Shaun?' she said. Jamie didn't react. She put a hand over his. 'Is it anything to do with Luke Atkinson?' she said.

'The little bastard!' The vehemence in Jamie's voice made her snap the hand back. 'Sorry.' He grabbed it convulsively. 'Sorry. How did you know?'

'I guessed. Luke was round seeing Liam the other night. He told him he was seeing someone who was already in a relationship and it was complicated.'

'It's not complicated.' The angry tone was back. 'Not for Lukey boy. He sees someone he wants, and he goes for him. Job done.' Pat very much wanted to say something along the lines of it taking two to tango, but it hardly seemed the moment and besides the first approaching voices of the cast could be heard outside. Both looked round.

'The thing is with Shaun . . .' Jamie was speaking fast, as if racing to get the words out, 'I know he's a bastard. I know what it is he's capable of. And okay, sometimes he scares me, but bottom line, Pat – I love him.' Pat looked at him. *Capable of what?* His eyes met hers, scared, childlike. 'I've no choice in the matter,' he said. 'I love him.'

'Oh. Jamie,' she said, holding his hand. She looked at him, realizing that now was not the time to ask what she'd come to ask.

The door opened. 'Salutations,' said the Reverend Mare cheerfully. 'I've had the Yorkshire Museum on. Seems like they can offer us a job lot of bonnets!'

★ ★ ★

272

Outside Pat sat in the Yeti for a full five minutes, regardless of the cold seeping into her feet. She'd gone there with a question that needed to be asked – and she hadn't asked it. And it still needed asking. What on earth should she do? To do nothing felt wrong on so many levels, but what was the *right* course of action? She thought of Jamie. Of Shaun – and Luke Atkinson. And the woman she'd never met, the woman she never would meet – Terri Stanley. Someone capable of provoking both affection and scorn.

She came out of her reverie with a start. How long had she been sitting here? Time seemed to have stood still. She took out her phone and realized she'd not turned it back on; sighing, she did and fished out her car keys.

The phone buzzed. Buzzed and buzzed again. Surely not the Amazon delivery? They knew to leave parcels in the barn.

But it wasn't Amazon, it was Liam. Thirteen missed calls. She felt a chill taking root round her chest area. *What on earth had happened?*

CHAPTER THIRTY-ONE

Sad memories and angry thoughts lead to a revelation in the charity shop.

It was one of those natural burial sites. Liz had somehow assumed it would be in a wood or on a hillside, but it wasn't; it was on a wide, windy stretch of the Fylde coastline near Knott End, looking over an expanse of wide, wind-bent grass with Morecambe Bay beyond. Liz sat on a bench looking out over the pearly sheen of tidal mud under vast grey skies. It was a place, she felt, where one felt somehow *free*. It was also a place where one felt very cold, despite her thickest fleece; however, she was determined to give no sign of this.

About twenty yards away was Tim. He had been standing a good twenty minutes, a lonely figure staring at the heap of fresh earth and fading bouquets. When the ground was levelled and the flowers removed there'd eventually be no trace of where the grave was. Which was, so Liz understood, the point of these places, but she couldn't help but feel it was all a bit sad.

Eventually he returned and sat next to her. For the longest time he didn't speak and Liz knew better than to break the silence, a silence that had characterized their journey over from

Thirsk. When he did speak his voice was tight and controlled in a way that vividly recalled Jacob.

'I didn't go into the service,' he said. 'I didn't dare. I just stood outside.'

Liz squeezed his hand. Even through her gloves his skin felt as cold as the winds sweeping in from the north.

'Thank you for coming with me,' he said.

'I'm sorry I wasn't more understanding,' said Liz. 'Now . . . and back then. I was just thinking about you. And before you say anything, I know what a cliché that sounds.'

Tim squeezed her hand. 'Thing is, Mum,' he said, 'I catch myself looking at Jay sometimes, and I think how I'd feel if he met someone a lot older, when he was only eighteen. I don't know what I'd do. I wouldn't be happy, I know that.' He sighed. 'But then . . . at the time . . . I couldn't think about anything else.'

Liz nodded. Only too well she remembered.

'I'd not thought about Rochelle for years,' he continued. 'Years and years. Not more than a passing thought. But then, two months ago, I saw some random Facebook post from someone we both knew, saying how she was in a hospice on end-of-life care. And . . . He paused, frowning 'And it really got to me. All at once, it was like no time at all had gone past and she was all I could think about.'

'And you told Leoni?'

He nodded. 'I had to. She tried to understand . . . but I didn't understand myself.' There was a pause and he stared bleakly out at where the tide was beginning to cut silver traceries across the grey mud.

'And you went to see her?' prompted Liz, remembering the till receipt.

To her surprise he shook his head vehemently. He opened his mouth to speak but emotion clogged his throat and he

275

dropped his head into his hand. Liz gently laid a gloved hand on his twitching shoulders. Eventually he looked up. 'She wouldn't see me,' he said. 'I asked but she said no. Her sister called me and said how she couldn't really face seeing anyone.'

That seemed to be that. In the silence that followed Liz was desperate to ask whether he was now going to go back to Leoni and Jacob, but again wisdom prevailed. Besides, she suspected he didn't really know himself. All Liz could sense in that present moment was his grief – that and her own unconditional love for him.

'I know you think it wouldn't have worked out,' said Tim. 'I know, an eighteen-year-old and a nearly thirty-something – total car crash. But with me and Rochelle, it would. It *would*.'

'I've always wondered,' said Liz, 'what made you break it off? Listening to what you're saying now I'm wondering even more.'

There was a pause. 'I didn't break it off,' he said. '*She* broke it off with me.'

Liz stared at him.

'She said I needed to be with people my own age.' Tim's voice was quiet. 'How I had my whole future in front of me – and how being with her would hold me back. What she didn't realize was that she *was* my future.' He turned and looked at her and with a shock she noticed the first faint tracings of old age on his face, greying hair round the temples, fine lines round the eyes and mouth. 'At the time I thought she'd just got tired of me, and it was all an excuse. Now . . . I can see where she was coming from.'

He looked away, at the sea. It was turning pewter in the waning January daylight. 'But it would still have worked.'

Liz frowned at the distant sea. All these years a belief that had been steadily burning inside her proved to be other than she'd thought. While Tim nipped to the toilet (carbon-neutral eco-friendly) she rang Thelma. It went to voicemail. Normally she wouldn't bother leaving a message, but this felt important. 'It's me,' she said, hoping the wind wasn't distorting her voice too much. 'I've been having some thoughts. About how you can think one thing only to find out it's not true at all.'

As she ended the call Tim appeared. 'Are we fit?' he said, sounding just like his father.

'We are,' she said, and gave him a hug.

'Listen,' he said, 'thanks again for coming with me, Mum.'

'You're very welcome,' said Liz.

As she was getting into the car she paused and took one final look at the burial ground, grey and green and peaceful.

'Thank you,' she said in a low voice towards the distant heap of soil and flowers.

The harmonized voices of the choir soared aloft to the curves and sweeps of the vaulted cathedral ceiling, high above where Thelma was sitting in still contemplation.

The strains of 'You Raise Me Up' didn't so much end as drop down gently into silence, and Thelma exhaled, relishing the space and peace. These Lunchtime Sing Up Sessions were something that had been happening at Ripon Cathedral every Monday and Thursday since New Year; different local choirs coming and singing to raise money for designated causes. This Thursday was the turn of 'Here comes Treble!' – a group of ladies raising money for the women's refuge.

As the choir coughed and fumbled with their music, Thelma spoke quietly. 'I know the *what*,' she said, 'and maybe the *who*.' An image of Pat came before her. 'What I *don't* know is the *why*.' She paused. '*Is* it for me to know the why?'

In the distance candles shimmered and glowed on the high altar.

'Guide my actions,' she prayed. 'Your word is a lamp to my feet.'

With a smart double click of a baton the women in their bright jumpers began singing again, their words once more soaring and swooping high above Thelma and her tired, muddled thoughts, bringing to life one of her favourite songs.

Be thou my vision, Lord of my heart, naught be all else to me save that thou art—

Visions. That's what it all seemed to come back to – that vision of Marguerite's . . .

The *what* . . . the *who* . . . but the *why* . . . *Why?*

Be thou my father, be thou my son . . .

Fathers and sons . . . and daughters. Mal Stanley and his children . . . *Why?* That's what she couldn't see.

After the song had finished, she sat bathed in the peace and stillness. She felt no further forward, but at the same time she felt soothed and refreshed and reassured.

Your word is a lamp to my feet.

Stepping out of the cathedral into Minster Road, Thelma experienced that momentary dislocation one gets when stepping from darker into the lighter. A buzz from her phone showed she had a voicemail from Liz. Odd, she normally never left voice messages. Hurrying down Kirkgate she listened, her pace slowing.

You can think one thing only to find out it's not true at all.

The town hall clock striking one brought her smartly out of her reverie . . .

The charity shop! She very much didn't want to be late, not in the current fraught atmosphere. She hurried to the shop, registering that the display in the window had been changed. Polly was standing behind the counter, her back chair-straight, lips squeezed grimly together. 'I'm so sorry,' began Thelma, but Polly it seemed wasn't concerned about Thelma's timekeeping.

'Have you seen,' she said loudly and clearly, 'what that *bitch* has done?'

Thelma stared at her askance, as did the customers in the shop.

'What?' She dropped her voice, hoping this would calm Polly's tones, and certainly moderate her angry language.

'You mean you didn't see it?' There was incredulous outrage in Polly's voice. Thelma looked at her blankly. '*The window display*,' said Polly, voice trembling. 'She's gone too far this time.'

Wordlessly, Thelma retraced her steps back out into the street and looked at Verna's latest creation. At first glance it seemed innocuous enough – a clock surrounded by various objects with a placard advising the people of Ripon *not* to be late for bargains! A bit of an odd choice of words was Thelma's first thought. She looked a bit more closely.

There were some books – *The Case of the Late Pig* by Margery Allingham, a rather lurid paperback entitled *Too Late for Love*, and *Alice in Wonderland* open at the page where the White Rabbit checks his watch in panic. And a cookbook open to a list of 'Last-minute Suppers'. Thelma looked at the clocks, which were all arranged at the same time – 1.30. The exact time Polly was supposed to have started the other day. Though there were no written comments about her timekeeping – none were necessary. It really was very clever.

Thelma went back into the shop.

'I am absolutely livid,' pronounced Polly. 'Verna Craig can stuff her shifts where the sun don't shine.'

'It must have taken a lot of thought,' said Thelma, not sure what to say.

This was not the response Polly wanted; she eyed Thelma coldly.

'I mean,' said Thelma hastily. 'It's a lot of effort. One wonders *why* she'd go to so much trouble.'

'That's easy,' said Polly. 'Spite.' She virtually spat the word out.

Spite. All that time and effort.
Hang on . . .
Spite . . .
Of course!

CHAPTER THIRTY-TWO

Pat has two surprise visitors and one welcome reconciliation.

Pat flew into the kitchen to find Liam hunched by Larson's basket, wide-eyed, looking about six years old. She took his hand, forcing her voice to be calm. 'Did you get through to the vet?' she said. Liam nodded, opened his mouth, but was overwhelmed by a great heaving gasp rendering him dumb.

'Take a deep breath,' she said, her voice low and calm and even, as it had been countless times during his childhood.

'I got through to someone called a triage vet,' he said unevenly. 'He said to take him in, but—' Another heaving breath choked him and she tightened her grip on his hand. 'But when I described his symptoms he said not to rule out the possibility of a tumour, in which case the kindest thing might be . . . might be . . .' Emotion and a fit of coughing overcame Liam and he fell back on his heels, pressing his face into his hands. Larson lay prone in his basket, oblivious. Pat rubbed a hand between her son's heaving shoulder blades, feeling icy still from head to toe. A tumour. Of course when anyone, human or animal, was ill that was the one screaming scenario that came immediately slamming into the mind. But even so . . . She took

281

a deep breath herself and took his hand again, as if trying to infuse him with her own frozen calm.

'Your dad's over at Olga's,' she said. 'Go and get him; he says he'll drive us in to Richmond.' He looked up, eyes red and wet.

'Go on,' she said. 'I'll wait with Larson.'

Once Liam had gone she fully expected to crumple – indeed that had been her chief reason for dispatching him – instead, however, cold calm persisted. The ringing, shocked calm that follows a sudden out-of-the-blue blow. Pat looked down at the prone figure in the basket, eyes half closed. She had a sudden vision of Larson as a puppy, emerging from the utility room, a pair of Justin's boxers swathed round his head and neck. 'Oh Larson,' she murmured, feeling her calm starting to pucker. A tumour! He wasn't *that* old – ten, maybe eleven?

But then, Rod hadn't been that old when he was diagnosed with cancer.

There was a faint, tentative knock on the back door.

'Come in,' she heard a voice saying before realizing it was her own. 'It's not locked.' A tall, young man holding an Amazon parcel appeared, looking uncertainly round.

Of course. The inflatable neck cushion.

'Thank you,' she said. 'Just leave it on the table. I don't need to sign for it or anything do I?' She felt her voice beginning to crack and forced in a massive, calming breath; she couldn't break down, not in front of the Amazon delivery man.

'Is something the matter?' The young man looked down at her, frank concern on his face. He was a tall, gangly lad with crisply curled hair and blue-grey eyes magnified behind enormous, thick lenses.

'I'm sorry,' she said. 'It's just my dog's not very well; we need to take him to the vet. My son's just fetching my husband—' Her voice caught as Liam's had before.

'I'm sorry to hear that.' He genuinely was, his face frowning, worried. 'Is it bad?'

'They say it might be—' Like Liam before, she felt her breath well up in her chest and jam her voice. She couldn't say the word, just as she hadn't been able to with Rod's illness.

'Poor wee fella.' The young man knelt down beside the basket. 'D'you mind if I take a look?' She nodded. He had, she noticed, a trace of a Northern Irish accent.

'Now then, my man, what's the matter?' He ran gentle but expert hands over Larson who licked his fingers feebly. He looked across at her. 'I wonder,' he said, 'd'you mind if I gave my brother a quick ring? He's a vet.'

'Where?' Somewhere inside an impossible crazy hope flickered, but she stamped it firmly back down.

'Oh, well, Northern Ireland, but I can describe how he is over the phone.'

A bizarre few minutes followed, involving Pat holding Amazon man's phone, as Amazon man gently probed Larson in response to a series of instructions from his brother, via a video call to Northern Ireland. At the conclusion of all this, Amazon Man's brother — a plumper, more jovial version of Amazon Man — spoke to Pat.

'I'd certainly take the wee fella in pronto,' he said, 'but I really don't think it's a tumour. He'd be in more pain. I think it's more likely to be something like a virus. Tell them to check for something like hypothyroidism.'

'Let me write that down,' said Pat, flustered, but Amazon man was already scribbling into a notebook he'd magically produced. Maybe something he used to write delivery things on?

'Thank you so much,' she said at the conclusion to all this. 'You must let me—' She stopped. Do what? Pay him? Finding out his bank details felt a bit like overkill, but she could hardly

283

send a bottle of wine to Northern Ireland. Maybe send something by Amazon? She found herself smiling at the irony.

'Don't be daft,' said the vet cheerfully. 'Just go easy on that brother of mine.'

Go easy? What did he mean by that?

'I can go to the vet's with you if you'd like.' Amazon man's voice broke into her thoughts. Pat looked at him uneasily. What was he talking about?

'Look, I've held you up enough as it is,' she said. 'You must be way behind with your deliveries.'

The young man looked at her, the magnified blue-grey eyes puzzled. Then the face broke into a delighted grin that filled with room with light and optimism. 'Bless your heart,' he said. 'No, you've the wrong end of the stick. I happened to see the delivery man at the gate and I said I'd bring the parcel in for him, save him a bit of time.'

At that moment the back door opened and Liam appeared, followed by Rod. Liam's mouth fell open, the way it did when he was thoroughly surprised.

'Bern,' he said.

In the end, Rod drove to the vet accompanied by Bern and Liam, the latter tenderly cradling Larson. Pat sat at her wooden kitchen table, hands clutching the sides as if holding on to a raft in a stormy sea. Every single thought – Liam, Bern, Larson, Jamie – felt way too big to do anything but twist tiredly away from. To calm herself she opened her Angela Hartnett *Cooking for Real Life* cookbook, pressing her hands against the well-thumbed cover, running her fingers down the creased spine, seeking *something* her brain could engage with. She flicked open a page to sausage rigatoni, one of Liam's favourites, a recipe she knew virtually by heart.

Out of the corner of her eye she saw something flutter from

the table, a page from a notebook – Bern's. He must have ripped it out when he was scribbling down his brother's instructions. On it was the legend 'Direct or Change?' – a sentence that would have been mysterious had it not been accompanied by the train times from Durham to Thirsk.

For the second time in twenty-four hours something clicked in her brain.

Of course.

There was a second tentative knock on the door. Probably the Amazon man – no, he'd been . . . well, not him, but Bern.

'Come in,' she said, stamping on the weary trails of thought.

'I'm sorry to just turn up like this,' said Thelma. 'I wanted to apologize. And to talk to you.'

And suddenly Pat was weeping, fat tears splashing and blurring the instructions for trimming fennel.

Many tissues, many incoherent and interrupted apologies later, the two faced each other across the table. Between them was an empty cafetiere of Farm Shop Arabian blend and the remains of two Dalton slices.

'More coffee, I think,' said Pat. 'I know I need one.'

As she stood and put the kettle on, Thelma looked round the kitchen. Despite their years together, it was a place she'd only visited a handful of times; the basis of their friendship had been the staffroom, the classroom and now latterly the garden centre. The room struck her as a place of peace and love, of coats crammed and overhung on pegs, of muddy boots willynilly by the door, a place of meals and bickering and chat and, she was sure, an awful lot of laughter.

Part of her longed not to have to say what she was going to say, but she knew she had to.

Cafetiere replenished, Pat sat back down and Thelma regarded her friend. Her very good friend.

'Go on,' said Pat. 'And don't say "what?" I can tell you've something you want to talk about.'

'The thing is.' Thelma stared fixedly at the crumbs on her plate 'The thing is, I think I know what happened – with Marguerite and the charity shop.'

'Actually,' broke in Pat, 'so do I.'

Thelma looked up, and somewhere inside all the billowing clouds of emotion and uncertainty she felt a beat of relief, as you do when you realize someone is on the same page as you – no matter how dark or upsetting that page might be.

To finish her account Pat waved the page from Bern's notebook and was rewarded by a vehement nod and a look of enlightenment from Thelma. Then Thelma added a few of her own observations and it was Pat's turn to nod.

Eventually she said, 'Given that we're right – and I'm sure we are – what are we going to do about it?'

Thelma frowned. 'I'm not really sure,' she said.

'I can just hear the police,' said Pat. 'Even your DS Donna. They'd laugh us right out of court and I can't say I'd blame them.'

Thelma nodded. 'And it's not even as if we've any proof,' she said. She looked at her friend. 'I do realize,' she said, 'how hard this is for you.'

Pat briefly nodded, her eyes shut. 'But,' she said, 'it's important for Marguerite to know. She deserves that. She's running around thinking all sorts, and although she's very happy with that, she really ought to know the truth.'

Thelma nodded and for a moment was silent. Then she looked directly at Pat. 'I know I was dismissive of all that side of things,' she said. 'The supernatural. But I do want you to know that I really respect your views.'

'There's no need to apologize,' said Pat. 'If you think something's a load of hooey, you should say so.'

'That's just it,' said Thelma. '*I don't.*' She paused and Pat suddenly found herself holding her breath. 'When I lost the children,' said Thelma, 'the miscarriages. It was very very hard.' There was something about the simplicity of her words that brought an ache to Pat's throat. 'And I visited a spiritualist. Just like you did. I wanted—' She paused, collecting her thoughts. 'I suppose I wanted some comfort – some *certainty*.' She smiled in a self-deprecating way. 'Perhaps some vision of them playing in some eternal nursery.' She said nothing for a moment, then resumed. 'The experience I had when I visited that woman – I've never been properly able to describe it. I felt . . . something akin to standing on a *threshold*. There was darkness; there was also light . . . I don't know what I felt, not even now. It was a very powerful experience. And even to this day, I'm not sure what I think about it.'

Pat covered her friend's hand with her own. She said nothing, because what was there she *could* say?

The moment was shattered by a buzz of noise. Pat snatched up the phone and Thelma watched as the light gradually returned to her face.

'Larson's going to be okay,' said Pat eventually.

'Praise God!' said Thelma and hugged her friend tight.

CHAPTER THIRTY-THREE

As the Village Voices prepare to speak there is more than one surprise encounter.

On a winter's evening, with lit windows glowing through the rising mist, Marley presented an altogether cheerier and more hopeful aspect than it did during daylight hours. Parking the mussel-blue Corsair on the lane outside the church, Thelma noted Liz's white Fiat already there. Hurrying up the path to St Jude's Church, she could see her friend hovering by the door, worriedly scanning the path. How late was she?

'I'm so sorry,' she said, wheezing slightly in the damp air. 'Deliveries took longer than planned.' It had indeed been a full-on day she'd spent with Teddy attacking the never-shrinking stacks of WAMMP parcels but now, after some ten solid hours, they were done. With a great sense of giddy achievement, the last parcel had been handed over to a woman who'd been almost tearful in her relief. 'It's come!' she'd said. 'Thank the Lord!'

'It makes you wonder what it was and who it was for,' she'd said to Teddy in the car driving home. In the failing January light the sky had been great swirls of apricot and grey; above the mist rising from the river, floodlights had picked out the lines and angles of the cathedral in shades of gold.

'I love all this,' Teddy said, changing gear for the roundabout by the bridge.

'I can tell,' said Thelma.

'All those years,' said Teddy. 'All those years doing what I felt I *ought* to do . . .'

'I didn't know you felt like that,' said Thelma.

'No,' said Teddy. 'I don't think even I did. But sometimes—' he glanced at his wife, his rugby player face lit by the lights on North Road '—sometimes you have to give yourself permission to live your best life.'

She'd left him in a hot bath listening to his 'Goon Show Volume 11' CD. Big Cyn was due to make a drop early doors but for now Thelma's study, dining room and blanket box were freshly polished and totally devoid of parcels.

'I'm sorry,' she said again now to Liz.

'I've only just got here myself,' her friend responded. 'Leoni dropped in.' There was a small but significant pause. Thelma had heard all about the trip to Garstang and indeed had nipped into church that lunchtime between drop-offs to light a candle for the couple.

'And how are things, do you think?' she said carefully.

'We'll have to see,' said Liz, her all-purpose comment on situations that had the potential to fall disastrously flat. 'But they've gone to Curry-tastic, her and our Tim—'

'And Jacob?'

'I left him with Derek making vegan flapjack for the anti-frackers stall.' She frowned looking down the path, her mind clearly on a more pressing worry. 'I've not seen anything of Pat or Rod yet.'

'They'll be here,' said Thelma. 'And it's not like there's any problem parking.'

Liz nodded. 'The Reverend Mare was telling me; there's only fifteen or so booked.' Thelma shook her head, thinking of the

National Rural Hardship Fund. For whatever reason, Jamie's production didn't seem to be attracting the crowds.

At that moment a familiar figure appeared on the path, obviously recognizing Thelma, but equally obviously looking less than thrilled to see her.

'What are *you* doing here?' Michelle Stanley sounded almost accusing. 'I didn't know *you* were coming.'

'Good evening, Michelle,' said Thelma. 'Of course we wanted to support such a good cause. Jamie's been working so hard I hear.'

'I'm looking for Shaun,' said Michelle, disregarding her completely and peering into the porch. Shrugging ungraciously she went on into the church.

'That,' said Thelma, 'was Michelle Stanley. And none too pleased to see me.'

Liz frowned worriedly. 'Are we sure all this is such a good idea?' she said.

'I know it's not ideal,' said Thelma, 'but Marguerite has a right to know the truth, so she can move on, if nothing else.'

Liz snorted slightly. 'I'm not so sure she'd *want* to move on,' she said. 'Knowing Marguerite McAllister, she's probably having a high old time exactly where she is.'

'Sorry! Sorry!' Pat came hurrying up the path, breath pluming out in the light of the porch. 'Rod's just parking up. Am I very late?' She smiled at Liz. 'Hello, stranger,' she said. 'Sorry not to reply to your texts.'

Liz took her hand. 'I've that bulb catalogue for you in the car,' she said.

As an exchange it was casual and quick, but nevertheless it spoke volumes.

'Get your breath back,' said Thelma. 'Marguerite's not even here yet.'

'Do we know she's definitely coming?' said Liz.

'She sent me a WhatsApp earlier,' said Pat. 'She's definitely coming, her and this mysterious plus-one.'

'Have you any idea who he might be?' said Liz.

'My money's on someone from the Yorkshire Paranormals,' said Pat. 'It has to be.'

'I have to say,' said Thelma, 'when I saw her the other night, she seemed very enamoured.'

Liz shook her head. 'Well, I hope for her sake it all works out,' she said. 'Let's face it, it's taken her the best part of twenty years to get over the last one.'

'Now, ladies, are you coming in? The view's a whole heap better from inside, or so I'm told!' The Reverend Mare laughed brightly at her own joke.

'We're just waiting on our friend,' said Liz.

'Ah yes – the extra two tickets! All welcome, more than welcome! You've pretty much doubled our audience numbers tonight!' She gave a bray of laughter but nevertheless looked hopefully down the path. 'You've not seen Shaun Stanley?' she asked. 'Or that lad who works for him?'

'No,' said Thelma. 'His sister was looking for him just now.'

'Oh well, no matter.' Mare shrugged and turned to go back inside. 'You've a couple of minutes yet,' she said. 'I understand there's been a wee technical hiccup.' And with that she went back in, leaving all three to wonder about the exact nature of the wee technical hiccup.

'Hello, hello, hello!' The bright, unflurried voice made them all turn. If Marguerite had any awareness of being late, she felt no need to apologize for it. She was wearing a sort of crimson cape with a fake-fur-lined hood, looking, so Thelma thought, like an ageing Red Riding Hood. She immediately chided herself for the uncharitable thought and turned her attention to the man standing next to her, the mysterious plus-one.

With a shock she realized the face was familiar – the same

291

brown eyes, the same slightly lopsided smile – but looking out from a balder, plumper head than she remembered. She could tell from both her friends they'd reached the same point of recognition.

'Hello,' he said, somewhat shyly. 'You probably don't remember me.'

'I certainly do,' said Thelma. 'You used to fix our photocopier.'

'He'd not been happy – not for ages and ages and *ages*.' Marguerite spoke in low tones that weren't actually very low at all. 'Well, neither of them were happy – they'd both been playing away. The physical side of things had pretty much *dried up*.' As usual there was little internal filter with Marguerite's recount. Next to her Pat was aware of Rod doggedly studying his programme and guessed he – and the audience in their vicinity – were finding this as embarrassing as she was. Still, she was grateful for *something* to occupy her attention and take her mind off the humongous faux pas she'd made that afternoon. She wondered if Liam was still angry with her.

'. . . anyway, that was when the clock arrived.'

'Clock?' Pat looked at her blankly.

'The one I sent him.' Marguerite's voice was patient. 'Exactly like the one I saw in my vision. And I sent it to him, just like I'd planned. Anyway, I was sitting there at home one night last week and there's this knocking and there he was on the doorstep. "Marguerite," he said. "This is the play, not the rehearsal."'

Pat winced. This was also a play, and one she wished would start, to both shut Marguerite up and take her mind off what had happened – her 'gob before brains' moment, as Rod had referred to it.

In the short space of time in which she'd known him, Pat had really taken to Bern; in his quiet way he'd slotted right

into life at Borrowby. It was the manner in which he just got
on with things in an unfussy, efficient way – emptying the
dishwasher, giving Larson his medication. And he was also good
for Liam – she could see that within ten minutes of him stepping inside the house. There was a stillness about her son, in
his eyes, in his posture, a sense of him being comfortable in his
own skin that she hadn't really seen since those far-off days of
his Dungeons and Dragons club.

But the fact remained that Liam had been upset by Bern.
And despite her son telling her in a hissed aside Everything
was Sorted and not to say ANYTHING, she was determined
not to start a relationship with Liam's partner by ignoring any
sort of elephant in the room.

She had been in the kitchen, turning out the ginger and
pistachio thins made for a family tea party, and Bern had been
sitting at the kitchen table fixing her rotary whisk. They had
been on their own and she'd suddenly known that it was the
moment to speak.

'It's great having you here, Bern,' she'd said. The sentence
had been genuinely meant; however, it was one of those
sentences where 'but' is clearly signalled, neon-pink and glowing.

Bern had smiled, put down the screwdriver and given her
his full attention.

'It's good of you to make me feel so welcome,' he'd said.

'And I'm really glad you made things up with our Liam.'

'So am I.'

Pat began arranging the ginger thins precisely on the wire
tray and plunged right in. 'I don't know if you're aware that
Liam . . . he's . . .' Here she paused, wondering how on earth
to convey the complex precious truth that was her son – the
sleepwalking, the asthma attacks, the brittle, feverish vulnerability
when the world was bewildering him. 'He needs someone he
can rely on,' she concluded, somewhat lamely.

293

'I understand you, Pat,' said Bern gravely.

'I mean, a few too many drinks, getting carried away in the heat of the moment — we've all been there.' Was she being clear enough? He was regarding her gravely, big glasses reflecting the kitchen light. Did he understand what she was getting at? 'Kissing the wrong person,' she said in a rush. 'We've all been there.' (*Apart from Liz and Thelma* came the sudden irrelevant thought.) 'But, I mean, kissing the wrong person,' she said again in order to make herself crystal clear. 'It's a big deal to someone like Liam.'

'*MOTHER!*'

She'd spun round, catching the edge of the baking tray and sending ginger and pistachio thins skittering across the work surface. How long had Liam been standing there in the doorway?

'We were just having a wee chat,' said Bern easily, beginning to gather up the biscuits, with his deft, long fingers. 'It's nothing.'

Pat looked at her son. She had no choice but to carry on. 'I had to say something,' she said, 'After Luke, I had to say something.'

'Your mam was just looking out for you,' said Bern. 'Sure, it's fine.'

'Oh God.' Liam was looking his familiar pink, tense self again.

'Liam, it's fine, really it is,' said Bern.

'Mother,' said Liam. 'It wasn't Bern kissing someone else. *It was me.*'

The silence had been broken by Bern crossing the kitchen and encasing Liam in an easy hug. 'It was just that barman at Yo-yos,' he said. 'He'd kiss anyone, that one.'

In the semi-darkness of the church Pat closed her eyes. How could she have been so thick? At that moment the lights faded into blackness and Marguerite finished her sentences about physical compatibility, twined her hand into that of Gary the photocopier man, and joined the rest of the audience in expectant silence.

Nothing happened.

Liz sighed; she was also keen for the play to start – not that she held out any great hopes of enjoying it. From what she'd heard she didn't think it'd be her cup of tea at all, not like *Jersey Boys*, which had been the last thing she'd seen. Her thoughts strayed to Curry-tastic where all being well Tim and Leoni would just be finishing their starters. And talking. Hopefully about nothing special. Because everything was all out there, all out in the open for the pair of them to pick over and process and deal within their own time, and she had no illusions that ninety minutes in Curry-tastic would actually *resolve* anything. What Tim and Leoni needed to do was focus on the mundane – the mundane and the trivial, like leaking radiators and queues in Aldi, new school trousers for Jacob and whether Tim should commit to the cricket team this summer. Just the ordinary trivial things that were in fact the building blocks of a life. A shared life, she hoped.

She stole a glance across at Marguerite and Gary, fingers firmly knotted together. She still couldn't believe it – and yet somehow, they looked so *right* together. She thought of Marguerite's belief, a belief that had lasted all those years, a belief they'd all pitied and derided her for. And yet all the time those feelings were so very real. Like with Tim and . . . Rochelle. Even here in the dark, even with the thought of that windy burial ground in Garstang, she still hesitated to say those two names in the same breath. And all that time – Rochelle had been the one to finish it.

A shout made her look up at the stage. A circle of people came on walking in a circle, groaning.

'Voices of the past, voices of the present,' shouted someone.

'Speak to us on this dark winter's night,' said someone else.

There was more groaning. Liz sighed slightly; her worst fears confirmed. Not a patch on *Jersey Boys*.

In contrast to her friends, Thelma found herself enjoying the play. She'd been expecting at least some of the traditions of a ghost story – a soundtrack of wind, maybe a plastic skull or two – but nothing like this – a group of people creating something that felt dark and disturbing. She looked around the half-empty church. More than one person was reading their programme; obviously she was in the minority.

Abruptly the stage fell into blackness. A single white beam picked out a face, a face she recognized as Jamie's and yet was at the same time a white, unearthly death's head. Somewhere behind her a child started crying. As an effect it was massively powerful . . . There was a ripple of tension – fear even – amongst the audience.

'Why.' The voice was low, deep, resonant, seemingly coming from the darkness itself. A figure materialized under the white face. 'Why have you called me on this dark night?' As he spoke Thelma became aware of the beginnings of a commotion. She hoped that the crying child had been taken out.

But the commotion was not in fact coming from behind her, but to her left. Before anyone quite realized what was happening, Marguerite had jumped to her feet.

'But that's him,' she cried out in a startled voice. '*That's the man in the charity shop!*'

CHAPTER THIRTY-FOUR

*Confrontation follows confrontation and
electrical safety advice is offered.*

Pat almost ran through the clammy night, down through the
misty streets of Marley, followed at a slower pace by Rod.

'Hang on a sec,' he called. 'Slow down.'

Impatiently Pat paused by the shuttered-up pub. Out of the
darkness the drumbeat of the *EastEnders* theme tune could be
heard.

'What's going on?' he said. 'What was all that about in the
church?'

'That charity shop Marguerite saw,' she said. 'It was all a
set-up by Jamie.' Even as she spoke, she knew he wouldn't have
taken it on board. She barely had herself.

'*Jamie?*' he said.

'I'll explain later,' she said and began jogging up the road
again. Rod fell into breathless step beside her.

'Why?'

'To scare the pants off Terri Stanley.'

'Look—' His hand on her elbow forced her to slow, and
impatiently she shrugged it off. 'Look, going after him. Is that
such a good idea?'

'I don't know.' Pat spoke shortly because there was so much about her relationship with Jamie she didn't really understand herself and certainly couldn't get into with Rod, not now. All she knew was that she couldn't let him go disappearing off into the night without making *some* sort of attempt to follow him – though what she'd say when and if she caught up with him, she had no idea.

The front door of Mallory Square was wide open and lights – the bright lights of crisis – blazed forth from the downstairs windows. Luke's grey Mini was tucked discreetly to the side and Jamie's cherry red Lexus was parked, or more accurately left, at an angle, the driver's door open. As they approached, raised voices could clearly be heard coming from the house.

'Are you sure about this?' said Rod. 'They sound like they don't want to be interrupted.'

'Just let me do the talking,' she said. The angry voices were loud, discordant. She rang and knocked, but they carried on unabated. She was about to push the door, when it opened from within to reveal Luke Atkinson looking very young and very scared.

'Now's not a good time,' he said but Pat simply walked past him, disregarding him completely.

From behind her she could hear the indignant beginnings of a sentence, then Rod's voice cutting in, reasonably and peaceably. 'Tell you what, son, let's you and me go and wait in the kitchen.'

In the living room the coffee table was on its side and an overturned bottle was splodging an enormous purple stain across the white carpet.

'I can't believe . . .' Jamie faced Shaun, eyes blazing. 'I can't believe you and that *shit* actually . . . And in our own living room!' His voice rose to a pained shriek and he hurled one of the Waterford crystal glasses into the fireplace where it exploded into diamond shards.

'You're just a fucking nutjob.' Shaun was standing by the enormous TV, clutching a laptop to his chest, as if shielding both the machine and himself from Jamie.

'Me? You're the nutjob, taking up with that toxic little shit.'

Shaun half closed his eyes and shook his head; in that instant Pat had a sudden flashback to Mal Stanley ripping off his Batman mask all those years ago.

'You're pathetic,' he said dismissively, and turned to go.

'Don't leave me.' Jamie's voice was low, heartbreakingly low, utterly flat and desperate. Shaun ignored him and suddenly Jamie launched himself on him, clutching his back, a crazy, sick parody of the picture above the fireplace. This was a pistol crack as one of them stepped on a fallen piece of glass.

'Get OFF!' Shaun gave a violent shrug and Jamie fell back onto the sofa. 'It's OVER.'

He walked past Pat and out of the room. In an instant Jamie had sprung to his feet, yelling after him, 'You don't know what I've done for you!'

'Jamie.' Pat's voice was quiet. As if he was registering her presence for the first time, he looked at her, uncertain, then blank. He held up one hand, as if warding her off and walked out. An instant later feet could be heard clattering up the stairs.

Rod looked out of the kitchen as she came into the hall.

'Everything okay?' he said.

'Just keep Luke with you,' she said and started up the stairs after the person who in spite of everything she thought of as her friend.

A moment later Pat found herself – as she had all those years ago – paused uncertainly, halfway up a flight of open-tread stairs. These stairs were straight, unlike the ones at Sunny View Lodge, but nevertheless she felt the same paralysing indecision, along with a powerful sense of déjà vu at the sound of muffled sobbing.

Get a grip, Pat, she said to herself.

Abruptly, the sobbing was masked as drawers and wardrobes began slamming open.

In the bedroom Jamie was frantically heaping clothes into a couple of cases – jumpers, shirts and trousers losing their neat folds as they were thrown in all willy-nilly and anyhow. Part of Pat itched to step in and make sure everything was properly folded.

Jamie caught sight of her reflection in the angle of the mirrored wardrobe door. Then he turned, carefully, deliberately and shut the door in her face. She stood perplexed – what to do? With a mighty breath, she knocked and firmly pushed open the door.

'Pat, I can't talk, not now.'

'That's fine,' she said and sat herself down on a chair. She knew what she wanted to say, and she knew she could only say it if he was prepared to listen – which he plainly wasn't. And if he wanted to talk, he would.

Jamie didn't pause but kept giving her increasingly irritated and uneasy glances.

'Pat . . .' he said eventually.

'I know,' she said. 'You don't want to talk. I get it. But I'm not leaving you on your own.'

'No.' He took a long, shuddering breath. 'No.' He began putting trainers – very expensive-looking trainers – in a holdall. Then he stopped and looked her in the eye. 'I have to get away,' he said. 'I realize that. I have to get away from that man. I see that now.'

Pat said nothing.

Jamie resumed his packing, putting bottles of aftershave in the holdall – Calvin Klein, Paco Rabanne, David Beckham. He abruptly stopped and looked at her. 'The reason I ran out of the play,' he said, 'was that I realized Shaun and that toxic shit weren't in the audience. And you didn't have to be a genius to work out where they were. And sure enough . . . *La voilà* – there they were curled up and loved up on the fucking sofa that I fucking chose from fucking Artemis.' He sounded bitter, but the look he gave Pat was appraising, almost sly. Pat returned his gaze.

'Jamie,' she said determinedly. 'About church. About what that woman called out.'

'I love him, Pat!' He cut across her, his voice sharp and urgent. 'I know what he's like – and God knows all my friends told me to steer well clear – but when you love someone you don't think straight.' He zipped up the holdall and hoisted it over a shoulder. It clanked like a bag heading for the bottle bank. 'I've put up with stuff – stuff I should never have had to put up with, but I did.'

He paused for breath, again gave that sly, appraising glance and Pat found herself looking at a frightened, guilty boy. It reminded her of Ryan McGann, Year Two, with a broken window behind him, glass on the playground, his voice whiney with panic. *'I didn't do it, Mrs Taylor, I didn't do it!'*

'Jamie,' she said again.

'Pat! I said I'm in no place to talk!'

I didn't do it, Mrs Taylor; I didn't do it!

What to say? What on earth to say? In *Line of Duty* everyone knew exactly what to say and how to say it, when to break in supported by a plethora of PowerPoints. But this wasn't *Line of Duty*, this was a man the wrong side of forty, facing a car crash of a relationship and the realization the man he loved and had done such dreadful things for was trading him in for a younger model.

'Look.' Jamie was babbling, almost snatching up the cases.

301

'Look, I don't know what's been going on. I have no idea. White vans parked up . . . That's none of my business. What Luke was doing getting rid of a load of coat hangers . . . It has nothing to do with me.'

'Jamie,' she said in the calm firm voice she'd used countless times with countless children over the years. 'Jamie, I know what happened. *I know what you did.*'

He stopped dead, put the holdall down and finally faced her. It was one of those timeless moments that come so rarely where all pretence and superficiality is stripped away. There was a long pause.

'I'm guessing you heard what went off between me and her at the funeral?'

Pat nodded.

'I wasn't bothered for *me*. Okay, it'd have been nice, some money, but it was Meesh . . . and Shaun. Mal was their dad. They deserved *something*. So I goes up to her planning to be quite reasonable. But the second I started talking, this *look* comes on her face. You know that look – it's the one you see when you get someone on a crowded bus who's not going to give up their seat for some old biddy who can barely stand upright. I says to her, "Come on, Terri," and then . . .' He shut his eyes, shook his head in disgust. 'Then she screams at the top of her voice, "I can't handle this" – not because she actually felt like that but to make everyone think I was giving her a hard time. The greedy son-in-law hassling the poor, grieving widow.'

Pat nodded. It was a tactic she'd seen used many times by both children and adults. 'Was that when she threw the drink over you?' she asked.

Jamie nodded. 'Just to make sure everyone in that golf club knew I was bothering her. I thought, "classy, love".' He hoisted up the case and holdalls and took a final bleak look round the room, no doubt torturing himself with memories of happier times.

Pat knew there was all sorts she should have said – neat, precise sentences setting out what he'd done. She also knew they would all come to her eventually, probably in the small hours of the morning, but for now all she could do was look at him.

He looked back at her, the ghost of a smile on his lips. 'Not that I'm admitting *anything*.'

'Where are you going?' said Pat. 'Do you need somewhere to stay?'

He shook his head. 'I'm going to drop out of contact for a bit. I need some time and space away from here. I'll be okay.'

On the threshold, he paused. 'Liam,' he said. 'I thought if Luke saw him, he'd leave Shaun alone. I'm so sorry. Because—' his voice faltered '—because if he's anything like his mother, he's way above slime like Luke Atkinson.'

'Oh, Jamie,' she said. He looked at her, eyes bright with unshed tears. He made as if to speak again, couldn't manage it and was gone.

She waited until she heard the front door close and the cherry red Lexus roaring off into the night before going downstairs. Her legs felt as heavy and tired as if she'd just completed a ten-mile hike. Rod and Luke had moved into the living room; Luke was hovering nervously by the door and Rod was on his knees, extracting shards of glass from the carpet. 'You want to get some white vinegar and hand soap on that asap,' he was saying. 'Red wine's a bugger to get out.'

They both looked at her as she entered the room. 'He's gone?' Rod said questioningly.

Pat nodded. 'I don't think he'll be coming back.'

'I was saying to Mr Taylor,' said Luke, his voice high and

shaky as he made an attempt at normality, 'I was saying they need to be getting this room redone. All this grey – it's a bit depressing, you know? It needs something brighter – maybe two-tone.' He reminded Pat of nothing so much as a small boy showing off a complicated Lego model.

'Luke,' she said seriously. 'Listen to me. If you ever, *ever* need a place to stay, you can always come to ours, no questions asked.' Rod gave a startled jerk of his head, but nonetheless nodded. It was probably as well, thought Pat, that he didn't realize this was the second time she'd made this offer in the past ten minutes. She deliberately ignored her husband and focused on meeting Luke's eyes and making hers as steady and sincere as she could so that on some possible dark future day, he'd maybe remember her words. As it was, however, he merely forced a puzzled, questioning smile onto his nervous face. 'Uh, okay?' he said, trying to sound bemused and amused and sneering. *Trying*.

The living room door opened, and Shaun marched in holding the open laptop. 'Right,' he said, 'the little fucker's drained the current account but I've managed to put a block on the rest.'

'How much has he got?' said Luke, his face suddenly sharp.

'About 10k.' Shaun sounded casual. 'Not that much. God, I need a drink.'

'Why don't I make us all coffee?' said Luke. 'Or maybe even open a bottle of wine.'

'Actually, we need to be going,' said Pat. She had no desire to remain in that house one second longer.

'I suppose,' said Shaun, suddenly fixing her with that pale, intimidating stare, 'I suppose he's been saying all sorts about me.'

'A fair bit.' Pat met his gaze full on. The Shaun Stanleys of this world had no power over her.

'I suppose he said I hit him. That bruise on his head. Well, for the record, that wasn't me.'

'I know,' said Pat and turned to go.

'I've disconnected your lamp,' said Rod. 'It took a fair old whack and the plug seemed to be getting warm. If I were you, I'd ditch it.'

'Thanks, mate,' said Shaun Stanley.

They walked back to the car in silence.

'Are we going back into the church?' said Rod. Pat shook her head; she had no wish to be part of whatever was going on in there. 'Please,' she said, 'take me home.'

Starting the engine Rod let out a breath. 'Well,' he said, 'that was like no village play I've ever seen.'

'No,' said Pat. She looked out at the lights of Marley passing by. 'I don't like leaving Luke there.'

'I'd've thought,' said Rod, 'you'd be glad he was nowhere near our Liam.'

Pat's phone buzzed. Six missed calls, three from Liz and three from Thelma. She put her phone in her bag. Not now.

'Poor Jamie,' she said. 'And I *know* what you're going to say. I know what he's done. A woman died – I know. It's just . . . the thought of him driving off into the dark like that . . .' Rod said nothing. 'I just can't help feeling I've let him down,' she said quietly.

'Okay,' he said, slowing for the Pickhill turn. 'I wasn't going to tell you this but I think you should know before you go beating yourself up too much.'

'Know what?' she said tiredly.

'He made a pass at me.'

Pat jerked up in her seat. 'Shaun did?' she said.

'Jamie. Your mate.'

'*Jamie?* Are you sure?' It wouldn't be the first time that Rod had got the wrong end of the stick.

'I'm sure. It was when he was showing me that hot tub of

305

theirs, which by the way is plumbed in all wrong; they're going to have a shedload of problems down the line.'

Pat broke in with some impatience. 'What did he actually *say* to you?'

'Something about whether I fancied trying it, and how maybe I should come round some time on my own when Shaun was out.'

'And what did you say?' She was surprised by how little she felt about the news. Maybe her emotions had all been used up for one night.

'I told him his plumbing was all up the spout.'

In spite of everything, Pat smiled. 'Why didn't you tell me?'

'I would have if he'd done it again. But I knew he was your big buddy. And I don't know, I felt sort of sorry for the guy. He seemed kind of lost.'

Pat nodded in the darkness. 'He is,' she said. 'Very much so.'

'One thing that's puzzling me,' said Rod. 'If Shaun didn't give him that bruise, then who the hell did?'

'I rather suspect,' said Pat, 'he did it himself. Smacking his head against the wall probably.' Was it the mizzle on the window or were her eyes blurring with cold foolishness? She knew that Key West had gone from her sight for good, leaving a world that felt infinitely grey and sad.

Rod reached out his hand and took hers. She held tightly to a rough warm reality in a night that had turned so very dark.

CHAPTER THIRTY-FIVE

In the garden centre explanations are given.

'So?' The Reverend Mare took a final appreciative sip of her gingerbread latte. 'When did you all start to suspect it was Jamie?'

Instinctively Liz and Thelma looked across to the counter where Pat could be seen queuing for another round of drinks, but she was too far away to hear and indeed seemed lost in her own thoughts. Although the weather was still as clammy and grey as ever this Thursday morning there was in the garden centre a feeling of optimism, showcased in the bright displays of spring bulbs: pink, purple and yellow.

'In a way,' said Thelma, 'Jamie was always the obvious culprit. The whole set-up with the fake charity shop, leaving the tarot card in the empty unit, and of course all those candles at Sunny View Lodge – all so *theatrical*.'

'Nasty, the whole thing,' said Liz.

'But slightly *wrong* in the details,' said Thelma. 'The wrong bedroom at Sunny View Lodge, and tarot cards are used in a pack, not left in corners, like calling cards, which all just drew attention to the fact it was in essence just an elaborate stage set.'

'But why go to all these great lengths?' Mare pushed back her fringe and frowned.

'Spite,' said Liz conclusively. 'Sheer spite. Jamie and Michelle wanted to scare the pants off Terri, poor love.'

'They'd both approached Terri after Mal's death and she refused to give them any of his money,' said Thelma. 'All that about them getting on with her was a lie from start to finish. For a long time, I was puzzling and puzzling thinking there must be some practical reason – some financial gain, some legal loophole whereby the Stanleys would benefit from Terri's death in some way. But I suddenly realized it was in fact all very simple – they wanted to get their own back on the woman who they saw as having stolen their inheritance.'

Mare frowned. 'How would setting up a charity shop achieve that?' she said.

'*A charity shop full of her dead husband's possessions*,' said Thelma. 'Remember there were only *men's* clothes in there. She must have recognized several items straight away.'

'Even so,' said Mare. 'Surely it was all a bit convoluted.'

'But effective,' said Thelma picturing the dim space.

'Terri was susceptible to all that supernatural malarkey, remember?' said Liz. 'That whole Flaxby Hall ghost project was her idea.'

'She'd more or less walked out of Sunny View Lodge and just left everything of Mal's for the house clearers,' said Thelma. 'So, it was easy enough for Jamie to borrow a van from Shaun's garage and take what they needed. I imagine, having looked through her windows, it's still all stashed away in Michelle's house.'

'Derek – my husband – he reckons Michelle could have easily found somewhere for them to stage their deception through her work in the planning department,' said Liz. 'Somewhere isolated where they could go unnoticed.'

'I see.' Mare looked as though she might say more but thought better of it. 'So how did they manage to get her to go there in the first place? It's not like they could have rung and invited her.'

'eBay, I'm guessing,' said Thelma. 'We do click and collect at our charity shop.'

'According to our Jacob it's perfectly possible to wangle it so a certain person gets the sale,' said Liz. 'Tate Bishop said she'd gone to collect something. I'm guessing shoes. She was mad on collecting shoes, poor love. Collecting, not keeping it seems. She left a whole load in the house.' She shook her head sadly, picturing the forlorn ranks of abandoned footwear.

The Reverend Mare nodded. 'So, Terri fell for their lure, and off she pops to their so-called shop.'

'It was a foggy night,' said Thelma. 'Which would have greatly helped things.'

'Then the whole scheme started to go pear-shaped,' said Liz. 'First off – totally by chance – our friend Marguerite happened on the shop and goes blundering on in. And at first, they thought it was Terri. Michelle locked her in and Jamie appeared doing his whole ridiculous voice of doom performance. It was only when she started screaming the place down that they realized their mistake. Marguerite runs out into the night, and they decided that as they'd soon be gone anyway, it hopefully wouldn't matter that much.'

'And then,' said Thelma, 'Terri arrived as planned. We know from Marguerite what must have happened – the doors locked; the lights dimmed. The voice in the darkness.'

'*Why did you do it?*' intoned Liz, her face grim. 'Totally over the top.'

Mare nodded. 'And I'm guessing,' she said, 'that their plan worked a bit *too* well?'

'You can just never be sure how people are going to react to things.' Thelma took a final sip of coffee.

'I remember at school,' said Liz. 'We had a theatre company in doing *The Wizard of Oz*. Most of the children were loving it, but we had this one girl—'

'Ellie Benson,' supplied Thelma.

'—the moment the Wicked Witch appeared she stands up and begins screaming the place down. Talk about blue murder. And that's how it must have been with Terri.'

'And this wasn't in a theatre,' said Thelma. 'This was in a lonely building on a foggy night. They'd even wired it for sound so she'd hear the tick of a clock. Pure theatrics—'

'Pure nastiness,' said Liz grimly. 'That clock stuck at ten to three – the time her husband died. *Wicked*.'

Again, the Reverend Mare looked very much on the point of saying something else.

Thelma interlaced her fingers. 'Terri was quite literally terrified out of her wits. She ran out, got into her car and fled . . . And we all know what happened next.'

There was a pause as all three pictured that broken wall with its bunch of flowers by the railway station.

'When she was being attended to after the crash, all she could think about was asking the saints to protect her,' said Liz sadly.

'Poor soul,' the Reverend Mare said, her eyes gazing into some faraway dark distance. 'Poor, poor soul.'

Thelma looked at her curiously.

'Of course, one can only imagine what Jamie and Michelle thought,' said Liz. 'Whatever they'd intended for Terri Stanley, it wasn't killing the poor woman. All they could do was stick to their plan – packing everything up and driving off, leaving no trace of what they'd done.'

'Okay,' said Mare. 'Don't get me wrong, ladies, I'm not doubting you for one minute – but my question is, how can you be *sure* of all this? As far as I can see there's no actual *evidence*.'

'Nothing that would stand up in court,' agreed Thelma.

'*SS Redemption*,' said Liz. 'It's the title of a book I found on the waste ground. *By the same author as a stack of books left behind at Sunny View Lodge*. They must have dropped it when taking stuff in and out of the building.'

'And then there was this,' said Thelma. She handed Mare the scrap of paper. 'I found it on the waste ground as well. It's from Jamie's notebook.'

'The one he used in rehearsals?' Mare took the scrap of paper. She frowned and read the words aloud 'Past and present – both the same?'

'At first we all thought it was an allusion to the supernatural,' said Thelma.

'It's the play, isn't it?' said Mare. '*Village Voices*. His plan of having the two Voices played by the same person.'

Thelma nodded. 'As I say,' she said, 'nothing that would stand up in any court of law.'

'And that would have been that,' said Liz, 'if Michelle Stanley hadn't stuck her oar in, trying to put paid to the sale of Sunny View Lodge, with that ridiculous phone call. Looking to make trouble for the woman even after she was dead.'

'When Pat and I were talking to her,' said Thelma, 'Pat asked if Terri had ever mentioned anything strange happening. She meant in the house, but in her guilty mind, Michelle assumed she was referring to the charity shop. She was completely panicked and started stressing how sinister Tate was – she even told Pat later he was stalking her, which I realized was a complete fabrication.'

'How?' said Mare.

'She told Pat she'd seen Tate *from her front window*. When I saw the amount of stuff she'd got in there I realized that the window was completely inaccessible.'

'She must have rung Jamie in a flat panic,' said Liz. 'And when Jamie heard Thelma had contacted that Mairead Hope-

311

Whatsit from Open Fist Arts, he must have thought we knew something. Which is why he agreed to meet us, feeding us all sorts of ideas about Mal and Terri and Tate Bishop to throw us off the scent.' Her voice was grim, her lips tight. 'One of them must have sent Pat that WhatsApp message saying Terri Stanley was a murderer.' She shook her head.

The Reverend Mare nodded sombrely. '"Although they plot against you and devise wicked schemes, they cannot succeed,"' she quoted.

'Very apt,' said Thelma.

'Though really,' said Mare reflectively 'They *did* succeed – in that they got away with it.'

Thelma looked at her. 'It depends what you mean by "got away" with it. It's true they won't be brought to book for what they've done, but you have to consider what that means.'

Mare shrugged. 'They go on as they were I suppose,' she said.

'Exactly,' said Thelma. 'As they were. Growing older year on year. Michelle in that sad, cluttered house surrounded by junk—'

'With rats,' put in Liz.

'On her own.' Thelma's voice held a finality of judgement. 'And as for Jamie . . .'

'What about him?' Pat had approached without them seeing or hearing her. She put the tray of drinks on the table.

There was a slight constraint amongst those present. 'How he made friends with me to find out how much we knew?' she said, handing out the drinks.

'He gaslighted you,' said Liz firmly, putting a protective hand on her friend's arm.

Pat rolled her eyes. 'Liz Newsome, he did *not*,' she said in fond exasperation. '*I* asked to meet *him* remember? And what was there? One night in a wine bar, and a meal. Plus, some texts and a trawl round a haunted house.' She stopped. She so wanted to say it was nothing but couldn't. Because it wasn't. She also wanted to say something along the lines of there being no fool like an old fool but she was assailed by a sudden fear she might start crying. 'I honestly don't think he was in his right mind,' she said quickly. 'Realizing he was losing Shaun, that devastated him. I think with that, and with what had happened with Terri, he wasn't in control. That ridiculous story about the brakes of his car not working, hinting Shaun was trying to kill him. Trying to implicate Luke Atkinson – forcing him to dump all those coat hangers they'd used in their so-called shop. Nicking the poor lad's hat and leaving it in Sunny View Lodge.'

Both Liz and Thelma clocked the labelling of Luke as a 'poor lad', but neither of them said anything.

'You sound sorry for him,' said Mare.

Pat shrugged. 'I'm sorry for all that energy and talent wasted in such a nasty direction,' she said. 'You know he even wrote a fake university paper to send to Marguerite to make her think her so-called vision was an actual scientific phenomenon?'

'So what are you going to do?' asked Mare.

'There's not a lot we can do,' said Thelma. 'There's not enough to tell the police. Terri's estate has presumably gone to Tate Bishop. I don't think either Michelle or Shaun will have any interest in pursuing it, not with everything that's happened.'

'And you think that's the reason they wanted revenge?' said Mare, her voice carefully neutral. 'The inheritance?'

Thelma looked at her closely. 'Do you?' she said.

Mare looked at her gingerbread latte. 'I'm thinking about those words your friend heard,' she said. Her voice was serious, the words carefully chosen.

'*I know what you did*,' supplied Liz.

Mare nodded.

There was a pause.

Thelma looked at her.

'Do you maybe think,' she said, 'that Terri murdered Mal Stanley?'

Mare looked at them for a long moment. '*I know she did,*' she said.

CHAPTER THIRTY-SIX

*In the garden centre car park there are dreams
of summer afternoons in beautiful places.*

There was another pause, this one considerably longer.

'Did Terri tell you?' asked Pat eventually.

'No, but I *know*.' Mare gazed out of the window but they all knew it wasn't the damp car park she was seeing. 'I'm not as clever as you three ladies, but in my job you come across many human emotions – grief, anger, love . . . and guilt. And Terri's guilt, well, I'm afraid it was absolutely *shining*.' She sighed and the three had a sense she was putting down a burden she had carried for a long time.

'After Mal died, when she called me over to the house, I spent some time with her.' She paused, marshalling her words. 'Some people when they do wrong, they're as happy as Larry – no qualms, sleep like a baby. I could fill this coffee shop with such people. But others . . . even though they've done wrong they have a conscience that kicks in. When I saw the state Terri was in, well, I just knew what she'd done.'

'She asked you to bless that house, didn't she?' asked Liz.

Mare nodded. 'But really,' she said, 'I think she was asking me to bless her. Absolve her, if you like.'

315

'But *how* did she kill him,' said Pat. 'Didn't DS Donna say Terri left Mal with the district nurse? And he called her at Charlotte's office? And *before* she came back, she called the neighbour, Mrs What's-er-face who saw him at the foot of the stairs. I don't see how she *can* have killed him.'

'I don't know,' said Mare. 'All I know is that she did . . .'

The noise of Thelma's spoon going round and round her cup made them all look at her. 'What strikes me,' she said, 'is that everyone was told about all the reasons why Terri *couldn't* have killed Mal. As you say, all those people were prepared to say where she was and where she *wasn't* – the district nurse, Charlotte, that neighbour – but really, we need to be thinking about it in a whole different way. We need to think about how she *could* have done it.'

'So how *could* she have done it?' repeated Pat, not without a trace of impatience.

'Well, I can't be sure,' said Thelma, 'but I imagine Terri left Mal with the district nurse and instead of going straight to Thirsk she parked up at the pull-in at the edge of the village – the one where I saw Luke that afternoon. If she drove a short way down, her car would have been quite out of sight. And if you walk down that track you quickly loop back to the village and get to the back of Sunny View Lodge. It's only about a five-minute walk so it'd have been easy enough for Terri to make sure the district nurse had gone and slip in unseen.'

There was a pause. No one particularly liked Mal Stanley but none of them like the thought of what must have happened when Terri went home.

'And then she'd have driven on to Thirsk?' said Liz.

'Wait a minute,' said Pat. 'Don't forget Mal rang her *when she was at the agency*.'

'*His* mobile rang her,' corrected Thelma. 'His mobile *used in the vicinity of Sunny View Lodge.'* There was another pause as various pennies dropped.

'Someone helped her?' said Mare.

'Tate Bishop.' Liz looked grim. 'That's what he meant when he said, "my conscience is clear". I *knew* he was hiding something. It's Andrew Collier all over.'

'They'd already done some small-scale pilfering on Terri's former clients,' said Thelma, 'but this was on a whole different level. And to all intents and purposes they got away with it.'

'Only Mal's children suspected,' said Mare. 'But couldn't prove anything.'

Liz shook her head. 'Wicked,' she pronounced.

'I keep thinking what Brid told us,' said Thelma. 'How she thought Tate made Terri do bad things.'

'It's easy enough to be led astray when you care for someone,' said Pat.

Her friends looked at her. 'Are you sure you're, okay?' said Liz.

Pat smiled, a forced wide smile. 'I'm fine,' she said, making jazz hands. 'Okay, I've been a prat, but I'm okay.'

Alone in the car park Pat let the smile go with a pent-up sigh. She looked across the Hambleton Hills towards Sutton Bank, seeing that the damp fuzzy weather had largely cleared, leaving the outlines sharp and distinct. Colder weather was on the way. She took a deep deep breath, feeling her bright persona slip and fall back into something saggier and infinitely sadder.

'I've been a prat,' she said aloud, 'and I'm very much *not* okay.'

She sighed, seeing a boy-band face in a sky blue shirt, topping up her empty glass with a never-ending bottle of prosecco. Part of her felt puzzled. This was the man who'd shown no hesitation in trying to upend her life – Liam, *Rod* – and she knew she should hate him for that. But she couldn't shake off that feeling of connection, that feeling of being with someone who made her feel like that girl in purple Doc Martens and dirndl skirts drinking Saltaire Blonde and burning incense sticks.

'I may be about to turn sixty,' she said to the hills, 'but I still feel just as stupid. *Stupider.*'

'Pat!'

She turned at the sound of the cheerful hailing to see the Reverend Mare striding purposefully between the parked cars towards her. 'Pat.' Her face grew serious as she drew nearer. 'I didn't like to say in front of the others but Jamie came back to the church. He must have come in the night or first thing because when I went in, he'd taken his equipment . . . and I found this.' She handed her a cream-coloured envelope with her name written on it in bold, unapologetic green biro.

'Thank you.' Half reluctantly Pat took the envelope. 'By the way,' she said, 'I'm sorry that we managed to ruin the play.'

'Oh no! You haven't.' The Reverend Mare gave a bark of laughter. 'In fact, just the opposite. Young Raymond, he stepped in after Jamie exited stage left, as it were.'

'You mean the Grey Waif of Pickhill?' said Pat.

Mare nodded. 'And he was really rather good. Dare I say, he brought a bit of much-needed humour to the proceedings. "I have plans for you," says the Lord! "Plans to prosper you!" And we certainly have. Prospered, that is. Word has gone out,' she said. 'Ticket sales have gone through the roof. All of his chums from Cubs have booked tickets.' She fumbled in the voluminous pocket of her anorak, and produced her car keys, cocooned in shredded tissue. 'I have to go now and put out more seats for tonight.'

But walking away the Reverend Mare paused, turned. 'There was something about him,' she said simply. 'About Jamie. Don't get me wrong, he drove me up the wall and down again, but for all that . . . I'm going to miss him in that old church.'

318

Pat nodded. 'He was very loyal to those he cared about,' she said. An image of Rod came into her mind. 'In his own way,' she added. 'His own dark way. When we went out, there was a woman who spilt a drink on me. I'm sure he tripped her up, to get back at her. And stand up for me.'

Mare nodded reflectively. 'People like that,' she observed, 'are very dangerous. No real self-control. Which of course was what made him such a good actor.'

Sitting in the Yeti Pat looked at the envelope a long moment, before taking a breath, steeling herself and opening it. Inside was a postcard showing a sunset, a dramatic gaudy affair, the sky whorls of grey and orange and purple. A crowd watching the sunset were in the front and bizarrely a man was silhouetted, walking across some sort of tightrope. Lemon serif font announced this to be *Sunset in Key West*.

There was no writing on the back.

Pat smiled.

Rod picked up on the third ring. 'So, Liam and Bern got off all right,' he said. 'The train wasn't cancelled, miracle of miracles.'

'Listen,' said Pat. 'Listen. I know what I want for my birthday.'

'At last!' he said. 'And what's that?'

'A shawl,' she said. 'A summer shawl.'

'I thought you had loads of shawls,' he said.

'No,' she said. 'And I want this one to be red and sparkly and floaty. For when we go to Chateau Ooh-la-la or wherever it is.'

'Oh,' he said. 'So, you're coming now, are you?'

'I warn you,' she said, 'I'm going to load ten books on the Kindle and whenever you go round some medieval walled whatever I'm going to sit outside a café in the sun, sip wine and read.'

'Anything else?' he said.

'One thing,' she said. 'At these here wine tastings I shall get gloriously drunk and when I do, I want you to look at me and realize how lucky you are.'

'I do that every single day of my life,' he said.

EPILOGUE

Two weeks into February the weather changed. 'We've a right arctic blast on its way,' warned the *Look North* weatherman. 'Better be digging out those winter woollies!'

It had indeed grown much colder, and waiting in the garden of Sunny View Lodge it felt colder still. Through the kitchen window Thelma could see Val Carpenter talking to Brid – or rather, judging by Val's superior expression and Brid's uneasy one, talking *at* her.

At least, thought Thelma, Brid seemed in better shape than she had been at her sister's funeral. She remembered the huddled figure sobbing against the reassuring mauve-haired presence of bezzie mate Jade. It had been a surprisingly full service; she, Liz and Pat had fully expected the church to be half-empty but in the event they did well to find seats together in St Jude's (now cleared of any trace of *Village Voices*). Both Charlotte Sykes and her assistant Veronica from the agency had been there, as had that gentleman Pat knew from the golf club. There had been no sign of either of the Stanleys – or Jamie – but standing away at the back had been a dishevelled, red-eyed man Liz had identified as Tate Bishop.

And it had been a lovely service; everyone had said so. The villagers, under the supervision of the Reverend Mare, had bedecked the altar with bunches of winter evergreens, and in every window burnt clusters of red candles. Because the hymns had been so well known everyone had felt confident joining in and the swell of noise had given a heartfelt send-off to Theresa Mary Stanley nee Matheson.

Thelma had felt very glad that Brid had agreed to have the service at St Jude's and ask the Reverend Mare to conduct it. The vicar's eulogy had been expert in its construction, dwelling heavily on Terri's early life and love of animals. It had struck just the right note, when there were, as Pat put it, so many *wrong* notes in the late Mrs Stanley's life that could have been sounded.

Thelma looked round the darkening garden for the two children she was keeping an eye on. There was Archie running round the patio, and over by the gate there was Grace deep in conversation with Jean from next door.

'Here I am!' Archie ran past her, face solemn, arms pistoning at his sides, his face determined. He'd already done three circuits of the house and was now completing his second lap of the garden and grounds. He reminded Thelma of when they'd first acquired Snaffles, how once he'd mustered the courage to leave the cat basket, he'd undertaken a similar solemn tour of 32 College Gardens.

The back door opened, spilling a golden portal over the mossy gravel. Brid emerged, frowning as behind her Val switched off the light and locked up. The pair crossed the gravel towards Thelma, Val's feet crunching confidently, Brid lingering looking uncertain. 'I've advised Ms Matheson that early March is the ideal time to be getting the place back on the market,' she said airily. 'That's when the spring surge really gets going.' She spoke directly to Thelma who got the distinct impression that Val perceived Brid as a child who needed to let the grown-ups sort things out.

'Anyway, folks,' concluded Val. 'I'll be on my way. Before this snow starts!'

Watching her driving off, Thelma looked at Brid. 'How are you feeling?' she said.

Brid gave a short laugh. 'All over the place if I'm honest, Mrs Cooper. I still can't get over our Terri leaving *me* all that money. Or this place.' She waved an incredulous hand towards Sunny View Lodge.

'It's a lot to take in,' said Thelma gently.

'The thing is . . .' Brid looked troubled. 'I can't help feeling guilty. It's not as if it were properly my money—'

'It's yours as much as it's anyone's,' said Thelma firmly. 'Mal wanted your sister to have it – and she wanted *you* to have it. Not Tate Bishop.' She looked at the troubled girl, shivering in the deepening cold. Just how Terri had acquired the money was a burden she had no intention of allowing her to shoulder.

At that moment Archie jogged by. 'Three,' he shouted.

'Go easy, Arch,' said Brid. She looked at Thelma apologetically. 'It's the space, Mrs Cooper. We don't have a garden at the flat.' She stopped as the thought struck her squarely. 'Though I suppose . . . well, when the money comes through, of course we'll be able to move somewhere.'

'You could,' said Thelma. 'Move here.'

'*Here*?' Brid sounded startled.

'You're twenty minutes from both Northallerton and Thirsk when you buy your car,' said Thelma. 'And there is, so I believe, a very good village school.'

'Right.' Brid sounded doubtful.

'I know,' said Thelma, 'that it's not to everyone's taste.'

'Oh no, it's not that, Mrs Cooper.' Brid sounded troubled.

'It's lush here. It's just . . . the way that Mrs Carpenter was talking, it made me think – are *we* suitable for a place like this?'

'In what way suitable?' asked Thelma.

'I don't know – me and the kids somewhere like this.'

'Your sister lived here,' reminded Thelma. 'And I'm perfectly sure you'd have no problem filling the space. You could always ask your friend Jade and her young one to move in with you.'

'But,' Brid looked troubled, 'would we fit in – in a village?'

Grace came running up to them, plaits flying behind her.

'I hope you weren't bothering that lady,' said Brid fearfully.

'Her name's Jean and I'm going to show her how to make fruit smoothies,' said Grace.

'Never mind that, go and find your brother; we need to be making a move. Mrs Cooper can't be waiting round all night to run us back – it's going to start snowing soon.'

As Grace ran off Brid looked again at the bulk of Sunny View Lodge. 'I don't know,' she said doubtfully.

'I believe,' said Thelma, 'that your sister had a lot of faith in you and your children. When she wanted to move in with you all . . . well, I think it wasn't so much about escaping Tate – or even here – but about being with *you* all.'

'Maybe.' Brid's eyes filled and she did that thing of flapping her hands in front of her face until Thelma handed her a tissue.

'I really do believe it's what your sister would have wanted,' she said.

'And you really think we'd be all right living here?' said Brid.

'I do,' said Thelma. And indeed, it was a conviction that had been growing on her standing there in the frosty garden as the winter dusk deepened. It almost felt – and Thelma was not a fanciful woman – that the house itself welcomed the prospect of being filled with light and lunchboxes and noise and prosecco and laughter. Lots and lots of laughter. 'Sometimes,' she said, 'you can feel afraid of what you want. And sometimes you have to give yourself permission to live your best life.'

Shortly afterwards the mussel-blue Corsair could be seen nosing its way back up the drive and once again the house was left alone, though possibly not for long. It sat patiently, a dark speck in amongst the many many glittering ones that lay in the valley between the Pennines and the Moors. Away in the north snow clouds were swelling, and high in the winter night sky a single bright star shone.

ACKNOWLEDGEMENTS

It's just after 7am, and I'm sitting here in the Year Four classroom having just arrived at work. For one of the last times. Next week I stop being Deputy Head and retire from a life of teaching. I'll still be doing some work here at the school but essentially, I've the feeling of being at the end of a journey, a journey of many happy years and as I write this, I'm remembering the many, many people who have been a part of that journey.

Similarly, I'm almost at the end of another journey- the journey of writing book three (book three! Mum and Dad, I wish you knew!) and I'm thinking of, and wanting to thank, the many people who have been a part of that much shorter (!) journey.

First and foremost, I want to thank the team at Avon for their sterling, tireless support and graft in bringing this next story of Pat, Liz and Thelma into the world, and for their consistent reminders that yes, there *is* a world beyond staff meetings and achievement assemblies. Thanks to my two editors, the much-missed Molly and the much-welcomed Sarah for their insights, suggestions, and lifelines! Thanks also to the brilliant (and much missed!) publicist Gaby, to Raphaella, to Maddie, Ella and of course to Emily without whom there wouldn't be a book!

Thanks also to my powerhouse of an agent, Stan. For the hard work, for the advice, the support, and for his rock-solid belief in me as a writer and the worlds I'm trying to create.

I also want to thank all those people who have contributed such valuable help as I've realized all over again that the journey of writing is never ever a straightforward one. Thanks to Philip Hey for his illuminating insights into life as a delivery driver. To my crime-o-pedia sister Judith who first talked me through the notions of a disappearing Charity shop. To the brilliant Gary Brown from the BBC for again (and again!) teaching me so much about the nitty-gritty craft of storytelling. And of course, to Julie Hesmondhalgh for once more imbuing the audio world of Pat, Liz and Thelma with so much energy and light and life.

And of course, big thanks to my faithful team of grammar police, whose gentle (and sometimes not so gentle!) corrections and notes helped me so much. To Peter Dodd and to Maureen from church. To the wonderful and – yes, I'm saying it again – evergreen Audrey Coldron. And of course, to Sandra Appleton still valiantly battling with the excesses of my prose some (gulp) fifty years on.

I also want to thank those fellow creatives I'm so fortunate to have in my life for their support, their encouragement, their texts and emails and conversations, and for the fact they *get it* when the days (and weeks) don't go so well. Big thanks to Mark Wright, to my cosy-crime bro-in-arms Jonathan, and to my fellow travellers for all these years, Louise Fletcher and Catherine Johnson.

Thanks also to this wonderful new community I've been introduced to this year, the world of Crime Festivals, where I've met so very many lovely fellow crime writers (and crime readers!) It's been great getting to know you! Thanks to Donna, Adrian and the team at Crimefest, to Bob and the team at Bloody Scotland – these events are five-star terrific and are thoroughly recommended!

And the indie bookshops! I don't think they know the value

of the environments they've afforded me as a writer – relaxed, inspiring worlds that leave me in a place of wanting to read – and write – all the more. Thanks to the Beverley Bookshop, to The Stripy Badger in Grassington, to Darling Reads in Horbury, to St Ives Bookseller, to Waterstones in Northallerton (not strictly an indie but definitely needs a mention!) to the new places (to me) I've encountered, The Wonky Tree Bookshop in Leyburn and The Grove bookshop in Ilkley. And of course, the wonderful White Rose Book Cafe in Thirsk and my original number one fan, The Little Ripon Bookshop. Visit them, and see for yourself what terrific places they are.

And of course, thanks to my huge, lovely family. My gorgeous cousin Ruth, my wonderful Aunties, Lee, Mary and Cath, to Babs and Tracey, Maisie, Elise and Trevor, Dan, Anja, Robin and Lawrence, to Caitlin and Andy, Conor, Niall and Jess, to John and Rozzi.

And again (and again) Judith. And Simon. I couldn't have written a word without you.

So, it's now nearly 7.45 a.m. and I'm way behind setting up for the day. The milk has been delivered, and I can hear Mr O unlocking the ICT suite. For one last time I have to struggle with teaching Bridging Through One Hundred.

But there's one more thanks I need to make. To Foxhill School, here on the tops. To its staff, parents and pupils. Its past head Sally, its present head Sarah. It's the best place I could have imagined spending the past twenty-five years.

By the sink on the towel dispenser, I can see a tacky-backed notice. It's one I put up within the first few weeks of being here all those years ago. One paper towel PLEASE. I'm thinking . . . even way back then . . . Liz, Pat and Thelma were there in my mind, waiting to come to life . . .

Introducing the three unlikeliest sleuths you'll ever meet . . .

Every Thursday, three retired school teachers have their 'coffee o'clock' sessions at the Thirsk Garden Centre café.

But one fateful week, as they are catching up with a slice of cake, they bump into their ex-colleague, Topsy.

By the next Thursday, Topsy's dead.

The last thing Liz, Thelma and Pat imagined was that they would become involved in a murder.

But they know there's more to Topsy's death than meets the eye – and it's down to them to prove it . . .

Don't miss J.M. Hall's debut cosy mystery – available now!

Signed. Sealed. Dead?

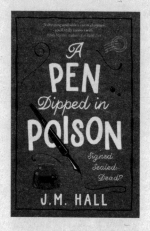

Curious white envelopes have been delivered to
friends and neighbours. Inside are letters revealing
the deepest secrets they have tried to hide.

As one by one, careers are ended, marriages destroyed
and no one is beyond suspicion, the three friends
decide enough is enough. They must take matters
into their own hands before more damage is done.

But as they work to uncover the truth, they begin to wonder
just how far someone will go to silence this poison pen . . .

Could a murderer be in their midst once again?

**The second addictive and page-turning cosy
mystery from J.M. Hall – available now!**